CANADIAN
STORIES
OF THE SEA

Edited by
Victor Suthren

Toronto   Oxford   New York
OXFORD UNIVERSITY PRESS
1993

Oxford University Press, 70 Wynford Drive, Don Mills, Ontario M3C 1J9

Toronto   Oxford   New York
Delhi   Bombay   Calcutta   Madras   Karachi   Kuala Lumpur
Singapore   Hong Kong   Tokyo   Nairobi   Dar es Salaam
Cape Town   Melbourne   Auckland   Madrid

and associated companies in
Berlin   Ibadan

This book is printed on permanent (acid-free) paper ∞

Canadian Cataloguing in Publication Data

Main entry under title:

Canadian stories of the sea

ISBN 0-19-540849-7

1. Sea stories, Canadian.   I. Suthren, Victor, 1942-

PS8323.S4C35 1993   C813'.010832162   C93-094563-8
PR9197.35.S4C35 1993

Design: Marie Bartholomew

Cover Photograph: Freeman Patterson/Masterfile

1   2   3   4 — 96   95   94   93

Printed in Canada

Contents

Acknowledgements

JOHN BAKELESS. 'Cartier Comes to Canada' from *The Eyes of Discovery* (New York: Dover Publications Inc, 1961). Reprinted by permission.

KEN COATES and BILL MORRISON. 'The Sinking of the Princess Sophia' from *The Sinking of the Princess Sophia: Taking the North Down With Her*. Copyright © 1990 by Ken Coates and Bill Morrison. Reprinted by permission of Oxford University Press Canada.

JAMES COOK. 'The North American Coast' from *The Explorations of Captain James Cook in the Pacific as told by selections from his own journals, 1768-1779* edited by A. Grenfell Price (Dover Publications, Inc, 1971). Used by permission of the publisher.

SIEUR DE LA POTHERIE. 'The Letter of the Sieur de la Potherie, to Monseigneur the Duke of Orleans, Regent of the Kingdom of France', *Ordeal by Ice* by Farley Mowat (1973). By permission of Farley Mowat.

DONALD GRAHAM. 'The Sisters' from *Lights of the Inside Passage: A History of British Columbia's Lighthouses and their Keepers* (Harbour Publishing, 1986). Reprinted by permission.

GEORGE H. GRIFFIN. 'How the Crane Fought the South-east Wind' and 'The Children of the Moon', *Legends of the Evergreen Coast* (Vancouver: Clarke & Stuart Co. Ltd, 1934).

GWYN JONES. 'The Greenlanders' Sage' from *The Norse Atlantic Saga* (2nd ed., 1986) © Oxford University Press 1964, 1986. Reprinted by permission of Oxford University Press.

JAMES B. LAMB. 'Slip and Proceed' from *The Corvette Navy* by James Lamb, © 1977. Reprinted by permission of Macmillan Canada.

HAL LAWRENCE. 'Early Patrols', *Victory at Sea: Tales of His Majesty's Coastal Forces* by Hal Lawrence. Used by permission of The Canadian Publishers, McClelland & Stewart, Toronto and Hal Lawrence.

MICHAEL LOK. 'Michael Lok's Account of the First Voyage', *Ordeal by Ice* by Farley Mowat (1973). By permission of Farley Mowat.

R. KEITH McLAREN. 'Bluenose and Bluenose II' from *Bluenose & Bluenose II* (Hounslow Press, 1981). Reprinted by permission of the author.

ROBERT and THOMAS MALCOMSON. 'The Battle', copyright © 1990 by Robert Malcomson and Thomas Malcomson. Reprinted from *HMS Detroit: The Battle for Lake Erie* by Robert Malcomson and Thomas Malcomson, by permission of Vanwell Publishing Limited.

FARLEY MOWAT. 'The Foggy, Foggy Dew', *The Boat Who Wouldn't Float* (1969). Reprinted by permission of the author.

NED MYERS. 'Loss of the Sourge' from Emily Cain, *Ghost Ships Hamilton and Scourge: Historical Treasures from the War of 1812*. Reprinted by permission of Emily Cain.

THOMAS H. RADDALL. 'A Quiet Way' excerpt from *In My Time* by Thomas Raddall. Used by permission of The Canadian Publishers, McClelland & Stewart, Toronto.

JOSEPH SCHULL. 'Masters and Men', 'Mighty on the Waters', and 'The Ship That Wouldn't Sail' from *The Salt-Water Men* (Macmillan of Canada, 1957). Reprinted by permission of Hélène Gougeon Schull. 'The Tribals—The Loss of "Athabaskan"' excerpt from *The Far Distant Ships: An Official Account of Canadian Naval Operations in the Second World War* (Queen's Printer, 1952). Reprinted by permission of Canada Communications Group.

WILLIAM SCORESBY. 'The Northern Whale-Fishery', *Ordeal by Ice* by Farley Mowat (1973). By permission of Farley Mowat.

C.H.J. SNIDER. '"Matilda" and "Loyal Sam"' from *Under the Red Jack*. Hodder & Stoughton Ltd. 'The Burlington Races', *In the Wake of the Eighteen-Twelvers* (The Bodley Head).

HOWARD WHITE. 'Nootka Whaling' and 'Skiffs, Gillnets, and Poverty-Sticks', *Raincoast Chronicles First Five* (Harbour Publishing, 1975). Reprinted by permission.

STEWART EDWARD WHITE. 'On the Big Sea Water', *Yachting: A Turn of the Century Treasury* edited by Tony Meisel. (Castle, 1987). Reprinted by permission of Book Sales, Inc.

GEORGE WHITELEY. 'Levi's Story' and 'Working on the Offshore Banks' excerpt from 'Working on the Offshore Banks', *Northern Seas Hardy Sailors* (W.W. Norton & Company Inc. 1982).

DEREK WILSON. 'The Money Pit', *The World Atlas of Treasure* by Derek Wilson. Pan Books.

Every effort has been made to determine and contact copyright owners. In the case of any omissions, the publisher will be pleased to make suitable acknowledgement in future editions.

Introduction

The Canadian coastline is washed by three oceans and the waters of the vast Great Lakes. But it has been a characteristic of Canadians that they have expressed very little of the romantic fascination with the sea which has been a part of other cultures. There have been no lack of seafaring Canadians, whether in the fishing fleets of the Maritimes or British Columbia, the sailing freighters and 'fish tugs' of the Great Lakes, or the deep-sea sailors who went abroad in the vanished Canadian Mercantile Marine, or the fighting ships of the Royal Canadian Navy. And in the fortitude and skill of a Bernier or a Slocum is found ample evidence that Canadians belong in seafaring halls of fame. But there has been little romantic rhapsodizing over the encounter of Canadians with the sea, perhaps because that encounter has so much been with the cold and pitiless waters of the northern oceans, or the treacherous chill depths of the Great Lakes, fully able to match the sea in ship-killing fury. There have been for most Canadians at sea no sparkling, sun-kissed seas beneath placid rows of Trade Wind clouds or sunny beaches washed by aquamarine wavelets. The North Atlantic and North Pacific, the icebound Arctic Ocean and Beaufort Sea, and the frigid expanse of Lake Superior have been more likely the Canadian experience, and it has been one of a hard-fought and often fatal battle with an inhospitable and unforgiving element. In its way, the story of the Canadian encounter with the sea provides a mirror as much of Canadian character as it does of the killing oceans which surround the country. In it are revealed tenacity; courage; an unvarnished practicality and stark realism; an unsentimental acceptance of hardship, discomfort, and loss; and very little lyrical romanticism.

It was common among nationalist Canadian writers of the nineteenth century to hymn the nordic virtues of Canadians as a product of the bracing northern environment, and while there was a great deal of chauvinist silliness in such talk—and not a small whiff of racism—there is a gem of truth in the concept of a people shaped in thought, mood and manner by their environment. Canada's has been one in which an internalized self-discipline has had to be present in its inhabitants, whether an Inuit hunter stalking a harp seal, or a suburban family readying a station wagon for a long January drive. The country is prepared, for almost half the year, to kill anyone who does not take some precaution or preparation. In this rigorous atmosphere of practicality the needed attributes of seamen are bred, for neither lassitude nor romanticism have been sufficient tools for survival in the northern seas. Given the opportunity to learn the professional seagoing skills, the Canadian brings to the sea a good preparation for the self-denial, harshness, and endurance he or she will find there. The resulting seamanship can be second to none, as the abilities of the Canadian Escort Groups by 1945, the achievements of Bernier's or Larsen's crews in the North, or the taciturn worth of Angus Walters' men in working and sailing the unforgettable *Bluenose* attest.

But the very workaday practicality of the Canadian approach to the sea has also meant that the notion of the sea as a romantic and adventurous universe has had to arise, for the most part, in writers in other cultures. Few Canadian writers of the sea, with some exceptions such as Farley Mowat or Thomas Raddall, have approached the lyricality of expression that has come from a Conrad or a Melville, a Jack London or a Patrick O'Bryan. It is possible that the potential lethality of the Canadian struggle with the sea has made wordless those all too aware of what seafaring threatens.

It may be that the rhapsodic hymning of the sea's romance must be left to other peoples to whose shores the sea shows a more benign and gentle face. A Lunenburg is no place for the daydreams of a Nantucket or a Hawaii.

The reality, of course, is that Canada's history is full of stirring tales of heroism, endurance, and courage at sea. From the legends of Nootka whalers to the schooner battles of the War of 1812; from the grim struggle of corvette and U-boat in 1943 to the gallant escape of *Aréthuse* from a besieged Louisbourg; or from the rockribbed defence by *Bluenose* of her schooner racing crown to the steady, unpretentious heroism of *St Roch*'s career in the Arctic, the brilliant colours of Canada's sea panorama stand out. But it seems too readily a characteristic of Canadians that they leave the telling of these sorts of tales to others, even while they are no stranger to the experience of the sea, whether blood-stirring accounts of action, or the quiet reflectivity that contact with the frontier of the sea can bring.

In this collection of stories and vignettes, an attempt has been made to provide a glimpse, however incomplete, of this panorama. Whether taken from recent or earlier works, whether fiction or fact, they are meant to give not an overview of the Canadian experience of the sea, but rather a series of glances; glances which can be read either one at a time or together, but with an ultimate aim of heightening the reader's awareness that this panorama is a broad, exciting, intricate and involving one. It is also intended to provide, in the actions and achievements of the men and women found in these stories, a small mirror of the Canadian character as well as of the awesome and fierce environment which is Canada. The seas which wash its shores are vast, beautiful and deadly; but upon them and beside them, remarkable things have happened.

The First Peoples

It may have been before the last great glaciations retreated from Canada, and it certainly occurred afterward; across the forbidding straits dividing Asia and America, neolithic family and tribal groups of sturdy, dark-haired nomads crossed to the North American continent, and began the southward march of thousands of years that would lead them to the farthest rockbound coves of Tierra del Fuego, and to the glittering brilliance of the pyramided Central American civilizations. As they spread across the vast landscape of Canada, they came to settle in numbers on the lush West Coast, where the bounty of nature allowed a flowering of art and culture more complex than the more austere societies in the snowgirt interior, and eastward. But whether in the Eastern Woodlands people's old tales of the land being borne up on the waters by a great turtle, or in the following West Coast tale, there was a distant, collective memory *of some vital conflict with the sea that echoed European and Middle Eastern traditions.*

The Deep Waters
E. Pauline Johnson

Far over your left shoulder as your boat leaves the Narrows to thread the beautiful waterways that lead to Vancouver Island, you will see the summit of Mount Baker robed in its everlasting whiteness and always reflecting some wonderful glory from the rising sun, the golden noontide, or the violet and amber sunset. This is the Mount Ararat of the Pacific Coast peoples; for those readers who are familiar with the ways and beliefs and faiths of primitive races will agree that it is difficult to discover anywhere in the world a race that has not some story of the Deluge, which they have chronicled and localized to fit the understanding and the conditions of the nation that composes their own immediate world.

Amongst the red nations of America I doubt if any two tribes have the same ideas regarding the Flood. Some of the traditions concerning this vast whim of Nature are grotesque in the extreme; some are impressive; some even profound; but of all the stories of the Deluge that I have been able to collect I know of not a single one that can even begin to equal in beauty of conception, let alone rival in possible reality and truth, the Squamish legend of 'The Deep Waters'.

I here quote the legend of 'mine own people', the Iroquois tribes of Ontario, regarding the Deluge. I do this to paint the colour of contrast in richer shades, for I am bound to admit that we who pride ourselves on ancient intellectuality have but a childish tale of the Flood when compared with the jealously preserved annals of the Squamish, which savour more of history than tradition. With 'mine own people', animals always play a much more important role and are endowed with a finer intelligence than humans. I do not find amid my notes a single tradition of the Iroquois wherein animals do not figure, and our story of the Deluge rests entirely with the intelligence of sea-going and river-going creatures. With us, animals in olden times were greater than man; but it is not so with the Coast Indians, except in rare instances.

When a Coast Indian consents to tell you a legend he will, without variation, begin it with, 'It was before the white people came.'

2

The natural thing for you then to ask is, 'But who were here then?'

He will reply, 'Indians, and just the trees, and animals, and fishes, and a few birds.'

So you are prepared to accept the animal world as intelligent co-habitants of the Pacific slope, but he will not lead you to think he regards them as equals, much less superiors. But to revert to 'mine own people': they hold the intelligence of wild animals far above that of man, for perhaps the one reason that when an animal is sick it effects its own cure; it knows what grasses and herbs to eat, what to avoid, while the sick human calls the medicine man, whose wisdom is not only the result of years of study, but also heredity; consequently any great natural event, such as the Deluge, has much to do with the wisdom of the creatures of the forests and the rivers.

Iroquois tradition tells us that once this earth was entirely submerged in water, and during this period for many days a busy little muskrat swam about vainly looking for a foothold of earth wherein to build his house. In his search he encountered a turtle also leisurely swimming, so they had speech together, and the muskrat complained of weariness; he could find no foothold; he was tired of incessant swimming, and longed for land such as his ancestors enjoyed. The turtle suggested that the muskrat should dive and endeavour to find earth at the bottom of the sea. Acting on this advice the muskrat plunged down, then arose with his two little forepaws grasping some earth he had found beneath the waters.

'Place it on my shell and dive again for more,' directed the turtle. The muskrat did so, but when he returned with his paws filled with earth he discovered the small quantity he had first deposited on the turtle's shell had doubled in size. The return from the third trip found the turtle's load again doubled. So the building went on at double compound increase, and the world grew its continents and its islands with great rapidity, and now rests on the shell of a turtle.

If you ask an Iroquois, 'And did no men survive this flood?' he will reply, 'Why should men survive? The animals are wiser than men; let the wisest live.'

How, then, was the earth repeopled?

The Iroquois will tell you that the otter was a medicine man; that in swimming and diving about he found corpses of men and women; he sang his medicine songs and they came to life, and the otter brought them fish for food until they were strong enough to provide for themselves. Then the Iroquois will conclude his tale with, 'You know well that the otter has greater wisdom than a man.'

So much for 'mine own people' and our profound respect for the superior intelligence of our little brothers of the animal world.

But the Squamish tribe hold other ideas. It was on a February day that I first listened to this beautiful, humane story of the Deluge. My royal old tillicum had come to see me through the rains and mists of late winter days. The gateways of my wigwam always stood open—very widely open—for his feet to enter, and this especial day he came with the worst downpour of the season.

Womanlike, I protested with a thousand contradictions in my voice that he should venture out to see me on such a day. It was 'Oh! Chief, I am so glad to see you' and it was 'Oh! Chief, why didn't you stay at home on such a wet day—your poor throat will suffer.' But I soon had quantities of hot tea for him, and the huge cup my own father always used was his—as long as the Sagalie Tyee allowed his dear feet to wander my way. The immense cup stands idle and empty now for the second time.

Helping him off with his great-coat, I chatted on about the deluge of rain, and he remarked it was not so very bad, as one could yet walk.

'Fortunately, yes, for I cannot swim,' I told him.

He laughed, replying, 'Well, it is not so bad as when the Great Deep Waters covered the world.'

Immediately I foresaw the coming legend, so crept into the shell of mono-syllables.

'No?' I questioned.

'No,' he replied. 'For one time there was no land here at all; everywhere there was just water.'

'I can quite believe it,' I remarked caustically.

He laughed—that irresistible, though silent, David Warfield laugh of his that always brought a responsive smile from his listeners. Then he plunged directly into the tradition, with no preface save a comprehensive sweep of his wonderful hands towards my wide window, against which the rains were beating.

'It was after a long, long time of this—this rain. The mountain streams were swollen, the rivers choked, the sea began to rise—and yet it rained; for weeks and weeks it rained.' He ceased speaking, while the shadows of centuries gone crept into his eyes. Tales of the misty past always inspired him.

'Yes,' he continued. 'It rained for weeks and weeks, while the mountain torrents roared thunderingly down, and the sea crept silently up. The level lands were first to float in sea water, then to disappear. The slopes were next to slip into the sea. The world was slowly being flooded. Hurriedly the Indian tribes gathered in one spot, a place of safety far above the reach of the on-creeping sea. The spot was the circling shore of Lake Beautiful, up the North Arm. They held a Great Council and decided at once upon a plan of action. A giant canoe should be built, and some means contrived to anchor it in case the waters mounted to the heights. The men undertook the canoe, the women the anchorage.

'A giant tree was felled, and day and night the men toiled over its construction into the most stupendous canoe the world has ever known. Not an hour, not a moment, but many worked, while the toil-wearied ones slept, only to awake to renewed toil. Meanwhile the women also worked at a cable—the largest, the longest, the strongest that Indian hands and teeth had ever made. Scores of them gathered and prepared the cedar fibre; scores of them plaited, rolled and seasoned it; scores of them chewed upon it inch by inch to make it pliable; scores of them oiled and worked, oiled and worked, oiled and worked it into a sea-resisting fabric. And still the sea crept up, and up, and up. It was the last day; hope of life for the tribe, of land for the world, was doomed. Strong hands, self-sacrificing hands fastened the cable the women had made—one end to the giant canoe, the other about an enormous boulder, a vast immovable rock as firm as the foundations of the world—for might not the canoe with its priceless freight drift out, far out, to sea, and when the water subsided might not this ship of safety be leagues and leagues beyond the sight of land on the storm-driven Pacific?

'Then with the bravest hearts that ever beat, noble hands lifted every child of the tribe into this vast canoe; not one single baby was overlooked. The canoe was stocked with food and fresh water, and lastly, the ancient men and women of the race selected as guardians to these children the bravest, most stalwart, handsomest young man of the tribe, and the mother of the youngest baby in the camp—she was but a girl of sixteen, her child but two weeks old; but she, too, was brave and very beautiful. These two were placed, she at the bow of the canoe to watch, he at the stern to guide, and all the little children crowded between.

'And still the sea crept up, and up, and up. At the crest of the bluffs about Lake Beautiful the doomed tribes crowded. Not a single person attempted to enter the canoe. There was no wailing, no crying out for safety. "Let the little children, the young mother, and the bravest and best of our young men live," was all the farewell those in the canoe heard as the waters reached the summit, and—the canoe floated. Last of all to be seen was the top of the tallest tree, then—all was a world of water.

'For days and days there was no land—just the rush of swirling, snarling sea; but the canoe rode safely at anchor, the cable those scores of dead, faithful women had made held true as the hearts that beat behind the toil and labour of it all.

'But one morning at sunrise, far to the south a speck floated on the breast of the waters; at midday it was larger, at evening it was yet larger. The moon arose, and in its magic light the man at the stern saw it was a patch of land. All night he watched it grow, and at daybreak looked with glad eyes upon the summit of Mount Baker. He cut the cable, grasped his paddle in his strong, young hands and steered for the south. When they landed, the waters were sunken half down the mountain side. The children were lifted out; the beautiful young mother, the stalwart young brave, turned to each other, clasped hands, looked into each others' eyes—and smiled.

'And down in the vast country that lies between Mount Baker and the Fraser River they made a new camp, built new lodges, where the little children grew and thrived, and lived and loved, and the earth was repeopled by them.

'The Squamish say that in a gigantic crevice halfway to the crest of Mount Baker may yet be seen the outlines of an enormous canoe, but I have never seen it myself.'

He ceased speaking with that far-off cadence in his voice with which he always ended a legend, and for a long time we both sat in silence listening to the rains that were still beating against the window.

As the First Peoples settled and prospered in the new continents, their remembrances and awareness of the world in which they lived grew and expanded in their stories and tales, so many of which were little more than warnings of how to live at peace and in harmony with the forces about them. Whether the Micmac on the Atlantic Coast, Iroquoian or Algonquian canoe-builders on the Great Lakes, or the seafarers of the West Coast, the people wove into their oral traditions clear lessons in respecting the sea and wind elements, and their power. It is evident in the charm of this West Coast story of how the Crane fought the South-east Wind.

How the Crane Fought the South-east Wind
George H. Griffin

Because the South-east Wind was a boisterous fellow and respected neither man's life nor property, Gas-ga, the Crane, determined to punish him. Gas-ga was a long time making up his mind but, when the last party of halibut fishermen failed to return after a violent storm, the Master Carpenter, as Gas-ga was sometimes called, set to work on his plans.

Now the South-east Wind was a wily fellow and chose for his home a barren rocky island far out across the waters many a moon's journey away, and it was necessary for Gas-ga to build a large and strong canoe for the journey. It was also necessary for him to go alone as he possessed magic which the other members of the tribe did not know, and which he did not wish to reveal.

It took him a long time to find just the right kind of log for the canoe, and many a weary hour did he spend in shaping it to his needs. Unfortunately, when the canoe was finished, it split from stem to stern. The Master Carpenter was ready to give up in despair. However, after he had rested for a few days, he set to work to make another vessel. Hour after hour he toiled away at the task and it was only when the sun set over the western Pacific that he left off working until dawn. Finally, when he had painted the canoe in gorgeous colours and fitted it with paddles, he placed it at the water's edge, intending the very next day to set out upon his quest.

But it was not to be. During the night a storm sprang up and smashed his handiwork to pieces. Gas-ga then realized that his enemy was working against him, and he wept with anger. The summer was nearly spent and, if he was to set out on his mission, it would have to be soon, for, when winter came, it would be almost impossible to make the journey. He was pondering these things, while seated upon a sun-bleached log in the sun, when Lana, the Greatest Fool, approached him.

'Why are you so sad, Master Carpenter?' Lana asked.

'Because my enemy, the South-east Wind, is stronger than I am. Twice now he has defeated me, for the first canoe split before it was placed in the water, and the second was smashed to splinters ere I set out upon my voyage,' replied Gas-ga.

'Be of good cheer, my friend. Although everybody takes me for a fool, you only have ever given me friendship. For this I am grateful, and willing to help you. I learned how to make the long canoes from my father, and, as you know, he was the only man living in these islands who could make a serviceable one. It is easy when one knows how. Come, let us start at once.'

Buoyed up by this good news, the Master Carpenter plucked up his spirits. At heart he was a little afraid that, when the job was finished, Lana would want to accompany him on his long voyage, and he did not want that to happen.

Lana led the way to a stately red cedar growing near the beach, and the two, working at the butt of the tree with stone axes and wedges, soon felled the giant. Then they measured off the correct length and cut the log to dimensions needed to form a splendid canoe. The outside took shape after many days' careful labour and, with fire and crude adzes, they hollowed it out, being careful to keep the sides of uniform thickness. Next a curving prow and stern were added by mitring carven pieces of wood to the hull.

'Now,' said Lana, 'We must be careful. The next step is to spread the sides to make the canoe wide enough to be seaworthy. This is the point where so many of our people have failed in the past. They are usually in too much of a hurry to do the work properly, and the result is a split that they can never hope to mend.'

Gas-ga did not reply to this for he remembered his first failure. Lana instructed him to fill the canoe with water and, when he had done so, both collected rocks and flung them into a large fire they had kindled. While the rocks were being heated, they built fires all around the hull of the vessel but not close enough to burn the wood of the sides. When these were burning steadily, they commenced dropping the red hot stones into the water within the craft. Very shortly clouds of steam told them that the water was nearly boiling. They kept adding stones and replenishing their fires.

Lana now told Gas-ga that the time had come to spread the sides, so taking especially prepared sticks fashioned to the correct width of the finished canoe, the sides were spread apart and some of the sticks fastened in place to prevent them closing together when the water cooled and the fires died down.

The workers did not let their work cool too rapidly, but attended to it all the night through, and, when morning came, they removed the debris and sanded down the outside of the vessel with dried shark's skin. Next they painted and carved the totems of the Crane, the crest of the owner, on its prow.

Before they placed the canoe in the water, they smeared the outside of it with oolachan grease to make it glide smoothly and then, last of all, they fashioned two sets of paddles.

'Now my work with you is ended,' announced Lana, when they stood back and admired the fine lines of their handicraft. 'My honest wishes for success are yours. Should you meet with the enemy, give him the beating he deserves.' When he had said these words, Lana left and went to his mean lodge at the end of the village.

Delighted with the results of their labours, Gas-ga forgot to thank the Greatest Fool for the aid he had given him.

Before setting out on his hazardous mission, the Crane betook himself to the forest, where he spent four days and nights in meditation and fasting, and at the end of that time he came back. He dressed himself in his best garments and taking a spear, club, and stone knife, he set out upon his undertaking.

Now the South-east wind was not idle all this time. Indeed, through a medium best known to himself, he had learned of the preparations that Gas-ga was making. He chuckled as he sat perched upon a rock on the lonely island that was his home.

It was a barren place; no trees or shrubs, but only mosses and lichen grew there. The island was really formed of two enormous rocks, or so it seemed at high tide. When the waters were in and running strongly, they swirled through the gap which cut the barren island in two and caused the sinuous kelp to wave back and forth like the coils of some hideous sea snake. It was on the highest of these two crags that the South-east Wind sat and saw his enemy approaching over the rim of the distant horizon.

When he was sure it was Gas-ga, he slithered down from his lofty perch and plunged into the swirling surf. His hair, a brownish yellow in colour, floated on the surface and looked like a mass of floating dead weed. With incredible swiftness, he propelled himself towards the approaching canoe, leaving little whirlpools in his wake. It was his intention to take Gas-ga by surprise.

The Master Carpenter saw the jagged fangs of rock and within himself he experienced a feeling of dread and awe. The very place made him shiver, brave adventurer though he was. He was not near enough to see the South-east Wind scramble down from his perch, but was keen-sighted enough to notice the sea fowl rise in clouds and wheel screaming aloft. Something unusual had disturbed them, unless—and the very thought chilled the marrow in his bones—his enemy had instructed them to tell him of the coming of the strange canoe.

Keeping this in his mind, he stopped paddling and scrutinized the oily surface of the waves. The South-east Wind, because he was busy and had hidden his face under the water, forgot for a moment to practise his wiles. He was impatient to reach his quarry and increased his speed. Just at that moment, Gas-ga saw a clump of floating weed acting rather strangely. It was travelling in the opposite direction to the current.

He suspected that it was his enemy, and quickly turned the stem of his craft to approach the floating mass from the rear. Expertly, Gas-ga brought the canoe alongside and, before the South-east Wind realized what was happening, Gas-ga had seized him by his snaky locks. The South-east Wind was helpless. Being in the water and being held there with an implacable grasp, he could not act.

Calling upon his nephew for aid, the South-east Wind commenced to tow the canoe towards the rocks which formed his abode. Instantly, the sky turned a saffron hue and a black archway of cloud formed in the south. The winds rose in a harsh murmur and hastened to aid their kinsman. The Ocean, heeding their commands, ruffled his crest. The low murmur increased to a roar, but still Gas-ga hung on.

The roar was soon mingled with a tremendous howling and shrieking as the South Winds, acting together in their unleashed might, bore down upon the frail craft. They hurled it like a chip. The waters, surprised at the lashing they were receiving, responded. They dashed spray like pellets into the face of the Master Carpenter and blinded him.

Gas-ga felt his grasp slipping, and his heart grew cold within him. He thought that his last moment had come. The waves, which up to this time had come singly, each capped with a fringe of creamy spume, now massed their forces and joined as one. A huge wall of water, so high that it seemed to reach the lowering sky, now bore down upon the helpless hero. Gas-ga felt the canoe rise on the watery slope. Higher, and still higher, he was carried. He looked down the valley with its smooth, jet black, glassy sides, and shuddered. The very bed of the ocean was visible. He could see the enormous halibut and hideous crab-like monsters moving in the depths. All this vanished in a smother of foam as the canoe took the crest. The winds shrieked a paean of triumph in his ears. His hand let go the slimy hair of his enemy, and he felt himself being hurried along with the speed of lightning.

Presently his rate of travel slackened and gave way as the angry waves abated their wrath, but not before the canoe grounded in the shoal waters of the island in front of the village in which he lived. Gas-ga waded ashore, thankful to reach dry land once more. His arch enemy, mortified at being held a prisoner for even a short period, retired to his abode to nurse his wounded pride.

From that day to this the People of the Islands remember when Gas-ga, the Crane, fought with the South-east Wind, and they always speak of their enemy in awed whispers. If they offend him by even the slightest trifle and forget to offer him their prayers, he will arise in his wrath, even as he did with Gas-ga, and destroy them.

The spiritual strength and wisdom of the First Peoples were aspects of them that the Europeans were slow to appreciate fully; that appreciation is still developing today. But the technical skill of their adaptations to the demands of the sea were more immediately recognized. And as this modern description of Nootka whaling technology reveals, it was a skill and technical competence worthy in itself of respect, and worthy of respect for the men who took this technology to sea, and trusted their lives to it.

Nootka Whaling
Howard White

When Captain Cook touched land at Nootka Sound in 1778, he found the Indians there engaged in methodical and effective whaling operations which they told him their forefathers had begun ages before. Technologically, these Nootkas were living in the stone age. The methods of their whaling industry bear witness to a capacity for adapting primitive technology to the most complex and demanding tasks.

The challenge of the whale hunt, it should be noted, was one European man avoided until after the development of ocean-going ships and the discovery of America. The industry did not really become efficient until the development of the American whaling ship in the early 1800s, a vessel described by Charles Olson as 'one of the most successful machines developed up to that time'.

When the reader comes across the details of Indian whaling methods related in this article, it may be worthwhile for him to imagine himself in the role of a native whaler, attacking a beast five times the size of the greatest dinosaur with minimum safeguards to his own person and with heavy odds against his success.

The canoes used in Nootka whaling varied little from tribe to tribe. The main body was hewn from a cedar log with fitted pieces bow and stern. Days might be spent wandering through forests far from the village in search of a suitable tree. Only in thick stands did the trunks grow straight and free of limbs. If a likely candidate were found, a hole would be chiselled into the stump to test for soundness. On rare occasions the entire tree might be felled but this was very hazardous. More often a scaffolding was erected around the trunk to the height desired in the canoe and a cut made halfway through the tree, top and bottom. A vertical split was started at the top with hard wood wedges and a pole inserted in the crack. The carver would then return home to other business. As the tree swayed, the pole would work its way down the trunk until a half-round block of just the right size broke loose. If the whole tree was being felled, surrounding timber was cleared away, limbs cut, and the chips of the cut scattered in the direction intended for the drop. After doing everything physically possible to assure a soft landing the carver sang out, imploring the tree to go gently.

For the rough shaping heavy stone mauls and nephrite or jade chisels were used. For the finer work the carver had stone or bone adzes and chisels of mussel shell. While he was working on a canoe the carver had to be very watchful of his own behaviour. He dared not touch women or rotten spots would appear at crucial points in the log. If he combed his hair, or dropped a hair, splits would appear.

When the outer hull was finished, holes were bored at all the critical bends and plugged with carefully measured coloured dowels. The hull was then righted and the hollowing begun. When his adze shaved the tip of a dowel, the carver knew he had dug far enough. This technique assured even thickness throughout the hull. The hull was humped up in the middle so it would level out upon spreading, which was accomplished by inserting long crosspieces anglewise between the walls and banging them straight after the wood had been softened with hot water. If the carver had been anywhere remiss in his duty, from choosing a cross-grained tree to winking at a girl, the canoe might at this point snap in two. No one but he dared look until the spreaders were firmly fixed and the wood dried. The bow and stern pieces were tightly fitted then laced down with spruce roots set in pitch.

When all carving and fitting was finished, the hull was singed with a torch flame to remove tiny slivers and sanded with dogfish skin. A final finish of seal oil and red ochre was baked on with torches. Narrow with straight gunwales, long prow and square stern, the Nootka whaling design greatly impressed early white shipmen with its speed and, according to some scholars, inspired the famous 'clipper bow' so popular in the mid-19th century.

The canoe was carried to the water on fir poles padded with cedar bark. It was never dragged or touched on the ground. The Nootka standards of craftsmanship were such that the largest 60-foot dugout, brought through such involved labours by purely instinctive judgement, was expected to float in perfect balance. There were no excuses and no ballast.

The Nootka harpoon was an awesome weapon four inches in diameter and eighteen feet long. It was made of two or three pieces of yew wood joined with interlocking curves and wrapped with whale sinew. The sinew was sewed together with yellow cedar bark, creating a tight binding that held the segments into a rigid whole. The harpoon head was made of a mussel shell with two carefully fitted pieces of elkhorn as barbs, and connected to a lanyard of whale or sea lion sinew covered with yellow cedar bark and, finally, overlaid with cherry bark.

The lanyard was spliced and served with nettle fiber string on a 240-foot length of line nearly one and a half inches in diameter. This line was spliced on to a second line of lighter cedar rope 360 feet in length. The combined strength of these lines was greater than a hemp rope of similar dimensions; also, the line had a certain rigidity which prevented it from fouling when played out after a strike.

Floats were the key of the Nootka method of whaling, and a special person was assigned to prepare and maintain them. Essentially they were whole sealskins sewn up and inflated like balloons.

Fresh skins were scraped with a pecten shell and tanned with warm urine. The hair was left intact and apertures closed with yew wood plugs; the skin was turned inside out and left with a small opening for inflation later on.

Other equipment included paddles of yew or maple which were tapered to lessen noise when striking the ocean's surface.

The canoe also carried bailing scoops and boxes for food and water supplies. Special bags filled with cedar shavings held human excreta which, it was believed, would anger the sea spirits if placed in the ocean. A large lance was included for administering the *coup de grace*. All of the canoe's gear was maintained in perfect order by the crewmen since inefficiency might spell disaster or result in the loss of a whale.

The Nootkas were hunting the seven species of whale which frequented coastal waters at the time of European contact. The largest variety of cetacean was the blue or sulphur-bottom whale. The largest animal ever to live on earth, blues measuring 100 feet in length and weighing over 100 tons have been recorded. By comparison, the largest of all dinosaurs attained a length of only 60 feet and weighed a paltry 20 tons.

The smaller, more common types of whale hunted by the Indians included the California grey whale (50 feet), sperm whales (60 feet), right whales (50 to 60 feet), humpback whales (45 feet), finbacks (80 feet) and the killer whale or blackfish (30 feet).

Sperm whales and killer whales are true carnivores with predatory habits and fully developed teeth, but the other species are baleen whales which filter microscopic plants and animals called plankton through the myriad rows of whalebone lining their mouths. Normally very difficult to catch, killer whales were sometimes taken by young Nootkas out to assert their prowess at whaling. The killer whale's flesh was considered a delicacy with a rich flavour like that of porpoise.

The whaling season lasted from the beginning of May to the end of June, corresponding with the whale's migrating habits.

The principal figure of every whaling expedition was the chief, who served as harpooner on the lead canoe. Supposedly having inherited his powers from his father, the chief was considered the greatest whaler of the tribe and all whaling equipment belonged to him. The strictest rituals of preparation for the hunt were reserved for the chief and his wife, who were required to live separately and abstain from sexual contact for weeks prior to the whaling excursion.

The couple spent days in singing and praying to the whale before the canoes actually disembarked, and rubbed each other's bodies vigorously with hemlock branches until the plant's needles had been torn off. With blood flowing freely from their scratches, they entered a special fresh-water bathing pool. Submerging and surfacing four times, the pair spouted water in imitation of the whale and moved in the direction that they wished the whale to follow after being harpooned. The wife repeatedly chanted a chorus of 'This is the way the whale will act' as her husband sang to the unseen animal. The ritual reflected their great concern to have the whale stay close to the village after being struck. If it headed out to sea it might take days of laborious paddling to bring it back, or it might run out of range, taking the prized harpoon head with it.

Besides living apart from his wife, the chief was required to avoid contact with all women during his preparations because of possible association with women who were ceremonially unclean. Both the chief and his wife tried to avoid the thought of sex as a means of obtaining further purification.

When the whaling canoes finally left for the long expedition, the chief's wife retired to her house, lay down and was covered with a cedar bark mat. She could neither move, eat, nor drink until her husband returned.

The chief's whaling regalia included a bundle of hemlock twigs tied to his forehead, a bearskin robe, and a ceremonial whaling hat woven for him by his wife. His hair was tied in a knot at the back.

The expedition left before dawn in order to arrive at the main whaling grounds at daybreak. The lead canoe carried the chief and his massive harpoon, a steersman and six paddlers. The second canoe was usually captained by a relative of the chief. Sometimes a small, fast-moving sealing canoe accompanied the other boats; it would return quickly to the village if a strike was made so the Indians on shore could offer prayers and sing as the men in the canoes struggled at sea with their giant catch.

The whaling grounds were often a shallow area such as a bay or cove where the whales were lazing near the surface. The animals would often select these quiet, sheltered waters to briefly rest on the annual migratory journeys from South Pacific regions to the icy Arctic waters.

After reaching the proximity of the whaling grounds, the Indian crews sat with all eyes trained on the horizon for the telltale spout of water marking the presence of a whale resting on the surface. The steersman, often an older and more experienced whaler, had a firm understanding of the whale's sounding habits and could predict with some accuracy the creature's underwater movements.

A whale resting will normally submerge and swim between 200 and 300 yards before surfacing again. These short periods of submerging and reappearance may be repeated three or four times before the creature finally sounds, disappearing beneath the surface for as long as 20 minutes.

The steersman was required to make a calculated judgement where the whale would surface and then direct the crewmen to row there with maximum speed. The striking position had to be exact because the cumbersome harpoon was thrust from above, never thrown. Close wasn't good enough; the canoe must be exactly positioned or the harpooner held his hand.

The account of John Jewitt, an English sailor who spent three years as a slave of the Moachat chief, Maquinna, gives an idea of a Nootka whaling party's day to day chances of success. According to Jewitt, Maquinna diligently hunted whales a total of 53 days between 1803 and 1805. His crews harpoooned nine whales but only managed to kill one and bring it to the village. The greatest whalers of ancient times, according to early informants, might have reached ten catches a season.

The best striking angle was to the whale's left with the harpooner having relatively free access to the area under the animal's left flipper. The crew tried to approach from the monster's rear where they would be out of its field of vision. At the exact moment of the strike, each crewman had a specific function which had to be carried out with clockwork precision.

The steersman shouted out to the harpooner when the tail was exactly the right distance under water for the strike to take place. Since the whale's flukes usually flipped up when the harpoon hit, the steersman would have to judge when the tail would miss the canoe if it made a sudden movement out of the water.

Responding to the steersman's call, the harpooner would ram his weapon down with all his strength into the whale's body below the left flipper. The harpooner immediately flattened out in the front of the canoe to avoid the wildly careening shaft.

Three pairs of paddlers sat between the harpooner at the bow and the steersman at the rear of the canoe. The starboard paddler occupying the most forward position, directly behind the harpooning chief of his tribe, would throw over the first float after the strike. The third starboard paddler, next to the steersman, played out the line for this float with his paddle to avoid fouling.

Paddler number two, occupying the middle position between his fellows and also on the starboard side, steadied the canoe with his paddle. The paddlers on the port side of the canoe backed water to port to keep the canoe away from the walloping flukes of the wounded beast.

After the canoe was backed out of danger and the floats and lines secured, the harpooner retreated to his role of chief and sang to the whale, imploring the thrashing, angry creature to head towards the shore.

'Whale, I have given you what you are wishing to get—my good harpoon. And now you have it. Please hold it with your strong hands and do not let go. Whale, turn toward the beach of Yahksis and you will be proud to see the young men come down to the fine sandy beach of my village at Yahksis to see you; and the young men will say to one another "What a great whale he is! What a fat whale he is! What a strong whale he is!" And you, whale, will be proud of all that you hear them say of your greatness. This is what you are wishing, and this is what you are trying to find from one end of the world to the other, every day you are travelling and spouting.'

The whale's initial struggle was a violent, dangerous period of the hunt in which the animal often would jump completely out of the water in attempts to escape the stinging harpoon. The line flew from the boat as if snagged on a runaway locomotive; crewmen careless enough to get in the bight might have an arm torn from its socket. The canoe itself would often be capsized or split in two by a blow of the flukes. Cases have been recorded where a split canoe was righted, bound together, the chase resumed and the whale ultimately overcome.

If no accidents occurred, the second canoe usually moved in for another strike.

Ideally, the whale would swim towards the village but often it broke for the open sea. The crew regarded this as a sign of some error in their preparations. As the whale tired and surfaced, the crew would make attempts to turn it around by poking its head or eye with a shaft. If nothing could be done, the forward paddler on the starboard side used the canoe's lance to slash the main tendons controlling the flukes. The paddler then drove the killing lance under the flipper. The great creature spouted blood and died.

A crewman would then dive into the water and hack holes through the snout and lower jaw so the mouth could be sewn shut. This prevented the dead carcass from filling with water and sinking. Additional floats would also be attached with small harpoons. Then the long tow back to the village began.

The entire tribe responded to the arrival of the whale with the ceremony and celebration of a great religious event. The whale was welcomed by a chorus of tribe members who praised its greatness in song as the chief's wife made offerings of water and eagle down.

The 'ceremonial hump', a wide piece of choice meat taken off the back near the fin, was presented to the chief. Considered taboo for eating, this blubber was hung on a rack outside the chief's house and decorated with eagle feathers and down. He also received a small piece of the tail for eating purposes. In order of their supposed 'gourmet value' other pieces were presented to visitors, crew members, and visitors who assisted in the hunt.

Ritual singing and formal chants of praise to the whale were made in front of the carcass continuously for several days.

Blubber was boiled in wooden boxes and the oil skimmed off for storage in bags made from the whale's stomach and bladders. The meat and blubber were dried, smoked and stored. The bones and waste portions of the flesh were left on the beach for scavengers.

Five days after the hunt a blubber feast was given. Visitors received gifts of choice cuts but neither the chief nor his wife could partake lest their luck in future hunts be affected.

Whaling among the Nootka Indians fell into a decline around 1860, probably owing to the greater attractions of white sealing. However, a revival of Nootkan culture renewed activity early in this century and some west coast tribes were taking the occasional whale as late as 1940. When Phillip Drucker made a study of contemporary Indian whaling in 1951, he found eight remaining whalers on the coast, only two of whom had been successful. One, named Ahousat Amos, had taken one whale, and another, Aliyu, had taken three.

It is difficult to say now whether the final demise of the art was a result of the ultimate deterioration of Nootkan traditional culture or of the west coast whale population itself. Perhaps in some cosmically ironic way it was fitting that both hunter and prey fell victim to the age of technology about the same moment in history.

But there were others on the earth's surface who had made themselves sailors. Far to the south, the great double-hulled canoes of neolithic Polynesians were carrying out the millennia-long voyaging trek up the 'wind corridor' from South-East Asia to Easter Island, and sailing north and south from Tahiti and the Marquesas to Hawaii and New Zealand. And in Northern Europe, the graceful open ships of the Norse quested out from Scandinavia, touching only briefly at North America, but followed in a few hundred years by other men who had married the skills of the Norse to the lateen sails and carvel hulls of the Arabs, and were ploughing the oceans outward from Europe in quest of gold, other riches, and finally the lands themselves that they came upon. When the first Canadians met them, they brought strange new experiences to the latter's minds as well as bodies, as this West Coast legend tells. Not evident to the Nootka and others was the scale of the upheaval that the coming of the 'Children of the Moon' would bring.

The Children of the Moon
George H. Griffin

STELLO-WALTH was a petty chief of the Nootka Nation and dwelt with his people at the edge of a sheltered cove on the West Coast of what is now known as Vancouver Island. By leaving his lodge and mounting a small promontory, Stello-walth could gaze out over the illimitable blue of the Pacific Ocean.

It happened on a fine morning in the early spring that the chief wandered down to the shore in search of a cedar log suitable to make a canoe. He took infinite pains with his beachcombing and it was some time before he came upon a log that would serve the purpose. He examined it carefully and walked around it, prying in the loose shingle to make sure that it was sound. Near one end of the bulky stick and resting across it was a small log. Stello-walth was about to throw it off when he paused and eyed it with growing wonder.

The things which held his attention were many. In the first place he noted that, in spite of the length of the slim pole, it was uniform in diameter and contained no knots. Again, it seemed to be covered with a shiny substance except in places where it had been worn off by fretting on the rocks and by the action of the water, but the thing that captivated him most was a band of some black material that was fastened about it. In great haste, Stello-walth went back to his lodge and, without telling any of the villagers of his remarkable find, he returned to the beach bearing sundry tools with him.

He peered at the black substance closely. It seemed to be very hard and fairly thick. He pounded it with his stone hammer, but made no impression on it. He now attempted to lever it away from the wood. For a long time he laboured, but he was forced to give up his task when the daylight failed. Early next morning he approached it again, and before nightfall he had succeeded in getting it off. All at once he recognized its possibilities. Here was a substance far harder than anything he had encountered before and, by rubbing it upon a rock, he found that the outer surface could be removed, revealing a bright under-coat.

Stello-walth was beside himself with delight. If he could only fashion a tool out of this material, he would have wonderful magic to build a canoe! It was with this in mind that he went to work. Day in and day out he toiled, always in secret, until at last he completed a cutting-head. The results were far beyond his fondest expectations. Skilfully he made a handle out of a crooked stick and lashed his new magic firmly to it with sinew. What a wonderful adze it made!

He was now ready to carry out his original intention—that of canoe building. He set to work with a will and, in a remarkably short space of time, he had carved a splendid vessel out of a cedar log. The elders of the tribe inspected it when it was finished. They congratulated him upon his superior workmanship.

'How did you make it so quickly?' they asked. 'See how smooth it is, inside and out. Tell us, O Chief, that we may do likewise.'

Stello-walth drew himself up to his full height, for this praise sounded like sweet music in his ears.

'My people, I possess magic that no man knows of. I am mighty, but the secret is mine. I, and only I, control it.'

They stared at him in amazement. Some, a little more sceptical than the rest, were inclined to misbelieve him. But here was the proof! No living person had ever built a canoe in such a short time. Undoubtedly their chief was mighty.

Everything progressed favourably for a moon or two, until a suspicion began to creep into Stello-walth's mind that the young men of the tribe were spying on him. Convinced that they were trying to discover his precious secret, he carried his magic about with him everywhere he went. He always took the precaution to keep it out of their sight by hiding it in the folds of his cloak, and not for one moment was it out of his sight or touch. In one way, it became a burden to him, but he did not seem to mind.

Early one morning, Stello-walth decided to go hunting. He bore his fish-spear, and, of course, his magic. He went alone to the sea front and clambered over many rocky pine-clad bluffs. In order to have the free use of both hands, he had fastened the precious adze to his waist with a length of twine. It was not until he resolved to go home that he missed it. The hunting had proven good and he was, therefore, bearing a burden besides the spear, so it was not strange that the tool had dropped without his realizing it.

Immediately upon discovering his loss, he laid down the load he was carrying and began to retrace his footsteps but, search as he might, he did not succeed in finding his magic tool. Disconsolate and unhappy, he returned with dragging steps to his abode and would speak with no person. Many wondered at the strange conduct of their chief, but were too prudent to question him about it.

Now Stello-walth had no intention of giving up so easily. He dared not elicit the help of any of the men, for it would mean the revelation of his secret and loss in prestige would follow. He must hunt for it alone and this he proceeded to do. Day after day, he pried into every nook and cranny along the beach, but his efforts were not rewarded, and so it was that he found hmself, late one afternoon, far from his lodge. He set out to return after eating a simple repast, but it was dark when he reached the last headland which formed the northern barrier of the village cove.

The moon had just risen. Her silvery disc was half-way over the rim of the horizon, and the ripples on the broad swells of the ocean glittered and glinted in the radiance. Stello-walth paused, a solitary figure, and contemplated the beauty before him. With preoccupied thoughts he stood perfectly still and let his vision wander outward across the waters, following the pathway of light. Suddenly he started, and passed a hand across his eyes. He looked again. There, slowly moving across the face of the moon, was a great canoe. Now it was framed within the lunar semi-circle, and Stello-walth saw that the canoe had wings. He could hardly credit his senses, but there it was. Ever so slowly the vessel passed out of the screen of light, and he observed that it carried with it a part of the moon, which showed like pin-pricks just below the billowing wings. He waited no longer, but hurried to the lodges clustered under the brow of the bluff upon which he stood. Arriving in the village, he summoned the tribe and told them of the vision he had seen.

Somewhere in the remote darkness of the room, hidden within the audience, a warrior laughed. Stello-walth was angered.

'Who dares laugh at my story?' he demanded.

There was an ominous silence. The man who had given way to merriment held his peace.

Shortly afterwards the meeting was broken up, and the people composed themselves to rest.

The sun had barely risen the following morning, when Stello-walth was awakened by the shrill shouts of children scampering outside the building. Someone was calling him. Hurriedly throwing his cloak about his shoulders, he went outside. All the villagers were gathered on the beach and there, at anchor in the little cove, was his canoe of the moon. With pride lighting up his features he walked to the edge of the water, the people falling back to form a pathway down which he strode. He turned and faced them.

'Does Stello-walth speak truth?' he said. 'Yonder is the sight I beheld.'

They shouted in approval.

'Assemble, warriors, and tell the shaman to come to me.'

His orders were obeyed.

'We must go out to greet the Children of the Moon with due ceremony as befits our station.'

He was interrupted by several of the men. Some suggested that they wait to see what would happen; others made it plain that they should arm themselves, but in the end Stello-walth's counsel prevailed.

Twelve young warriors were selected who were pure in heart and body. They were attired in the best costumes the tribe could offer. The chief placed over his head a ceremonial mask with bristles of the walrus standing erect so as to form a kind of crest. In his hand he bore a rattle. All of them stepped into the finest war canoe and slowly paddled out towards the moon bird. When they were within hailing distance, Stello-walth made a long speech in which he welcomed the strangers.

After it was finished, the tribesmen resumed their paddling and brought up alongside the vessel. The next problem was to get aboard the canoe with the splendid white wings, but assistance was offered to them by the Moon Children who let down pieces of material very like cedar rope and signed for them to come aboard. They obeyed and, in a short time, were assembled upon the deck. They stared about them with amazement, and Stello-walth was quick to note an abundance of the black stuff which he had found in his beachcombing. The Moon Chief now came up and spoke to them in a strange tongue. Like the hissing of snakes, it sounded to the warriors.

Stello-walth gazed intently at the white face and the eyes the colour of the blue sky and the hair that looked like grass when it is yellow after the drought of summer. The Moon Chief made signs for them to be seated and, when they had done so, slaves appeared who also had white faces and placed before them on the deck, shining discs, hollow in the centre and containing dark blood and bleached bones. The Moon Chief signified that they should eat.

Stello-walth turned to his warriors and saw the look of dismay on their faces. Solemnly he shook his head in disapproval. Never before had they feasted on raw blood and bones. At last, one of the Moon Children placed some of the vile stuff in his mouth and ate it. A warrior, younger than the rest of his companions, followed the example of the sailor. Spurred on by this, Stello-walth began to eat. How crumbly the bones were, and how sweet the dark blood!

While they were feasting, several of the Moon People took the opportunity to examine the clothes of the warriors. They fingered the rich texture of the sea-otter cloaks, and made strange sounds to themselves. Stello-walth, perceiving their interest, commanded his men to take off their robes. And thus it came about that each visitor had the shining disc in front of him in trade for his cloak.

After this exchange, a Moon Child brought forth a long, black stick and, placing it to his shoulder, pointed it at a gull perched on the log supporting one of the wings of the big canoe. A loud bang followed and the bird dropped dead at Stello-walth's feet. He reached out for the black rod and handled it gingerly. It was formed of the familiar black substance!

The Moon Chief now took the weapon and piled the traded cloaks beside it and made signs to Stello-walth, who understood. He immediately ordered some of his men to go ashore and bring back with them from his lodge bundles of sea-otter skins. When they returned and the pile had reached the top of the gun which was held in an erect position, the White Chief gave it to Stello-walth. No longer need people fear the roving bears and wolves.

At sunset, they crowded on the beach to watch the majestic canoe spread its wings to make its return journey to the moon, and that evening Stello-walth held a feast.

This was the tribe's first acquaintance with the white strangers from over the sea. They had partaken of the food of the Moon Children— molasses and biscuits—and had eaten this from tin plates. Their chief was the fortunate owner of a firearm, and was reverenced for his loftiness.

The Newcomers

It may have been that storm-blown Phoenician galleys, or the craft of an unknown long-vanished North Atlantic sea culture, may have touched at the dark, serrated evergreen shores of Canada. There is no confirming record of such visits, nor any certainty that ancient Chinese voyagers in their sturdy junks may have touched Canada's west in their search for the legendary land of Fu-sang. But more concrete is the record of discovery—in their eyes—of North America by the Norse, about the year 1000 A.D. Driven by population pressures in the narrow fjords of Scandinavia, and encouraged by a warming climate, the Iron Age Norse had developed their double-ended rowing boats into two types of formidable ships: the 'snake ship', or long, narrow attack craft powered by oars and a single squaresail, swift and flexible, but unsuited for ocean passage-making; and the knorr, a strong and more amply proportioned trading boat, double-ended and either rowed or sailed under a single wool and leather squaresail. Pressing outward from Scandinavia in search of plunder, trade, or settlement — the Norse were practical, and would consider any mix of the three — the Nordic adventurers reached Iceland, then Greenland, and finally Canada in a tale captured and kept by a rich storytelling tradition.

The Greenlanders' Saga
Gwyn Jones

Bjarni brought his ship to Eyrar that same summer his father had sailed away in the spring. He was taken heavily aback by the news, and had no mind to discharge his ship's cargo. His shipmates asked him what he proposed to do, and he replied that he meant to carry on as usual and enjoy winter quarters at his father's home. 'I shall steer my ship for Greenland, if you are prepared to go along with me.' They all said they would stand by his decision. 'Our voyage will appear foolhardy,' said Bjarni, 'since no one of us has entered the Greenland Sea.' Even so they put out the moment they were ready, and sailed for three days before losing sight of land. Then their following wind died down, and north winds and fogs overtook them, so that they had no idea which way they were going. This continued over many days, but eventually they saw the sun and could then get their bearings [*or* determine the quarters of the heavens]. They now hoisted sail, and sailed that day before sighting land, and debated among themselves what this land could be. To his way of thinking, said Bjarni, it could not be Greenland. They asked him whether he proposed to sail to this land or not. 'My intention', he replied, 'is to sail close in to the land.' Which they did, and could soon see that the land was not mountainous and was covered with forest, with low hills there, so they left the land to port of them and let their sheet turn towards the land.

After this they sailed for two days before sighting another land. They asked whether Bjarni thought this in its turn was Greenland. In his opinion, he said, this was no more Greenland than the first place — 'For there are very big glaciers reported to be in Greenland.' They soon drew near to this land, and could see that it was flat country and covered with woods. Then their following wind died on them. The crew talked things over and said they thought it common sense to put ashore there; but this Bjarni would not allow. They reckoned they were in need of both wood and water. 'You lack for neither,' said Bjarni, and got some hard words for this from his crew.

He gave orders to hoist sail, which was done; they turned their prow from the land and sailed out to sea three days with a south-west wind, and then they saw the third land, and this land was high, mountainous, and glaciered. They asked whether Bjarni would put ashore there, but no, he said, he had no wish to. 'For to me this land looks good for nothing.' So without so much as lowering their sail they held on along the land, and came to see that it was an island.

Once more they turned their prow from the land and held out to sea with the same following wind. Soon the wind freshened, so Bjarni ordered them to reef, and not crowd more sail than was safe for their ship and tackle. This time they sailed for four days, and then saw the fourth land. They asked Bjarni whether he thought this was Greenland or not. 'This is very like what I am told about Greenland,' replied Bjarni, 'and here we will make for the land.'

So that is what they did, and came to land under a certain cape in the evening of the day. There was a boat on the cape, and there too on the cape lived Herjolf, Bjarni's father. It was for this reason the ness got its name, and has been known ever since as Herjolfsnes. Bjarni now went to his father's, gave over his sailing and stayed with him for the rest of Herjolf's life, and later lived there as his father's successor.

The next thing that happened was that Bjarni Herjolfsson came over from Greenland to see earl Eirik, and the earl made him welcome. Bjarni gave an account of those travels of his on which he had seen these lands, and people thought how lacking in enterprise and curiosity he had been in that he had nothing to report of them, and he won some reproach for this. Bjarni became a retainer of the earl's, and next summer returned to Greenland.

There was now much talk about voyages of discovery. Leif, son of Eirik the Red of Brattahlid, went to see Bjarni Herjolfsson, bought his ship from him, and found her a crew, so that they were thirty-five all told. Leif invited Eirik his father to lead this expedition too, but Eirik begged off rather, reckoning he was now getting on in years, and was less able to stand the rigours of bad times at sea than he used to be. Leif argued that of all their family he would still command the best luck, so Eirik gave way to him, and once they were ready for their voyage came riding from home. When he had only a short way to cover to the ship, the horse he was riding on stumbled, Eirik fell off, and damaged his foot. 'It is not in my destiny', said Eirik then, 'to discover more lands than this we are now living in. Nor may we continue further this time all together.' Eirik returned home to Brattahlid, but Leif rode on to the ship and his comrades with him, thirty-five of them all told. There was a German on the expedition named Tyrkir.

They now prepared their ship and sailed out to sea once they were ready, and they lighted on that land first which Bjarni and his people had lighted on last. They sailed to land there, cast anchor and put off a boat, then went ashore, and could see no grass there. The background was all great glaciers, and right up to the glaciers from the sea as it were a single slab of rock. The land impressed them as barren and useless. 'At least,' said Leif, 'it has not happened to us as to Bjarni over this land, that we failed to get ourselves ashore. I shall now give the land a name, and call it Helluland, Flatstone Land.' After which they returned to the ship.

After that they sailed out to sea and lighted on another land. This time too they sailed to land, cast anchor, then put off a boat and went ashore. The country was flat and covered with forest, with extensive white sands wherever they went, and shelving gently to the sea. 'This land,' said Leif, 'shall be given a name in accordance with its nature, and be called Markland, Wood Land.' After which they got back down to the ship as fast as they could.

From there they now sailed out to sea with a north-east wind and were at sea two days before catching sight of land. They sailed to land, reaching an island which lay north of it, where they went ashore and looked about them in fine weather, and found that there was dew on the grass, whereupon it happened to them that they set their hands to the dew, then carried it to their mouths, and thought they had never known anything so sweet as that was. After which they returned to their ship and sailed into the sound which lay between the island and the cape projecting north from the land itself. They made headway west round the cape. There were big shallows there at low water; their ship went aground, and it was a long way to look to get sight of the sea from the ship. But they were so curious to get ashore they had no mind to wait for the tide to rise under their ship, but went hurrying off to land where a river flowed out of a lake, where they cast anchor, carried their skin sleeping-bags off board, and built themselves booths. Later they decided to winter there and built a big house.

There was no lack of salmon there in river or lake, and salmon bigger than they had ever seen before. The nature of the land was so choice, it seemed to them that none of the cattle would require fodder for the winter. No frost came during the winter, and the grass was hardly withered. Day and night were of a more equal length there than in Greenland or Iceland. On the shortest day of winter the sun was visible in the middle of the afternoon as well as at breakfast time.

Once they had finished their house-building Leif made an announcement to his comrades. 'I intend to have our company divided now in two, and get the land explored. Half our band shall remain here at the hall, and the other half reconnoitre the countryside—yet go no further than they can get back home in the evening, and not get separated.' So for a while that is what they did, Leif going off with them or remaining in camp by turns. Leif was big and strong, of striking appearance, shrewd, and in every respect a temperate, fair-dealing man.

One evening it turned out that a man of their company was missing. This ws Tyrkir the German. Leif was greatly put out by this, for Tyrkir had lived a long while with him and his father, and had shown great affection for Leif as a child. He gave his shipmates the rough edge of his tongue, then turned out to go and look for him, taking a dozen men with him. But when they had got only a short way from the hall there was Tyrkir coming to meet them. His welcome was a joyous one. Leif could see at once that his foster-father was in fine fettle. He was a man with a bulging forehead, rolling eyes, and an insignificant little face, short and not much to look at, but handy at all sorts of crafts.

'Why are you so late, foster-father,' Leif asked him, 'and parted this way from your companions?'

By way of a start Tyrkir held forth a long while in German, rolling his eyes all ways, and pulling faces. They had no notion what he was talking about. Then after a while he spoke in Norse. 'I went no great way further than you, yet I have a real novelty to report. I have found vines and grapes.'

'Is that the truth, foster-father?' Leif asked.

'Of course it's the truth,' he replied. 'I was born where wine and grapes are no rarity.'

They slept overnight, then in the morning Leif made this announcement to his crew. 'We now have two jobs to get on with, and on alternate days must gather grapes or cut vines and fell timber, so as to provide a cargo of such things for my ship.' They acted upon these orders, and report has it that their towboat was filled with grapes [raisins?]. A full ship's cargo was cut, and in the spring they made ready and sailed away. Leif gave the land a name in accordance with the good things they found in it, calling it Vinland, Wineland; after which they sailed out to sea and had a good wind till they sighted Greenland and the mountains under the glaciers.

The small Norse settlements in Canada which followed their discovery of 'Vinland' did not survive. Even with their Iron Age weapons, the Norse had no real technological superiority over the Canadian First Nations who met, and ultimately resisted, the Norse settlement efforts. Faced with a resolute hostility from the 'Skraelings', as the Norse called the inhabitants, the Scandinavians abandoned their efforts at settlement, and a worsening climate, the Black Death, and the Mongol hordes put an end to European expansion by sea for a time. The Crusades, however, had awakened European tastes to the riches of the Middle East. With the fall of Constantinople in 1453 and the Ottoman Turk astride the trade routes to the East, the Europeans were faced with reliance upon expensive Venetian or Genoese merchants for their Eastern spices or goods— or trying to get around the Ottoman barrier by getting to the East themselves, by sea. When Europeans married the Northern squaresail to the Arab lateen, they created a ship capable, with the right hull, of open-ocean voyaging. By the 1470s, Basque fishermen may have already been to the great fishing banks off Canada's east coast. But it was Columbus' 1492 voyage to the Americas, and the flood of Aztec and Inca wealth into Spain as the Spanish looted their new possessions, that spurred the French, English, and Dutch to see what could be found beyond the Western Ocean. And Jacques Cartier was the first European to see in any depth the land that would become Canada.

Cartier Comes to Canada
John Bakeless

Two little French sailing vessels, hardly more than yachts, hove to while they were still some leagues off the grim Newfoundland coast. It was late spring or early summer of 1534, and Jacques Cartier was just beginning his adventurous exploration along the St Lawrence, which other and later Frenchmen were to carry inland across the continent, for more than two hundred years.

Of Cartier the man almost nothing is known. He was a Breton, of the stout seafaring breed. He was born at St Malo in 1491. He could command enough capital to outfit an ambitious expedition. He was a skilled and fearless navigator. Beyond that practically nothing is known of his early life, before the moment when he steered out of St Malo for a new world, brave and strange and perilous.

From the decks of their low-riding craft, neither of more than sixty tons burden, with gunwales that barely cleared the rolling waves, Cartier and some sixty bearded sailors gazed in amazement at what they saw. The new world they had sailed from France to explore was beginning to reveal its expected wonders already—while they were still far from shore.

Birds. Sea birds.

Sea birds swarming over and around one lonely rocky island, far at sea, in such numbers that 'all the ships of France might load a cargo of them without once perceiving that any had been removed', while at the same time in the air and round about fluttered other birds till they seemed 'an hundred times as many more as on the island itself'. The numbers were 'so great as to be incredible unless one has seen them'— in fact, a Jesuit father who tried to land on the same island a few years later found that 'if you do not obtain a good foothold, they rise in such numbers that they may knock you over.'

Not all the birds on this marvellous, seagirt rock—the modern Funk Island—could fly. The French sailors, who had been living on salt meat all the way from Normandy, looked hungrily at queer, large, black and white fowl, obviously and appetizingly edible, as big as geese and 'so fat that it is marvellous'. Some of them were settled comfortably among the rocks, others swimming along shore. None of them were flying, for, as the sailors would see when they came closer, the birds had 'only small wings about the size of a man's hand'.

These were the great auks, a species completely extinct for the last hundred years, but common in primitive North America along the coast from far north in Canada to Cape Cod and probably a good deal farther south. There were plenty of them in this whole range in 1534 and they were especially numerous on this lonely island, far at sea, for here they were perfectly safe. No Indian was foolish enough to paddle his canoe over thirty miles of sea, just to lay in a stock of eggs and poultry, when both were to be had for the taking, along the river near his *wiggiwam*.

On their wave-beaten cliffs, none of these birds had ever encountered any human enemies. It is doubtful if any of them had so much as seen a human being, until the fatal day when two big longboats put off from the French ships. Within half an hour, the capacious craft were loaded down with fat birds, 'as with stones'. Each of the ships could salt down four or five casks of them for future use, while the crews feasted on fresh poultry.

Though the great auk was helpless on land, so that it could be caught and clubbed with no effort at all, the sailors found to their dismay that other birds, especially the gannets, fought back, and 'bit like dogs'. They were even more surprised by a huge white polar bear, 'as big as a calf and as white as a swan that sprung into the sea in front of them'. Apparently the bear had also come to feast on birds and birds' eggs. The big white beast escaped from this first encounter, but next day, as the ships went on toward the coast, they found him swimming desperately for shore; caught up with the fugitive by lowering away the longboats—the ships themselves being too clumsy to manoeuvre as the brute twisted and turned in the water, and were soon feasting on red meat as well as poultry. 'His flesh was as good to eat as that of a two-year-old heifer,' says Cartier, with all a Frenchman's gastronomic enthusiasm, heightened a little by a long voyage on ship's diet.

(One of the amusing things about French explorers is how very French they were. Amid all their hardships and dangers, whatever else they noted down, they never missed good food, the prospects of good food, or a chance to make wine. Some of the missionary French priests, who had given up for their cause almost everything else that makes life worth living, nevertheless took along a little stock of savoury herbs.)

Today, polar bears would not ordinarily be found so far south, but in the sixteenth century they were not uncommon around the gulf of the St Lawrence, and a few may even have come down as far as what today is the United States. Their meat was not always so wholesome as Cartier found it. Much later French explorers, who killed an enormous specimen in Hudson Bay, ate ravenously of the fresh meat, and immediately became so ill that they expected to die, though they were able to save themselves with medicine and Indian sweat-baths. Just what was wrong is by no means clear, for other explorers ate white bear's meat with much satisfaction. Probably Radisson's hungry men had simply gorged themselves and were suffering nothing worse than a stomach-ache, though a friendly Indian explained to the sufferers that the white bear had poison in his liver.

Until white men reached North America with firearms, the polar bears had little to fear. Originally—like the grizzly, which white men would not encounter for two centuries to come—the white bears had no great fear of human kind. Indian arrows were no real danger, and at first the huge animals treated the white man and his arquebus with equal indifference. An English observer notes in 1578 that 'the beares also be as bold, which will not spare at midday to take your fish before your face.'

Rejoicing that his first landfall on the mysterious shore had been so auspicious, Cartier and his sixty men sailed on up the Newfoundland coast, passed its northern tip, and then turned southwest, through the Strait of Belle Isle, until the Gulf of St Lawrence began to open out before them.

Here they came to another 'Isle des Ouaiseaulx', or Bird Island, now identified as the Greenly Island of modern days, on which they noted with interest as many birds as ever, including a new species, the red-beaked puffins, burrowing into the earth under the flat rocks to make their nests. The steep sides of the island were perforated with their burrows—as they still are. Leaving the ships and going on in longboats, Cartier and some of the men camped for the night on another island, where they were delighted to find the eggs of eider ducks 'in great quantity'.

Though the first to leave a record, they were by no means the first white men to visit these waters, a fact of which they had evidence the next day when they ran into a large fishing vessel from La Rochelle. Frenchmen had been fishing here for at least thirty years, together with Basques; and it is by no means impossible that they knew all about them long before Columbus, though—like all fishermen—they kept their choicest fishing grounds a secret. Certainly Bretons were off the Newfoundland coast and in the St Lawrence by 1504, and as early as 1508 a Norman sea captain had ascended the St. Lawrence for more than two hundred miles, bringing Indians back to France, though no record of his adventurous voyages has come down to us.

Feeling their way cautiously and recording soundings of these unknown waters when they could, Cartier's two little ships crept down the west coast of Newfoundland, delighted to find that they could catch a hundred cod in an hour. Whatever else this new land might yield, it was proving endlessly rich in things to eat. Half way across the bay they had new proof of this. They came upon more islands, covered with sea birds, the modern Bird Rocks.

'These islands', Cartier noted, 'were as completely covered with birds, which nest there, as a field is covered with grass.' Like the bird islands they had already seen, these were—and are—perfect natural refuges. Great Bird Rock rises sheer for 105 feet, offering a landing place to small boats only in the calmest sea, with only one or two difficult routes to the top. 'The birds sit there as thicke as stones lie on a paved street,' wrote a visitor in 1597. When Audubon visited the rocks in 1833, he found the nests still so thick that they were 'almost touching each other'. A scientific bird census made in 1870 showed 100,000 gannets.

Although Funk Island, the first Cartier had seen, was a little too far out to sea for birchbark canoes, the Indians swarmed to these more accessible islands whenever they craved a change of diet. It was not really hunting. They killed a supply of wild poultry with clubs or, if that was too much trouble, trampled them to death, bringing back canoes 'filled with sumptuous food acquired without prices'. No slaughter ever seemed to diminish the supply of birds in those days, for it was, as a Jesuit historian wrote as late as 1710, 'impossible to count their numbers'.

All along the shores of the St Lawrence, waterfowl were nearly as numerous and there were more along the chains of lakes that stretched west and north, and still more, west and west, and then great flocks in the Columbia and north and south along the coast of the Pacific. 'Everywhere,' says our Jesuit, 'may be seen sporting in the water, geese, ducks, herons, cranes, swans, coots, and other birds whose habit it is to seek their living from the waves.' Even in the twentieth century, something like this may still be seen in the protected area of the Missouri River, near Great Falls, Montana.

The ornithological Jesuit is perhaps the first to put on record a queer old story about a strange sea bird, probably the great auk: 'One of its feet is armed with hooked claws, the other has webbed toes, like those of a duck; with the latter it swims, with the former it seizes and disembowels fishes.' This zoological fantasy seems to have been widely believed, mainly because no one thought of anything so simple as examining a few specimens.

The safety of the upper rocks was inaccessible to the auks. Unable to climb or fly, they had to nest on the lower levels, where their enemies could reach them. So long as only Indians hunted them there, they could survive, but when the wasteful, ruthless white man came, the great auk was doomed, though even so it bred rapidly enough to maintain itself for three hundred years after Cartier.

Cartier's sailors, who had by this time pretty well eaten up their casks of salted wild poultry, landed again—this time to kill about one thousand wildfowl, leaving regretfully when their longboats were full, for 'one might have loaded in an hour thirty such long-boats.'

Cartier's Frenchmen had at first been horrified by the barren, rocky shores past which they sailed, 'stones and horrible rocks', with a little sour earth, in which grew nothing but moss and stunted shrubs. Cartier, as he gazed at it, rather wondered whether this might not be 'the land God gave to Cain', so grim was the first impression it produced.

Now the land began to improve, for they were approaching the rich alluvial meadows of the St Lawrence River. Landing on Bryon Island, almost in the middle of the Bay, they were delighted to find it 'covered with fine trees and meadows, fields of wild oats, and of pease in flower, as thick and fine as ever I saw in Brittany, which might have been sown by husbandmen'. There were also wild roses, strawberries, 'gooseberry' bushes, which may have been merely chokecherries, 'parsley and other strong-smelling herbs'.

Most astonishing of all were the walruses, 'great beasts like large oxen, which have two tusks in their jaw like elephant's tusks and swim about in the water'. The sailors tried to catch one they found asleep near the water, 'but as soon as we drew near, he threw himself into the sea.' It is perhaps just as well that he did, for walruses were often just as willing as grizzly bears to stand and fight it out. An English crew, passing the Bird Rocks some years later, rashly annoyed the 'Sea Oxen' they found sleeping by the water's edge; and 'when we approached nere unto them with our boate they cast themselves into the sea and pursued us with such furie as that we were glad to flee from them.'

Cartier's men, as they cruised slowly around the gulf, continued to encounter the giant, tusked beasts, but seem to have kept at a respectful distance. There were also whales and belugas (small, white whales). All three animals have since vanished from these waters.

Coasting along Prince Edward Island, Cartier was so impressed by the primeval forest that he landed four times to examine the trees—cedar, yew, pine, elm, ash, willow, and still others whose identity he could not even guess at, with wild pigeons and other birds fluttering in their branches. On the Gaspé Peninsula they were again impressed by the towering trees of the virgin forest, 'as excellent for making masts for ships of three hundred tons and more, as it is possible to find'.

So far, Cartier had had no real contact with Indians. His men had for some time been catching distant, occasional glimpses of 'wild and savage folk', clad in furs, painted 'with certain tan colours', wearing feathers in their hair—the Beothucks, a long-since vanished tribe. Once, on Prince Edward Island, they saw Indians crossing a river in canoes. A little later one warrior ran along shore, beckoning them to land, but when the longboats turned in toward him, the man lost his courage and vanished into the shelter of the forest. Leaving a knife and a woollen girdle tied to a branch, to show that the white strangers were friendly, Cartier turned back to his ships.

Then two little fleets, totalling forty or fifty canoes, appeared, the men at the paddles making signs of friendship and calling out a greeting which Cartier wrote down as *Napou tou daman asurtat*, words which were identified four hundred years later as Micmac, conveying an offer of friendship. But Cartier himself could make nothing of them, and there were so many Indians that he was afraid to let them get very close. In the end, he had to frighten them away with light artillery.

Next day, in spite of this bombardment, more Indians appeared, this time in nine canoes, holding up furs, as if they wished to trade. Cartier sent two men ashore, carrying knives and other iron articles. Trade was so brisk that the Indians sold even the furs on their backs and had to go home to their camps completely naked. Next day, the Frenchman had another friendly meeting with the Indians, and Cartier wrote down the words *cochy* (hatchet) and *bacan* (knife), which identify these Indians as more Micmacs.

On the Gaspé Peninsula they soon met about three hundred more Indians, whom Cartier surveyed without any approval at all—'the sorriest folk there can be in the world, and the whole lot of them had not anything above the value of five sous, their canoes and fishing nets excepted.'

Bits of vocabulary, which he again set down, show that these were a new tribe, speaking some kind of Iroquoian language. Perhaps they were Hurons, for Cartier describes them as 'wonderful thieves'. The French explorers were to become tiresomely familiar with the gift for petty larceny of this talented tribe, who, when they couldn't steal with their light fingers, did nearly as well with their prehensile toes.

Cartier completed his first voyage in the next few days, missing the entrance to the St Lawrence River entirely, because he sailed up the wrong side of Anticosti Island. Having found nothing but more magnificent forest and beautiful, green, empty meadows, he sailed for Normandy, taking with him two young Indians, whom he had—more or less—kidnapped, though he had tried to do it in a friendly way.

Eight months later, in May of 1535, eager for more North American adventure, he returned from France, bringing back with him the two Indians. During their sojourn in France, they had been studying French, and Cartier hoped to use them as interpreters. He had failed to realize how bitterly they resented the original kidnapping, in spite of subsequent good treatment.

Again he halted at the Isle of Birds (Funk Island) to secure two boatloads of wild poultry, before steering into the Gulf of St Lawrence.

This time he followed the northern coast, a course which brought him directly into the mouth of the river, which was to open the way for French explorers reaching southward from the St Lawrence Valley to the Susquehanna, the Ohio, the Mississippi, and the Gulf of Mexico, and westward through the Great Lakes almost to the Rockies, during the next two hundred years.

Listening eagerly to what his two Indians, who in eight months had learned a good deal of French, could tell him about the country they were passing, Cartier and his men crept up the river, sometimes in their ships, sometimes rowing their longboats close in to shore. Twice they made complete circles, so as to see both banks. It was slow going, for Cartier was desperately afraid of uncharted rocks and shoals. Any damage to his ships now would be hard to repair; serious damage to their hulls could not be repaired at all.

Animal life was as abundant in the river as it had been in the gulf. Whales were everywhere—'none of us remembers having seen so many.' Up the Moisie river were many walruses—'fish in appearance like horses which go on land at night'. Soon they encountered more beluga. In a little while the water would grow fresh, the Indians said. They were now entering 'the great river of Hochelaga'—a name that the St Lawrence bore for some time. Yonder was the mouth of the Saguenay river, marked by 'lofty mountains of bare rock with but little soil', yet with astonishingly high trees. There was copper (*caignetdazé*) in that country, said the Indians.

Just below the Indian village of Stadacona (Quebec) they met their first large group of Indians, Hurons, who fled until the two Indians called out to them from Cartier's ship. Then the white men were welcomed with dances and gifts of eels, fish, corn, and melons. Other Indians came swarming in as the news spread, and next day came the great Huron chief, Donnaconna himself, paddling out to the ships with twelve canoes.

The quest for 'Cathay and the Indies' continued unabated, even with the discovery of the vast New World. So rapid was European exploration after Columbus that by 1522 the world had been circumnavigated, a strait round the bottom of South America had been found, and the Indian Ocean had become virtually a Portuguese lake. The restless Elizabethan Age dawned in England, characterized by a bitter struggle with the Spanish, and a product of that age was a York-

shireman and seaman named Martin Frobisher. His determination to make a successful 'Northwest Passage' around North America to Cathay and the Indies, and thereby avoid Spaniard, Portuguese, and Ottoman alike, brought him into Canada's north in 1576. It was a world that soon challenged him beyond expectation in its 'Icie Seas'.

Account of Frobisher's First Voyage
Michael Lok

Of the matters that chiefly moved me to enterprise and advance this voyage of Captain Frobisher and to venture my money therein so largely; I will say briefly that two things moved me thereto. First: The great hope to find our English seas do open into the seas of East India by the north-west way, whereby we might have passage by sea to those rich countries for traffic of merchandise, which was the thing I chiefly desired. Secondly: I was assured by manifold good proofs of divers travellers and histories that Canada, and the new found lands thereto adjoining, were full of people and full of such commodities and merchandise as are found in the countries of Lapland, Russia, and Moscovia, which are furs, hides, wax, tallow, oil, and other. Whereby if it should happen those new lands should stretch to the north pole, so that we could not have passage by sea that way, yet in those same new lands to the northwestward might be established trade of merchandise.

Now, in this voyage of which I write, Captain Martin Frobisher, being furnished with two ships of thirty tons burthen, the *Michael* and the *Gabriel*, and one pinnace of ten tons, and all other things necessary, in as ample manner as the funds supplied would reach, he set sail from England on the 19th day of June, anno domini 1576.

On the 30th day of June, the weather grew to a great storm which continued until the 8th day of July, in which time they could bear no manner of sail. In this great storm they lost sight of their small pinnace (she having three men therein) which they could never since hear of, though they used all possible diligence and means that the weather would suffer to seek and save the same.

When the storm ceased they passed along on their way again, and on the 11th day of July they had sight of land unknown to them. They could not come close enough to set foot thereon because of the marvellous abundance of monstrous great islands of ice which lay driving all along the coast thereof.

Bearing in nearer, in order to explore the same, they found it marvellous high, and full of high ragged rocks all along the coast, and some of the islands of ice near it were of such height as the clouds hung about the tops of them, and the birds that flew about them were out of sight.

Here they lost the ship *Michael*, to their great discomfiture, for the people of that ship, being loath to make discovery of new lands, set their course back again homeward to London.

In the meantime the said Captain Frobisher, in his remaining ship the *Gabriel*, was overset with a sea which they shipped on the thirteenth day of July during the rage of an extreme storm which cast the ship flat on her side. And being open in the waist, she filled with water so that she lay as good as sunk; and would not wear nor steer.

In this distress, when all the men in the ship had lost their courage and did despair of life, the Captain, with valiant courage, stood up and passed along the ship's side on the gunwale of her flat side, and caught hold on the weather leach of the foresail thereby to help her to her feet. And to lighten the ship, they cut away the mizzen mast. And the mariners also would have cut over the main mast, which the Captain refused to allow. At last the ship became upright again, but being full of water, with the rolling of the seas, the water issued out of her and withal many things floated over the ship's sides. And so they put the ship to run before the sea all that day and next night in the storm. Also they broke their main mast afterward, but mended it again.

The storm being ceased, and being now out of hope any more to meet with his other ship the *Michael*: still the Captain determined to follow his enterprise and voyage, according to the uttermost of his power, and rather to make a sacrifice unto God of his life than to return home without the discovery of Cathay, except by compulsion of extreme force and necessity.

And so they returned to a course according to their commission. And on the 29th day of July the Captain himself first had sight of a new land of a marvellous great height, the headland whereof he named Elizabeth Foreland in memory of the Queen's Majesty.

When they approached near they found the seashore full of monstrous high islands and mountains of ice, floating and driving with the winds and tides so as they durst not yet approach with their ship to land thereon. Nevertheless, remaining still in hope to find a safe place to enter with the ship, they passed to and fro along the coast, still in the sight of land, for sixteen days, until the ice was well consumed and gone.

On the 19th day of August they found an island which they liked, in a great strait which they named Frobisher's Strait. The Captain and six of his men landed thereon and went to the top of a high mountain thereof to discover the land about them: and there they espied seven strange boats with men therein rowing toward the island. Whereupon in great haste they ran down again to recover their own boat, which hardly had they recovered before the arrival of those seven boats. The Captain returned to his ship with his boat to put all in readiness for defence if need should be; but sent his skiff crew to view the strange men and have speech with them if they could.

The strangers made offer of friendship, whereupon, by signs, it was agreed that one of their men should come in the skiff aboard the ship, while in pledge for him, one of our men went on land.

The stranger being in the ship made great wondering at all things: and the Captain gave him to taste of the ship's meat and drink and wine, but he made no countenance of liking these. Then the Captain gave him some trifles, which he liked well and took them with him to land where he was delivered, and our man received back again.

Hereby the Captain, perceiving these strange people to be of countenance and conversation proceeding from a nature given to fierceness and rapine, and he being not yet well prepared in his ship for defence, he set sail presently and departed thence to take more time to prepare for defence.

They passed to the southern side of the strait, and there anchored and prepared to defend themselves the best they could as need should be; which was not easily to be done, having so small a ship, and she now armed with so few and weakened men, who had so great labours and diseases suffered at the sea.

On this southern shore the Captain with some of his men went on shore on an island, and climbed to the top of a high mountain to discover what he could of the straits, of the sea, and of the land about. From there he saw two headlands at the furthest end of the straits and a great opening between them which, by reason of the great flooding tides which they found coming out of the same, they judged to be the West Sea, whereby to pass to Cathay and to East India.

Withal they also espied in a valley right under them three houses covered with leather of seal skins, like tents, and also two dogs. And presently, to avoid danger, Captain Frobisher with his men repaired to the boat at the sea shore, but as soon as they had entered it they espied a great boat of that country, with men therein, hard by them, who made signs of friendship. But the Captain would not trust them, and made signs to one of them to come into his boat, which the stranger did. Thereafter the master of our ship went on land to the people who received him and led him by the hand into their houses, or rather cottages.

Thus, having got the master among them, some of them made secret signs to the savage who was held for pledge in our boat that he should escape into the water, which signs Captain Frobisher perceived. And, therefore, having in his hand a fair long dagger, he held the point thereof to the strange man's breast threatening by signs to kill him if he did once stir.

Meantime the master was led into their houses and there saw their manner of food and life, which is very strange and beastly. And the master being returned to the boat and entered therein, the stranger kept for pledge was delivered on land, and presently another of those strange men went willingly in the Captain's boat aboard the ship to see the same: to whom was given many trifles of haberdashery, which pleased him well.

And he being in the ship, Captain Frobisher had talk with him by signs that he should be their pilot through the straits into the West Sea, which he agreed unto. This strange pilot was then carried back again to land to prepare himself and his own boat. But because the Captain did wisely foresee that these strange people were not to be trusted, he told the boat crew that they should set that strange pilot on the point of a certain rock of an island which he assigned them: which was within his own sight so he might have rescued them if any force should have been offered against them.

But these foolish men (being five of them in all in the boat) having set on land this stranger at the place appointed, immediately, and contrary to the Captain's command, rowed further beyond that point and out of his sight. And after that the Captain never saw them again, nor could hear anything of them.

Thus the Captain, having lost his boat and five of his best men (to his great discomfort) still remained with the ship there at anchor all that day and next night hoping to hear of them again. But he could not hear or know anything of them, and thereby he judged they were taken and kept by force.

Wherefore the next morning, which was the 20th day of August, he set sail with the ship and passed along by their houses, as near as he could, and caused his trumpet to sound and shot a piece of ordnance over the houses. But with all this he could see nothing nor hear of his boat or men. But he heard the people of the land laugh, and then he swore not to make peace again with them, but rather to depart from thence to other places, there to try and find some other people of that land to whom these late doings were unknown, and of them to take some prisoners in reprisal for his own men.

He sailed for the space of three days, and finding no other people, he then returned again to the same place where he lost his boat and men.

Being come there he perceived that all the men of the land were gone from thence, and their houses also, which was to his greatest discomfort: for now he was in despair of the recovery of his boat and men any more.

Also being thus maimed by the loss he had suffered, he utterly despaired how to proceed further on his voyage towards Cathay. And most of all he was oppressed with sorrow that he should return back again to his country without bringing any evidence or token of any place whereby to certify to the world where he had been.

So, remaining in this great perplexity and sorrow, more willing to die than to live in that state; suddenly he espied a number of the boats and men of that country coming towards the ship. Whereat he was pleased (though, his ship's weak state being duly considered, he had the more cause to be afraid). But he presented, armed and prepared his ship with all things necessary for defence; and also he covered the chainways and shrouds, and all other places where the enemy might take hold to clamber into the ship. And in the waist of the ship he placed a piece of ordnance, intending to shoot and sink one of their great boats, of which some had twenty men therein, and to have recovered some of them for prisoners with which to redeem his own men.

But when their great boats approached and perceived the defence made against them, only one small boat with one man therein (which was he that first of all came into the ship) dared approach very near to the ship's side, making signs of friendship the while. Whereat the Captain likewise made him signs of friendship, and thus entertained the stranger while he placed himself at the waist of the ship, having at his feet in secret his weapons. The Captain then caused all his men to withdraw from him, whereby he might appear to be alone and without any malice. He made offer of some small things to bring the stranger to the ship's side, but for a long time the man would not approach, which was no small grief to the Captain and the rest. Yet at the last, with the fair offers and enticement with gifts of the Captain, he approached to the ship's side, but stood upon guard with his oar in one hand ready to put off his boat again suddenly if need should be. Now Captain Frobisher called for a bell which he held toward him as a gift, but with a short arm, and when the stranger reached for it the Captain caught hold of the man's wrist and suddenly, by main force of strength, plucked both the man and his light boat out of the sea into the ship in a trice.

So the Captain kept him, without any show of enmity, and made signs to him presently that if he would bring his five back he should go again at liberty, but he would not seem to understand the Captain's meaning, and therefore he was still kept in the ship with sure guard.

This act was done in the presence of all the rest of his fellows, they being within an arrow shot of the ship; whereat they were all marvellously amazed and thereupon presently cast themselves into council and so departed in great haste toward the land, with great hallowing or howling shouts after their manner, like the howling of wolves or other beasts in the woods.

The Captain with his ship remained there all that day and the next day, but could hear no news of his boat and men. Whereupon, having this strange man prisoner in his ship, he took counsel with the master and others what were best to be done. And they all agreed that, considering their evil and weakened state, (being but thirteen men and boys remaining, and they so tired and sick with the labours of their hard voyage) that to proceed any further would bring great danger to the utter loss of the enterprise.

Therefore on the 25th day of August they set sail with their ship, keeping their course back toward England, and so came to London the 9th day of October, and there were joyfully received with the great admiration of the people, having brought with them their strange man and his boat, which was a great wonder unto the whole city and to the rest of the realm that heard of it.

The quest for the Northwest Passage remained a fixation of European exploration of the Canadian coast. Barring the many—and often disastrous— expeditions to the Arctic in the 19th century, it was the exploration of Captain James Cook of the Royal Navy in the late 18th century that brought a practical end to the search for an easy route to Asia. Cook coasted along Canada's western shores under orders to search for a strait leading into Hudson Bay. He did not find it, but he did meet with the peoples who had thought of him and his kind as the 'Children of the Moon'; his observations of British Columbia's inhabitants in 1778 were no less interesting than theirs of him and his ships.

The North American Coast
Captain James Cook

At the end of March [1778] Cook regained the coast and entered King George's or Nootka Sound,the northern entrance of the channel which forms Vancouver Island. He remained there until 26th April, using the abundant supply of local timber to repair the disgraceful condition of his ships and trading with the natives of whom Dr Anderson left interesting descriptions.

MONDAY 30th March. In the Morning I sent three armed boats under the command of Mr King to look for a harbour for the Ships and soon after I went my self in a small boat on the same service. On the NW side of the Arm we were in and not far from the Ship, I found a pretty snug Cove, and Mr King who returned about Noon found one still better on the NW side of the Sound; but as it would have required more time to get to it than the other, it was resolved to make the nearest serve. But being too late in the day to transport the Ships thither before night, I ordered the sails to be unbent, the Topmast to be struck and the Foremast to be unrig'd in order to fix a new bib, one of the old ones being decayed. A great many Canoes filled with the Natives were about the Ships all day, and a trade commenced betwixt us and them, which was carried on with the Strictest honisty on boath sides. Their articles were the Skins of various animals, such as Bears, Wolfs, Foxes, Dear, Rackoons, Polecats, Martins and in particular the Sea Beaver, the same as is found on the coast of Kamtchatka. Cloathing made of their skins and a nother sort made, either of the bark of a tree or some plant like hemp; Weapons, such as Bows and Arrows, Spears &c^a Fish hooks and Instruments of various kinds, pieces of carved work and even human sculs and hands, and a variety of little articles too tedious to mention. For these things they took in exchange, Knives, chissels, pieces of iron & Tin, Nails, Buttons, or any kind of metal. Beads they were not fond of and cloth of all kinds they rejected.

TUESDAY 31st March. The next day the Ships were got into the Cove and their moored head and stern most of the Moorings being fast to the shore. We found on heaving up the anchor that notwithstanding the great depth of water it was let go in, there were rocks at the bottom which had done some considerable damage to the Cable, and the hawsers that were carried out to warp the Ship into the cove got also foul of rocks, so that it appeared that the whole bottom was strewed with them. As we found the Ship again very leaky in her upper works, the Caulkers were set to work to caulk her and repair such other defects as were wanting.

SATURDAY 4th April. In the afternoon we resumed our work and the next day rigged the Foremast; the head of which being rather too small for the Cap, the Carpenter went to work to bring, or fix a piece on one side to fill up the Cap. In cutting into the mast head for this purpose, and examining a little farther into it, both Cheeks were found so rotton that there was no possibility of repairing them without getting the mast out and fixing on new ones. It was evedent that one of the Cheeks had been defective at the first, and the defective part had been cut out and a piece put [in], what had not only weakened the mast head, but had in a great measure been the occasion of roting all the other part. Thus when we were almost ready to put to Sea, we had all our work to do over again, and what was worse a job of work to perform that required some time to finish, but as there was no remedy we immidiately set about it. It was lucky these defects were descovered in a place where wood, the principal thing wanting was to be had, for among the drift wood in the Cove where we lay, were some well seasoned trees and very proper for our purpose, one of which was pitched upon and the Carpenters went to work to make out of it two new Cheeks.

MONDAY 13th April. In the after noon of the next day, I went into the woods with a party of men and cut down a tree for a Mizen Mast and the next morning it was got to the place where the Carpenters were at work upon the Fore-mast. In the evening the wind which had been for some time westerly, veered to SE and increased to a very hard gale with rain which continued till 8 oclock the next morning when it abated and veered again to the West. On the Morning of the 15th the Foremast being finished got it along side and set the Carpenters to work to make a new Mizen Mast, but the weather was so bad that the Foremast could not be got in till the afternoon. At this time several Indians were about the Ship who looked on with more silent attention than is usual with Indians.

It is quite possible to follow Cook's course from the statements in his Journal, although some of his names remain on the map and some do not. H. R. Wagner in his *Cartography of the North West Coast of America*, notes that Cook, in all probability, had knowledge of the recent Spanish expeditions, and was very possibly instructed to follow the route taken by Bering the great Danish explorer sent out by the Russians, particularly as Cook followed this route. Leaving Nootka Sound on 26th April 1778, Cook sighted land on 1st May in 55° 20′ north; named Mt Edgecumbe, Edgecumbe Bay and Cross Sound; saw Mt St Elias, which he thought was Bering's mountain, and following the coast westwards, landed on Keyes Island, which he named after the Royal Chaplain. He then sailed into the inlet which he first named Sandwich, and later King William Sound, spending some days in Snug Corner Cove. On 18th May he named Montague and Green Islands and on 21st May Cape Elizabeth. He later named Point Banks; the Barren Islands, and Cape Douglas, the last in honour of his friend Canon Douglas of Windsor whose editing of the Second Journal had met with Cook's approval. On 28th May he sailed up Cook's Inlet and Cook's River, and landing at Possession Point, in the Southern inlet, took possession of the region for the British Crown.

Cook then sailed westwards along the Alaskan coast, naming prominent geographical features; sighted Shishaldan Volcano on Unimak Island and was very nearly wrecked on the northern point of Unalaska Island which he named Providence. On the north end of Unalaska he found a harbour which he named Samganooda and is now known as Samganuda. After this Cook passed through Bering Strait into the Arctic, where, as Christopher Lloyd points out, he spent the last part of August tacking backwards and forwards off the American and Asian Coasts in an effort to break through an impenetrable ice pack. He saw Cape Prince of Wales, the western point of Alaska; Icy Cape in the American Arctic, his farthest north, and North Cape on the north eastern Siberian Coast. It was a magnificent achievement, which not only demonstrated Cook's abilities as an explorer and cartographer, but also the very fair accuracy of Bering's cartography considering the circumstances under which he worked.

On 29th August in latitude 69° 17′ north Cook decided that he could do no more that season but must return to the Hawaiian Islands to refit for a second effort. On the way he stopped at Unalaska in the Aleutians to refit as the *Resolution* was leaking badly from her disgraceful caulking, and her masts, rigging and sails were in a sorry plight. Russian traders had tried to contact Cook on his voyage northwards; now they met him at Unalaska and gave him most useful information, from their knowledge, or ignorance, of the geographical features northwards, and were most open and honest in handing him their charts. Wagner asks the pertinent question as to why the British Government behaved so very differently in concealing Cook's achievements in the Arctic, and delaying the publication of his Third Journal after his death. Perhaps, as Wagner suggests, the furs which Cook's crews sold to the Chinese, had already brought a rush of British fur traders to the Pacific, and disputes with Spain and further Anglo-French rivalries were imminent. We return to the Journals.

WEDNESDAY 22nd April. Here I must observe that I have no were met with Indians who had such high notions of every thing the Country produced being their exclusive property as these; the very wood and water we took on board they at first wanted us to pay for, and we had certainly done it, had I been upon the spot when the demands were made; but as I never happened to be there the workmen took but little notice of their importunities and at last they ceased applying. But made a Merit on necessity and frequently afterwards told us they had given us Wood and Water out of friendship.

SUNDAY 6th April. The 26th in the Morning every thing being ready, I intended to have sailed, but both wind and Tide being against us was obliged to wait till noon, when the sw Wind was succeeded by a Calm and the tide turning in our favour, we cast off the Moorings and with our boats towed the Ships out of the Cove . . . *Nautical remarks*. The inlet I honoured with the name of *King Georges Sound*, but its name, with the Natives is *Nook ka*. The entrance is situated in the East corner of *Hope Bay*, in the latitude of 49° 33′ N, Long 233° 12′ E . . . . The land boardering upon the Sea Coast is of a middling hieght and livel, but about the Sound it consits of high hills and deep Vallies, for the most part cloathed with large timber, such as Spruce fir and white Cedar. The more inland Mountains were covered with Snow, in other respects they seemed to be naked. When ever it rained with us Snow fell on the Neighbouring hills, the Clemate is however infinately milder than on the East coast of America under the same parallel of latitude. The Mercury in the Thermometre never even in the night fell lower than 42 and very often in the day it rose to 60; no such thing as frost was percieved in any of the low ground, on the Contrary Vegetation had made considerable progress, I met with grass that was already above a foot long . . . . *Inhabitants their Persons and Habits*. I can form no estimate of the number of Inhabitants that may be in this

Sound, they however appeared to be pretty numerous. And they as also all other who visited us are, both men and Women, of a small Stature, some, Women in particular, very much so and hardly one, even of the younger sort, had the least pretentions to being call'd beauties. Thier face is rather broad and flat, with highish Cheek Bones and plump cheeks. Their mouth is little and round, the nose niether flat nor prominent; their eyes are black little and devoid of sparkling fire. But in general they have not a bad shape except in the legs which in the most of them are Crooked and may probably arise from their much siting. Their Complextion is swarthy, but this seems not alltogether natural but proceeds partly from smoke dirt and pai[n]t, for they paint with a liberal hand, and are slovenly and dirty to the last degree . . . . The men on some occasions wore Masks of which they have many and of various sorts such as the human face, the head of birds and other Animals, the most of them both well designed and executed. Whether these masks are worn as an Ornament in their public entertainments, or as some thought, to guard the face against the arrows of the enimy, or as decoys in hunting, I shall not pretend to say; probably on all these occasions. The only times however we saw them used was by some of the Chiefs when they made us a ceremonious and in some of thier Songs . . . . *Canoes.* Thier Canoes are 40 feet long, 7 broad and about 3 deep, some greater some less; they are made out of one tree hollowed out to an inch or an inch and a half in the sides, and in shape very much resemble a Norway yawl only longer in proportion to their breadth, and the head and stern is higher. In the upper part of the former, or prow, is a groove or hollow, for the conveniency of laying their Spears, darts, harpoons &cᵃ. They are generally without carving or any other ornament except paint and but few have it. The paddles are small and light; the shape in some measure resembling a large leaf, pointed at the bottom, broadest in the middle, and gradually losing it self in the shaft, the whole being about five feet long. . . . *Food and Habitations.* As the food of these people seems to consist chiefly of fish and other Sea animals, their houses or dwelings are situated close to the shore. They consist in a long range of buildings, some of which are one hundred and fifty feet in length, twenty four or thirty broad and seven or eight high from the floor to the roof, which in them all is flat and covered with loose boards. The Walls or sides and ends, are also built up of boards and the framing consits of large trees or logs . . . . *Large Images.* At the upper end of many of the appartments, were two large images, or statues placed abreast of each other and 3 or 4 feet asunder, they bore some resemblance to the human figure, but monsterous large; the best idea will be had of them in a drawing which Mr Webber made of the inside of one of thir appartments wherein two of them stood. They call them Acweeks which signifies supreme, or Chief; a curtin or mat for the most part hung before them which they were not willing at all times to remove, and when they did shew us them or speak of them, it was in such a Mysterious manner that we could not comprehend their meaning. This made some of our gentlemen think they were their gods, but I am not altogether of that opinion, at least if they were they hild them very cheap, for with a small matters of iron or brass, I could have purchased all the gods in the place, for I did not see one that was not offered me, and two or three of the the very smalest sort I got.

SUNDAY 26*th* April. Having put to Sea on the evening of the 26th as before related, with strong signs of an approaching Storm; these signs did not dicieve us: we were hardly out of the Sound before the Wind in an instant shifted from NE to SEBE and increased to a Strong gale with Squals and rain and so dark that we could not see the length of the Ship. Being apprehensive of the wind veering more to the South, as usual, and puting us in danger of a lee shore, got the tacks on board and stretched off to the SW under all the sail the Ships could bear. Fortunatly the Wind veered no farther Southerly than SSE so that at day light the next Morning we were quite clear of the Coast . . . .

A. Grenfell Price, ed.

By the end of the time of the Cook expeditions, the American Revolution and treaties signed in Europe had established the essential limits of what would become Canadian territory. But the seeds of conflict sown by the newcomers in dividing up the continent would grow in a few years into the dark foliage of war. The waters of Canada were soon to be stained with the hues of blood far beyond anything seen before the coming of the 'Children of the Moon'.

chapter three

Blood On The Waters

The Treaty of Paris in 1783 essentially established the eastern border between Canada and the United States, leaving western aspects of the line to be settled later. But the process of deciding which Europeans would rule what parts of North America had been a bloody one from the start: an almost uninterrupted series of wars from the 1690s (when it really got going in earnest) to 1815, first between the British and the French, and later between the breakaway American colonies and the British. The vast Civil War still loomed ahead for the United States, but by 1815 the shadow of war had essentially passed from Canadian waters. The struggle of over a century and more had produced some remarkable stories of courage and determination, not in the least of which was the Canadian d'Iberville's 1697 expedition to root out the English on Hudson Bay, as related in the official report of an observer, the Sieur de la Potherie, to the Regent of France.

French Guns Amidst the Ice
Sieur de la Potherie

Monseigneur,

The expedition to Hudson Bay, an account of which I have the honour to present to Your Royal Highness, is one of the most singular which has yet appeared; Your Highness will find in it nothing but storms, battles, and ship-wrecks.

The royal squadron fitted out for this enterprise in 1697, has had to contend not so much with the savages who inhabit this extreme northern part of America as with waves, storms, ice, sand banks, and mountains of snow. It was here that the French showed their full courage and triumphed over the most terrible obstacles that nature could present to the most famous heroes. In fact, to arrive in Hudson Bay we had to pass through a great sea rendered inaccessible, even in the dog-days of summer, by currents, sand banks, continued storms and icebergs. These difficulties, insuperable by any other people, served only to excite the valour of the French, who, like the heroes that govern them, find nothing that can repel their attack.

What a joy it is for the members of this expedition to see their country again after passing through such perils, and to hear that Your Royal Highness has been pleased to listen to their tale! No one can better appreciate the extraordinary deeds recorded in these narratives than those who have themselves performed heroic deeds. Wherefore I am in duty bound to dedicate to Your Royal Highness this work, which having been written by the Sieur de la Potherie, the King's commissioner in the fleet, who took part in all the expeditions described in it, cannot be suspected of being untrue.

We set sail from Newfoundland to the northward on July 8, and on the 17th we perceived, three leagues to windward, a floating iceberg three hundred feet in height, in the shape of a sugar loaf.

Now nothing is more disagreeable than to find yourself in a storm, but it is much worse when storms happen in these northern places. On the 24th, in latitude 60° 9', we met a gale from the north-north-west which lasted eight hours. All our rigging was covered with ice and our crews suffered a great deal. The *Palmier* had her bowsprit broken. This, however, was but the beginning of the difficulties and hardships we were to endure in the course of the most dangerous navigation. On the 25th, we knew from the current that we were approaching the frigid zone; and on that day we saw nothing but terrifying sights for, as we were making our way north-north-west, we began about eight o'clock in the morning to run into a field of ice.

The first land in this clime that we became acquainted with was Resolution Island at the mouth of Hudson's Strait.

Nothing could be more frightful than to see ourselves in this vast strait where we could scarcely discern the water for the many ice-floes against which our ships struck every moment. The *Pelican*, which was always ahead (the three others following us in line), did her utmost to lessen the difficulties. She made openings crossways by main force, but the others, not being able to follow us, often found themselves shut in. It was very distressing, Sir, to find ourselves unable to give them any assistance. They anchored at once; so did we, drawing alongside an iceberg four or five hundred feet in length, on which we landed some sailors with anchors to make fast our vessel. At that time there was no night. We had the pleasure of seeing the sun set and rise almost at the same time, and you could read with ease at midnight.

On one occasion, while we were moored to the ice, we put in forty barrels of fresh water, very good to drink. This, Sir, is not surprising, for the rain, falling upon the ice, makes a kind of cistern and, when the snow melts, the water formed has none of the acrid and salty taste of sea water. Still we had to put brandy in the casks in order to remove its crudeness; otherwise it would be dangerous to drink it pure and one would run the risk of having violent colics.

At times there occur such sudden movements of the ice, that, just as you think yourself properly moored, the whole pack opens up. Once, as we were waiting for a favourable moment to continue our journey, the ice to which we were moored was unfortunately broken up by great currents. Our ship was carried away, without any possibility of steering her, and ran poop to poop against the *Palmier* at four o'clock in the morning. This mishap was followed by a far more cruel accident, for our brigantine, the *Esquimaux*, of thirty tons, which had always followed us through the ice, was crushed near the *Palmier* and the twelve men on board barely saved their lives.

However, after being carried along the coast and constantly flung from side to side of the strait for many days, we at last found ourselves quite close to Cape Digges.

For a long while we had been longing to see Eskimos. They are a very cruel people with whom, up to that time, no one had had any commercial dealings. On the 19th, however, we saw some of them on the ice, crying aloud to us from a great distance and leaping up with dresses of caribou and other skins which they were showing to us.

The opportunity was too good to be lost. M. Martigny, after taking all precautions not to be made their victim, embarked in a skiff with four or five well armed men. Landing on the ice where they were, he found nine of them, with their canoe which they had drawn up on the ice. On landing, he presented the calumet to two who had come forward while the others remained at the edge of the ice.

The calumet is something very mysterious among the savages of the north; it is the symbol of peace. It is a kind of large pipe made of red, black, or white stone. The head is well polished and made in the form of a war club. The stem is ornamented with porcupine quills and little threads of skins of various colours.

So, at this meeting, Martigny presented them with a pipe like a calumet and a tobacco-pouch, smoked for a little, and then gave them the pipe to smoke. The seven other natives, who had kept away, when they saw the good faith in which we were acting, came to him with exclamations of joy, crying out in very clear tones, leaping and rubbing their stomachs as most convincing signs of friendship and of the good trade they wished to carry on with us. They gave him to understand that they were well enough off to trade. But, as he wished to have them on our ship, he told them he had nothing and asked them to come with him. But no matter how he insisted and welcomed them, they would not trust him. Martigny finally lay down on the ice to indicate that he would give himself as a hostage on condition that one of them would be sent. They wished to have two for one, and Grandville, a marine guard, remained also as a hostage.

When this Eskimo was at the top of the ladder of our ship, he saw one of our men who was dressed in black, of whom he was so much afraid that he hesitated whether to throw himself into the sea. The man, seeing his terror, offered him a knife, after which he decided to come aboard. On finding himself surrounded by a crowd of the crew, he did not seem at all put out but kept dancing and crying out in amazement at a machine which seemed to him so surprising. But when he saw the fire burning in the kitchen, he gave a dreadful cry, not being able to conceive how such a flame should not cause a conflagration. For, as far as we could conjecture, these people must rarely warm themselves at a fire for there was not an inch of soil in the strait, nor the smallest shrub. If they make a fire, they must burn the fat of seals and walruses.

We gave a pie to the Eskimo! He did his utmost to show his gratitude. I think there is no other nation that speaks faster. His accent resembled the Basque; he hardly opened his teeth, and yet he articulated quite distinctly. They gave him a small piece of bread which he slipped adroitly under his chin between his coat and his skin, pretending to eat it. We pretended not to notice, but we saw that he was afraid of being poisoned. We therefore tasted another piece, which we gave him, and he ate it afterwards. However, we neglected to taste a glass of wine, which he, as a result of our neglect, poured again under his chin. We had to drink some, and to taste beforehand everything we wished to give him. The sound of a silver fork pleased him so much that he hid it very cunningly between a piece of pie and a bit of bread. I embarked with him, and, when we had arrived on the ice where his comrades were, they all crowded around me, crying and jumping. I made them several presents, and, willy-nilly, they insisted on stripping themselves naked in order to give me their clothes, and I grew anxious to know if they were sensitive to the cold.

The reception we gave them led them to send two others on board. They met with as agreeable a reception as the first. They stripped themselves as bare as my hand, and I observed that, when looked at in this condition, they had a sense of modesty. They were given knee-breeches and they showed no sign of suffering from cold. Yet they had to go three leagues to get to Digges Islands. One of them, as he was going, gave me a piece of the raw flesh of a sea-fowl which I had to eat in his presence. He gave a cry of joy, and, at the same time, sucked a raw beef heart which we had given to him.

Two others came in the afternoon to the ice-field where we were hunting. These also traded their clothing for knives, scissors, needles, bells, farthings, playing cards, old sheet music, and, in general, everything we gave them was precious to them. As these people have no trade with anybody, they did not bring any skins, but they must have the finest furs in the world in those regions.

Although we were now at the entrance of Hudson's Bay, we could not get in. All the ice in that vast body of water was passing out into this strait. The continual movements of the icebergs in the current forced us also to take a capricious course and the currents drove the *Pelican* back more than eight leagues into the strait. On August 25 we made all sail through the ice because we were quite a distance behind the other three ships which were by then at the end of the strait, and we were anxious to join them.

Now the *Profond* saw three vessels approaching. Dugue, who was in command of her, thought at first that they were the other three ships of our squadron. They came up to him gradually with the currents. Then he was surprised to see a sudden change, for they were three English ships of fifty-six, thirty-six, and thirty-two guns. He ungrappled from the ice immediately and ran at all hazards into a field of ice rather than surrender, for he had on board all our munitions and provisions for the Fort Nelson expedition. The English gave chase. Serigny and Chartrier in the *Weesph* and *Palmier* wanted to go to his assistance but they were fast in the ice. The *Profond* was now also fast and close to the English ships *Dering* and *Hudson's Bay*. Then, on August 26, at about nine in the morning, the battle began. Dugue attacked them; the enemy riddled him with balls, cutting his rigging in pieces, because he could only fight with two cannon which had been placed in the rear of the gunroom.

The *Hampshire* of fifty-six guns was not able to join the other English ships till the evening. After ten hours of intermittent fighting all three fired broadsides at the *Profond* and left her, thinking she was certain to go down. Four men were killed on the *Profond*. The English must also have lost some, because several human arms were found on the ice. As to our own ship, we were not in this glorious battle, which may be said to have been the first sea fight ever waged amid the ice.

The currents now brought the *Pelican* out into Hudson's Bay, and our sailors had reason to be pleased at seeing themselves freed from the ice. A fresh breeze arose which helped us greatly as we sailed to the south-west.

On September 3, 1697, we in the *Pelican* arrived within sight of Fort Nelson, from which the English fired some cannon-shots, which were apparently signals for the ships they were expecting from England. We anchored three leagues and a half to the south-west of this fort, in the open sea. We were surprised not to find there the *Palmier*, the *Weesph*, and the *Profond*, which ought to have arrived before us, as they had been off Cape Digges while we were still detained in the ice.

At daybreak on the 5th we perceived three vessels to leeward that we took to be ours. After weighing anchor about seven in the morning, we sailed down on them and made signals to which they made no response. This made us think they were English and so they were, being the *Hampshire*, the *Dering*, and the *Hudson's Bay*.

Every man was at his post. La Salle, the ship's ensign, and Grandville, a marine guard, commanded the lower battery; Bienville, the brother of

M. d'Iberville, and the Chevalier de Ligondez, a marine guard, the upper battery. M. d'Iberville asked me to take command of the forecastle and, with a detachment of *Canadiens* that he gave me, to meet the enemy as they tried to come on board.

The enemy drew up in line. The *Hampshire* was at the head, the *Dering* followed, and the *Hudson's Bay* came behind, all three close together. The fight began at half past nine in the morning. We made straight for the *Hampshire*, which, thinking we were going to board her, let fall her mainsail and shook out her topsails. After this refusal, we went to the *Dering* and our fire cut the tackle of her mainsail, and then, the *Hudson's Bay* coming in front, we sent her the rest of our broadside. The *Hampshire*, putting about to windward, fired a volley of musketry on our forecastle and sent a broadside of grape which cut the halliards of our fore-topsail, a back stay of our top gallant mast, and our mizzen stay. The fight grew stubborn, the three vessels keeping up a continual fire on us, with the object of demasting our ship.

Now the *Hampshire*, seeing that she could not engage us between a shoal and their own two vessels, and that all the efforts they had made during two hours and a half were useless, determined to run us down, and, for that purpose, tried to get windward of us (which she was unable to do), but we ran alongside of her, yard-arm to yard-arm. As we were so close to each other, I ordered a volley of musketry to be fired at her forecastle where there were many sailors who called out for us to leap aboard. They immediately returned our volley with a discharge of grape which cut nearly all our rigging in pieces and wounded many of our men. As they ran along by our ship, we fired our batteries, which were so well aimed that they proved most effective, for we were no sooner separated from one another than the *Hampshire* immediately foundered. The *Dering*, which was close to us, sent us her broadside, but the encounter was a cruel catastrophe for the English, because the *Hudson's Bay* lowered her flag, and the *Dering* took to flight.

We had fourteen men wounded by two discharges of shot from the last broadside of the *Hampshire*, which fell into the lower battery. We had seven shots below the water-line and the water came pouring in, not to speak of several shots which passed through the *Pelican* from side to side. We had been so overwhelmed with their musketry fire and the discharges of grape-shot which they fired at us from pistol range, that our mizzen mast was filled with musket balls on all sides to the height of ten or twelve feet; and if I had not looked after my men we should not have had four people left on the forecastle. I got off very cheaply myself with having my coat all tattered, and my cap pierced by a ball. In fact I was in as good condition and with as much coolness after the battle as when M. d'Iberville bade us enter the lists, except that one would have mistaken me for a veritable blackamoor, my face was so peppered with powder. I think the English took me for some prince of Guinea, for I heard someone crying out: 'Fire at that fine-looking darkey from Guinea.'

We gave chase to the *Dering*, and we should have captured her if we had not, three days before, had our mainyard broken in half by a squall. In any case, our prize, the *Hudson's Bay*, which was a league distant, might have got away into the mouth of the river on which Fort Nelson is situated, so we put about and, after having put a price crew on board, we went towards the *Hampshire* in order to save her sailors. We found that she had stranded on the shoal where the enemy had wished to engage us, and the weather became so rough after the battle that it was impossible for us to lower a boat. We anchored close to the *Hampshire* with the chagrin of being unable to aid her in so dangerous and unfortunate a situation.

The east-north-east wind, which was then blowing, kept getting stronger and stronger. A frightful sea arose, driving us steadily towards the shore till the next morning between nine and ten o'clock, when our rudder struck bottom a couple of times. We were obliged to cut our cable at midday so as to make sail, and drove before the wind till four o'clock in the afternoon. The bitter cold, the snow, and the ice which covered our rigging were cruel obstacles. As we could not reach the shore, we anchored in nine fathoms of water. Our anchors held till nine in the evening, when the great anchor broke. I cannot express to you the sad state of the crew. Some were suffering from disease. The very strongest were in desperate straits. It was night, and the horror of darkness was added to the fear of death. The tossing and the disorder reacted quickly upon people in so downcast a state, and when the panic spread we could not reassure them.

The vessel was headed into the wind and anchored again, but the kedge anchor broke. As the small remaining anchor could not hold, we had to cut the cable and get under way again. A wave swept off our stern galley, and broke the table and benches which were in the main cabin. At ten o'clock in the evening our rudder was carried away and we thought ourselves utterly lost. As the tide rose, our ship, which was drawn along in the current, went aground. All these various movements made the hair of the most careless stand on end. Finally, about midnight, the ship split across the middle of the keel and filled with water above the between-decks. We spent the night in this wretched state and, at daybreak, we saw the land two leagues away.

In our cruel situation we did not lose hope of saving our lives. M. d'Iberville, who had all the forethought possible in such a catastrophe, was bent on saving his crew. He begged me to take the canoe and try where we could make a landing in some safety.

So, on September 8, the Nativity of the Virgin, I embarked in a canoe with some *Canadiens*, and after we had leapt into the sea, which was up to our shoulders, with our muskets and powder-horns on our heads, and some balls, I sent the canoe back to the ship. Meanwhile, rafts and floats were being made to save the sick. We drew ourselves as well as we could out of the water, which was extremely cold.

For all my vigour and presence of mind, I felt myself suffering keenly and, as I was utterly exhausted, I wished to find somewhere to rest. I was suddenly overcome with hunger which forced me, in my despair, to eat the weeds floating on the sea.

After having crossed more than a league of sea, we came to a snow bank more than two feet thick under which was mud. Our passage was very rough and cost the lives of eighteen soldiers who died of cold, and I myself should have succumbed but for the help of some *Canadiens* who found me lying on the snow.

The next day, we crossed over a marsh which would have been impassable for horses and then we made another camp at a place we called the 'Outpost'. I forgot to state that the *Hudson's Bay* had met the same fate as ourselves, having foundered eight leagues further south.

In the meantime, the *Palmier*, the *Weesph*, and the *Profond* arrived at the mouth of the river. The first had lost her rudder forty leagues to the west of this, having been steered these forty leagues with oars and outriggers.

M. d'Iberville with some others of us went to reconnoitre Fort Nelson about eleven o'clock in the morning. We could not manage it without drawing the musket fire of the English, and they would have fired grape-shot at us if we had not defiled by narrow paths. We kept under cover till we were almost at the foot of the fort. Then d'Iberville sent for Martigny and ordered him to go and demand two Iroquois and two Frenchmen whom he knew to be in this place; for they had not been able to get away last year before it had been recaptured by the English from the *Canadiens*.

When Martigny arrived with the white flag at the gates of the fort, the governor had his eyes bandaged and had him led into the place. He held a council of war. It was decided that the four men could not be given up under such circumstances. Some of the men from the *Hudson's Bay* had taken refuge in the fort after their shipwreck, and this had strengthened the garrison.

That afternoon we set up a mortar battery in the wood two hundred paces from the fort, without letting the enemy become aware of what we were doing. When the platform was almost finished, they heard the noise of two or three blows of a sledge-hammer, which quickly brought upon us three cannon-shots, one of which came near killing M. d'Iberville.

On the night between the 11th and the 12th, we cut off some English who were going to and fro to fetch the sailors of the *Hudson's Bay*, who kept arriving every now and then. The clerk of the Hudson's Bay Company was killed in this encounter.

We began our bombardment of the fort at ten in the morning of the 12th. When we saw the third bombshell fall at the base of the fort, Serigny went to summon the governor to surrender. The latter declared that he did not wish to have his throat cut, and that he preferred to see the place burned rather than give it up. He admitted that there was no chance of his receiving any aid from England, and that, if he were forced to capitulate, it would be due to his bad luck.

We began to fire anew between one and two o'clock. They kept up a continual fire on us with cannon and with two mortars. They have very able cannoneers. They had nothing but the sound of our bombs to enable them to conjecture where we were, because the thick copse, in which our battery was, prevented them from getting an accurate knowledge of its position. This did not prevent two of their cannon-balls from hitting the parapet and another from covering us with earth.

Serigny summoned the English again at four o'clock and told the governor that it would be the last time he would do so. We had resolve to make a general assault and, if he should then make any proposals, they would not be received. We had surrounded their fort and with storming axes we would have cut down their palisades and bastions, and they might have expected that, had we stormed them sword in hand, they would have had no chance of escape. Serigny even assured the governor that, although the season would not allow our ships to remain more than ten or twelve days, forces would be left more than sufficient to capture the fort in the winter.

The English governor told Serigny that he was not wholly his own master and that he would give him an answer at sundown. We did not cease setting up a new battery on the south-south-west side, which would have thrown them into utter disorder, but, at six o'clock, the governor sent a Protestant minister, Mr Morison, to bring a capitulation, in which he asked to keep all the beavers that belonged to the Hudson's Bay Company.

I was willing to act as interpreter, but I soon saw that I was wasting my Latin on this minister who could scarcely decline Musa. I was not surprised at it afterwards as there are very few Scottish ministers who know Latin.

This proposal of their was too advantageous for people who were at our mercy, and our gentle dealing with them was rather due to our natural French generosity. So we refused their demand.

They held a council of war, and at eight p.m. the governor sent Mr Henry Kelsey, a King's Lieutenant, and the deputy governor with a letter in which he asked to be allowed to retain two mortars and four cannon (five-pounders), which they had brought last year from England. We would not let them have these. Finally, on the next day, the 13th, the governor sent us three hostages to tell us that he would surrender the place and to ask permission to evacuate it at an hour after midday.

The governor at the head of the garrison and part of the crew of the *Hudson's Bay* left the fort an hour after with drums beating, muskets loaded, matches lighted, banner waving (they had lowered it very quickly at the third bombshell we had fired at them, perceiving that we were using it as a target), and their arms and baggage.

I had the skins that were in the fort put on board the Hudson's Bay Company sloop *Albemarle*, which we had also captured. As our pilots were not well acquainted with the river, this vessel ran on a little rock which made a hole in her. There was a panic among our own people and the English who were on board. The barque filled with water. They tried to lighten her by jettisoning many cases and packages. It was a very dark night. Some threw themselves into the water, others, in trying to get safely to land, found themselves fast in the mud.

We left Fort Nelson on September 24, 1697, which is the date when the rivers and the sea begin to freeze over, or very fierce winds prevail.

We set sail with the wind south-south-west, at an hour after midday. The *Profond*—to which our crew had been transferred from the wreck of the *Pelican*, as well as a party from the *Hudson's Bay*, and from the garrison of the fort—went aground an hour later on the bank or shoal on the north side. However, as we still had an hour of flood tide, we got clear and continued our course. Otherwise, we should have been obliged to transfer some of our three hundred men to the *Weesph*, which had escaped our mischance, and to send back the rest to the fort. We should certainly in that event have suffered a famine there, and also on the *Weesph*, for the latter had only enough provisions for her own crew, and the fort no more than was necessary for the garrison we had left behind in it.

Next day the wind blew very hard. The cold increased because we were getting nearer the pole. The days became very short. The sun no longer was visible, so we could not get an altitude. A storm was indicated. We advanced without knowing where we were, and yet we had to get into Hudson's Strait. To enter it was a stumbling-block for us, as we were enclosed in a bay, the northern shore of which was quite unknown. We were wandering in a region full of dangers.

The constant working of our rigging exhausted the sailors. The wretched condition we were all in, owning to lack of linen and other clothes, due to our shipwreck, suddenly brought about an epidemic of scurvy; and I hardly venture to tell you, Sir, that we were all tormented with vermin to such an extent that some of our scurvy patients, who had become paralytics, actually died from this pest. When the sailors came down from the yards, they fell stiff with cold on the deck, and it required the use of fomentations to bring them around again.

We were running east when we found ourselves by good fortune in Hudson's Strait. We found no more ice-packs in the strait. There were still some icebergs of great height which had stranded a league or two from the land and had not been able to follow the current. The ice-packs in the bay and in the strait extend more than four hundred leagues. When they begin to break up, they pass out into the sea. These fragments are so large that five or six thousand men could be drawn up in order of battle upon them with ease. They usually break up in the month of July and they sometimes travel two hundred leagues in the open sea before being completely melted.

At this time the sea was clear, but the cold was so piercing that our crew could not endure it and nearly all the sailors took the scurvy. So few of us escaped that we were obliged to make use of our English prisoners in order to run the ship.

On October 5, at midday, we saw the Savage Isles to the north-east of us. They are on the north coast of the strait a mile or two distant from the mainland.

We began to find ourselves out of danger, freed from those anxieties which had kept us in dread of perishing every moment.

As the winds drove us along we found ourselves suddenly in another and even harsher climate. This sudden change caused so many deaths in our vessels that we threw five or six sailors into the sea every day.

It was a plague that had infected our ships. Perhaps you will not be displeased if I give you an idea of it. You will see that I have become a great doctor on this voyage, and that I have not altogether forgotten the study I made of anatomy while I was taking my course in philosophy.

You must know, then, that the sudden change which takes place in the temperature, after leaving the mildest and most agreeable season of the year, brings about an entire revolution, all at once, in the human body, which contracts a disease peculiar to those regions, called the scurvy.

The extreme cold, and especially the tremendous quantity of nitre that exists in the straits, form fixed salts which arrest the circulation of the blood. These corrosive spirits give rise to acids, which, little by little, undermine the part where they occur, and the chyle, which becomes viscous, acid, salt, and earthy, causes the thickening of the blood, which, being thus impeded in its circulation, gives rise at the same time to pains in the lower extremities, as in the legs, thighs and arms, which are the first parts to be attacked.

The parts affected become insensible, blackish, and, when one touches them, there remains a hollow such as one would make in a piece of dough.

It was most pitiful to see people completely paralysed, so that they could not move themselves in their hammocks, and yet their minds were perfectly sane and clear.

The food that one is obliged to take at sea contributes not a little to the malady. Thus the quantity of acid in the salt beef and pork that they give the sailors causes a swelling in the gums and an obstruction in the salivary glands, which are intended to filter the lymph with the blood and carry it into the mouth by little ducts so as to serve as the first solvent in digestion. And, as all these little passages are blocked up by the excess of these penetrating salts, there is then spread through the mouth a thick, gluey, and viscous humour. Then the blood, finding these ducts stopped, forms a mass of putrid matter which corrupts the gums, loosens the teeth and causes them all to drop out.

Some have a flux at the mouth, others have dysentry. The former drivel. The viscous matter which flows from the mouth causes gangrene in the glands and in the gums. They must then be given strong detergent gargles which can separate this thick matter. Lemon juice is very helpful.

Those who have dysentry are more liable to die. In these patients, there is formed in the region of the intestines an extremely corrosive humour. As soon as this juice is found to be corrupt, it follows of necessity that there are faintings and heart failures. For, as the heart can only exist by the circulation of a pure, clean, and active blood, any other matter that forms in it cannot help hindering its ordinary course. And the gangrene, which forms in these patients, arrests the laws of the circulation of the blood.

The brain, being no longer bathed in its mild influences, receives vapours which cause delirium, madness, and then death. I have seen several who seemed to have a strong voice, a clear eye, and a clear tongue without any blackening or excoriation, and yet died while they were speaking.

One must use foods, therefore, which can dissolve the mass of the blood and by their sulphurous and volatile parts carry off the acids. These foods, by an insensible transpiration, dissipate the crudities of the mass, and are able to rally together the fibres of the blood. One should give the patients very little salt meat, but rice, peas, dried beans, detersivent injections, and astringent opiates into which cordials enter; giving them plenty of fresh linen, which is a great relief in such cases.

This sickness only increases the appetite. The patients are as ravenous as dogs. I was not surprised, Sir, that this sudden change of climate on our return voyage should have caused so many deaths on our ships. There was a fermentation going on in the mass of the blood, which caused a gangrenous corruption. The heat wished to dilate what the cold had contracted; there was bound to be a combat. And nature, enfeebled by the dilation of the pores, caused an overflow which threw the whole machine out of gear.

Finally, after so many pains, labours, and misfortunes, we arrived at Belle Isle in Newfoundland on November 8. We proceeded to put our scurvied patients in the hospital of Port Louis, and we set out from there for Rochefort, where we discharged our ship.

By the time of the War of 1812, Canada had a small but resilient population of English-speaking inhabitants in Upper Canada and the Maritimes, balancing the French-speaking population of Lower Canada, or Quebec. The declaration of war by the United States was based on a justifiable annoyance that a hard-pressed Great Britain was not taking the new American nation seriously, particularly at sea; and a less justifiable greed for Canada's prime Upper Canadian agricultural land. Nova Scotia in particular responded to the war with the Yankee cousins by producing a number of enterprising 'privateers', or civilian warships licensed to attack enemy vessels; their successes and adventures against the cousins made many a Nova Scotia fortune, and made also for rich storytelling, as in this excerpt by Canadian maritime historian C.H.J. Snider.

'Matilda' and 'Loyal Sam'
C.H.J. Snider

The *Matilda*, fifty-ton privateer schooner out of Annapolis Royal in Nova Scotia, had been a month at sea, and all she had to show for it was a new hawser and a barrel of flour.

These trophies she had wrung from a little dubiously American shallop called the *Nymph*, of Marblehead, which she had sent into Digby. John Burkett, jr, and the *Matilda* were both new at the privateering trade. John got his commission on the 11th of May, 1813, and it was on the 11th of June that he had seized the reluctant *Nymph*, which had the protection of a British importation permit. Her flour cargo was a temptation, for a month at sea had left the *Matilda*'s bread-bin as empty as the *Matilda*'s prize-book.

There had been no luck before taking the *Nymph* and none after. For five days following the *Matilda* had been diligently and perilously combing the New England coast from Mount Desert to Portland. With half a mind to give up the cruise at the end of this day John Burkett tacked the *Matilda* offshore on the morning of June 16th.

Almost immediately his look-outs in the crosstrees sang out, 'Sail ho! Sail ho!' Even from the fifty-foot elevation of the *Matilda*'s mastheads against the morning brightness could be made out two dots, or perhaps one should say a very tiny dot and an up-ended dash.

John Burkett, jr, was not slow in deciphering this code-message. A ship, a large three-masted vessel, was the dash. The dot spelled a brig, a two-masted square-rigger, miles farther out to sea. The ship was racing for Sequin Light at the mouth of the Kennebeck, on the Maine coast. The brig was in pursuit. Both had to beat against the moderate June breeze into which the *Matilda* was nosing.

There was a chance, just a chance, that the *Matilda* could cross the bows of the oncoming ship and cut her off from the port. If both ship and brig should prove American the Nova Scotian privateer would indeed be in a trap; two enemies on one side, blocking escape to sea, and on the other the hostile shore. But with a great deal of luck she might catch the ship and sail off with her before her consort or chaser got within striking distance.

'When you've been out a month and got nothing it's time to make your own luck,' was John Burkett, jr's conclusion.

For hours then, with every sheet trimmed to the exact inch for best results, and picked helmsmen steering as through the eye of a needle, the *Matilda* clawed to windward. As the sun crossed the yardarm, in the old phrase for high noon, the breeze weakened and shifted. The *Matilda* was then to leeward of the ship, in a disadvantageous position; but she was between her and the land. The ship, nearly six times her size, looked British-built; but she was flying Stars and Stripes, and standing on for the American port. The brig was far off, seven miles to leeward, but pertinaciously beating in from sea.

Before the *Matilda* had sailed from where old Fort Anne stood glowering above the red mud of Annapolis Basin five small cannon had been mounted on her fifty-foot deck. In some doubt as to whether they would do more damage on board or to the enemy, Capt. Burkett now set his green crew to firing the pair on the weather side, and the one in the bow. They rocked the small schooner with their recoil, but they hurt neither the *Matilda* crew nor the strangers. The cannon balls splashed the water far short of their target. The privateer was too far leeward. The ship fired back. Most of her shot fell short, too. Some went through the schooner's sails.

For an hour and a half Burkett worked his roaring guns and used every art he knew to gain upon the Stars and Stripes which moved so tantalizingly ahead of him. In the light breeze that happened which an older sea-fighter would have expected. The little *Matilda*, reeling with every broadside, shook all the wind out of her low sails and halted herself with the jar of the explosions. The tall ship, steady in the water with her great bulk, and feeling the highest zephyrs with her lofty royals, steadily drew ahead, pushed on by each discharge of her stern guns.

It was after two o'clock now, and it looked as though the ship would escape. The brig, whether friend or foe, was still far out to sea, and making slow progress. The wallowing *Matilda* had fallen farther to leeward. John Burkett, jr, and his forty men—or the thirty-seven he had left after manning the *Nymph* for Digby—ceased firing and took to the sweeps. Manfully, by the hour, they pulled at the long oars under the burning sun. They kept the *Matilda* between the ship and the shore; and after hours of toil they drew abreast of the chase.

At five o'clock they rested, and began firing broadsides again. This time they had the satisfaction of seeing the white splinters fly from the sides of the ship. But she struck back viciously. She had eight guns to the *Matilda*'s five, and they were heavy ones. The privateer's sails and gear were ripped with bar and chainshot. Fortunately it flew high, and the stranger's guns, although well served, were not fired rapidly. She seemed to be short-handed.

They had crept to within a mile of the lighthouse by now; perilous proximity indeed for a Nova Scotian privateer on the Maine coast. The wind had all died away. Out to sea the brig was just able to move. Inshore the ship and the privateer were motionless, except when they rolled with the shock of their cannonading.

In a lull in the firing the creaking of yardarm tackles could be heard, and two boats were hoisted out over the great ship's rail and dropped into the water with a hurried splash. She was too big to row. Boat's oars thrust through her ports would hardly reach water. They were going to try to tow her in past the lighthouse.

They whitened the water with their oar-strokes, but the heavy ship did not budge. The boats were too light and the six rowers too few to move her. There was a consultation, and the men in the boats tossed their towlines back aboard and began to pull past the *Matilda* for the shore. They were going to get help.

'Twas a jest of the time that if one wanted to be perfectly safe when challenged to a duel one should choose nine-pounders for weapons. Ship guns could not be relied upon to hit with accuracy anything which was not tied to their muzzles. In the phrase of the gunners, the balls left the barrel all right but the Lord alone knew what happened to them after that. So it was with little confidence that John Burkett trained the hot nose of his bowchaser on the boats as they fled athwart the *Matilda*'s course with feverish strokes.

The cannon only succeeded in splashing the rowers. But the *Matilda* men had muskets, and without waiting for orders they blazed away. One man screamed and fell forward over his oar. The others dropped their and flung themselves under the shelter of the thwarts. The *Matilda* launched her own boarding boat, six men leapt into it and pushed off. Soon they returned, towing the first-fruits of victory—a gig and a jolly-boat, bullet-spattered, with six wounded and frightened prisoners.

But the cannonading and the musket-volley and the effort to reach the shore brought succour to the ship. Militiamen put out from the fort near the lighthouse, circled around the range of the *Matilda*'s fire, and flung themselves on board the becalmed vessel amid loud cheering. Gallant fellows; for Maine militiamen as a rule hated the water, and it was only to save countrymen in distress that they took the risk of British bullets.

'You'll never take her now,' the prisoners from the boats taunted Capt. Burkett, when this junction was effected. 'Her guns are too heavy for you as long as there's men enough to work 'em, and with the soldiers aboard of her to help you'll never carry her by the cutlass.'

'What is she?' demanded Capt. Burkett, in no happy mood, realizing that instead of practising cannonading all afternoon he should have laid the enemy aboard while the odds were forty pairs of fists to fifteen.

'A Britisher,' he was told, 'called the *Loyal Sam*, and prize to the *Siro* of Baltimore. All you'll ever get out of her are these two boats with the bullet-holes in them.'

As though to prove their words the remaining prize crew in the *Loyal Sam*, reinforced by the soldiers, now commenced to work the ship's eight guns in earnest. The ocean was lashed into foam by the plunging cannon balls. More rents and rips appeared in the *Matilda*'s drooping sails, but as by a miracle all the shot went overhead. She answered with her kicking nine-pounders, and the smoke of the combat made a rosy pavilion in the still air under the rays of the setting sun.

John Burkett, jr, decided to try belated boarding. To get the *Matilda* alongside with the sweeps meant that all hands would be breathless with labour at the very moment when they needed all their wind for a hand-to-hand fight. He resolved to board with his boats; he had three now, counting those he had captured.

Around the boarders' rum-tot, and under the rosy pall the boarders pulled away. The pall turned to purple as the sun dipped. Shadows spread seaward from the western shore. As they raced they chased or carried a revival of the breeze. The highest sails of the *Loyal Sam* rounded and swelled, and, responding to their urge, she began to slip quietly through the belt of calm. Far beyond the canopy of the cannonade, steel-blue upon the quicksilver of the sea, the line of the overshot of the evening breeze spread upon the face of the waters.

Five minutes more and the prize crew of the *Loyal Sam* would have their prey safe within the shelter of a home harbour. It was neck or nothing now with John Burkett, jr, and his men. They had to take this ship or be taken by her into an American port and prison. It seemed as though they would never cross that gap of water which had looked so narrow when they left the *Matilda*. They did not realize that the *Loyal Sam* was moving all the time. They were so close to the harbour light they could see the lighthouse keeper in the lantern as he kindled the lamp for the night.

When at length they dashed alongside the *Loyal Sam*, under her bellowing guns, they heard the long reverberation of another broadside, fired from the sea, one gun after another, as each bore on the target. By a caprice of the land breeze the *Loyal Sam*, close-hauled on it as hard as sheet and brace could be sweated, paid off a little, and prolonged the act of boarding. But the *Matilda*'s boats at last made fast, and up the channels and chain-plates along her sides the privateersmen swarmed. They were met with musket-butt and boarding pike, and tumbled back into their boats; but they sprang to the attack again, knowing that the next minute meant the difference between prize and prison.

Over the bulwarks they clambered, leaping down into a smoke-filled cannon-cluttered deck, crowded with confused militiamen and tired American tars; tired and confused, but fighting gamely with the assurance of dogs on their own doorstep. The lighthouse loomed large.

The Annapolis Royal men cheered as they charged.

'*Matilda! Matilda!*' they shouted, this being the word agreed on for in-fighting, where, in the close quarters of the mêlée, friend might easily pistol friend.

In answer, from the opposite bulwarks came the amazing cry: 'Freeman forever! *Sherbrooke! Sherbrooke!*'

On the midship hatch, half-way across the narrow field of battle, John Burkett, jr, of Annapolis Royal, met James Ledger, of Liverpool, N.S., cutlass to cutlass.

'Don't skewer me, partner,' panted Ledger, 'we both fly the Red Jack, I take it. Let's get this packet turned round before she runs over the lighthouse!'

It was a situation which required disentangling, but sailors of the sail learn to think clearly and act quickly. Before the bewildered Maine militiamen and Baltimore prize crew could realize what was happening Burkett and Ledger had raced to the helm and the *Loyal Sam* was standing seaward, with three boats dragging at each side. Through the twilight the tall spars of a large brig showed that the third entry in this all-day race had got in at the finish. The boats of the *Sir John Sherbrooke*, largest privateer out of Nova Scotia, had boarded the *Loyal Sam* from the opposite side at the same moment as the *Matilda*'s boats. Caught between two fires, out-numbered, and embarrassed by the *Loyal Sam*'s original crew, some of whom were held on board as prisoners of war, the Americans offered futile resistance. In a few minutes they were all overpowered, and the ship was hove to under the lee of the waiting *Sherbrooke*, for stock-taking.

She was a fine vessel of 280 tons, from the Clyde. She had been to New Providence in the Bahamas with dry-goods, beer, porter and coals, in the winter, and had started home for Greenock with a cargo of cotton, coffee, indigo, lignum vitae, hides, dyewoods and tortoise-shell. On May 17th, in a mid-Atlantic gale, a sailor was washed away by a boarding sea, and the captain, trying to save him, was also swept overboard. Three days afterwards, to the other trials of an overburdened first mate, was added a pursuit by an enemy privateer. Mounting ten guns, and manned by twenty-eight men and boys, the *Loyal Sam* should have been able to beat the privateer off. Although she had lost her captain and one man she had five able-bodied passengers. She was a smart vessel, and the first mate put her before the wind, which was a trying point of sailing for her schooner-rigged pursuer. The chase was long, but the privateer came up at the last as if by magic. After firing a few rounds the *Loyal Sam*'s crew—they were still exhausted from their labours of saving the ship in the gale—hauled down her colours. They had the mortification of finding that they had surrendered to a vessel which had only two guns mounted. Their captor was the privateer schooner, *Siro*, of Baltimore, Capt. David Gray. He had thrown overboard eight of his ten guns in order to get up with the prize. That was why the *Siro* sailed so fast at the end.

Capt. Gray found $24,000 in specie in the *Loyal Sam*'s cabin. He helped himself to the money, and to some coffee and cabin stores and pigs from her live stock, and to a couple of cannon, so as to be able to continue his cruise. He fell a prey to a British man-of-war soon afterwards, but by this time the *Loyal Sam* was well on her way to the United States, with part of her crew and the five passengers still on board as prisoners, snuffing the fresh air on sufferance of prize-master George Franklin Williams and a dozen Baltimore privateersmen.

These were the facts which John Burkett, jr, and James Ledger pieced together from the log book, prisoners, and the rescued passengers, as the *Matilda*, sailed by the few hands left aboard as ship-keepers, toddled up to where the two great square-riggers lay in the deepening dusk. They were about of a size, the *Loyal Sam* and the *Sherbrooke*, and John Burkett's squat command looked particularly shabby and unimpressive under the shadow of the great wings of their waiting sails.

The *Sherbrooke* boarders—Freemans, Smiths, Barsses and Reeses, bristling with scriptural names—had no mind to share or surrender the capture. A large proportion of the *Sherbrooke*'s large crew (she berthed one hundred and fifty fighters) were foreigners, but the prize-masters and petty officers were all of deep-rooted Liverpool stock. They were already accustomed to precedence, although they had only been privateering three months. In the Vice-Admiralty Court records their captain was always enrolled as 'Joseph Freeman, Esqre, commander', like the captain of a man-of-war, while other privateersmen had to content themselves as a rule with 'So-and-so, master'. As for this Burkett fellow the Sherbrookes knew nothing of him and had never heard of his vessel.

'Who are you, anyway, captain, and where do you come from?' demanded James Ledger, as the *Matilda* joined the group.

'I'm John Burkett, of Annapolis Royal,' said the *Matilda*'s commander sturdily, 'and my father's John Burkett of Annapolis Royal, and I sail the *Matilda* and he owns her.'

'Never heard of her a-privateering,' quoth James Ledger, 'but I mind now she was in Halifax last year with a cargo of potatoes.'

'What if she was?' demanded John Burkett hotly. 'Everybody's got to make a beginning. The *Sherbrooke*'s not been in this trade so long as anyone from her has a right to put on airs. Where were you all last year when the *Liverpool Packet* was making prizes on the coast?'

'I was in her,' laughed Ledger. 'I only joined the *Sherbrooke* when she fitted out this spring. We never saw the *Matilda*'s nose outside the basin all the time I was in the *Packet*.'

'Well, you see it now,' retorted Burkett.

'So it seems,' Ledger chuckled, 'poked in other people's business. Where's your commission?'

'Here's commission enough for you!' answered Burkett angrily, flourishing his cutlass.

Blood might have been spilt between the two, but at this moment Capt. Freeman, of the *Sherbrooke*, arrive on board the prize. Grave, distinguished in manner and bearing, accustomed to command, of ancient family and experience in affairs, there was that about Joseph Freeman which explained at once the deference with which he was received in merchants' houses in Halifax and in Admiralty courts. He listened courteously to John Burkett, jr, and then said:

'I dare say you will be able to place all this in evidence before the prize court, sir. We have also claims for its consideration. What say you to this? You put a prize-master and crew on board, and we shall do the same. Let them carry this vessel into Halifax together. The prisoners, it seems, are many, and there are wounded men, and half the passengers, and the original crew. Will you take half of them aboard your vessel?'

The commander of the *Matilda* swallowed hard. A score of such guests would seriously encumber his small craft. That barrel of flour they had taken out of the *Nymph* could not last forever. But, not wishing to seem less than a full partner in the capture, he agreed. That night the division and transfer was made, and the three vessels separated. By morning they were out of sight of the coast. A week later the *Matilda* anchored at Digby, at the entrance to the Annapolis Basin, and her first cruise was over. She was crowded from keelson to carlin with prisoners, and she did not anchor alone. Two American sloops of nearly double her size, ninety tons burthen each, came in with her, further trophies of her bow and spear. They were the *Henry*, of Harpswell, lumber-laden, and the *Packet*, of Salem, and she had captured them on her way home.

John Burkett, jr, had to go to Halifax to fight for his rights in the *Loyal Sam*. It was necessary for David Shaw Clarke, proctor on his behalf, to prove before the Court of Vice-Admiralty that the *Matilda* was indeed a regularly commissioned privateer, and that she had five carriage guns mounted at the time of the *Loyal Sam*'s capture. The prize court decided that the recapture of the ship for her Greenock owners called for generous salvage money, and allowed the high proportion of one sixth of the appraised value of the vessel and cargo. This was fixed at £9,424, so the *Sherbrooke* and the *Matilda* had approximately $7,850 to divide between them.

One would like to know who was the Samuel whose loyalty was so insistently proclaimed to all who sailed the salt seas; but on this point the court records are dumb.

What came to fascinate Snider and other Canadian maritime writers and historians was the growth and competition, during the War of 1812, of sizeable fleets of British-Canadian and American warships on the Great Lakes. Formations of warships manoeuvred on Lake Ontario and elsewhere to gain command of the lakes and give advantage to the allied land forces. And it was not simply skirmishes between clutches of small, hastily-armed merchant schooners; at the height of the competition the British launched a 112-gun ship of the line, the Saint Lawrence, at Kingston, Ontario, which was bigger than Horatio Nelson's Victory, and which was to be challenged by the awesome American New Orleans of 120 guns, not launched before the war ended. The rival commanders on the Lakes were cautious in coming to grips with one another, with so much to be lost in one battle; but their chases and manoeuvrings were the fodder of excited storytelling. In this tale by Snider, a Canadian lake veteran recounts the confrontation between Sir James Lucas Yeo's British Lake Ontario fleet, and the American one of Commodore Isaac Chauncey.

The Burlington Races
C.H.J. Snider

'What! You never heard tell of the Burlington races! Then I suppose your education was also neglected in the matter of the Ontario circuit, the Niagara Sweepstakes, and so on? Salt my old bones, the upbringing of the young has been of a strange sort, in these days of turf-guides and form charts.'

Like a Cyclops regarding the captives in his cavern, Malachi Malone glared from his bunkshelf in the schooner's forecastle upon the assembled 'watch-below', sitting smoking and yarning on the chain-lockers.

'Fill away, Malachi, on the 1812 tack,' Archie Nickerson, the second mate, fired back, folding up the sporting page of the day-before-last's paper, from which the boys were trying to pick the Queen's Plate winner. And Malachi went on.

'Second year of the war I got a berth in the new ship, the *Wolfe*, as powder boy, with an extra shilling a week from the captain of the starboard quarter battery for keepin' his shot-tally for him, because I was handy with a pen. The Admiralty was just as strict with us on the lakes as they were on salt water, with fines for every commander who went beyond his skimpy allowance of ammunition. That was why there was such wild shooting work in action sometimes. The crews never got a chance to exercise at the guns unless a foreign ensign made the target.

'I felt like a lord with my shilling a week for checking bar, chain, and round shot, just because I was handy with a pen and could read without spelling every other word; but the new commodore took the wind out of my sails in short order.

'Sir James Lucas Yeo, he was, and he had just come to the lakes after fairly setting the sea on fire with the privateer *Confiance*, which he had cut out from under the French guns at Muros Bay. He was a hummer.

Why, the King of Portugal made him a knight for the capture of the town of Cayenne! He was thirty when he reached the lakes, a long, thin, sulky-looking chap, with a chin as hard as the peak of the anchor, and eyes that spat black lightning. He was a hard fighter, a hard driver, and a hard loser. He went black in the face every time things went wrong, and that first season he went black very often. That new flagship of his, the *Wolfe*, was chaos afloat when he took her over—fresh from the ways, rigged out by torchlight, armed in the dark, and manned haphazard by hayseeds. First he made her a floating hell, then a progressing purgatory, and, before long, a well-oiled fighting-machine; but there was a lot of rawhide used in the process.

'Sir James fumed like a volcano, but took care the lava never scorched his own sides. He had the smaller fleet and fewer guns, and never once could old Chauncey nettle him into—'

'Who was old Chauncey?' piped up Bill Barrymore, the newly-shipped donkey-man, pulling off his last seaboot.

'Who was old Chauncey? Who was George Washington?' snorted Malachi in disgust at such ignorance, 'Who—'

'Don't cross his bows when he has the starboard tack, you engine driver,' warned Nickerson, 'or it'll be "eight bells" before Malachi gets under weigh again.'

'Isaac Chauncey,' rejoined Malachi deliberately, 'was the American Commodore on the lakes. It's all right, boys; he was dead before you were born, so no wonder you don't mind him. He was a jolly old dog was Chauncey—broad in the beam, with a round red face that had seen lots of wind and weather, and never forgot to laugh. There was only one thing he liked better than fighting and that was telling about it.

'He had a queer fleet, had Chauncey. To start with, he had that old wagon the *Oneida*, a brig that crawled like a tortoise going free, and slid sideways like a crab when she tried to beat to wind'ard. But she had sixteen twenty-four-pounders, and that made her a tough nut to crack. She was better at fighting than running away—and that suited Melancthon T. Woolsey, of Sacket's Harbor, the lieutenant who commanded her, to a knock-down. Chauncey built a twenty-four-gun ship, the *President Madison*, in fifty-eight days from the day the timber was felled in the bush. Later on he built another fine ship-rigged corvette, the *General Pike*, and a smart schooner called the *Sylph*. And he had a whole menagerie of little fore-'n'-afters of stone-hooker size—from a hundred tons down.

'They were coasters, bought up when the war broke out, and loaded with deck-jags of cannon. They were slow as molasses and tippy as soda-water bottles. All they were good for was long range work in smooth water. Then they were terrors. The guns they carried were all long 'uns, twice as powerful as the carronades our fleet had, meant for nigh-hand broadside work.

'In light weather, at long range, those schooners lived up to their names— *Scourge, Asp, Pert, Growler,* and *Conquest.* In a sailing breeze they were as harmless as might be expected of *Ontario, Julia, Hamilton, Fair American, Governor Tompkins,* or *Lady of the Lake.* All told, Chauncey had fifteen vessels that summer.

'Yeo had only eight at most. There was the *Wolfe,* not quite as big as either the *Pike* or the *Madison;* and the *Royal George,* ship-rigged like the *Wolfe,* but smaller. Then there were the brigs—the old *Earl of Moira,* and the *Lord Melville*—about half the size of the two ships; and the schooners, *Sir Sidney Smith, Beresford, Simcoe,* and *Seneca*—none of them much bigger than the larger Bay of Quinte traders to-day. The last two were kept for transport duty or harbour work. The squadron sailed in three pairs—two ships, two brigs, two schooners; and they held together like a bunch of trained dogs—after Yeo had sent one or two crews ashore to dig trenches, for shortening sail before the flagship signalled.

'But Chauncey's bunch—Lord love you, the only way he had of keeping them together was roping them up. The smart ones in the fleet could sail circles around the droghers, and what was worse for him, they liked to do it. He'd write home how hard he wanted to fight, but he'd forget to add that he wanted to fight in smooth water at long range. He'd tow that slug the *Oneida* by the hour, and make the *Madison* and the *Sylph* tow the schooners, so that he would have all his guns for a battle—if he ever got one. And Sir James took good care that they never closed up until it was blowing a good hickory and there was a chance of our short guns and musketry sweeping the decks of the low-bulwarked, wallowing schooners. *That* was why we had what we called the 'Ontario Circuit'.

'Old Chauncey had raised merry—begging your reverence's pardon.' This was jerked at the young divinity student who was earning a dollar a day before the mast in the *Albacore.* 'He'd slipped out of Sacket's with the ice, and raided York before Yeo reached the lake. He had swamped Fort George, filled the Niagara peninsula with Yankee soldiers, and got the penned-up Buffalo fleet free on Lake Erie by the time Yeo had the *Wolfe* ready and made his fizzle of an attack on Sacket's. Then Yeo had shelled out the American encampment at Forty-Mile Creek at the head of the lake and scoured the south shore, raided the Genesee settlement near Rochester, taken the fort and the supply depot at Sodus, captured two schooners and a brigade of boats, and gone back to Kingston to refit. While he was on the south shore, young Lieutenant Wolcott Chauncey slipped across in the *Lady of the Lake* and snapped up the transport *Lady Murray*, loaded with soldiers, sailors, and supplies, at Presqu'isle, on the north shore, near the Bay of Quinte.

'Yeo made another stab at Sacket's Harbor with no result. The *Pike* and the *Sylph* were just building then, and if he had destroyed them he would have had the whip hand. But he had to go back to Kingston, and the new *Pike*, the heaviest ship on the fresh water, joined Chauncey's fleet, and the old boy went up the lake, tried Burlington Heights and got his fingers burned, raided York again to fill his flour-bins, and went across to Niagara, to send sailors up to Lake Erie and taken on soldiers in their places.

'While we were at Burlington we heard how our whole Lake Erie fleet had been shot to pieces at Put-in-Bay. We found that Chauncey had reached Niagara again, and as he had got the habit of filling his flour-bins over at York we stood down the lake and anchored in Humber Bay in the lee of the Island—York Roads they called it then. Sure enough, next morning, the twenty-eighth of September, the lookouts sighted him, stretching across from Niagara under all sail, with stu'ns'ls out, in a smart east breeze. We hove up our anchors and stood out to meet him, close hauled on the port tack.

'We were about three miles apart when the fleets drew abreast. It looked as though our big chance had come. Here was the enemy, at least fifteen miles from shelter—and a good fresh breeze, rolling the sea ahead of it and promising a strong gale before night—just our conditions.

'"One, two, three, four, five, six, seven sail," I heard Sir James count to the first lieutenant, who was busy plotting out courses. "A pity he didn't bring the rest of his menagerie, but what's left in Niagara will stay there the rest of the war if this day's work is good!"

'The *Pike* was storming along, far in the lead, with the schooner *Asp* thrashing about after her on the end of a long towline. The *Governor Tompkins* followed under full sail. Next came the *Madison* and the *Sylph*, each with a wobbling schooner fast to them. Then, far back, the *Oneida* lumbered, with enough to do to look after herself. And last of all were two schooners, too far off to be made out.

'As the fleets lapped and began to pass the *Pike* steered for the *Beresford* and *Sir Sidney Smith*, two schooners, in the rear of our line. The *Wolfe* was at the head, and to give Chauncey a fight with a man of his size

Sir James signalled the fleet to wear ship. The *Wolfe* was the first to come round. This brought us and the *Pike* and *Tompkins* in range of one another. They opened with their long guns, and we tried our carronades.

'The boys burst into cheers as they saw the *Pike*'s main t'gallant mast, with its sail and the royal above it, pitch overboard after our first broadside. The splinters flew from the *Pike*'s bulwarks and we knew every shot of ours was telling. Her first broadside went high, spotting our topsails with shot-holes; and then with a roar her whole forecastle seemed to lift up. When she yawed to give us the starboard broadside the bow-chaser burst. That killed and wounded twenty-two of her men. But the rest of her broadside did terrible work with us. It was fired low, and it sheared the bulwarks like a scythe; the *Pike*, you know, threw the heaviest long-range broadside on fresh water—'

'How heavy?' interrupted Pan-faced Harry.

'Three hundred and sixty pounds, thrown a mile and a half; which isn't the weight of one shot maybe of a modern battleship, nor the range of a modern rifle, but it was a stunner in my day.

'Boys-oh-boys, how the splinters did fly! The captain of the port quarter-guns was scattered all over me; poor chap, a split ball fairly made mincemeat of him. I was on my knees, wiping the blood from my eyes and trying to get up, when there was a ripping crash overhead, and the mizzen topmast fell forward, with its yards, into the main rigging. It was blowing hard by this time, and the weight of the wind and the falling spars snapped the main topmast backstays. The maintopmast bent like a whip, and then it too came crashing down, bringing the main yard with it.

'In all my sailing I've never seen such a mess—the deck filled with screaming, groaning, cursing, cheering men, splintered spars as big as tree-trunks, tangled ropes, and loosened sails, thrashing about and smothering everything like a collapsed circus tent.

'Sir James, black and bloody, seized the wheel himself. "She won't steer!" he hissed, as he whirled the spokes over, to keep her from falling into the trough and rolling her one remaining mast out. "No wonder, with all her after sail gone, and that raffle of stuff dragging overboard! Quarter-master, put her dead before the wind, and keep her there! Sailing-master, set everything you can crowd on to the foremast! All hands to the quarter deck, except the foremast men and the stern-gun crews, to chop clear the wreck."

'And with that he gave up the wheel and seized a ship axe. There was another crash from the *Pike*, but the shot this time went whistling into the empty space where our topmasts had been.

'Then, through the powder smoke speared a long bowsprit, crowded with straining sails, and a short, blocky ship ranged across our stern.

'"Leave him to me, sir!" I heard a strong clear voice call, and peering out of a shattered gunport I saw it was the *Royal George*, and Sir William Howe Mulcaster was hanging by the mizzen t'gallant backstays, trumpet in hand.

'Sir James answered something, but I couldn't hear it, for just then the *George*'s broadside spoke. Then her headsails fluttered and went dead as they were blanketed, and she wore around, and ranged across our stern again, and gave them the other broadside. I heard a distant roar from the *Pike* and the splinters crackled from the *George*, and her fore topmast was shot away, at the head. But the yard stayed aloft, leaving her under control, and Captain Mulcaster kept swinging her, yawing to port and starboard as fast as his crews could load their guns, and covering our retreat.

'Just one glimpse I got at the *Pike* while I helped slash the lanyards of the trailing maintopmast rigging. She was all cut up forward, and steering wild. The schooner that had kept on her quarter, the *Tompkins*, had her foremast dragging over the bows. The *Sylph* and the *Madison* were hanging on to their towing schooners, glad of the chance of keeping out of reach of the spurs of that fighting-cock Mulcaster. Our own schooners and the brigs were running abeam of us, firing their stern guns.

'I've sometimes thought it only needed a little more nerve to have turned on those Yankees with our five fighting ships, leaving the *Wolfe* to sink or swing. The brigs and schooners and *Royal George* might have downed the *Pike*, cut up as she was, in spite of her heavy batteries; and once she was crippled as badly even as the *Wolfe*, the rest would have been easy, for it was blowing so hard the *Sylph* and the *Madison* were the only other real fighters. We could have sailed circles around the old *Oneida*, and the little schooners were rolling so their guns would have gone down the hatches or overboard the moment they tried to fire them.

'Of course, we didn't know then the *Pike* had twenty-seven men laid out, all told. We were hard hit ourselves, and ours was the Commodore's ship. Had Mulcaster been flying the broad pennant now—but what's the use—they're all dead, now, all but me.'

'Go on, Malachi,' said the second mate, 'you've got a hundred years of life in you yet.'

'Sure I have,' answered Malachi, relighting his pipe, 'and as I was saying, we ran on and on, with the *Royal George* swinging to port and starboard off our quarters and more splinters flying from Chauncey's fleet every time she did. Flamboro' Head, back of Burlington Bay, loomed up bigger with every lift of the sea.

'"Pilot, can you take us through the cut in this sea?" asked Sir James.

'"I'm a bit doubtful," said an old lake sailor, who had a berth in the chart room just for his knowledge of the anchorages. They were all natural harbours then, mind you, and beacons as scarce as hens' teeth. "Well, if you do, here's five golden guineas," said Sir James, "and if you don't, there's the fore yardarm, with a whip rove and a noose at the end."

'"I'll take the guineas," said the old chap. And Sir James paid him then and there.

'"Now, Jonathan," he said, with a look at the pursuing fleet astern, and the breakers bursting on the beach ahead, "follow as hard as you like. *You* can't make the entrance to the bay, even if *we* can. If we all drive ashore, we are wrecked on our own coast, you on a foreign one, and your fleet is just as much destroyed as if I had captured it in midlake—as I hoped to do this accursed day."

'You might have thought Chauncey heard him, for the *Pike* was next moment flying a string of flags, and the whole fleet hauled on the wind— the *Oneida* first of all—and started to thrash back to Niagara from the perils of the lee-shore. We watched them dip and lunge and roll, and began to make bets that Melancthon Woolsey's old brig would never claw clear, even with six miles offing; but next moment our own troubles engaged us.

'The surf went seething up the beach in great bursts of white foam, retreating in a creamy lacework of sandy backwash, and spouting high again in the next breaker. Straight as an arrow for the gap in the sand the *Beresford* steered. She went through on the crest of a comber, and the *Sir Sidney Smith* followed. We could see them across the sandbar as they rounded up to guard the entrance. Then the *Moira* tried it, and passed, and the *Melville*, with the water spouting from her scuppers, as her crew pumped her of the burden trickling in through the loosened shot plugs. Then it was our turn, for with all our aftersail gone we had to drive straight before the wind, and couldn't turn aside to give the gallant Mulcaster the next chance. A rush on a comber, a sickening pause as the backwash on the bar caught us, then a triumphant forward plunge—and the pilot laughed at the noose on the foreyard, and jingled the guineas in his pocket.

'And in our wake, with never a zig-zag now, the *Royal George* came roaring, bow and stern resting on the travelling crests of two giant seas. Up, up, up she lifted, as the two combined under her keel; a forward spring, a rush like an avalanche, and the last and bravest ship of all was through, safe over the hurdles in the steeplechase that ended the Burlington Races.'

'Oh, so *that's* what you call the Burlington Races,' said Pan-faced Harry in a relieved voice. 'I was wondering—'

But what he was wondering the watch never knew. For on the scuttle hood there was a banging, and the first mate was heard calling:

Heigh below you sleepers,

Don't you hear the news?

It's *eight b-e-l-l-s!*

Notwithstanding the Saint Lawrence and other purpose-built ships, both Lake fleets pressed into service commercial vessels which often became top-heavy with the addition of the heavy iron naval guns to their decks. Two American vessels, the Hamilton *and the* Scourge, *were lost one summer evening in 1813 in a line squall on Lake Ontario, in an event remembered by Ned Myers, a seaman in one of the ships. In recent years, underwater archaeology has revealed that both vessels remain intact on the dark floor of Lake Ontario, awaiting recovery or whatever study technological advances will allow. Myers' account, from James Fenimore Cooper's* Ned Myers: or A Life Before the Mast *(1852), is simple, graphic, and moving.*

The Loss of the 'Scourge'
Ned Myers

It was a lovely evening, not a cloud visible, and the lake being as smooth as a looking-glass. The English fleet was but a short distance to the northward of us; so near, indeed, that we could almost count their ports. They were becalmed, like ourselves, and a little scattered.

Towards evening, all light craft were doing the same, to close with the Commodore. Our object was to get together, lest the enemy should cut off some of our small vessels during the night . . .

A little before sunset, Mr Osgood [the captain] ordered us to pull in our sweeps . . . we took [them] in as ordered, laying them athwart the deck, in readiness to be used when wanted. The vessels ahead and stern of us were, generally, within speaking distance. Just as the sun went below the horizon, George Turnblatt, a Swede, who was our gunner, came to me, and said he thought we ought to secure our guns, for we had been cleared for action all day, and the crew at quarters. We were still at quarters, in name, but the petty officers were allowed to move about, and as much license was given to the people as was wanted. I answered that I would gladly secure mine if he would get an order for it; but as we were still at quarters, and there lay John Bull, we might get a slap at him in the night. On this the gunner said he would go aft and speak to Mr Osgood on the subject. He did so, but met the captain (as we always called Mr Osgood) at the break of the quarter-deck. When George had told his errand, the captain looked at the heavens, and remarked that the night was so calm there could be no great use in securing the guns, and the English were so near we should certainly engage, if there came a breeze; that the men would sleep at their quarters, of course, and would be ready to take care of their guns, but that he might catch a turn with the side-tackle-falls around the pommelions of the guns, which would be sufficient. He then ordered the boatswain to call all hands aft, to the break of the quarter-deck.

As soon as the people had collected, Mr Osgood said: 'You must be pretty well fagged out, men; I think we may have a hard night's work yet, and I wish you to get your suppers, and then catch as much sleep as you can, at your guns.' He then ordered the purser's steward to splice the main-brace. These were the last words I ever heard from Mr Osgood. As soon as he gave the order he went below . . .

The schooner, at this time, was under her mainsail, jib, and fore-topsail. The foresail was brailed, and the foot stopped, and the flying-jib was stowed. None of the halyards were racked, nor sheets stopped. This was a precaution we always took, on account of the craft's being so tender.

We first spliced the main-brace, and then got our suppers, eating between the guns, where we generally messed, indeed. One of my messmates, Tom Goldsmith, was captain of the gun next to me, and as we sat there finishing our suppers, I says to him, 'Tom, bring up that rug that you pinned at Little York, and that will do for both of us to stow ourselves away under.' Tom went down and got the rug, which was an article for the camp that he had laid hands on, and it made us a capital bed-quilt. As all hands were pretty well tired, we lay down, with our heads on shot-boxes, and soon went to sleep.

In speaking of the canvas that was set, I ought to have said something of the state of our decks. The guns had the side-tackles fastened as I have mentioned. There was a box of canister, and another of grape, at each gun, besides extra stands of both, under the shot-racks. There was also one grummet of round-shot at every gun, besides the racks being filled. Each gun's crew slept at the gun and its opposite, thus dividing the people pretty equally on both sides of the deck. Those who were stationed below, slept below. I think it probable that, as the night grew cool, as it always does on fresh waters, some of the men stole below to get warmer berths. This was easily done in that craft, as we had but two regular officers on boardr, the acting boatswain and gunner being little more than two of ourselves.

I was soon asleep, as sound as if lying in the bed of a king. How long my nap lasted, or what took place in the interval, I cannot say. I awoke, however, in consequence of large drops of rain falling on my face. Tom Goldsmith awoke at the same moment. When I opened my eyes, it was so dark I could not see the length of the deck. I arose and spoke to Tom, telling him it was about to rain, and that I meant to go down and get a nip, out of a little stuff we kept in our mess-chest, and I would bring up the bottle if he wanted a taste. Tom answered, 'This is nothing; we're neither pepper nor salt.' One of the black men spoke, and asked me to bring up the bottle, and give him a nip too. All this took half a minute, perhaps. I now remember to have heard a strange rushing noise to windward as I went towards the forward hatch, though it made no impression on me at the time. We had been lying between the starboard guns, which was the weather side of the vessel, if there were any weather side to it, there not being a breath of air, and no motion to the water, and I passed round to the larboard side in order to find the ladder which led up in that direction. The hatch was so small that two men could not pass at a time, and I felt my way to it, in no haste. One hand was on the bitts, and a foot was on the ladder, when a flash of lightning almost blinded me. The thunder came at the next instant, and with it a rushing of winds that fairly smothered the clap.

The instant I was aware there was a squall, I sprang for the jib-sheet. Being captain of the forecastle, I knew where to find it, and threw it loose at a jerk. In doing this, I jumped on a man named Leonard Lewis, and called on him to lend me a hand. I next let fly the larboard, or lee top-sail-sheet, got hold of the clew-line, and, assisted by Lewis, got the clew half up. All this time I kept shouting to the man at the wheel to put his helm 'hard down'. The water was now up to my breast, and I knew the schooner must go over. Lewis had not said a word, but I called out to him to shift for himself, and belaying the clew-line, in hauling myself forward of the foremast, I received a blow from the jib-sheet that came near to breaking my arm. . . .

All this occupied less than a minute. The flashes of lightning were incessant, and nearly blinded me. Our decks seemed on fire, and yet I could see nothing. I heard no hail, no order, no call; but the schooner was filled with the shrieks and cries of the men to leeward, who were lying jammed under the guns, shot-boxes, shot, and other heavy things that had gone down as the vessel fell over. The starboard second gun, from forward, had capsized, and come down directly over the hatch, and I caught a glimpse of a man struggling to get past it. Apprehension of this gun had induced me to drag myself forward of the mast where I received the blow mentioned.

I succeeded in hauling myself up to windward, and in getting in to the schooner's fore-channels. Here I met William Deer, the boatswain, and a black boy of the name of Philips, who was the powder-boy of our gun. 'Deer, she's gone!' I said. The boatswain made no answer, but walked out on the forerigging, towards the head-mast. He probably had some vague notion that the schooner's masts would be out of the water if she went down, and took this course as the safest. The boy was in the chains the last I saw of him.

I now crawled aft, on the upper side of the bulwarks, amid a most awful and infernal din of thunder, and shrieks, and dazzling flashes of lightning; the wind blowing all the while like a tornado. When I reached the port of my own gun, I put a foot in, thinking to step on the muzzle of the piece; but it had gone to leeward with all the rest, and I fell through the port, until I brought up with my arms. I struggled up again, and continued working my way aft. As I got abreast of the main-mast, I saw someone had let run the halyards. I soon reached the beckets of the sweeps, and found four in them. I could not swim a stroke, and it crossed my mind to get one of the sweeps to keep me afloat. In striving to jerk the becket clear, it parted, and the forward ends of the four sweeps rolled down the schooner's side into the water. This caused the other ends to slide, and all the sweeps got away from me. I then crawled quite aft, as far as the fashion-piece. The water was pouring down the cabin companionway like a sluice, and as I stood for an instant on the fashion-piece, I saw Mr Osgood, with his head and part of his shoulders through one of the cabin windows, struggling to get out. He must have been within six feet of me. I saw him but a moment, by means of a flash of lightning, and I think he must have seen me. At the same time, there was a man visible at the end of the main-boom, holding onto the clew of the sail. I do not know who it was. The man probably saw me, and that I was about to spring, for he called out, 'Don't jump overboard! — don't jump overboard! The schooner is righting.'

I was not in a state of mind to reflect much on anything. I do not think more than three or four minutes, if as many, had passed since the squall struck us, and there I was standing on the vessel's quarter, led by Providence more than by any discretion of my own. It now came across to me that if the schooner should right she was filled, and must go down, and that she might carry me with her in the suction. I made a spring, therefore, and fell into the water several feet from the place where I had stood. It is my opinion the schooner sank as I left her.

I went down some distance myself, and when I came up to the surface, I began to swim vigorously for the first time in my life. I think I swam several yards, but of course will not pretend to be certain of such a thing, at such a moment, until I felt my hand hit something hard. I made another stroke and felt my hand pass down the side of an object that I knew at once to be a clincher-built boat. I belonged to this boat, and now I recollected that she had been towing astern. Until that instant I had not thought of her, but thus was I led in the dark to the best possible means of saving my life. I made a grab at the gunwale, and caught in the stern-sheets. Had I swum another yard, I should have passed the boat, and missed her altogether! I got in without any difficulty, being all alive and much excited.

My first look was for the schooner. She had disappeared, and I suppose she was just settling under water. It rained as if the flood-gates of heaven were opened, and it lightninged awfully. It did not seem to me that there was a breath of air, and the water was unruffled, the effects of the rain excepted. All this I saw, as it might be, at a glance. But my chief concern was to preserve my own life. I was coxswain of this very boat, and had made it fast to the taffrail that same afternoon, with a round turn and two half-hitches, by its best painter. Of course I expected the vessel would drag the boat down with her, for I had no knife to cut the painter. There was a gang-board in the boat, however, which lay fore and aft, and I thought this might keep me afloat until some of the fleet should pick me up. To clear this gang-board , then, and get into the water, was my first object. I ran forward to throw off the lazy-painter that was coiled on its end, and in doing this, I caught the boat's painter in my hand by accident. A pull satisfied me that it was all clear! Someone on board must have cast off this painter, and then lost the chance of getting into the boat by accident. At all events I was safe, and I now dared to look about me.

My only chance of seeing was during the flashes, and these left me almost blind. I had thrown the gang-board into the water, and I now called out to encourage the men, telling them I was in the boat. I could hear many around me, and occasionally I saw the heads of men struggling in the lake. There being no proper place to scull in, I got an oar in the after rowlock and made out to scull a little in that fashion. I now saw a man quite near the boat, and, hauling in the oar, made a spring amidships, catching this poor fellow by the collar. He was very near gone, and I had a great deal of difficulty in getting him in over the gunwale. Our joint weight brought the boat down, so low that she shipped a good deal of water. This turned out to be Leonard Lewis, the young man who had helped me to clew up the fore-topsail. He could not stand, and spoke with difficulty. I asked him to crawl aft, out of the water, which he did, lying down in the stern-sheets.

I now looked about me and heard another; leaning over the gunwale, I got a glimpse of a man, struggling, quite near the boat. I caught him by the collar too, and had to drag him in very much in the way I had done with Lewis. This proved to be Lemuel Bryant, the man who had been wounded by a hot shot, at York, while the commodore was on board us. His wound had not yet healed, but he was less exhausted than Lewis. He could not help me, however, lying down in the bottom of the boat, the instant he was able.

For a few moments I now heard no more in the water, and I began to scull again. By my calculations I moved a few yards, and must have got over the spot where the schooner went down. Here, in the flashes, I saw many heads, the men swimming in confusion and at random. By this time little was said, the whole scene being one of fearful struggle and frightful silence. It still rained, but the flashes were less frequent and less fierce. They told me, afterwards, in the squadron, that it thundered awfully, but I cannot say I heard a clap after I struck the water. The next man caught the boat himself. It was a mulatto, from Martinique, who was Mr. Osgood's steward, and I helped him in. He was much exhausted, though an excellent swimmer, but alarm nearly deprived him of his strength. He kept saying, 'Oh! Masser Ned—Oh! Masser Ned!' and lay down in the bottom of the boat like the two others, I taking care to shove him over to the larboard side, so as to trim our small craft.

I kept calling out to encourage the swimmers, and presently I heard a voice saying, 'Ned, I'm here, close by you.' This was Tom Goldsmith, a messmate, and the very man under whose rug I had been sleeping at quarters. He did not want much help, getting in, pretty much, by himself.

I asked him if he were able to help me. 'Yes, Ned,' he answered, 'I'll stand by you to the last; what shall I do?' I told him to take his tarpaulin and to bail the boat, which, by this time, was a third full of water. This he did, while I sculled a little ahead. 'Ned,' says Tom, 'she's gone down with her colours flying, for her pennant came near getting a round turn around my body, and carrying me down with her. Davy has made a good haul, and he gave us a close shave, but he didn't get you and me.' In this manner did the thoughtless sailor express himself, as soon as rescued from the grasp of death! Seeing something on the water, I asked Tom to take my oar, while I sprang to the gunwale and caught Mr Bogardus, the master's mate, who was clinging to one of the sweeps. I hauled him in, and he told me he thought someone had hold of the other end of the sweep. It was so dark, however, we could not see even that distance. I hauled the sweep along until I found Ebenezer Duffy, a mulatto, and the ship's cook. He could not swim a stroke, and was nearly gone. I got him in alone, Tom bailing, lest the boat, which was quite small, should swamp us.

As the boat drifted along, she reached another man, whom I caught also by the collar. I was afraid to haul this person in amidships, the boat being now so deep, and so small, and so I dragged him ahead, and hauled him in over the bows. This man was the pilot, whose name I never knew. He was a lake-man and had been aboard with us the whole summer. The poor fellow was almost gone, and like all the rest, with the exception of Tom, he lay down and said not a word.

We had now as many in the boat as it would carry, and Tom and myself thought it would not do to take in any more. It is true we saw no more, everything around us appearing still as death, the pattering of the rain excepted. Tom began to bail again, and I commenced hallooing. I sculled about several minutes thinking of giving others a tow, or of even hauling in one or two more, after we got the water out of the boat; but we found no one else. I think it probable I sculled away from the spot, as there was nothing to guide me. I suppose, however, that by this time all the Scourges had gone down, for no more were ever heard from.

Tom Goldsmith and myself now put our heads together as to what best to be done. We were both afraid of falling into the enemy's hands, for they might have bore up in the squall and run down near us. On the whole, however, we thought the distance between the two squadrons was too great for this; at all events, something must be done at once. So we began to row, in what direction even we did not know. It still rained as hard as it could pour, though there was not a breath of wind. The lightning came now at considerable intervals, and the gust was evidently passing away towards the broader parts of the lake. While we were rowing and talking about our chance of falling in with the enemy, Tom cried out to me to 'avast pulling'. He had seen a vessel by a flash, and he thought she was English, from her size. As he said she was a schooner, however, I thought it must be one of our own craft, and got her direction from him. At the next flash, I saw her, and felt satisfied she belonged to us. Before we began to pull, however, we were hailed. 'Boat ahoy!' I answered. 'If you pull another stroke, I'll fire into you,' came back. 'What boat's that? Lay on your oars or I'll fire into you.' It was clear we were mistaken ourselves for an enemy, and I called out to know what schooner it was. No answer was given, though the threat to fire was repeated, if we pulled another stroke. I now turned to Tom and said, 'I know that voice—that is old Trant.' Tom thought we were 'in the wrong shop'. I now sang out, 'This is the *Scourge*'s boat; our schooner is gone down, and we want to come alongside.' A voice now called from the schooner— 'Is that you, Ned?' This I knew was my old shipmate and schoolfellow, Jack Mallet, who was acting as boatswain on the *Julia*, the schooner commanded by Sailing-Master James Trant, one of the oddities of the service, and a man with whom the blow often came as soon as the word. I had know Mr Trant's voice, and felt more afraid he would fire into us than I had done of anything which had occurred that fearful night. Mr Trant himself now called out, 'Oh-ho; give way, boys, and come alongside.' This we did, and a very few strokes took us up to the *Julia*, where we were received with the utmost kindness. The men were passed out of the boat, while I gave Mr Trant an account of all that had happened. This took but a minute or two.

Mr Trant now enquired in what direction the *Scourge* had gone down, and as soon as I told him, in the best manner I could, he called out to Jack Mallet: "Oh-ho, Mallet—take four hands, and go in the boat and see what you can do—take a lantern, and I will show a light on the water's edge, so you may know me.' Mallet did as ordered, and was off in less than three minutes after we got alongside. . . .

Mr Trant now called the Scourges aft, and asked more of the particulars. He then gave us a glass of grog all round, and made his own crew splice the main-brace. The Julias now offered us dry clothes. I got a change from Jack Reilly, who had been an old messmate, and with whom I had always been on good terms. It knocked off raining, but we shifted ourselves at the galley fire below. I then went on deck and presently we hear the boat pulling back. It soon came alongside, bringing in it four more men that had been found floating about on sweeps and gratings. On inquiry, it turned out that these men belonged to the *Hamilton*, [commanded by] Lieutenant Winter—a schooner that had gone down in the same squall that carried us over. These men were very much exhausted, too, and we all went below and were told to turn in.

I had been so much excited during the scenes through which I had just passed, and had been so much stimulated by grog that, as yet, I had not felt much of the depression natural to such events. I even slept soundly that night, nor did I turn out until six the next morning.

When I got on deck, there was a fine breeze; it was a lovely day, and the lake was perfectly smooth. Our fleet was in good line, in pretty close order, with the exception of the *Governor Tompkins* [commanded by] Lieutenant Tom Brown, which was a little to leeward, but carrying a press of sail to close with the commodore. Mr Trant, perceiving that the *Tompkins* wished to speak to us in passing, brailed his foresail and let her luff up close under our lee. 'Two of the schooners, the *Hamilton* and the *Scourge*, have gone down in the night,' called out Mr Brown, 'for I have picked up four of the *Hamilton*'s.' 'Oh-ho!' answered Mr Trant, 'that's no news at all, for I have picked up twelve, eight of the *Scourge*'s and four of the *Hamilton*'s—aft fore-sheet."

These were all that were ever saved from the two schooners, which must have had near a hundred souls on board them. The two commanders, Lieutenant Winter and Mr Osgood, we both lost, and with Mr Winter went down, I believe, one or two young gentlemen. The squadron could not have moved much between the time when the accidents happened and that when I came on deck, or we must have come round and gone over the same ground again, for we now passed many relics of the scene, floating about in the water. I saw sponges, gratings, sweeps, hats, etc., scattered about, and in passing ahead we saw one of the last that we tried to catch; Mr Trant ordering it done, as he said it must have been Lieutenant Winter's. We did not succeed, however, nor was any article taken on board. A good look-out was kept for men from aloft, but none were seen from any of the vessels. The lake had swallowed up the rest of the two crews, and the *Scourge*, as had been often predicted, had literally become a coffin to a large portion of her people.

But there was loss of life at the hand of man as well as the whims of weather. On Lake Champlain and Lake Erie, the rival fleets did come to toe-to-toe punching, producing a tragic and horrifying experience for all who took part. Most significant for Canada was the loss on Lake Erie at Put-in-Bay, Ohio, in September of 1813, suffered by an ill-prepared British-Canadian squadron under Captain Robert Barclay, a Trafalgar veteran, at the hands of an American one under Commodore Oliver Hazard Perry. That loss opened what was later southern Ontario to an invasion and occupation, and its horror was amplified by the similarity of the combatants to one another, the courage and gallantry of the crews, and the respect and kindness which followed the killing.

The Battle for Lake Erie
Robert and Thomas Malcomson

At dawn on September 10, 1813, the lookout perched on the heights of Gibraltar Point, one of the rocky outcroppings scattered among the Bass Islands, signalled to the American squadron lying at Put-in-Bay that ships were approaching from the northwest. Oliver Hazard Perry, realizing instantly that it was Barclay come out to fight, quickly passed the word for his vessels to weigh anchor.

The breeze was baffling and light as the American squadron struggled to leave its anchorage that morning. Besides being weak, it was also blowing from the southwest and that placed Perry at an immediate disadvantage. Usually the opening stage of any confrontation between warships undersail was taken up with careful manoeuvring by the opponents as each strove to make sure the wind was in his favour. Capturing the weather gauge (being between the wind and the enemy) allowed a commander to control how fast or slowly to press action, which left his antagonist with the choice of setting all sails and fleeing or fighting against the wind to get into a preferred position. That undesirable alternative, not unlike running up a hill to meet an enemy charging down, was the one that Perry chose rather than escaping downwind. Beneath a pristine summer sky the two squadrons plodded toward each other, their full sets of sails filling gently in the three-knot breeze. At 10 a.m. they were still more than five kilometres apart when that faint wind died away and abruptly returned, blowing this time from the southeast. Perry became the first recipient of good luck as the advantage of the wind gauge fell into his hands.

It was a moment of critical importance for the British. If they held their position and engaged, they were allowing Perry to set the scene and pacing for the battle. If the British tried to run, they might be able to escape, but to what effect? Robert Barclay, ever mindful of the need to relieve the supply shortages at Amherstburg, made his choice and ordered his commanders to lay to. Aboard each ship the men rushed to reduce and back the sails so that they brought their vessels to a virtual standstill in the water. Lying in close quarters at regular intervals, the *Chippawa, Detroit, General Hunter, Queen Charlotte, Lady Prevost* and *Little Belt* waited for the enemy to come downwind to them. From the American squadron, little could be detected of the circumstances under which Barclay had left Amherstburg. Across the lightly rippled water, his ships appeared 'all newly painted, their sales were new and their bright red ensigns were tending to the breeze, all looking splendidly in the bright September sun. Their appearance and movements showed that a seaman and master spirit held them in hand.'

Earlier Perry observed that the British had not formed the line of battle that he expected. As his squadron crept forward, he ordered the *Niagara*, which according to his strategy had taken the van, to heave to while the *Lawrence* caught up, whereupon he called over to Elliott that he would take the lead. *Scorpion* and *Ariel* were told to move ahead to support the flagship. With those changes the American squadron proceeded. At about 11:00 a.m., amid a chorus of cheers, Perry raised the flag bearing James Lawrence's heroic words to the masthead and then ordered the crews to be fed, since the normal hour for their meal would probably find them fighting for their lives.

Aboard HMS *Detroit*, Barclay, accompanied by Lieutenants John Garland and George Inglis and Provincial Lieutenant Francis Purvis, inspected his ship to ensure that unnecessary furniture and stores had been stowed out of the way and that cartridges and balls were on hand at each gun. Below deck the passageway to the magazine was guarded, the opening to the stuffy compartment itself shrouded with water-soaked fabric to prohibit any errant spark or flame reaching that highly inflammable storeroom. Just like in the American ships, the British crews were fed early and their meal topped off with the final draughts of spirits remaining in the ships' casks. A stillness fell aboard the *Detroit* and its sister ships as the men consumed what many of them must have feared would be their last meals. Tidings of good luck and final bequests were given as the soldiers and seamen crouched between the guns on the deck, where sand had been spread intended to provide footholds later when the planks became streaked with blood. In the final tense moments as the Americans approached, led by one of their powerful brigs, Barclay looked over the ships of his command and perhaps gave a silent salute for success to his colleagues Finnis, Buchan, Bignell and the others.

Just before 11:45 a.m. a bugle sounded aboard the *Detroit*, followed by song and cheers along the British line. The ships in that squadron had reset their sails to get underway in a south-southwest direction. Perry's vessels, coming out of the southeast in a line that straggled across three kilometres of lightly rippling water, were altering course to run on a path parallel to their opponents. At 11:45, with the Americans about two kilometres distant, Captain Barclay gave the order to try a shot from *Detroit*'s long 24-pounder.

From the deck of the *Lawrence*, which Perry was steering to engage the British flagship, the smoke of the long gun could be seen drifting away on the light wind. A splash well ahead of the brig showed where the ball had fallen short. The American crews waited stoically for their turn to reply. A few minutes later a second puff of smoke appeared on the larboard side of the *Detroit*. There was a pause lasting several moments and then the ball smashed through the forward bulwark of the *Lawrence*, sending jagged splinters across the deck. It was followed with the first American reply as twenty-four-year-old Stephen Champlin called for *Scorpion*'s long 32-pounder to be fired. The *Scorpion* and *Ariel* had moved up to a station just ahead of the larboard bow of the *Lawrence*, which itself entered the bombardment at 11:55 a.m. with shots from its two 12-pound cannons; the port bow chaser gun had been moved over to the starboard side during the hour prior to the starting of the fighting. After this preliminary exchange of shots, the action became general as all the vessels began to fire at various rates at the opponents; to which they had been assigned.

This opening stage of the battle saw Perry struggling to manoeuvre the *Lawrence* into close quarters with the *Detroit*, so that the full impact of his battery of carronades could be inflicted upon the British. As he closed on Barclay's flagship he kept his two 12-pounders busy, but they offered little opposition to the hail of iron that was being thrown at the *Lawrence* from the British line. That fire, the strongest aspect of the British gunnery, began to take effect as the round shot blasted through the American bulwarks, tearing men apart, slashing the gun crews with knife-sharp splinters of wood, crushing them beneath overturned carronades and under the rigging that had been ripped from above. Perry ordered that the ships following him be signalled by means of a speaking trumpet to get in close to the enemy.

Master's Mate John Campbell had the crew of the *Chippawa* popping away with its little 9-pounder at the *Lawrence*. Champlin in the *Scorpion* and Packet in the *Ariel* kept their batteries blazing at the *Detroit*, but made the error of overloading their guns. On board the *Scorpion* a cannon blew off its mounts and fell into a hatchway. Also on that schooner, Midshipman John Clarke was killed by a round of shot. Another gun, this time aboard the *Ariel*, burst, wounding some of its crew. Perry ordered his tillermen to bring the *Lawrence*'s bow more towards the wind, so that he could try the range with his carronades. Slowly the brig turned toward the left. The starboard battery fired, but the shells fell short. Again, the helm was put down, and the brig was brought back on the course that angled towards the *Detroit*. A second time Perry called for his vessel to be yawed, but again the broadside proved ineffective. At about 12:20 p.m. the *Lawrence* was pulled in line parallel with the British once more and took up a station opposite the *General Hunter* at a distance that First Lieutenant Yarnell later judged to be about 255 metres. The full weight of her starboard carronades was divided among the ships in the British line. In Yarnell's words, 'Our first division [the carronades on the forward part of the starboard side] was fought against the *Detroit* and our second against the *Queen Charlotte*, occasionally directed guns at the *Hunter*.'

Meanwhile, at the rear of the American line, the three schooners and the sloop *Trippe* were throwing their 24- and 32-pound balls at the *Little Belt* and the *Lady Prevost*. This shelling was taking place at well over 1,000 metres, a range at which Lieutenant Buchan's carronades were totally ineffective, leaving his crews open to a killing fire without the opportunity to respond.

In between the action at the two ends of the lines a curious series of events was beginning to develop. According to Perry's in-transit revision of the line of battle, Jesse Elliott had steered the *Niagara* to follow after the *Caledonia*, which would stay between the twin brigs. As the action commenced, Perry signalled the commanders of his squadron to engage the ships identified beforehand as their opponents. By 12:30, most of the American commanders had done just that, although Perry himself, totally involved in a tremendous cannonade with the main strength of the British line and assisted by the *Ariel* and *Scorpion*, was most closely engaged. The *Niagara*, however, was still well out of the fight. Elliott had not brought his brig to run opposite the *Queen Charlotte* as planned. Instead, he maintained his station behind the *Caledonia* using his two 12-pound long guns to lob shots at his adversary. To Robert Barclay's eye, the *Niagara* 'kept so far to Windward as to render the *Queen Charlotte*'s 24 Pounder Carronades useless.' Thomas Stokoe, executive officer aboard the *Queen Charlotte*, supported this view of events. A year later, at Barclay's court martial, he recalled that the *Caledonia*'s long guns, fired from a considerable distance had more effect than the long guns of the *Niagara*. Aboard the *Lawrence* Lieutenant John Yarnell agreed with these estimates, putting Elliott's brig just more than one kilometre astern of the *Lawrence*. At that distance, Elliott followed so closely behind *Caledonia* that at one point the *Niagara*'s main topsail had to be backed in order to prevent a collision with the more sluggishly sailing *Caledonia*. Yarnell remembered seeing the sail laying back against the mast; indeed the same procedure was being used to keep the *Lawrence* in the centre of the fight.

In opposition to the distant *Niagara* and the *Caledonia*, the *Queen Charlotte* was answering with its two long 12-pounders. Aboard the *Queen Charlotte* the expectation had been that the second American brig would close in fast and hard, but this was not happening. And just as well, because Lieutenant Thomas Stokoe had suddenly found himself in charge of the second British corvette. Tragically, in the first minutes of the fight, a round shot from either the *Niagara* or the *Caledonia* had come whistling aboard, simultaneously killing Commander Robert Finnis and the ranking officer of the Royal Newfoundland Regiment, Lieutenant James Garden, 'mingling the blood of the one and the brains of the other, on the bulwark, in one melancholy and undistinguishable mass.' It was a decisive point in the combat, as Robert Barclay later stated, 'Too soon, alas, was I deprived of the Services of the Noble and intrepid Captain Finnis . . . with him fell my greatest Support.'

Taking control of the situation, Thomas Stokoe waited for the *Niagara* to move in on his ship. When this did not happen Stokoe ordered more sail to be set and promptly passed to the port side of the *General Hunter*, leapfrogging in line to support the *Detroit*, which was very heavily engaged. At about this time, more than an hour into the battle, Stokoe himself fell to the deck, wounded severely by a large splinter. As the first lieutenant was taken below, the command of the *Queen Charlotte* devolved to Provincial Marine Lieutenant Robert Irvine.

The second hour of the battle wore on and the casualties on board the *Detroit* and the *Lawrence* began to mount. A disproportionate number of the seamen aboard the British corvette were falling compared to the soldiers in the crew. Robert Barclay was thrown off his feet by a musket ball or a piece of wreckage that tore a gash in his thigh. He went below for medical attention from surgeon George Young, but soon returned to the deck. The *Detroit* was being ripped apart by the broadsides of the *Lawrence*. The rigging and sails were hanging in shreds, the bulwarks pierced by the 32-pound balls that had crashed through them. The crews of the guns were losing man after man as canister and splinters mowed them down. Marines posted in the toptrees of the brig's masts were picking off the unsheltered British, whose blood was beginning to smear the sanded deck. Purser Hoffmenster, who had volunteered to join a gun crew, crumpled screaming to the deck, his knee torn apart. Able Seaman Daniel Mead and John Barnes, a landsman, were killed outright.

Aboard the *Lawrence*, the slaughter was just as nightmarish. His luck holding out, Perry strode his deck unharmed while all around him others were falling. A splinter knocked young James Perry on his back, but the lad was soon up again. Second Lieutenant Dulaney Forrest, one of the men sent from the *Constitution*, was struck by a musket ball and collapsed, stunned. Seeing that Forrest was only winded, Perry helped him to his feet, whereupon the lieutenant coolly picked the ball out from where it had been tangled in his coat and put it in his pocket. Many others were less fortunate than these two officers, and along the deck of the *Lawrence* the dead and wounded began to pile up. Commandant Perry walked to the skylight and called below to the surgeon's assistant, Usher Parsons, to send up one of the attendants who had been assigned to help him.

Below deck Parsons was immersed in a hell of his own. With no sedatives, no concern for septic conditions and wielding a gruesome set of tools more typical of a shoemaker than a doctor, Parsons ministered to the wounded and dying. Splinters were picked out of gaping wounds, which were then roughly sutured together. Arteries pulsing blood were clamped off with tourniquets and fractured bones hastily set and splinted. Where such techniques offered no help, Parson's assistants seized the seamen while the doctor sliced through flesh with scissors and knives and then completed amputation with a saw. Less dangerous scrapes were bandaged and the patient sent back to his station. For some, however, there was no salvation. Lieutenant John Brooks, one of the marine officers serving aboard, was stricken by a cannon ball that tore into his upper leg, destroying his hip joint. Screaming in agony, he was carried below where Parsons could do little more than cover his ghastly wound and assure him that the end would not be long in coming. Brooks expired just before the close of the battle.

Somehow in this madhouse the men found reason for mirth. One of the three wounds that John Yarnell received was a jagged gash to his scalp. As he descended into Parson's operating theatre, he passed through a cloud of stuffing that had been ripped from a bank of hammocks. The feather-like stuffing stuck to the blood of his wound, forming a mantle around his head and causing the wounded to 'roar out with laughter that the devil had come.'

Parsons had more than just the wounded and dying to worry about. Usually the place in warships that was alloted for a surgeon's grisly work was the cockpit, a portion of one of the lower decks well below the waterline of the vessel. The *Lawrence* did not offer this sanctuary. Since it drew just less than three metres of water, the operating theatre was positioned above the water line in the officer's wardroom. As a result, no fewer than six cannon balls crashed through the hull and into the tiny space Parsons occupied. They too took their toll. 'When the battle was raging most severely,' Parsons recalled, 'Midshipman Laub came down with his arm badly frac-tured; I applied a splint and requested him to go forward and lie down; as he was leaving me, and while my hand was on him, a cannon-ball struck him in the side, and dashed him against the other side of the room, which instantly terminated his sufferings.'

The action continued on toward 2:00 p.m. The schooners at the rear of the American line were gradually catching up and simultaneously having effect on the *Lady Prevost* and the *General Hunter*. Lieutenant George Bignell, newly appointed commander of the *Hunter*, was severely wounded and fell, followed shortly after by his second in command, Master's Mate Henry Gateshill. What little impact the weak batteries of the small brig could have on the distant enemy was further reduced with the loss of its officers. The *Lady Prevost* had also suffered badly and began to fall out of the line, drifting to the right of the corvettes, its rudder disabled. On board eight crew members were killed, nineteen wounded. Among the casualties were the severely injured Frederic Rolette and Lieutenant Edward Buchan, shot through the face. Only the *Little Belt* was escaping the kind of lethal drubbing that had already stripped three of the British ships of their commanding officers. The little sloop began to head toward the leeward side of the bigger ships.

The two squadrons continued to crawl along in a southwesterly direction beneath a massive pall of smoke. The cannonade at the centre of the action had not let up for nearly two hours, but was becoming less regular. The murderous exchange of round shot, canister and grape was sweeping the decks of men and dismantling the guns their mates were left to handle.

Aboard the *Queen Charlotte* Seamen Jones, Tadley and Willsbrook joined their captain in death. Three of the late James Garden's Royal Newfoundlanders were killed, seven men of the 41st Regiment died, the eventual death toll on the *Queen Charlotte* rising to eighteen. On the *Detroit* the cost was no less grim. The number of wounded was approaching three dozen. Commander Barclay still held the deck, but his situation was precarious. First Lieutenant John Garland was cut down with a wound that left him dying, as was Master's Mate Thomas Clarke.

In spite of the murderous cost the fighting had taken, victory seemed faintly within the grasp of the British at that point. Their chief opponent, the *Lawrence*, was beginning to wither and was seen to fall back away from the *Detroit*. Perry's sailing master, William Taylor, explained the appearance of his ship as 'presenting a picture too horrid for description — nearly the whole crew and officers and all prostrated on the deck, intermingled with broken spars, riggings, sails and in fact one confused heap of horrid ruins. Some of the guns were dismounted and mounted five times in action — some of these guns were mann'd three different times in action.' The number of killed and wounded was surpassing eighty. Somehow, Oliver Hazard Perry was escaping injury of any sort. Just before 2:30, together with the chaplain and the purser, Perry fired a shot from the last of the *Lawrence*'s starboard carronades and then told Yarnell that he had resolved to give up his flagship and to head for the *Niagara*. A shot-pierced boat that had been towed behind the brig was pulled along the port side of the ship. Perry quickly changed out of the plain sailor's jacket he had worn since the fighting began and put on his uniform coat. The flag, bearing 'Don't Give Up The Ship', was hauled down and the young commandant stepped into the boat, which struck out for the *Niagara*. Standing in the stern, in full view of the British sharpshooters, Perry defiantly held his battle flag, until he was begged by his boat crew to sit down.

As Perry drew away from the *Lawrence*, Yarnell called for the Stars and Stripes to be lowered. Rather than take any more beating, the lieutenant was resolved to surrender. Aboard the *Detroit* the sign of surrender was not missed, but no ship's boat had survived the cannonade and there were scarcely enough men left to be spared for taking possession of the American flagship. Perry's departure from the *Lawrence* was clearly visible from the deck of the *Detroit*, and the British marksmen sniped at him. Also seen was the more ominous movement of the *Niagara* as it set more canvas in order to close on the faltering *Lawrence*. Robert Barclay saw that 'the *Niagara* . . . was at this time perfectly fresh.' The *Detroit* was in a 'very defenceless state . . . a perfect Wreck' and support from the other ships in the squadron was weak at most. As he watched Perry's boat being rowed to the *Niagara*, the British commander probably wondered how he was going to handle the imminent attack of the enemy's second brig. The situation must have looked very dark, but it suddenly got darker. From some direction, perhaps from the *Scorpion* or *Ariel*, which had faithfully maintained their stations throughout the fray, came another salvo of canister or round shot. Again the *Detroit* absorbed the blow, but some part of that blast tore into Robert Barclay's back ripping his right shoulder blade asunder. He was carried below, his authority passing to Second Lieutenant George Inglis and his subordinate Francis Purvis.

Little time was lost in Perry's transfer to the *Niagara*. That ship had been the object of some questions as the heat of the battle had risen. Usher Parsons observed that Jesse Elliott's ship 'did not make sail when the *Lawrence* did, but hung back for two hours, when she should have followed the example of the *Lawrence*, and grappled with the *Queen Charlotte*.' The men on the flagship had been dismayed by this lack of support. 'I expressed my surprise that the *Niagara* was not brought into close action,' recalled John Yarnell. 'The crew also expressed their surprise, but were encouraged by the officers to fight on till she should come down and take part with us.' The exact distance at which the *Niagara* held station is difficult to pin down. Perry's crew felt more effort could have been made by their cohorts to render them some support. On board the *Niagara* men felt that no inappropriate hesitation had been allowed. 'The lightness of the wind prevented our getting as close to the *Lawrence* as it was supposed, we intended,' explained Midshipman Montgomery of the *Niagara*. Elliott's own explanation was that the line of battle, once dictated, is an order that 'no captain has a right to change, without authority, or a signal from the commanding vessel.' Breaking out of that line, as he did after 2:00 p.m. he perceived to be at risk to his own head. Furthermore, Elliott later asked Perry why he had taken position opposite the *Hunter*, rather than moving further up so that the following ships could take their places. Elliott apparently did not question Lieutenant Stokoe's moving the *Queen Charlotte* past the *Hunter* in order to lend more support to his flagship, nor did he take it as an example of what he could do. Instead, for more than two hours Elliott kept the *Niagara* so distant from the main action that in the warships on both sides of the fight, and especially aboard the *Lawrence*, men viewed his conduct with doubt.

When he decided to make his move, Jesse Elliott hailed Lieutenant Daniel Turner for the *Caledonia* to bear up, which Turner did, setting more sail to move out of Elliott's way and to get in closer to the enemy. The *Niagara* let fall its foresail and cruised down toward the head of the British line. Elliott did not select a direct route for charging at the *Detroit*, however. From the *Scorpion* Stephen Champlin saw the *Niagara* range 'ahead of the *Lawrence*, and to windward of her, thus bringing the commodore's ship between her and the enemy, when she might have passed to leeward and relieved the *Lawrence* from any destructive fire of the enemy.' The breeze, during this time, had freshened and most of the ships began to move at a faster pace toward the southwest, while the *Lawrence* with its sails and rigging cut to shreds, fell behind, 'lying like a log upon the water.'

It was during this move to pass around the windward of the wrecked flagship that Commandant Perry's boat intercepted the *Niagara*. He hurried up the side of the brig and was met by Elliott. The two men were seen to shake hands and exchange words, after which Elliott himself got into Perry's boat and directed it to be rowed toward the schooners in the rear of the squadron. Perry had ordered him to speed them on, while he planned to steer the *Niagara* through the British line.

Perry found the *Niagara* to be in very good order, further evidence of its lack of involvement in the battle that had started nearly three hours before. Some damage had been inflicted upon the rigging, including the cutting of backstays and shrouds. Two men had been killed, several wounded. The vessel was quite manageable, however, and continued the sweep that brought the *Niagara* bearing down upon the British. Perry steered to pass across the bow of the *Detroit*.

Aboard the British flagship George Inglis watched the American approach and felt the effect of the mightly blast of its starboard carronades. The order in the British line of battle had been completely lost. With a steadier breeze the schooner *Lady Prevost* had wallowed past the *Detroit* and was now close to the tiny *Chippawa*. The *Queen Charlotte* was ranging up near the *Detroit*'s stern, aiming to pass on that ship's starboard side. Further back was the *Hunter*, while the *Little Belt* was making way towards the west. Urged on by Elliott, the American schooners had put out their sweeps and begun the strenuous task of rowing their vessels to bring them up to the British as fast as possible.

Inglis decided that his best strategy would be to get his starboard battery into action. It had stood unused all afternoon, though not undamaged, and could at least offer some fresh resistance to the oncoming *Niagara*. Inglis passed the order to bring the bow of the *Detroit* across the wind. Among the tattered rigging the survivors of his crew fought to turn the wounded corvette. Halfway through the procedure, as the wind pressed the sails against the mast, pushing the ship itself into reverse, cries of alarm rang out and the *Detroit* rammed backwards into *Queen Charlotte*'s larboard side, their spars tangling. With its starboard battery still ineffective the *Detroit* lay impotent in the water, as Perry's *Niagara* crossed in front of it raking it from stem to stern with a deadly cannonade.

As the hour of three approached, the climactic moments of the battle for control of Lake Erie were played out. The *Niagara* broke through the British line, its well-crewed batteries on both sides of the ship blazing away at a range of less than one hundred metres. To larboard the *Chippawa* and the *Lady Prevost* received the full force of the unscathed carronades. Only five casualties had accumulated on the smaller of the two schooners, among them the *Chippawa*'s commander, Master's Mate John Campbell, wounded slightly. The deck of the *Lady Prevost* was empty, however, all the men having run below. Deserted, Lieutenant Edward Buchan could be seen hanging over the rail, screaming in torment from his horrible wound. Perry saw this pathetic sight and ordered his larboard guns silenced.

Meanwhile, the starboard carronades of the *Niagara* continued to pound the two British corvettes. The Royal Ensign, flapping in the rigging of the *Queen Charlotte*, came down in defeat. On the *Detroit* Inglis had managed to break free of the *Queen*, but could get no more control of his ship. 'Laying completely unmanageable, every Brace cut away, the Mizen Topmast, and Gaff down, all the other Masts badly Wounded, not a stay left forward, Hull shattered very much, a number of the Guns disabled, and the Enemy's Squadron Raking both Ships, ahead and astern, none of our own in a situation to support us, I was under the painful necessity,' Inglis explained, 'of answering the Enemy to say we had struck.' Since the Royal Ensign had been nailed to the mast, Inglis ordered one of the survivors to tie a white cloth to a boarding pike and wave it back and forth to indicate his surrender.

As the guns were stilled, the *Chippawa* and the *Little Belt* attempted to escape by fleeing leeward. But the *Trippe*, which had come up ahead of the other schooners, pursued the *Chippawa*; the *Scorpion* went after the *Little Belt*. In time, after being fired at, the British vessels hauled down their flags. The battle ended and a silence fell over the intermingled cluster of British and American warships; a silence broken by some cheers of victory and many cries of men wounded and dying.

Jesse Elliott had boarded the schooner *Somers* and taken over command of its forward gun. When the surrender had been signalled, the aft gunner wanted to take one last shot at the British. Elliott berated him for so cowardly an act, but the man roared back that the British had pressed him into service nine times and he wanted revenge. The cannons remained silent and Elliott was rowed over to the ravaged *Detroit*. There he found a scene that provoked this anecdote years later:

> I went on board the *Detroit*, to take possession, and such was the quantity of blood on the deck, that in crossing it, my feet slipped under me, and I fell; my clothing became completely saturated and covered with gore! I went below to see Capt. Barclay, who tendered me his sword; but I refused it, and anticipated the wishes of Capt. Perry, by assuring him that every kindness would be shown himself and the other prisoners.

At 4:00 Oliver Hazard Perry returned to the shattered *Lawrence*. His surviving comrades met him at the gangway, but the violent nature of their experience left them mute. As Usher Parsons remembered, 'The battle was won and he was safe, but the deck was slippery with blood, and strewn with the bodies of twenty officers and men, some of whom had set at table with us at our last meal, and the ship resounded everywhere with the groans of the wounded.' Perry went to his cabin where he penned a quick message to General Harrison and, in so doing, created one of his own memorials: 'We have met the enemy and they are ours—Two Ships, two Brigs, one Schooner and one Sloop.'

Soon the surviving senior officers from each of the British vessels arrived at the *Lawrence* to tender their formal surrenders. Robert Barclay sent Lieutenant O'Keefe of the 41st Regiment to represent him. O'Keefe appeared in full dress and, despite Elliott's comment, offered Barclay's sword to the conquering Perry. Commandant Perry, accepted the surrender, but bade O'Keefe and the others to keep their weapons. Later, he went over to see Barclay in person and found him dangerously wounded and despondent.

As evening approached the vessels were anchored, their position now near Western Sister Island. Guards were organized to secure the British prisoners. Work details hustled to repair torn rigging and to splint damaged masts and spars. It was decided that a prompt burial was the best way to deal with the dead, except for the fallen officers, who would be buried ashore. Accordingly, each man who had lost his life during the battle was sewn into his hammock with a cannonball at his feet. With the rites of an Episcopal Service read over them, the dead were committed one by one to the deep.

As most men collapsed from exhaustion, the last little drama of the day was played out. After a long chase, Stephen Champlin's *Scorpion* returned with the *Little Belt* in tow and anchored under the stern of the *Niagara*, just as the ship's bell struck midnight.

It has been fortunate for Canada that, excepting only the Canadian ships and people lost to German U-boats in Canadian waters during the Second World War, no bloodletting equal to the War of 1812's slaughter has stained the country's waters.

chapter four

Making a Living
on the Sea

Before and after the great struggles of the 18th and 19th centuries over Canada's lands and waters, the greater concern for all who sailed on the latter was somehow to make them pay; to earn a living, however laborious, by either using them as a highway or plundering their depths of fish and whales. As this early 19th century account by whaling man William Scoresby illustrates, this could be a challenging process indeed.

The Northern Whale-Fishery
Captain William Scoresby

The ship *Esk*, which I then commanded, sailed from Whitby on the 29th of March, 1816. We entered the frigid confines of the Icy Sea and killed our first whale on the 25th of April. On the 30th of April we forced our way into the ice with a favourable wind, and after passing through a large body of it, entered an extensive open sea. The wind then blowing hard south-south-east, we kept our reach to the eastward until three o'clock in the afternoon when we unexpectedly met with a quantity of ice which interrupted our course. We then wared, by the way of avoiding it, but soon found, though the weather was thick with snow, that we were completely embayed in a situation that was truly terrific.

In the course of fourteen voyages in which I had before visited this inhospitable country, I passed through many dangers wherein my own life, together with those of my companions, had been threatened; but the present case far surpassed in awfulness, as well as actual hazard, anything that I had before witnessed. Dangers which occur unexpectedly and terminate suddenly, though of the most awful description, appear like a dream when they are past; but horrors which have a long continuance leave an impression on the memory which time itself cannot altogether efface. Such was the effect of the present scene. Whilst the wind howled through the rigging with tempestuous roar, the sea was so mountainous that the mast-heads of some accompanying ships, within the distance of a quarter of a mile, were intercepted and rendered invisible by the swells, and our ship frequently rolled the lee-boats into the water, that were suspended by their keels above the rough-tree rail!

At the same time we were rapidly approaching a body of ice, the masses of which, as hard as rocks, might be seen at one instant covered with foam, the next concealed from sight by the waves, and instantly afterwards reared to a prodigious height above the surface of the sea. It is needless to relate the means by which we attempted to keep the ship clear of the threatened danger because those means were without avail. At eleven p.m. we were close to the ice, when perceiving through the mist an opening a short distance within, we directed the drift of the ship towards it. In this place the pieces of ice were happily of smaller dimensions; at least all the larger masses we were able to avoid, so that after receiving a number of shocks we escaped without any particular accident into the opening or slack part of the ice above noticed. This opening, as far as we could see, promised a safe and permanent release.

But in this we were grievously disappointed: for when we attempted to ware the ship, which soon became necessary, she refused to turn round, notwithstanding every effort. In consequence of this accident, which arose partly from the bad trim of the ship, and partly from the great violence of the wind, she fell to leeward into a close body of ice, to which we could see no termination. The *Mars*, of Whitby, and another vessel which closely followed us as we penetrated the exterior of the ice, being in better trim than the *Esk*, performed the evolution with ease, and were in a few minutes out of sight. In this dreadful situation we lay beating against the opposing ice with terrible force, during eight successive hours, all which time I was at the top-gallant masthead directing the management of the sails in order to avoid the largest masses of ice, any one of which would have perforated the side of the ship. By the blessing of God, we succeeded wonderfully; and at eight a.m. the 2nd of May, gained a small opening where we contrived to navigate the ship until the wind subsided, and we had the opportunity of forcing into a more commodious place. On examining the ship we found our only apparent damage to consist in the destruction of most of our rudder works, a few slight bruises on the sides, and a cut on the lower part of the stern of the ship.

From this time to the 20th of May, the fishery was generally interrupted by the formation of new ice, insomuch that during this interval we killed but one whale, while few of our neighbours succeeded so well. During the succeeding week we became so fixed that we never moved except occasionally a few yards. The next twelve days were spent in most arduous labour in forcing the ship through the ice. At length, on the 12th of June, we happily escaped. On the 27th of June, we had secured thirteen fish, and our quantity of oil was about 125 tuns.

After proceeding to the westward for the greater part of the 28th, we arrived at the borders of a compact body of field-ice, consisting of immense sheets of prodigious thickness. As I considered the situation not favourable for fishing, the ship was allowed to drift to the eastward all night. In the morning of the 29th I found, however, that she was very little removed from the place where she lay when I went to bed. I perceived that the floes, between which there had been extensive spaces, were now in the act of closing, and attempted by lowering four boats to tow the ship through an opening at a short distance from us. At the moment when we were about to enter it, it closed. In attempting to get the ship into the safety of an indentation which appeared calculated to afford a secure retreat, a small piece of ice came athwart her bow, stopped her progress, and she was in a minute afterwards subjected to a considerable squeeze.

From none of the pieces of ice around us did we apprehend any danger. There was a danger, however, on the larboard quarter, of which we were totally unconscious. The piece of ice that touched the ship in that part, though of itself scarcely six yards square, and more than one yard above the water, concealed beneath the surface of the sea, at the depth of ten or twelve feet, a hard pointed projection of ice which pressed against the keel, lifted the rudder, and caused a damage that had nearly occasioned the loss of the ship. About an hour and a half after the accident, the carpenter, having sounded the pump, discovered to our great concern and amazement a depth of eight and a half feet of water in the hold. This was most alarming; with despair pictured in every face the crew set on the pumps; a signal of distress was at the same time hoisted, and a dozen boats approached us form the surrounding ships. In the space of four hours the water had lowered to nearly four feet, but one of the pumps becoming useless, and bailing being less effectual than at first, the water once more resumed its superiority and gained upon us.

As the pumping and bailing could not possibly be continued by our own ship's company, it was necessary to make use of some means to attempt a speedy remedy whilst our assistants were numerous. As there was a probability that a bunch of rope-yarns, straw, or oakum, might enter some of the larger leaks and retard the influx of water if applied near the place through the medium of a fothering-sail (that is, a sail drawn by means of ropes at the four corners, beneath the damaged or leaky part) we prepared a lower studding-sail, by sewing bunches of these materials which, together with sheets of old thin canvas, whalebone-hair, and a quantity of ashes, fitted it well for the purpose. Thus prepared it was hauled beneath the damaged place, but not the least effect was produced. We therefore set about unrigging the ship and discharging the cargo and stores upon a flat place of the floe, against which we had moored, with the intention of turning the ship keel upwards. My own sailors were completely worn out, and most of our auxiliaries wearied and discouraged; some of them evinced by their improper conduct their wish that the ship should be abandoned.

Before putting our plan in execution, we placed twenty empty casks in the hold to act against a quantity of iron ballast which was in the ship; caulked the dark lights, removed all the dry goods and provisions that would injure with the wet, secured all the hatches, skuttles, companion, etc., then, erecting two tents on the ice, one for sheltering myself, and the other for the crew, we ceased pumping, and permitted the ship to fill. At this crisis, men of whom I had conceived the highest opinion for firmness and bravery greatly disappointed by expectations. Among the whole crew, indeed, scarcely a dozen spirited fellows were to be seen.

As no ship could with propriety venture near us to assist in turning the *Esk* over, on account of the hazardous position of the ice around her, we had no other means of attempting this singular evolution than by attaching purchases to the ice from the ship. Everything being prepared, while the water flowed into the ship, I sent our exhausted crew to seek a little rest. For my own part, necessity impelled me to endeavour to obtain some repose. I had already been fifty hours without rest, and this unusual exertion, together with the anxiety of mind I endured, caused my legs to swell and become so extremely painful that I could scarcely walk. Spreading a mattress upon a few boards laid on the snow within one of the tents, and notwithstanding the coldness of the situation and the excessive dampness that prevailed from the constant fog, I enjoyed a comfortable repose for four hours, and arose considerably refreshed.

About 3 p.m. on the 1st of July, I proceeded with all hands to the ship which, to our surprise, we found had only sunk a little below the sixteenth mark externally, while the water but barely covered a part of 'tween decks within'. Perceiving that it was not likely to sink much further on account of the buoyancy of the empty casks, and the materials of which the ship was composed, we applied all our purchases; but even with the strength of 150 men we could not heel her more than five or six strakes. When thus partly careened, with the weight of two anchors suspended from the mast acting with the effect of powerful levers on the ship, I accompanied about 120 men on board. All these being arranged on the high side of the deck, ran suddenly to the lower side, when the ship fell so suddenly on one side that we were apprehensive she was about to upset; but after turning a little way the motion ceased. The tackles on the ice being then hauled tight, the heeling position of the ship was preserved until we mounted the higher part of the deck, and ran to the lower as before. At length, after a few repetitions of this manoeuvre, no further impression whatever was produced, and the plan of upsetting the ship appeared quite impracticable.

The situation of the ship being now desperate, there could be no impropriety in attempting to remove the keel and garboard strake, which prevented the application of the fothering. Whatever might be the result, it could scarcely be for the worse. These encumbrances being removed, the sail for fothering was immediately applied to the place, and a vast quantity of fothering materials thrown into its cavity, when it was fairly underneath. Over this sail we spread a fore-sail, and braced the whole as tight to the ship as the keel-bolts, which yet remained in position, would admit. The effect was as happy as we could possibly have anticipated. Some time before all these preparations were completed, our people, assisted by the crew of the *John*, commanded by my brother-in-law, who after a short rest had returned to us, put the three pumps and bailing tubs in motion and applied their energies with such effect that in eleven hours the pumps sucked! The *John's* crew on this occasion exerted themselves with a spirit and zeal which was truly praiseworthy.

As the assistance of carpenters was particularly needed, we fired a gun and repeated our signal of distress, which brought very opportunely two boats, with six men each, from the *Prescot*, and the same number from our tried friend, Mr Allen, of the *North Britain*. As we likewise procured the carpenters of these ships, together with those of the *John*, they commenced operations by cutting through the sealing, between two frames of timbers directly across the hold; a situation which was on the fore part of the leak, or between the leak of the body of the ship. The timbers in this place were unhappily found so closely connected that we had to cut away part of one of the floors so that we might come at the outside plank, and caulk the crevices between it and the timbers. This operation, on account of the great depth of timber and the vast flow of water that issued at the sealing, was extremely difficult, tedious, and disagreeable.

Meanwhile seeing that we had good assistance, I allowed our crew four hours' rest, half of them at a time, for which purpose some of their beds were removed from the ice to the ship. Here, for the first time during four days they enjoyed their repose; for on account of the cold and damp that prevailed when they rested on the ice, several of them, I believe, never slept.

Some of the *John's* people returning to us, swayed up the topmast, and rigged most of the yards, while our men were employed stowing the main-hold which, by the floating of the casks, was thrown into a singular state of disorder. Some of the casks were found without heads and all the blubber lost, and many were found bilged, or otherwise damaged.

After the carpenters had completely cleared the space between the ribs, or frames of timbers, they drove oakum into it, along with an improved woollen sheathing substance; and occasionally, where the spaces were very large, pieces of fat pork. The spaces or crevices being then filled, all the above substances were firmly driven down by means of pine wedges, and the spaces between each of the wedges caulked. This would have been very complete had not the increased flow of the water overcome the pumps, and covered the sealing where the carpenters were at work. They were therefore obliged to wedge up the place with great expedition; and being at the same time greatly fatigued, the latter part of the operation was accomplished with much less perfection than I could have wished.

Hitherto calm weather with thick fog having constantly prevailed, was the occasion of several ships remaining by us and affording assistance, which would otherwise have left us. But the weather having now become clear, and a prospect of prosecuting the fishery being present, every ship deserted us except the *John*, and she was preparing to leave us likewise. In the state of extreme jeopardy in which we were still placed, the love of life on the part of the crew determined them to attempt to quit the ship and take refuge in the *John* as soon as she should attempt to leave us. I was confident that unless the assistance of the *John* was secured, the *Esk*, after all the labour bestowed on her, and the progress which had been made towards her preservation, must yet be abandoned as a wreck.

At length I yielded to the request of my whole crew and made a proposal to Captain Jackson of the *John*, who agreed, on certain conditions involving the surrender of a large proportion of our cargo, to stay by us and assist us until our arrival at some port of Shetland.

These agreements being fully understood and signed, the *John* hauled alongside of the ice, which had now opened near the *Esk* for the first time since the accident, and took on board the whole of our loose blubber, together with half our whalebone, as agreed. Everything now went on favourable, and whilst our crew and assistants were in full and vigorous employment, I retired to seek that repose which my wearied frame stood greatly in need of.

On the 5th of July, assisted by all hands from the *John*, the stowing of the hold and the rigging of the ship were completed and, under a moderate breeze of wind, we left the floe; but what was our astonishment and mortification to find that the ship could not be guided! The rudder had become perfectly useless, so that the ship could not be turned round or diverted in the least from the course in which the impetus of the wind on the sails was the most naturally balanced. This was an alarming disappointment. However, as the ship was in such constant danger of being crushed in the situation where she lay, the *John*, with the greatest difficulty imaginable, towed us three or four miles to the eastward into a place of comparative safety. Here we rectified our rudder and arranged for the trimming of the ship more by the stern, to compensate in some degree for the loss of the after-keel. When these matters were completed, on account of strong wind and thick weather we could not, without imminent danger, attempt to penetrate the compact body of ice which at this time barred our escape to the sea.

However, after various other alarms, and careful attention to the leakage, together with the unremitting diligence of the crew in the use of the pumps, we eventually descried land on the 23rd of July and approached within three or four miles of the coast of Shetland. In the evening the *John*, having fulfilled the articles of agreement as far as was required, we sent the twelve men belonging to her crew on board, and they left us with three cheers and the usual display of colours. We were now left to sail by ourselves; our progress was in consequence rather slow. At daylight on the 27th we were rejoiced with a sight of our port. We pressed towards it with every sail we could set, and having received a pilot as we approached the pier, we immediately entered the harbour and grounded at half-past five a.m. in a place of safety.

Nonetheless the sturdy communities of Canada's sea and lake shores grew steadily through the 19th century as Canadians developed their inshore and offshore fisheries, and were increasingly involved in the great transoceanic trading relationships. And the Canadian presence, for all that the sea was still a harsh and perilous place, was astonishing in its size.

Mighty on the Waters
Joseph Schull

In the year 1879, in Yarmouth alone, twenty-six families learned that 'the sea is made of mothers' tears'. Tales of disaster came back to Canada from the coastal waters and the Atlantic, from the Pacific and the Indian Ocean, from the East Indies and the China Seas. In the shipping-journals of ports around the world, translated into many languages for they concerned the cargoes of many nations, appeared the notices of Canadian vessels lost, abandoned, or destroyed. Yet many as they seem when counted up years later, they were a minute fraction deducted from a great total of routine departures and safe arrivals. Canada, in 1878, stood fourth among the ship-owning countries of the world, with a merchant navy of seven thousand vessels.

Ship-building was still the great industry in Quebec, and Quebec had been surpassed by New Brunswick and Nova Scotia. All along the Atlantic coast and the Fundy shore, ships were building. They were building along Minas Basin and Northumberland Strait; and the mouths of little rivers winding out of the woods to a bay, like Maitland at the head of Minas, were lined with ship-frames as far as the eye could see.

Ships built in other years came back on every tide to Quebec and Halifax, Yarmouth and Saint John. As they nosed into place among the crowded ranks looming along the docks, it must have seemed that the felled forests had returned by sea. Long lines of masts and spars and rigging clawed at the sky. Bowsprits and jib-booms, reaching in over the roofs of waterside sheds, made shady aisles of the streets along the wharves. Wagon-loads of cargo, inward and outward bound, clattered along the cobbles. Mates and captains bickered in the humming sheds of sail-makers and spar-makers, carpenters, riggers and caulkers. Sailors with pay burning in their pockets told each other in strange tongues of the places to spend it. Sailors whose pay was gone rolled back to their ships. Sailors without ships lolled around the docks and spun their yarns for anyone who would listen. The air was sharp with the smells of brine and fish, tar and hemp, and of strange, spicy cargoes tumbling from their slings. It was no wonder that so much of young Canada gravitated toward the sea. They were good places for a boy to go, those waterfronts of the seventies. It was a good time to live.

It was good in the little ports of the coast, too, and across in New-foundland. The fisheries went their ancient way. The West Indies and the Mediterranean and the nearer coasts of South America were only a step to long-familiar markets, and the ships of this short-run trade were a navy in themselves. Duder's, the great firm of St John's, Newfoundland, operated a fleet of three hundred and fifty-two vessels and proclaimed themselves the largest ship-owners in the world. Newfoundland, moreover, had another fleet distinctive to itself.

These were the sealers who went north each year to find the packs of the 'Whitecoats' and slaughter them for their oil.The Whitecoats were the infants of the Harp seals, born on the great raft of ice carried down along the Labrador coast by the polar currents. Toward the end of winter the ice began to move southward from the region of Baffin Bay, and the Harps came with it. February twenty-eighth, said old sealers, was the birthday of the Whitecoats; and as the first days of March came two hundred ships or more would file out through the high-cliffed gateway of St John's harbour. They would swing to the north, yard-arm to yard-arm, jostling for position in the long race up the Labrador coast; then as each captain guessed or smelled out the signs of seal, he would turn his armoured bow and double-timbered hull into the white waste of the ice.

They were crowded, dirty, reckless, jovial ships, the sealers, with sides of bacon hanging from their yards, and timbered 'pounds' built on the decks to hold the pelts that could not be jammed into the holds. Weeks before they sailed, the 'ice-blink' in the northern sky had warned all Newfoundland of the coming of the great raft. Men from every outport had gathered up their gear, loaded it onto barrel-stave sleds, and trudged to St John's as far as fifty miles through the snow. A berth in a sealer was hard to come by, for all the island wanted to go. It was first come, first served as the outport men crowded down Water Street to the wharves, and the rule still held when safe aboard and bound north. Nothing so formal as a mutiny was ever heard of in a sealer, but there were lively days. Edgar Kelland of Winterton, an outport lad of twenty at the time, remembered one in his old age.

'We sailed from Carbonear,' he says, 'in the afternoon of the first day of March, 1871. A gale came in from the northwest. The ship was flying along at a great rate with every topsail and every stitch of canvas that she was owner of set on her.

'When dark came, I was in the forecastle with about fifty more men. Now, very near all were what they call three sheets in the wind. The mate started to amuse himself by cracking a little funny joke on one and another of the men. There was no harm whatever in it, but one man took it as an insult and struck the mate between the eyes. Then the mate's nephew knocked out the fellow that struck his uncle. Then another fellow knocked him out. They went into it on both sides till the whole gang was a solid tangle.

'Now I never saw but one of them in my life before and I kept as clear of their blows as possible, but a fellow shouted, "Get on deck. There is no room to fight here!" Another fellow replied, saying, "Yes, the deck is the spot," so they made a mad rush for the ladder. I was pushed up with the rest, and all of them ahead of me were fighting furiously. Then I heard a fellow shout there was no one at the wheel. The ship was coming up into the wind and the topsails were beginning to slap, so I made a rush aft for the wheel. Just then, a fellow let go at me but I happened to be a little out of his reach and his fist only brushed my ear.

'I thought to myself that a miss was as good as a mile, so I rushed on and took the wheel and kept the vessel away on her course. It was blowing a storm and very frosty. After being at the spokes for about a half-hour I began to feel very cold, so I shouted for someone to take over, but all I saw was a fellow now and again tumbling heels in the air abaft the mainmast. A thought struck me just then, "Where is the Captain?" I did not have long to wait, for just then he darted his head up out of the cabin. There was a man crouched behind the companionway who sprang towards him and made a grab at his head. The Captain shot down again like a rat into a hole and locked the door.

'I glanced forward again and saw a man about half-way between myself and the mainmast, but when he saw me still at the wheel he turned to go towards that mad gang again. I sprang from the wheel and rushed after him, caught him by the shoulder and spun him around and told him to take her and be damned. Then I reached the mainmast and leaned against it.

'Of all the scenes I had witnessed or even read about, this beat them all. There were about sixty men, if you could call them that, kicking, cursing, screeching, falling together sometimes one and two, more times five and six together, and some of them getting kicked, some stripped naked to the waist. As far as I could see it was "hit the next man to you."

'Now what I wanted to do was get to my berth. For a long time I could see no vacancy. Then the ship gave a heavy lurch and a number of them fell to the deck. I made a dash for the hole and went through at a great rate. When I landed in the forecastle I found only one man there and he was swearing hard on one Pether Brien. He ripped off his blue jumper, tore it into two pieces and flung it on the floor. "There," he said, "that's what I'd serve Pether Brien!" Then two great feet came clumping down the ladder and a giant landed on the floor. "All right, Mickey McCannister, and what do you want of Pether Brien?"

'Poor Mickey got into an awful plight and said, "Go away now, Pether— don't touch me now, Pether!" But Pether closed his great fist on Mickey's throat and punched his face till the blood was all over it. Then he flung him on the floor like a dead rat and said, "There's Pether Brien for you now!" Mickey lay on the floor groaning, "Pether, I'm kilt! Pether, you've kilt me!"

'Then two more great burly-looking fellows came down the ladder and stepped over Mickey and made for me as I lay in my bunk. The first fellow that reached me lifted his fist and said, "What are ye laffen at?" But before he had time to smash my face, the other one that was close to his back said, "How dare you insult a stranger?" and hit him one behind the ear and knocked him on the floor. Now more and more men began to come down gashed and bleeding, and the fight was pretty well over. The next day what was able to get on deck was a hard-looking sight.'

Across the water in Nova Scotia, where the shores fold into little bays from Halifax to Yarmouth, the country is gentler and the memories are somewhat gentler too. From here the brigs and schooners ran to the West Indies, outward bound with lumber and fish, homeward bound with rum, molasses, sugar and salt. Captain William Henry Smith of Liverpool is one of the last of the lads who went there under sail, and his thoughts play much among the warm southern waters. He lived about a generation removed from the greatest days, but nothing had changed very much when he first sought a berth. And with him, as with sailors everywhere at all times, the memory of the first berth and the first departure remains the clearest.

Like every Liverpool boy, he spent much time around the harbour. It was pleasant to see the ships coming in and going out, with their tall negro chantymen whose singing often lured the faithful from the open doors of the church on a Sunday. It was good to talk with idling sailors, and hear the names of far ports that rang like bells. But as a boy grew too old to scrape the sweet seepings from a molasses barrel and lick the candy from his fingers, he began to think of sailing for himself.

Old Captain Zwicker had the brig *Georgina* loading for Trinidad, and he needed hands; but the captain was a gruff man. It took a week of watchful waiting before you summoned up the nerve to ask him if there might be a place for a boy on his ship. It seemed another week went by as he looked you over, but he nodded at last and said he could even maybe use two. There was the long run to the sawmill then for your friend, Ed. Mr Bell chased you from the sawmill when he saw you talking to Ed, because he wanted to keep a good worker, but Ed had heard enough. The two of you were off to Mr Zwicker, and then to the store to spend your ten dollars' advance pay on fitting out.

You came home with knee-boots, oilclothes, sou'wester, overalls and matches, and at home you got together your bed-tick, quilt, soap and towels, liniment and rags for bandages. The sea-chest had long been ready, and laid away in it by a mother who read your thoughts were knife, fork, spoons and the cup and pan you would eat from—the 'pint and pannikin'. Mr Anderson, the sail-maker, made you a canvas bag, and at last on the great day your older brother came down with you and Ed to the ship. He was already a seaman, and he looked at *Georgina* with a wise eye, cautiously approving. He saw you into the forecastle, saw your gear stowed under your bunk and your oilskins hung on your peg in the bulkhead. Then he shook hands and went ashore. You wouldn't be seeing him for quite a spell, because when your ship came in his would most likely be out. You and Ed sat on your bunks and looked at each other, grinning nervously.

The bellow for all hands came from above, and you climbed up to the deck. You stood around a little lost as the sails went up and the mate and the old hands bustled about. There was a cold lump of loneliness in your middle. It was followed by a shiver along your spine as the brig began to run under her sail and the mate's eye fell on you. 'Here boy, take the wheel.'

He stood on one side of you and the captain on the other as you took those spokes in your hand for the first time. You were inclined to look sideways at the officers, and Mr Zwicker barked as he caught one glance. 'Don't you look at me—keep your eyes on that wheel. Hold her so's you can feel the wind on the back of your neck.'

You set your face to the bow and tightened your grip while the school-house and the church steeple fell away, and the dull ache grew inside you and made your eyes wet. Then the last headland dropped astern. The sea heaved, the vessel slipped off a little, and you turned the wheel to bring her back on the wind. 'That's right,' said Mr Zwicker, and all at once the loneliness was gone. The wheel of a ship was in your hands, the deck beneath you, and the road to the West Indies lay ahead.

Each year from the little ports the boys went in their thousands to the little ships. There were other boys, and girls too, who scarcely knew the land. Some were born at sea, some had gone to sea as infants, and some learned their first lessons in mid-ocean at the hands of tutors or governesses. These were the children of the long voyagers, the masters of the great square-riggers, who took their families to sea.

There were many such children in the seventies and eighties. The captains of the ocean carriers were seamen, businessmen, and diplomats. Cargoes and the quest for cargoes took them from sea to sea and from port to port on voyages of two years or three or even longer. There were no cabled market reports or instructions from owners to guide them when they reached a port of call. The disposal of their freights, the collection of their bills, the unravelling of foreign port procedures, and the search for new freights were as much the problems of the master as the care of his ship. His life was on the sea, his thoughts were on the sea, and he wanted his family with him.

This was a good life too, well remembered by Captain Joseph C. Hilton of Yarmouth, who sailed with his father and mother in the barque *B. Hilton*. Young Joseph's first recollections were of the sweet-smelling pitch-pine after-cabin where the family lived, with the brass lamp suspended over the dining-table and the long barometer swinging from the deck-head. It was wide as the ship, this cabin, running from the stern forward almost to the mizzen- or after-mast. Its floor was a little below the level of the deck, and when you came into it by the forward door you descended a little stairway of two or three steps. Above it was the pilot-house on the poop, where the helmsman stood and the captain and the mates kept their watches beside him. A companionway, a longer stairway of bright, polished wood, led up from the cabin to the pilot-house, and on either side of the companionway were the smaller cabins which served as the family bedrooms.

In the cabin Joseph played his first games as the ship swung out across the oceans. The sound of the wind outside shrieking through the cordage, and the thud of waves against the hull, were so familiar that he hardly heard them; but sometimes he squealed with annoyance as his houses of blocks toppled and his toys ran away from him with the roll of the ship. Mother was often in her berth on these days, because she didn't care for the rough weather, but he would talk with her through the open doorway, and both would listen for the captain's steps overhead and the reassuring sound of his voice.

At seven-thirty each morning Joseph would wake to the striking of seven bells. Then the cabin-boy would ring the bell warning that breakfast was nearly ready. Father had already gone up the pilot-house for his morning look about, and soon the order would be heard, 'Relieve the wheel. Go below the watch.' There would be the stamping of men along the deck, going and coming as the watch changed. Then father would come down the companionway, wet and jovial. He would shrug out of his oilskins, and mother would join him at the table. Father would bow his head and there would be a long prayer, which always seemed to end sharp on eight bells. At the last 'Amen' the cabin-boy would come skating in with breakfast from the galley forward, and after breakfast there would be the anxious question of the weather.

Bad weather meant a long day in the cabin, but on fine days Joseph was allowed to stand beside his father in the pilot-house. He could never go forward from the poop without special permission. That was the crew's quarters and the working area, and no place for small boys on the loose. Sometimes father or one of the mates took you down along the deck and let you look into the forecastle, where the off-watch men lying in their bunks grinned and waved at you. Sometimes they turned you over for a while to the boatswain or one of the seamen, and you gave a hand with the work. You learned to 'hold a turn' while the men twisted a rope tight, or watched an old hand patching up a spare sail with his palm and needle. The best times, however, were always on the poop.

Standing with his father beside the helmsman, Joseph would wait expectantly through the long, easy silences of a fair day. When he felt his hair stir with a changing of the wind, he would look up, trying to read the captain's face. If there was change enough, it meant some moments of rare excitement.

First there would be a quiet word from the captain to the mate, 'Tack ship.' The mate's voice would rise in a bellow, 'All hands about ship,' and he would race for the forecastle head with two of the best hands after him. The second mate would go to the lee side, men would come tumbling up from below and swarm along the decks, making for the halyards and braces. Orders would come so fast you could hardly follow them. 'Haul up the mainsail,' 'Lay aft to the spanker sheet,' 'Ready about.' The ship would swing gently with a great flapping of loosened canvas as the helmsman bore down on the spokes of his wheel. More orders would rattle out from the forecastle head, where the mate stood with his eyes on the spars, 'Haul in the spanker sheet,' 'Hard a-lee.' The ship is changing her direction, sails are spilling out their wind, other sails are picking it up. 'Belay spanker,' 'sheet main braces,' 'tops'l haul.' The new alignment of the sails is taking shape as men haul on the ropes, chanting together. There is a great whine and rattle of pulley-blocks, yards groan and wheel above as the ship pays off slowly on her new tack. 'Belay main braces— lay forward'—'fore bowline! let go and haul'—and the men tramp along the deck, hauling round the fore and topsail braces. 'Way-hay-hay-hay-y' goes their chant as the ropes tighten home and the canvas swells out round and full again. The mate waves to the captain from the forecastle head; the ship is tacked, the yards are trimmed. 'Steady your helm,' says the captain, and the excitement is over for the day.

Saturdays were the dirty-work days when the men had to bring the pots of grease from the galley and climb into the rigging, 'slushing down' the masts so that the yards would run freely. Sundays were long because you had to dress up, and the men were expected to tidy themselves too. They did their washing in tubs on the deck, and books from the ship's library were set out for them on the booby-hatch. They were supposed to refrain from unnecessary work, though it didn't seem to make much difference, and on Sunday evenings they trooped self-consciously into the after-cabin for a long reading from the scriptures by father, and hymns which mother played on the organ.

There were other days which came anywhere in the week, and sometimes too often. These were the days when the weather began to make up. Father would be eyeing the sea and rigging, muttering a little to himself. The mate would come along the deck for a consultation, and then the hands would be turned out to shorten sail.

The flying jib, high at the fore, would be the first to come in. Then, looking very small among the yards crossing the tall masts, men would swing out along the foot-ropes to furl in the topgallant and topmast staysails, the fore-royal, the main royal and the gaff topsail. The ship was ready for a near gale now, and you hoped that would be enough. But if the sea began to heave over the weather rail amidships and spray came arching over the poop, you knew it wouldn't be. More hands would go aloft. The foretopsail would be reefed in, then the main topsail and the mainsail and the smaller sails that served and fed the wind to them. You would take a last resigned look at the bare spars against the dark sky, and wait for your father to notice you beside him. When he did, the order would be 'go below'. There you would stay, sometimes for weeks, and sometimes growing bored and cranky, but always you knew the good days would come again.

The land, for lads like Joseph, was always a destination; a place you talked of and looked for. You shouted with excitement when you saw the first smudge of it low down on the sea, but when you got there you didn't like it much. If it was home, there was always the dreaded talk of school ashore. If it was elsewhere, it was a place where cargo was unloaded and new cargo taken on. There would be sightseeing, and parties in the evening when other captains and their wives from home came across the harbour in their ships' boats to pay a call. But the sight-seeing was often tiresome, and the parties were for the grown-ups. Sailing-day was always the day you looked for.

Mother would be making ready for sea in the cabin, supervising the steward as he took up the carpets, beat them and put them away. Furniture had to be fastened into its sea positions, or stowed where it would be safe. Out on the deck tarpaulins would be settling down over the closed hatches, and father would be swearing over the mess the shoreside riggers had made of his sails.

The tug would puff noisily alongside, make her hawser fast, and ease ahead. The hawser would tighten and the ship begin to move while the mate was still booting some of the drunken men along the deck. They would be all right in the morning, and some of them would already be straightening up as the tug cast off. You were supposed to ignore them as mother did when she came up for her last look along the shore.

As the ship began to make sail it would be time for the pilot, standing beside the captain, to take his leave. You would watch for the pilot schooner, waiting on station at the harbour mouth. Down she would come, a beautiful little craft, beautifully handled, with a large black number painted on her mainsail. She would place herself just out of the ship's path to windward, and drop a boat. The boat would come skimming across the water to the ship's side and ride with her a little as she gathered way. The pilot would shake hands with father, touch his cap to mother, and pat you on the head. Then he would go down the rope ladder into the boat, and the pilot schooner would swoop down on the boat to pick it up. The last threads tying you to land were snapped again. The ship was forging ahead, and you were safe at sea.

They were great days for a lucky boy, and they were good for the captains and the owners too. The long voyagers in the wooden hulls were linked with the builders ashore, and all were prospering. The sea sent back its profits to the land, and the land returned them in more and bigger ships. The vessels of the great ship-owning families of Quebec and Halifax and Yarmouth and Saint John were now admired round the globe. Famous hulls carried the names of the tidal hamlets to the ends of the ear.

In the late 20th century, when Canadian seafaring is no longer a fraction of what it once was, it is remarkable to note that the success of Canadians at sea was a function, not only of their business acumen, but of their hardy natures, particularly that of the Nova Scotia 'Bluenose' men. That they lived a life of rough and tumble hardship is revealed in this wry description, and the tale that goes with it.

Masters and Men
Joseph Schull

By the early 1870s the carrying-trade had become a large and important part of Canadian life. The ships that went to England with timber were coming back with iron and coal. They were returning to Europe with cotton from Mobile, Charleston, and Galveston. They were moving outward again with coal bound round the Horn for South America and the coaling-stations of the Pacific. Cargoes of guano brought them back round the Horn to Europe. Guano, the petrified droppings of sea-birds, deposited through centuries on lonely headlands and islands along the South American coast, was in tremendous demand in Europe as a fertilizer, and the guano carrying-trade was an industry itself. Coal and oil and manufactured goods were also flooding out to the far east, and year by year a larger proportion of the cargoes was carried by Canadian vessels.

Ships from Yarmouth and Quebec and Saint John, from Hantsport and Windsor and Maitland and dozens of the smaller ports, passed each other on all the oceans. Their masters and men traded home gossip in Akyab and Shanghai, in Cardiff and Yokohama, in Valparaiso and Callao and Rio de Janeiro and Bombay. The names of little tidewater hamlets, hardly known the length of a province at home, became familiar to the vast and cosmopolitan community of the sea. Sailors who saw them on the stern-plates of a vessel told their mates in many languages, and sometimes warned them, that a Bluenose was in port.

They were not easy ships to sail in. You fed better in a Bluenose than in most vessels, and you never had to ask a mate's permission to take a drink from the big iron-bound casks on the deck. 'Full and plenty' was the rule so far as food and water were concerned. Sails, rigging, winches, pumps and deck-gear were always of the best. But the 'stiff' looking for a soft berth would be made uneasy by his first glimpse of spotless decks, gleaming ironwork, and fresh paint. It all spoke of a taut-run vessel, and it did not lie.

The discipline of the Bluenose merchant marine was soon a recognized and fearful thing. Gold lace and gilt buttons played no part in it, and neither did nautical academies. Masters and men wore the clothes that pleased them and learned their trade at sea. But in no merchant service and in few navies was the line between the forecastle hands and the 'afterguard' more sharply drawn.

Frederick William Wallace tells the story of a hardcase Nova Scotia captain who was signing on a crew in the shipping-office of a big port. Red-haired and bow-legged, looking like a stumpy farmer in his work-clothes, the master stepped up with his men to sign the articles before the shipping-master. He placed his signature at the head of the list and added, as required, the name of his home town, a backwoods Nova Scotia village. Then came the mates and the crew, among whom was the captain's younger brother, a lowly foremast hand.

'Home town?' asked the shipping-master, and the brother smirked side-wise at his mates with a touch of superiority. 'Indian Cove, sir—same as the captain. He's my brother.'

The crew grinned at each other, the shipping-master frowned and the captain flushed to the roots of his stubbly hair at this attempt to snuggle up to authority. Not a word was said, however, as the company left the shipping-office. The captain remained silent as they trooped aboard the vessel and prepared for sailing. Only when they were under canvas and running nicely before a fresh breeze did he refer to the matter on his mind. 'Go for'ard,' he said, 'and fetch that brother of mine.'

The mates came onto the poop with the brother between them. There was a length of rope in the captain's hands. 'Seize a-hold of that scow-banker,' he growled, 'till I get this bowlin' over him.' The brother emerged from a brief rough-and-tumble flat on the deck with a bowline over his shoulders. 'Naow, you Indian Cove gumphead,' came the voice of command, 'I'm a-goin' to wash the goldurned spruce gum smell out of you so's you'll look like a white man in future. Heave him over!' Over the side went the brother, and towed in the wake astern till the captain was satisfied that he knew the difference between master and man.

All captains were ready, if the need came, to insist with equal emphasis on respect for their authority. It was not often, however, that any question of authority came so near the poop. Squarely between the captain and crew, hard-fisted, quick-eyed and ready for anything, stood the two mates.

The 'Bluenose Bucko Mate' was soon the villain of a thousand yarns in seamen's taverns around the globe. Sometimes he deserved it, and more often not. His job was to sail the ship by the captain's orders, and to keep her like a Dutch housewife. A cargo badly stowed, a smear on the shining deck, or a rope's end flying loose meant disgrace for the mate and torment for the crew. The sight of an idle hand sent him roaring for paint pots or polishing rags. On the tougher ships a man who loafed on the halyards or showed an inclination to stay below in a gale was helped along to his station by a boot or a belaying-pin or a length of rope. The 'hobo' or 'sojer' who wished to stand and argue got the bare fist sometimes enclosed in the brass knuckle.

The second mate was a younger copy of the first, and both were made in the image of the captain. The three of them together were the brains and heart of the ship. Out of these triumvirates, multiplying on all the seas, grew the reputation of the Bluenose wind-jammers. 'Floating hells,' reported the bums as they reeled ashore after a voyage to recover in the shore-side taverns. 'Better than your limey hard-scrabble packets,' retorted the good sailors. If you knew your trade and did your work, you were all right with the Bluenoses. There was no nonsense about them. When they shipped a man they had paid out good money in advance wages for an able seaman, and an able seaman he was going to be.

Bluenose officers were tough because they always had a good proportion of tough men to deal with. They could no longer count exclusively on home boys to man their vessels. There were so many ships of all nations at sea in the 1870s that good sailors were becoming hard to find. The forecastles of Canadian vessels had begun to take on the cosmopolitan character of all other merchant navies. Vessels sailed from Canada to ports around the world, and in each port some or all of the crew would be paid off. For any one of the hundreds of reasons known to sailors, men would decide to change ship or jump ship, and the captain would have to replace them. He took what he could get, sailed again, and left some more of his crew behind at the next port.

Even if the men had all been virtuous sailors anxious to go to sea, the everlasting changes in ships' companies would have been a nuisance to the officers. A good proportion of the men in each port, however, were sea-going tramps. They were driven round the world by crimes somewhere behind them, by curiosity, or a rooted aversion to settled work. They preferred the land when they had money, and when their money was gone they took to the sea, hoping to be carried as painlessly as possible to the next place.

These were the men the 'crimps' thrived on; and crimps were soon as much a feature of Quebec and Halifax and Saint John as they were of the Old-World ports. A crimp was usually the keeper of a tavern or a sailors' boarding-house, but his principal occupation was to find crews for needy ships. When a captain had signed up all the good men he could find and was still short of a complement, he came in desperation to a crimp. The crimp provided the extra bodies; and bodies they sometimes were. Dead men had been heaved over a ship's side at night, and collected for; the living usually arrived dead drunk or drugged. All were out-of-work sailors who had fallen into the clutches of their host after a round of the taverns.

The crimp collected from the captain the first month's wages in advance. It was a profitable business, and some of the more enterprising extended their services to accommodate unemployed landlubbers. Paddy West of Liverpool, most famous of the crimps, conducted what he called a seamen's college; and those who passed through his hands have left the name 'Paddy Wester' to this day as the brand of a useless sailor.

Tuition was free at Paddy's college. The graduate was merely required to turn over his advance pay when he got a berth. During the week or so of his education he would first be set to turning a ship's wheel rigged up in Paddy's back yard. He would 'go aloft and furl sail' by running upstairs to the attic and making the window-blind fast. Finally he would march three times round a table on which Paddy had set a bullock's horn. The graduate was now equipped to tell his prospective captain that he had been three times round the Horn. His hands were stained with tar, he was equipped with old dungarees and a sheath knife, and delivered to the ship as an able seaman.

Crews liberally diluted with men like these often confronted masters and mates at the outset of a voyage. Men recovering from drugs and drink in the forecastle would be bellowing to get off the ship; ignorant imposters would be standing around helpless and scared. Even the good sailors, if there were any, would have taken full advantage of their stay ashore, and would be in no mood to jump when an order was given. It was hardly to be wondered at that mates usually strode into the middle of a new crew with fists flying and knuckle-dusters at work.

The wonder was that in most cases a good crew was kneaded together out of this sodden mass. The hard-handed officers could teach what they knew, and they were miracle-workers once a ship was at sea. Plentiful food, enforced cleanliness, and endless hours in the rigging or along the decks made many a stiff into a sailor in spite of himself. Bluenose ships might lurch out of harbour with their decks in pandemonium, but they usually came slanting home with a smart and disciplined crew.

There were, however, a few grim exceptions, and one of these was the ship *Lennie*. She had been built at Belliveau's Cove near Yarmouth, and was commanded by Captain Stanley Hatfield of Yarmouth. In the early autumn of 1875 *Lennie* sailed to Antwerp with timber. At Antwerp there was no return cargo to be had, and the vessel therefore left in ballast on October 23, bound for Sandy Hook. Unlucky in cargo, she had also been unlucky in crew. The mixed bag which manned her included four Greeks, three Turks, one Austrian, one Italian, one Dane, and one unsavoury Englishman. She also carried a young cabin-boy and, very fortunately for the owners as it turned out, a brawny Belgian by the name of Constant van Hoydonck. Van Hoydonck, for lack of a better berth, was serving as a steward, but he was a capable seaman already well on the way to his master's papers.

The *Lennie* towed down the Scheldt and headed out through the straits of Dover for the English Channel. By October 31, she was well into the Atlantic. The mates had had an unusually rough time with the crew, and with the Greeks in particular, but there was now a sullen quiet on the decks. Captain Hatfield took it to mean that his 'sojers' were in hand and would soon be acting like sailors. He was wrong.

On the morning of October 31, the mate was out on the foreyard clewing up some gear badly set by the incompetent men. The second mate was in his cabin, off watch. Captain Hatfield noticed one of the men loafing on the main braces. It was Big Harry, a ringleader of the Greeks and the chief trouble-maker on board. The captain shouted at him, but the Greek did not move. It was deliberate defiance, for the benefit of some of his mates who were watching.

Hatfield picked up a rope's end and started for the man, giving him the rough side of his tongue as he came. Big Harry waited till the captain was within a yard of him, then leaped forward like a cat, whipped out a knife and buried it to the hilt in the captain's chest. Hatfield slipped to the deck, struggled up on one knee, and fell on his face as another Greek darted in and stabbed him in the head.

The rest of the men on deck left their stations and ran to join the others round the dying captain. Men from below came hurrying up as if on signal. The mate dropped from the foreyard to the deck and the second mate came plunging from his cabin as a babble of shouts and curses rose in six tongues. They charged into the mêlée making for Big Harry, and for a moment the crew gave back before their fists and belaying-pins. Whatever plans had been made in the forecastle, some of the men were cowed by the sight of the bloody figure on the deck. Then a wave of murderous desperation seized them. Headed by the Greeks, they came on in a vicious rush. The second mate went down with a knife in his heart. The first mate was stabbed in the back as he grappled with the ringleader. Within five minutes of the first blow the three officers were dead and their bodies flung over the side. The mutineers were in command.

Van Hoydonck had been in his bunk when the wild flare-up began. Before he know what had happened, his cabin door was locked and the skylight above him battened down. Within an hour, however, the mutineers were knocking at his door. They did not know how to operate the ship.

Van Hoydonck was brought to the deck with Big Harry's knife at his back. There were no officers to be seen, the ship was floundering about in a rising wind, and the wild, scared faces which encircled him told clearly enough what had happened. He was the only man on board who knew anything about navigation, and his appearance from below was greeted with a medley of threats and promises. They would spare his life and give him a share of the profits they hoped for if he would sail the *Lennie* to Greece. One of the men had an uncle there, they told him, who would know where to sell the vessel.

Van Hoydonck agreed, with a number of private reservations. He told the men he would head for Gibraltar on the way to Greece. He gave over his own duties to the frightened cabin-boy, who had had no part in the murders, and took up the station of the dead captain on the poop. An hour or so without officers, in a vessel they could not sail, had already sobered the mutineers considerably. The helmsman obeyed Van Hoydonck more readily than he had ever obeyed the captain, and the rest meekly followed his instructions as he showed them how to square the yards. The bloodstained decks were swabbed up and the ship's name erased from her stern and from the lifeboats as she steered away on the new course Van Hoydonck had set. The men began to look at each other with an air of gloomy relief, which was hardly warranted. Their new master was taking them not to Gibraltar but straight up the Bristol Channel.

Bristol Channel is a wide stretch of water, but it is also a lane of heavy ship traffic. As vessel after vessel passed the *Lennie* the crew began to mutter together and glance ominously toward the poop. If they were in the open Atlantic they should not be seeing so many ships. Big Harry came up onto the poop, unsheathed his knife again, and demanded to see the chart. It meant nothing to him, but his knife and the look in his eyes told the Belgian that this plan had failed. Van Hoydonck took a sun sight, pretended that he had made a mistake, and altered course for the French coast.

Toward evening land was sighted and the ship came in to anchor. It was necessary, Van Hoydonck said, because the wind was against them for Gibraltar. This was true, but van Hoydonck with the assistance of the cabin-boy used the time to write some notes explaining the situation. These he sealed in bottles and threw overboard.

The captain's cabin was now the headquarters of Big Harry, and toward dark the most resolute of the mutineers were summoned there to meet with him. Van Hoydonck was not included, but through the night the sounds of angry debate reached the poop. In the morning Van Hoydonck was ordered to put to sea at once. He did so with obvious reluctance, and he looked back too anxiously at the shore. Abruptly four men seized him from behind, walked him from the poop and dumped him down the companionway to his cabin.

He lay there for three days and nights, coolly waiting. The cabin-boy was permitted to bring him food, and this was a reassuring sign. He would have been dead and overboard long since if the men had really believed they could spare him. The shouts and clatter above had a panicky ring. No one could work the ship, and it was bucketing helplessly about in the Bay of Biscay. At length angry seas slapping at the sides told of a gale on the way. Fists and knife-handles banged at Van Hoydonck's door again. He was to take over the ship once more.

He found the mutineers in a sad state. Beaten by the weather, terrified by the sight of passing ships, and exhausted by their attempts to make sail, they were quarrelling fiercely. Guilty fear was beginning to divide the leaders from the followers, and each man was suspicious of his mates. Van Hoydonck knew, however, that they trusted him least of all, and that one slip could send him overboard. None of them had anything to lose by another murder.

The gale was Van Hoydonck's excuse to run in again toward the French coast. He brought the ship off Isle de Re, and prepared to anchor in the shallow water. They were off the harbour of Cadiz, he said, which actually lay nearly a thousand miles to the south round the shoulder of Spain. Just as he was letting the anchor go, however, one of the men shouted that this was not Cadiz. He knew the look of the coast there, and if they were off Cadiz they should be in deep water.

Van Hoydonck was deposed again, but this time he was held on the poop. Three men stood with knives at his back as Big Harry took command and tried to get the ship to sea against a gale. He demanded instructions from Van Hoydonck, but Van Hoydonck refused to give help while he was a prisoner. The ship reeled back with fouled yards banging against the masts and canvas flapping uselessly. Big Harry was as hopelessly incompetent as the others. The knives which threatened Van Hoydonck went back into their sheaths. The Belgian, restored to authority, coolly ordered the anchor down, paying out sixty fathoms of chain to tangle itself in the eight fathoms of water and 'give them plenty of trouble in getting it up'.

For five nights and days they lay in the roadstead, battered by the gale. The mood of the men became more dangerous by the hour, and their first instinct was to settle things with the knife. Van Hoydonck played them off skilfully one against another. Some he promised to clear if the ship were captured. He warned others of plots being hatched against them by their mates. When the stew of suspicion boiled up into threats against him once more, he dared them to kill him and try to get to sea without him. They turned on the cabin-boy, always under Van Hoydonck's wing. The Belgian warned them there would be some necks cracked before they got to the boy. They looked at his big hands and brawny arms, looked at the weather, and sheathed their knives again.

There was a distress signal flying from the mast-head. Van Hoydonck had managed to get it up by telling the crew it was only a hoist to indicate that they were windbound. It almost became his death warrant on the morning of the sixth day. A French pilot-boat nosed out from the coast and came alongside, but as her master pointed to the *Lennie*'s signal the mutineers realized that it had been a summons. Van Hoydonck was dragged below before he could say a word to the pilot. Pushed to the rail by the other mutineers, the Italian and the Dane summoned a few broken words of French to explain that the signal had been hoisted by mistake. The pilot made little of what they said, but gathered that he was not wanted. He shrugged irritably, and turned his vessel toward shore again.

Below decks Van Hoydonck summoned his last resources of guile and daring. He really had made a mistake in his hoist, he told the men, and if they didn't believe him what did they propose to do about it? Could any of them handle the vessel without him? Once more he emerged master of the ship.

Each night while they lay anchored off Isle de Re, he and the cabin-boy had been industriously throwing over bottles with notes in them. There had been no indication that any of them had been found, and now the gale was beginning to let up. Van Hoydonck was afraid he would be forced to sea again. But there was a curious apathy about the crew now, and some of the men were eyeing the shore. What kind of country was this, asked Big Harry. 'Oh, a fine country,' said the Belgian largely. 'A republic, where they have no police.'

It was the most successful of his many fabrications. That night Big Harry and five of his closest associates launched a boat and pulled away for shore. When their departure was discovered in the morning, the morale of the remaining men fell apart. They began to plead with Van Hoydonck and ask for favourable testimony from him if they were caught.

One of the bottles had already been picked up. Shortly after dawn the following morning the French gunboat *Travailleur* appeared in the roadstead. She circled the *Lennie* slowly, then closed her, hull to hull. Her guns were small but evil-looking, and there was no fight left in the remnant of the mutineers. They tumbled over the side and began their journey to a French jail. By nightfall steel bars and hard-eyed custodians were advancing the political education of their mates who had sought the republic without police.

Big Harry and three of his companions were hanged, while several of the others went to prison for long terms. A new master and crew took *Lennie* back to Yarmouth, though for a long time men were reluctant to sail in the ill-fated ship. Van Hoydonck, decorated by four governments and with substantial salvage from the *Lennie's* owners, abandoned his ambition to be a shipmaster. Perhaps he had had enough. With his salvage money he opened a dockside pub in London, where his ale and yarns were much sought out by curious Yarmouth men.

As the 19th century ended, the great fleet of Canadian sailing vessels vanished from the world's oceans, as their owners turned to other economic pursuits. The steam-powered Canadian merchant marine laboured on until after the Second World War, until it too vanished, beset by foreign competition and union troubles. But in the 1920s and 1930s, when commercial sailing vessels had all but gone from the sea, Canadians still put to sea under sail, now almost exclusively to live the hard and perilous life of a Grand Banks dory fisherman. Stretching south and east of Newfoundland, the ancient fishery of the Grand Banks has teemed until recent years with fish drawn to the shallow waters and the rich mix of the Gulf Stream and Labrador Currents. Now its stocks are seriously overfished, but in the 1930s, in the depths of the Great Depression, a hard living could still be wrung from the sea, in the tall, dory-carrying form of a gaff-rigged fishing schooner. This is how the life appeared to a young marine biologist, sailing in such a vessel in March of 1932.

Working on the Off-Shore Banks
George Whiteley

The ship in which I sailed was named *Democracy*. She had been built in 1912 at Essex, Massachusetts, and her hard-pine planking and tall spars were still sound after twenty years of hard work. In length about one hundred twenty feet, with a displacement of one hundred fifty tons, she was able to stow two hundred thousand pounds of salt cod. Our crew consisted of captain, cook, twenty fishermen, and a deck boy. *Democracy* carried ten dories, with two fishermen manning each dory.

The first spring fishing trip is known locally as a 'frozen baiting'. Shore fishermen who live on the fjords at the head of Fortune Bay carry on a March herring fishery. Herring is the best bait available at this time of year. We bought eighty barrels at $1.50 per barrel. Placed on racks overnight the herring froze solid. In this condition, they were stowed in the ship's bait lockers.

We sailed from the harbour of Fortune at noon on Good Friday, March 25, with all sails set to a fresh northwest wind. During the afternoon, we put into the harbour of St Pierre, a French possession, located south of the Burin Peninsula, about forty miles from Fortune. The captain wished to pick up a spare storm staysail and a truckload of empty whiskey cases: firewood for the cabin stove. The St Pierre waterfront was busy loading rum runners with cases of liquor for deserted beaches on Long Island and other hideouts along the coast of the USA. Captain Hannrigan, *Democracy*'s skipper, a short burly man, active in spite of his sixty years, picked up information from one of the smugglers that the Nova Scotia banks were free of ice. He thought we would probably head in that direction to begin fishing.

My journal states: 'We are under way again; course SW by S from St Pierre's Gallantry Head; wind fair at ten knots. How pleasant to feel the ship under sail, moving with a gentle lifting motion. The mainsheet strains; blocks creak softly. A swirling pool of water marks our wake. We sail into the sunset of a peaceful evening. The main cabin is the gathering place for most of the crew. The ten dory skippers sleep here in cubbyhole-like bunks along each side of the cabin. The captain and I share a large wide bunk in a tiny stateroom on the starboard side. Crew not on watch busy themselves in various ways seated on a narrow shelf in front of the bunks; one fixes his lignum vitae trawl roller, another bends a new flag on his trawl buoy. Radio has just given weather report: "fresh NW wind becoming strong SW with snow tomorrow". On deck, wind is bitter cold. Seawater temperature must be close to thirty-three degrees. Sighted drift ice just before dark. We tacked to the south and east.'

The Nova Scotian fishing banks lie about one hundred fifty miles from Fortune Bay. Given average weather conditions, a vessel can reach the area in a day or two. We took nine days.

Day after day we met drift ice whether we tacked to the west or to the east. The ship had to heave-to in a series of gales. Captain Hannrigan decided to head northwest—to get inside the icepack near the mouth of Cabot Strait on the Newfoundland side. We skirted the ice-edge only to find that the heavy floes extended all the way to the coast. The ship was put about again to sail southward until drift ice was no longer a barrier. Constant fog had prevented Captain Hannrigan from getting a noon sun-sight or any celestial observation by which to establish a line of position. Having to heave-to and drift made accurate dead reckoning a real problem. We really did not know where we were with any reasonable degree of accuracy. In this uncertain, worrisome state, a sudden lift in the fog, one afternoon, disclosed that we might be nearing land. A sounding was made, but before the ship could bear off, we found *Democracy* surrounded by breakers; the schooner struck several times, but fortunately there was a heavy swell running which carried the ship over the back of the reef into deeper water. The grounding must have taken a slice out of the keel but there seemed to be no other damage.

Thankful for our narrow escape, we bore away south, resolved to continue in that direction.

Next morning, the fair wind dropped to a cold damp wheeze. Towering swells, like whaleback mountains, now beset the ship from several directions, creating a confused pattern. *Democracy* drifted with all sails set among thousands of small pans of ice like grossly overgrown white lily pads floating on the surface of the ocean. The schooner rolled first to one side, then to the other, rising up, up, on the swelling oily wave, then twisting and settling into the deep trough. The mainsail filled as the ship reached the crest, hung limp as the hull descended, then filled again with a thunderous report. The main boom swung outboard, wrenching the sheet bar-tight with such a jerk, I wondered how long the deck bolts securing the mainsheet blocks would hold. A diesel-powered trawler, out of New York, fishing for halibut, passed under our stern. She hailed us for any fishing news. When she reduced speed to speak to us, her hull and superstructure would completely disappear from sight as she sank into the trough of a sea. Moments later she would reappear on the back of a wave as if she were about to be launched into the air like a rocket.

The dreary day passed slowly until, at sunset, the night wind pushed us forward again.

On April 4 *Democracy* rounded the extreme south end of the icefield, and by tidal eddies on the surface of the ocean the captain judged we were nearing the edge of Banquereau, a Nova Scotian fishing ground. During the night, we came upon a small fleet of eleven Newfoundland schooners at anchor. Crews on most of the vessels were cleaning the day's catch. Around two small tables on the foredeck a team of three men gutted the cod, removed the head, and then cut out the backbone. The slitting tables were red with blood and gurry while on each side of the big deckhouse, in glistening black and yellow oilskins, fishermen armed with flashing knives were chopping mounds of frozen herring—tomorrow's bait for thousands of trawl hooks. In the rigging, like tea-kettles with two flaming spouts, small tin kerosene lamps cast over the shadowy scene an orange-tinted glare that mingled with reflections of green and red navigation lights in the dark ocean.

We sailed slowly through the fleet, Captain Hannrigan at the wheel. He ranged *Democracy* close to certain vessels to exchange fishing information. At midnight, we anchored in ninety fathoms.

About 3 a.m. next morning, our dorymen were roused by the captain. After a quick mug-up, the crew began to chop frozen herring to bait the long-line trawls. Each trawl consists of twenty-eight stout lines, and each line has about one hundred fifty hooks attached to it by short leaders. Before daylight, the dories were hoisted overboard and the dorymen rowed away from the ship to set trawl, each on a given compass course. *Democracy* was fishing at last.

During my four years with the Marine Laboratory, I gained a great deal of pleasure from various seagoing assignments by being an attentive listener. Many fishermen or sailors, afloat or ashore, were eager to describe incidents in their lives which may not have been too unusual in their view, but which, to me, were fascinating. I also found, in some cases, events meant a great deal to an individual, as if, at one point in time, this ordinary person, often inarticulate, even illiterate in the general sense, had achieved a high level of personal awareness and sense of worth.

During one rough night, when I was on deck, sheets of spray swept aft as *Democracy* plunged into and pushed aside the wind-blown crests of breaking seas. An elderly doryman, on watch at my side, said: 'I mind [remember] a terrible August gale when I was a young man. We were anchored on the eastern edge of Grand Bank; three hundred fathoms of cable out. Gale sprung on us without any warning. While we were at anchor, the schooner's riding sail was up, to help keep the vessel's head to windward. Somehow, the force of the first blast of wind tore the sail adrift from the sheet and the sail began to flog the main rigging. There was no way to muzzle the sail whipping around like that; it would cut off a man's head; so what with the rearing of the vessel in the seas and the strain on the rigging, the spar commenced to weave like a spintop. Before we could do much of anything to relieve the strain, the force of the sea and the twisting ship broke off the mainmast not much above the deck. There must have been a weak spot there. Anyhow, blue water poured over the bulwarks like a raging river. The captain, in his cabin below decks, thought the ship was sinking and wouldn't come on deck. I got an axe and cut the mooring cable (hated to see that fine cable go); called all hands to man the pumps; cut away the main rigging so the mainmast wouldn't punch a hole in the side of the ship. The broken spar lay across the deck, lodging on the bulwarks. With every sea it was like a battering ram, chewing up the taffrail; a threat to the vessel's survival. Somehow, we were able to clear away the mess of rigging and roll the spar overboard, so the sea could carry away the wreckage from the ship. Then, we turned to the foresail and double-reefed it; if we got the sail up, we could heave-to properly or run before the gale. But before we were able to rig the canvas, a great roaring monster of a wave broke over the bow. We all grabbed something solid for dear life. The sea broke up the nest of dories on the port side—swept them clean away, and drove one of the crew through a fish box. He was badly bruised but no broken bones, thanks be to God! A wild night, that way, boy! But we saved the schooner for the owners and for ourselves, I suppose. And they thanked me.'

The life of a Banks fisherman is filled with many hazards, especially during sudden winter storms that sweep over the cold ocean waters. On such a night, the laboratory's research trawler *Cape Aquihas* was hove-to on the Grand Banks. Our ship, although old in years, was a stout craft and we were in no danger. Captain Gabe Fudge and I shared a cabin located directly below the ship's helm. A gimballed overhead compass on the ceiling recorded the trawler's heading. Gabe glanced at the compass occasionally as he reminisced about his years in sailing bankers.

Gabe said: 'We had a rough time, one winter fishing trip. I remember it well. From Belleoram, Fortune Bay, we sailed the first day of February— a mighty cold day—with bait lockers filled with frozen herring. The *Santos* was about one hundred thirty tons, a fine-looking schooner, practically new, only two years old, built in Shelburne, Nova Scotia. For gear we had the best of everything—spanking fine sails, new running rigging, miles of trawl, spare equipment, ice axes and ice pounders and lots of grub. We sailed as far west as Rose Blanche Bank, swung over the dories, and each dory set a few tubs of trawl. The day started out fine, warmish for February. By the time the dories had taken back their gear, the sky was clouding, and before we had all the dories back on board, I could see the weather was making up for a dirty night. Soon, fog shut down thick . . . southeast wind with snow flurries. Later, the wind chopped around to the north and began to freshen fast. By dark, a living gale had hold of us. Salt spray froze on everything. No canvas could stand that wind. We wrestled the sails as best we could. The big mainsail had been furled early on. We handed the staysail but the foresail was iced up so much we couldn't get stops on it. We tied down the gaff as securely as possible and put a vang on the boom to ease strain on the foresheet, and I made sure every opening on the deck and cabin house was covered and snug, booby hatches and any other place through which water might enter the hull. Even though hove-to, the violence of the sea made any physical movement a slow strenuous effort, almost a struggle for existence.

'All night, under bare poles, we ran before the seas. While the vessel was hove-to, when we snugged her down, the man at the wheel, watching the breaking seas instead of the ship's head, let her broach a bit and a few big ones came on board. Two of the crew were thrown against the windlass and were injured. We did the best we could for them at the time. In the freezing weather and flying spray *Santos* iced up quickly. The foredeck was soon like an iceberg; the nested dories a solid mass. We had to take the cook out of the fo'c'sle. All hands gathered in the cabin with the hatch battened down. *Santos* was logging about ten knots but we couldn't do anything to slow her down. The vessel was deep in the water from weight of ice. Force of the gale tore off the tops of the seas and flying spindrift beat like hail on the helmsman.

'From our general heading, to be safe, we had to clear Seal Rocks off St Pierre. For seven hours I took the wheel myself. When the schooner was heading to windward while we snugged down, a man couldn't stand more than five minutes at the wheel; a face would freeze, even in that short time.

'When I was steering, my big sheepskin coat and collar, covered by oilclothes and sou'wester, were so coated with ice the wind didn't seem to get at me. Not that I was not uncomfortable, but I was not starving with cold. The worst nuisance was the slippery deck. When the ship would rear up on a sea and then plunge into those clumpers, it was a struggle to hang on to the wheel and at the same time keep a steady footing.

'And, of course, it was pitch dark.

'One of the crew, Jim Smith, stood by me (if I was near starving with limited food I couldn't refuse that man my share of grub). Jim crawled out of the cabin somehow and got the door shut between the worst seas.

He tied himself to a ring bolt in the deck; with a piece of oak he beat the spokes of the wheel, freeing them from the encasing ice. Otherwise, I would not have been able to continue steering. Jim was a Roman Catholic in a crew of Protestants. Every now and again, when he would feel the schooner rise on the back of a sea and catch sight of a terrifying mass of water foaming down on us, he'd make the sign of the Cross on that sea. I'd say to myself: "All right, old man. If you think that sign does any good, keep it up. I'm for you."

'Down in the cabin, the cold must have been as perishing as it was on deck. There was no fire; the stovepipe was stuffed shut. When *Santos* would bury herself in a foaming greybeard, the deadlights in the deck would reflect green sea, as water filled the scuppers and sluiced down the deck. The noise of rushing water must have sounded ominous to the men below. I'd hear a muffled shout from someone in the cabin, "She's gone this time . . . gone this time, boys." But I'd say to myself, as the stern rose again, "No, she's not gone yet." . . . But oh my, it was rough!

'One time, Smith looked forward and said, "Skipper, I can't see any dories on the port side."

'I kept looking between seas. Sure enough, the entire nest, all those six dories nested together, were clean gone. Certainly, I never saw them go. When the ship would be smothered by a sea, pieces of ice torn from the mass on the foredeck, pieces as big as a growler, would surge across the waist. With the air full of sea smoke, spray, and frost, I couldn't make out anything forward of the cabin house.

'Smith and I rigged a clever dodge to keep the compass-hole clear. The compass was in a tiny lighted space on the back of the cabin house, opposite the wheel. The opening to the compass was closed by a sliding wooden shutter. With all that water surging around and freezing where it landed, we'd never been able to keep the compass-hole free of ice. Smith found a long-handled string mop wedged in the scuppers. When the deck would fill with a sea, he would plug the compass-hole with the mop. Then, after a while, we would take a peek to see how the schooner was heading. It was a job to keep the mop from freezing stiff but somehow Smith would stamp off the ice. Anyhow, we kept the opening free enough so that we could check the course.

'Towards morning, I was beaten out, completely pooped. Had to lie down for a spell. I called George Mills, whom I could depend on, to take the wheel and to call me if he thought the schooner wasn't riding well. In oilclothes, sheepskin coat, rubber boots, I fell into bunk. But I wasn't down for long before George woke me to say the ship was listing badly to starboard. We had better do something quick.

'The nest of dories that remained on the starboard side was a mountain of ice and made the ship list quite a bit. Forward, she was as much like an iceberg as a vessel could be.

'I called the crew to come on deck. All hands turned out except for two men; the biggest fellows too. My God! I said things to those two men that I'd find hard to repeat. But they stayed in bunk, snivelling like spoiled children. They were frightened to death. "She's going to sink," they said, "there's no use doing anything to try to save her."

'Well, with the rest of the men working with ice hammers; breaking ice loose from dories, stanchions, scuppers, running rigging, and getting it overboard, all the while watching out and hanging on so as not to go overboard themselves, the ship was lightened considerable.

'When sea and wind began to moderate, I said, "Now boys, let's get the jumbo on her." Some job to set that staysail! We set a course for St Pierre and, at dusk, even in light snow, caught sight of Gallantry Head light.

'Next morning, after jogging around all night, I thought we'd get into St Pierre roadstead but I'damned if the wind didn't come down nor'west again . . . hard. We had to run off once more, but we hove-to that night and got some sleep. Next day, wind moderated and veered, permitting us to head towards Fortune Bay and our home port, Belleoram.

'I forgot to mention, that when we set the jumbo after that long struggle, the cook was able to get down in the galley through the forward booby hatch. We had some deer meat in a locker and the cook prepared a big meal; the first real food we had eaten in several days. I can tell you, that feed of venison was a tasty bit.

'After a few days home in Belleoram, we put on fresh supplies, picked up six new dories, and set sail again.'

The raw exposure to the force and power of the sea that formed the Banks fisherman's life gave him a unique perspective on survival, and what forces may be at work in such survival. Tales like the following were commonplace, and were shared with little comment and rarely disbelief. It was simply too dangerous to scoff.

Levi's Story
George Whiteley

While the ship was hove-to, one Sunday afternoon, to give the crew a rest, Levi confided to me an incident that had taken place some years ago when he was a doryman on the sailing banker *Poloma*.

'We went to sea in the early part of January,' he said. 'And in a gale on St Pierre Bank sprung the foremast a couple of inches, so the skipper decided to run for shelter and repair the damage. We made into the village of Harbour Buffet, a snug port on the south end of Long Island, Placentia Bay. While *Paloma* lay at anchor there, a man came aboard with a hardship story: he had been sick during the past summer; most of the codfish he had caught were sunburned on the flakes when he was drying the catch; he netted herring in the fall but hadn't enough to feed his family all winter; they were short of food, near starving. So the skipper gave him a barrel of flour, a few pounds of tea, salt beef, beans, and molasses, and the poor fellow rowed away overjoyed. A day or two later we sailed for the banks again, having put the ship to rights.

'Now, the weather that winter and spring was the worst you ever saw. Gale after gale; nor'east, sou'west, no matter the direction; wind, sea, and cold made hell of a doryman's life. Twice the western boats from Rose Blanche were caught in a norther. Coated in ice, with canvas shredded, several went aground and were broken up on the long beach of Miquelon.

'In spite of rough weather, our fishing was good. *Paloma* worked over the eastern side of Green Bank, that is, to the eastward of St Pierre Bank. Whenever the sea was civil enough to set gear and we were able to underrun our trawl twice in a day, we'd have a full doryload of cod every time. The skipper wanted the vessel loaded before we returned to Fortune Bay but our supply of bait ran low, so he decided to put into Harbour Buffet again to pick up enough herring to finish the voyage. Buffet is a great place for herring.

'*Paloma* had logged more than fifty miles heading landward when a howling nor'easter brought snow squalls and thick fog. The wind was on our starboard quarter. We could keep going fairly well under reefed foresail and reefed jumbo or staysail. The mainsail was snugged down before the canvas froze stiff. We had ample sea-room except for Lamb Rock—a three-fathom spot on our course in the middle of the ocean—and a treacherous breaking reef called St Mary's Cay offshore from Cape St Marys. Many a ship had been lost on that breaker.

'The old *Paloma* was making pretty good weather in the storm, although she was rolling quite a lot without the steady effect of the mainsail. An occasional sea broke over the bulwarks and a surge of white water across the deck. A bucket or two slopped over the high sill of the fo'c'sle companionway. I was off watch with five of the crew and the cook in the fo'c'sle. We lay in bunk all standing, you know—oilclothes and everything on, just in case we had to jump quick. The other fellows were asleep but the rolling and pitching made me nervous. The fo'c'sle's oil lamp flickered in the draft from the scuttle. Jackets and trousers, hung on a line to dry over the stove, swayed back and forward and twisted around with the motion of the vessel as if they were in some way live things.

'After a while, the ship's motion increased as if we were getting into shoal water or had changed course. I climbed out of bunk and stuck my head out of the companionway to have a look. In spite of the thick fog and the late afternoon, there was still enough daylight to see around. The wind had kicked up a savage sea. My dear man, the breaking crests of those combers were coming aboard with every roll now. Spray was flying. With the main boom tied down I couldn't see aft very well, but when the fore boom lifted, every now and then, I saw the skipper at the wheel. He was steering. He always like to steer in a storm. Then I caught sight of another figure crouching in the wind near the captain. I thought to myself, now, that is queer. The captain had said he wanted the watch on deck to stand right in the eyes of her, on the bow, to catch sight of anything ahead that would bring danger to ship.

'I crawled out of the hatch and looked forward. She was burying her bowsprit now, every time she pitched by the head. I counted the watch . . . one, two, three . . . three to port and three to starboard. That's peculiar, I said to myself. Six on watch, and two aft. Going below, I counted the sleeping crew; five and myself made six, and the cook. We only had fourteen all told on board, including captain and cook! Perhaps I was mistaken about seeing a man aft with the captain, although I was almost sure I saw one. As I was mulling over this puzzle, holding on the fo'c'sle ladder, I felt the schooner heel, a kind of shudder. Jumping up the steps, I heard the captain shout, "Hard down hard, sir," as if repeating an order.

'On deck there was noise and confusion. The schooner had jibed. Foresail and staysail booms crashed to starboard as the wind came over the stern. Before the ship settled on port tack, the booms swung back and forth with canvas rattling like cannon. The men on watch were yelling and pointing to starboard. About seventy-five yards astern, just visible in the fog, huge seas curled high and broke—a fearsome sight. Those breakers could only be the Key! St Mary's Cays!

'I stood in the companionway and watched as we drew away from danger. Then I looked aft at the captain. He was standing at the wheel. But he was alone. Just the captain at the wheel.

'I ran aft as he brought *Paloma* back on starboard tack, on our course to land.

'"What happened, skipper?" I cried, grabbing a handhold on the wheel-box.

'"My God, Lev," he said, "that was a close one! We were heading straight for the Cays, straight for the breaker, when I felt a touch on my arm. I glanced around. I could swear that a man stood by me . . . Hard down,' says he. 'Quick!' So I put the wheel over and she jibed. When I looked again . . . he was gone. We may have been well paid for that flour, I think!"

'I didn't know what to make of all that. But we just missed a bad job on the Cays, that's for sure.

'Two days later we reached Harbour Buffet. It appeared that they were holding a wake in one of the houses. Who had died? The very same poor fellow the skipper had helped with the food. And, would you believe it! The hour of his death was just about when he saved us from the Cays!

'Now adjust your mind to that.'

If it is true that many who know the power of the northern seas will stand on the shore and give thanks they are ashore, seamen in the sort of peril that faced Paloma *are equally thankful that lighthouses exist to mark the shoals and headlands which might otherwise kill an unwary ship. To all who strive to make a living from the sea, the lights and lighthouses of the Canadian coasts are beacons of surety in a dangerous world, and the keepers of the manned lights, now very few in number, have the sailor's gratitude and occasionally his envy. But the life surrounding a light's operation may be anything but tranquil and easy. Sisters Island Light lies to the northwest of Lasqueti Island in the Strait of Georgia on British Columbia's coast; its story is anything but uneventful.*

The Sisters
Donald Graham

In August 1932 Colonel Wilby reminded his deputy minister in Ottawa, 'It has always been our endeavour to keep a lightkeeper no longer than is absolutely necessary at Sisters Station.' Since the light had gone into operation in 1898, seventeen keepers had come and gone, taking few pleasant memories of their stay away with them. Reiterating the policy three years later, G.E.L. Robertson, director of pilotage on the West Coast, referred the commissioner of lights to Sisters' position. It would take some hunting even with a lens to find that 'speck on the chart . . . . In fact, Sisters Island has only a little bit of a walk around the rock,' Robertson pointed out, 'and it is a very hard place to get on and off in winter weather and a good place to leave a man on as short a time as possible.'

If the commissioner had taken the trouble to unroll the chart across his desk, he would have found Sisters Island marked as two small black rocks only seventeen feet above high water, two miles southwest of Lasqueti Island off Parksville. In 1897 Gaudin had warned Anderson to expect more 'urgent appeals for aids . . . owing to the increase of shipping to the North being caused by [the] rush to Alaska for gold . . . . This point,' he counselled, referred to Sisters, 'is the first that should be lit', and a small beacon, similar to those already operating at Bare Point and Berens Island, was installed that May. The light's range would be short, broken by surrounding points of land—to miles to the northwest and six miles southward. There was 'not a shadow of danger to the east or west of it,' the agent wrote, recalling an earlier inspection of the site, 'and no outlying dangers on the shore of Lasqueti.' A bell would suffice for a fog warning. It would be necessary, however, to provide room for a family and a means of storing potable water 'in such a manner that it . . . [would] not spoil through the spray which no doubt . . . [would] be pretty well carried over the roof in high winds.'

Gaudin visited Ronald McNiell, Sisters' first keeper, in March 1899. McNiell glumly reported 'a long and tedious winter' since he had 'not seen or spoken to any person since his installment in December.' McNiell resigned in August. Next came a man named Higgins and his common-law Indian wife. In March 1900 Higgins reported she had left him because of the clamour of the fog bell every thirty seconds, which cracked plaster throughout the interior. Higgins followed his wife in February 1901, and Alfred Jeffries left in his turn in October 1902, 'due to his wife's illness'. Sisters, five years old, was already a revolving door.

Gaudin had high hopes for Benjamin Blanchard, a qualified machinist and expert boat handler, a man who could 'perform repairs to the building without asking extra payment for every little bit he' executed. Blanchard stuck it out for two years with his wife and daughter—something of a record at Sisters. During that time, rain fell in the house long after the weather cleared outside, since the contractor had failed to use galvanized shingle nails. Blanchard resigned in June 1904. His daughter had seriously injured her arm, and the salary was far too low.

W.C. Ferneyhough came in June and went in November. The department dismissed his complaints about Sisters' sodden conditions as 'altogether exaggerated and misleading'. If he had only followed the example of previous keepers 'who took the precaution to place a pail under the drip to prevent any inconvenience', he would have had no grounds for complaint.

Meanwhile, Ben Blanchard had heard somewhere that lightkeepers' salaries were about to go up by 24 per cent. He came back to Sisters after Ferneyhough. The increase stemmed from Colonel Anderson's decision to build a fog alarm on the Rocks, and construction commenced in October 1907. Still, it was a long wait—almost too long. In March Gaudin received a desperate letter from Sisters by way of a fish packer. Blanchard was 'on the verge of starvation'. He implored the agent to send out the *Quadra* with provisions from Nanaimo. When the diaphones went into operation, Blanchard's salary rose from $500 to $800, out of which he was required to pay an assistant. Mrs Blanchard filled the bill and they achieved a measure of financial relief, but by May 1910 the keeper had decided to resign 'to obtain educational advantages for his young family'.

With waves constantly washing up and over the rocks, launching a boat and hauling it back up its ways was always a perilous venture. Walter Buss went out to pick up mail and to see a dentist on 19 November 1912 and was unable to land on his return. A fish boat was wrecked on one of the rocks around 7 p.m. that night and the crew cowered in the dark, screaming for help as the tide rose and heavy southeast swells tried to wash them off. By 8:30 p.m. on the twentieth, thinking their 'time was coming any minute', they waded across to the station after the wind suddenly changed direction. No one was home. 'Everybody in Nanaimo tell[s] me I have no business paying for the boat the way it was lost,' the infuriated skipper informed the minister of Marine and Fisheries. 'If Mr Buss had been there with the lighthouse boat there was no possible chance at all for us to lose our boat.'

Buss was immune to any reprimands. He had written asking for an increase in pay that August. When Robertson flatly turned him down, he decided, 'I cannot see my way clear to take on the duties of lightkeeper another year,' and sent in his resignation to take effect 28 September. He had only remained at Sisters awaiting a cheque, now a year overdue, for expenses incurred putting up two technicians for a week in November 1911. 'I am not by any means running a charity boarding house for the Flotsam and Jetsam of the lighthouse and Marine service,' he tersely reminded Robertson. 'Now to my mind I think it is casting reflections on the Marine and Fisheries Staff to have its employees beating the keepers out of board bills.'

Robertson tried to make the keepers' toehold on Sisters somewhat more bearable—and infinitely safer—by proposing a mail service to the rock in March 1912. It would cost $72 a year. The commissioner of lights in Ottawa scotched his plan. After all, Sisters lay in the inside channel. Since 'so many other points throughout the Dominion' were 'more unfavourably situated, . . . if the Sisters were supplied with a mail service, an inconvenient precedent might be established.'

As the topography virtually ruled out raising children, the department always had great trouble enticing married men out to Sisters. Allan Couldery was anxiously awaiting an appointment in July 1918 when Robertson dispatched Gordon Halkett to Vancouver to offer him Sisters light. One glance at Halkett's photograph of the station was enough. 'Reluctantly, very reluctantly,' Couldery was 'compelled to decline the Keepership of the Sisters Light Station.'

The department relied heavily upon bachelors, but men soon grew despondent alone out on that rock—with predictable results. Halkett reported in March 1915 that the station was 'kept in a disgraceful condition', and Robertson warned the keeper to give his 'pig sty . . . a thorough house cleaning', as he planned 'to be around in the vicinity . . . shortly'.

In June 1924 earwigs came ashore. Within a month of securing a beachhead, they completely overran the station. 'Towards evening they come out and spread all over,' Charles Clark reported. 'My wife's nerves are in such a shape I am afraid I shall have to send her away from the station.' The Clarks had a two-year-old child, and the boy was defenceless against these 'most repulsive creatures', confined as he was to the dwelling and the walkway around it.

The insects multiplied by the thousands, keeping pace with Clark's attempts to kill them. At sunset they poured out from under the shingles and up through the floors, a teeming bronze mass which cracked and splattered underfoot. Night after sleepless night, the Clarks lay in bed with the child between them, listening to the insects plop from the ceiling and cupboards. Summer was a sweltering siege. 'We have to keep all doors and windows tightly closed so you can imagine what it means living in a house during hot days without fresh air,' Clark told the agent. '[I am] sending my wife and child down the first opportunity . . . & I would not think of bringing them back again to this station.' Dallain, the acting agent, sent out coal oil, disinfectant, a mixture of flour and plaster of Paris, 'a deadly bait' which had proved 'effective for pests of this kind at other stations'. Clark seems to have won the battle against his tormentors, but it was a pyrrhic victory. He resigned.

Joseph Pettingell doubtless astonished Wilby with a letter from Sisters in January 1925, expressing how 'greatful' he and his wife were for their appointment, and promising to give his 'undivided attention' to duties at the station. His first duty was to draw drinking water from the engine room reservoir and tote it up to the house in pails, for the water was well down in the cistern when the Pettingells first came ashore. Gratitude dwindled further by May 1926. When the *Berens* brought supplies that month, Pettingell put his wife aboard the tender, to be taken to hospital. 'What is the sickness I am unable to say,' he wrote Wilby, 'but it has been coming for quite a few days, yesterday & last night, at times, her tongue clove and she could not move it.' In October the keeper reported that they were all covered 'with a terrible itching rash that spread over . . . [their] bodies with some rapidity'. Every balm and ointment from their medicine chest had been smeared on with no effect. 'With my wife it still comes on towards night, same with my oldest girl,' Pettingell said, 'with the younger one she is still covered from her feet up.' Wilby recommended the Pettingells be transferred to Cape Mudge the following May, since they had been at Sisters 'for some time [two years] and the environment . . . [was] beginning to affect their health.'

There was always the awareness of living just beyond the sea's reach, a sensation quite literally brought home to Jonathon Fleming during Christmas week 1932, when a 'terrific So. East gale' made him wonder if Sisters Rocks might be restored any minute to their pre-1898 condition. 'The following is a list of damage done by the storm,' the keeper wrote in a still-shaky hand:

> Boathouse wrecked and most of it washed away with equipment and personal effects. Boatways washed away and boat damaged. Owing to weight of oil drums the oil house was saved but was shifted on the foundation and sides and floor damaged. Outside walk of engine house badly damaged,

and drain pipes leading to water supply tanks broken and washed away. Toilet, sidewalks and platforms all wrecked and washed away. Pipe guard rail round dwelling twisted out of shape and broken. During the storm I could not get away from the dwelling as heavy seas were breaking over platforms.

'As the rowboat is out of commission,' Fleming concluded, 'I will have to signal for Mr Williams to come over from False Bay and get this letter for mailing.'

If there is anything more terrifying than being all alone and under assault by seas capable of twisting two-inch metal pipe like pretzels, Charles Lundgren experienced it in August 1944. He had replaced S. Greenall, who had fled Sisters after only one week that summer. At one in the morning Lundgren awoke to a distant rumbling somewhere far below his bed. The dwelling began to 'shake violent', shuddering on its foundation. All the windows smashed. Lundgren fled outside in his nightshirt, covered with plaster. The light was out and he climbed the tower to find a pane had fallen down and shattered the vapour tube. 'I putt in plase Aladdin lamps then 4:50 a.m. an other shock struck the house but not so violent,' Lundgren reported, 'i whent outside and it was 15 craks in the foundation and the plaster from the siding fell down onto the floor.' Six panes in the tower and 'som of the lens wher cracked'.

He had brought an assistant and fifteen dogs with him, turning the dwelling at Sisters into a reeking kennel, hopping with fleas. Victoria turned a blind eye to such conditions, knowing full well by now how difficult it was to lure people out to Sisters and keep them there. Art and Elsie Tolpitt took over in February 1945 and walked into a revolting situation. 'Often wish you could see us both in our mad scramble to get straightened out,' Elsie wrote W.L. Stamford, the agent.

Oh Boy! What fun we're having along with the dirt, fleas & old relics of furniture. The smell is vanishing by degrees, thanks to the simple things in life such as soap, fresh air & darned good elbow grease. While at Cape Beale & Cape Mudge I developed a spare tire around the middle, but I've lost it already with perpetual motion ten hrs. a day, but now I see my knees are like sand paper, but so long as we get this place sweet and clean I don't mind. We can't even handle a thing but what our hands are covered in filth & grime; Never in my life have I seen such a contaminated mess that those two partners made of this place. I'd like to string them up especially the dog owner, Every Floor was stained from his dogs.

Elsie looked forward to having Halkett come over, sometime in June, to witness the transformation they had wrought. First, though, she and Art promised to take their 'Life Buoy Soap and walk off the rocks and really go to town on [them]selves . . . . But with it all,' she confessed, 'I must admit I'm very happy & contented & really like the life of a light keeper's wife . . . .'

In March 1947 Elsie was seriously ill and the department granted the Tolpitts three weeks' leave. Art resigned and Lundgren, the detested dog owner, came back—just in time for one of the coldest winters ever on the West Coast. Water froze in the pumps, rupturing pipes. Lundgren warned, 'If this violent cold dont stopp the Coal Box will be empty.' He was shoveling two hundred pounds a day yet Sisters Rock was 'a iceberg . . . a decepart place to be in'. Moreover, Lundgren was now almost incapable of packing more coal. 'You have neglected to send hoist wire that i ordert 8 monts ago,' he reminded Morrison. 'Hoist wire rotten and brocke and the Raol [roll?] fell a topp of mi injured mi legs and left hand i have been crippled for a mont—Just for the neglegkt of the Department to send safe equipment.'

R.B. Roberts lost the station boat to a high tide and a fierce gale from the northwest in November 1959. 'The storm struck with such violence & so suddenly that I barely had time to secure a line to . . . [the boat] before it was swept over along with the part of the landing to which it was lashed,' Roberts recalled. 'Storm damage to all parts of the station, the dwelling excepted, is a regular occurrence.'

Half a century of such assault and battery had left the dwelling in a ramshackle condition. The department considered moving the station over to Lasqueti Island, with power supplied by submarine cable. Instead, a concrete structure combining engine room, tower, and living quarters, went up on the original site in 1967. Sisters was converted to a 'crib' station, like Sand Heads, with keepers landed by helicopter for two-week stints. Even at that, two weeks at the Sisters can seem too long.

Whether on the sea, or beside it, the elemental qualities which are called for in those who earn their living through the sea are courage, persistence, and endurance. To a degree sophisticated modern technology has begun to make this less so. It will remain to be seen if the country is not the worse for the loss of this 'school of hard knocks', even as we celebrate that there is much less necessity for 'widow's walks' on Canadian homes at the edge of the cold waters.

To those waiting in patient anxiety for the safe return of loved ones working at sea, the hymning of a vanished and romantic era of wooden ships and iron men is uninformed nonsense. That harsh practicality has been in all ways the most important thing about the Canadian experience of the sea. And like the struggle with the winter, it has shaped the country and its people to a degree they may not fully understand.

Special Ships

There have been thousands of ships in Canada's maritime history, from towering full-rigged clippers to rust-streaked corvettes. Some have had special magic; some have built careers of resolute service, like the RCMP schooner St Roch, which carried Larsen and his crew on wartime Northwest Passages full of adventure and challenge; some have been full of mystery, like the abandoned Canadian-built sailing vessel Marie Celeste; and some have simply been scenes of horror, like the passenger steamer Noronic, which burned on Lake Ontario, killing hundreds.

But a few ships hold, or deserve to hold, special attention in Canada's history; and foremost among these is the working Grand Banks schooner Bluenose. After the First World War, a race competition between a Canadian and an American working fishing schooner was held on the East Coast. To much surprise, the Canadian schooner Delawana was beaten handily by the American Esperanto.

Bluenose and Bluenose II
R. Keith McLaren

Nova Scotians were shocked and dismayed to be beaten so soundly by the Americans, so plans were quickly drawn up to build another schooner for the following year's competition. A vessel that would be acceptable to compete in the International Fisherman's Race had to meet conditions specified in the 'Deed of Gift', which governed the disposition of the Trophy. Since the most important requirement of the race was that the contestants be '*bona-fide* fishermen', the primary function of the vessel had to be fishing, not racing. Above all, the boat had to earn a living the rest of the year and prove that she was economically sound as a fishing vessel.

A young naval architect, W.J. Roué, was commissioned to design a fishing schooner for the competition. The product was the schooner *Bluenose*, a fine, sleek-looking craft. She was built at the Smith and Rhuland Yard in Lunenburg, Nova Scotia. One alteration made during construction that caused some comment was the raising of the forecastle head by eighteen inches to facilitate more head room for the crew, but no evidence shows that this improved the speed of the vessel; only possibly did it make her deck drier forward. The *Bluenose* was launched on March 26, 1921, in good time for her to put in a season fishing on the Banks and qualify her for the races in the fall.

The *Bluenose* was financed at a cost of $35,000 by Captain Angus Walters and four Halifax businessmen who formed the Bluenose Schooner Company. She immediately proved to be a successful venture. In her early trials she seemed a handy enough vessel under the capable command of Captain Walters, and during the first season fishing on the Banks she brought in 4,200 quintals (112 lbs to a quintal) of fish, a highly respectable amount.

Like the Canadians, the shipyards in the New England states were building new schooners. A new vessel had to be found for the upcoming competition, because the American champion, *Esperanto*, sank while fishing off Sable Island in June, 1921. Two of the new schooners were the *Yankee* and the *Mayflower*. The *Yankee*, unfortunately, turned out poorly, as her trials soon proved. She could not handle sail well and had to have engines installed to make her economical.

The *Mayflower*, designed by Starling Burgess, sported a yacht-like appearance with wire running rigging, a dolphin striker, and a slightly rakish design. Although she did put in a qualifying season on the Banks, the International Race committee considered her primarily a racing rather than a fishing vessel, and this contravened the conditions provided under the 'Deed of Gift'. Their decision to disqualify her from the race caused great controversy which at one point threatened to cancel the entire series. The committee in Gloucester finally adhered to the decision, but only after bitter argument.

The 1921 eliminations were held in October. In Gloucester a small, sprightly schooner named *Elsie* won out in a race against four other competitors: the *Elsie G. Silvia*, *Ralph Brown*, *Phillip P. Manta*, and *Arthur James*. In Halifax nine vessels were ready at the starting line for the 1921 eliminations. Two races determined the challenger of the cup, one on October 15 and the other on the 17th. The *Bluenose* became the unquestioned winner after beating the *Canadia* by four minutes in the first race and by seventeen minutes in the second. The other vessels in the race were the *Donald J. Corkum*, *Delawana*, *J. Duffy*, *Independence*, *Senora*, *Alcala*, and the *Uda R. Corkum*. The *Bluenose* had proven to be as successful a racer as she was a fisherman.

The success of the *Bluenose* was largely due to the capable captain and her excellent crew. *The Halifax Herald*, October 24, 1921, commented on Captain Walters, 'Aboard and during the race he is a martinet for discipline and order. The owner of a head that shows above the weather rail knows about it in a manner that leaves no room for back talk. He did his commanding with the aid of a megaphone and he has a caustic tongue. He is a driver from gun to gun.' His crew were seasoned 'salt-bankers' that knew their trade; no less than nine were captains of their own boats.

Captain Marty Welsh of the American schooner, *Elsie*, was a very capable skipper and his crew, like the crew of the *Bluenose*, were largely men who captained their own boats. Furthermore, the *Elsie* had a reputation of being swift for Captain Welsh astonished listeners by telling them of hauling his log at 13 knots on his trip up from Gloucester.

The first race on the 22nd was won by the *Bluenose*. She had gained the advantage during the first leg and kept it through to the end. Unfortunately, the *Elsie* lost her foretopmast during the latter part of the race, losing the use of her foretopsail and jibtopsail. Captain Walters, in the interests of keeping the race 'fair and square', doused his own foretopsail, but the *Bluenose* was already well in the lead and crossed the finish line thirteen minutes and fifteen seconds ahead of the *Elsie*.

The second race was a far more exciting contest. *Elsie* crossed the starting line several boat-lengths ahead of the *Bluenose* and held on to this lead, passing each mark half a minute ahead of her opponent. It was not until the fourth mark was passed and the windward race began from Shut-In Island Bell to the Inner Automatic Buoy that the *Bluenose* forged ahead. In her best sailing form, she drove down relentlessly upon the *Elsie* and took the race by eleven minutes. The crowds cheered from the shore as *Bluenose* flew across the finish line. Nova Scotians were jubilant. The *Bluenose* had proved to be a champion and had brought the International Fisherman's Trophy back home.

Through the winter, plans and construction began in various ports in the United States in hopes of having a brand-new challenger ready for the next year's race. In Essex, Massachusetts, a fine new schooner called the *Puritan* seemed to be a likely contender for the Fisherman's Race. During her trials and impromptu races she was found to be a very fast sailor, but her career was cut short. During a trip to the Banks in June, she hit the north-west bar of Sable Island and was lost. The *Henry Ford*, also built in Essex, was finished almost a month later than the *Puritan*. Her late launching and fitting out didn't allow the boat to put in a full season on the fishing grounds, as the Fisherman's Race rules demanded, but she fell in with every other condition specified in the 'Deed of Gift', so the Race committee decided it would be fair to allow the *Ford* to enter the year's competition.

The ruling on the *Ford* upset the owners of the previously disqualified *Mayflower*. They tried to enter the competition a second time and were again rejected. The owners felt their vessel had more than proven herself to be a *bona-fide* 'fisherman', but the race committee refused to alter their former decision, as further 'evidence' cited the title on the construction plans, which called the *Mayflower* a 'schooner-yacht'. The *Mayflower* reluctantly accepted the decision, but sent out a challenge to the winner of the 1922 race to compete against the *Mayflower* in a separate race.

The Americans held their eliminations on October 12, 13 and 14, and the *Henry Ford* under Captain Clayton Moissey won against the *Elizabeth Howard*, *Yankee*, and *L.A. Dutton*. The Canadian eliminations were held on October 7, 9 and 10, with the *Bluenose* competing against the *Canadia*, *Mahaska*, and *Margaret K. Smith*. During the first race, the *Bluenose* showed an astonishing display of speed. Leading the boats at the start, Walters made an error in navigation and passed the Inner Automatic Buoy on the starboard hand instead of to port. Following quickly upon the heels of the *Bluenose* was the *Mahaska*, making the same mistake, while the *Canadia* and *Margaret K. Smith* took the lead by passing on the proper side of the buoy. Recognizing his mistake, Walters immediately proceeded to correct it, yelling, 'Spit on your hands and never say die, boys,' and he swung the big vessel around to repass the buoy on the proper side. By the time she had come around, the *Canadia* was in the lead almost a mile ahead, with the *Smith* close behind. With a combination of the vessel's speed and Captain Walters' fierce determination to win, the *Bluenose* narrowed down the distance, passed the *Smith*, and finally caught up with the *Canadia* and forged ahead to cross the finish line seven minutes ahead of the rest. Due to light winds, the next two contests were not finished within the time limit and were called 'No Race' by the committee, but because of the superb performance of the *Bluenose* during the first race, it was decided that she be named the defender.

Four races were held in Gloucester in 1922. The first was unofficial; the sailing committee cancelled the race due to false starts of both vessels, but the Captains of the *Ford* and *Bluenose* decided to race anyway, ignoring both the recall signal and a Coast Guard boat sent out to bring them back. The *Ford* took an easy win beating *Bluenose* by almost twenty-two minutes, and although Captain Walters told the committee that it was a fair race and to 'tally one up for Clayte', the race committee wouldn't hear of it and declared the race unofficial.

The second race on the 23rd was won by the *Henry Ford*, beating the *Bluenose* by two-and-one-half minutes. Two days later the *Bluenose* beat the *Ford*, but the citizens of Gloucester were outraged at what they considered an unfair contest, because the *Ford* had lost her foretopmast in the event. The Race Committee considered the protest and decided that the wind was not strong enough to warrant a broken topmast and gave the race to the *Bluenose*. The next day the final and deciding race was won by the *Bluenose* by almost eight minutes. The *Bluenose* retained the Fisherman's Trophy and received a cash prize of $3,000. The defeated *Henry Ford* won $2,000.

The promised race with the *Mayflower* never happened, because at the end of the 1922 series a *Bluenose* crewman, Bert Demone, fell into the harbour and drowned. The *Bluenose* crewmen had no desire to engage in another race after this mishap and left for Lunenburg in mourning.

In September 1923 the fishing fleets had just finished another season on the Banks and were preparing themselves for the next international series. The Americans had built another schooner in the spring called the *Columbia*, which was designed by Burgess and Paine and built in Essex. She had put in a qualifying season on the Banks and was ready for the race. After winning a last-minute challenge from the *Henry Ford*, the

Columbia sailed to Halifax to race against the *Bluenose*, now established as the Cup's defender.

The first race, run on October 29, 1923, was one of the most exciting of all the series. The *Bluenose* led at the start by thirty seconds, and increased the lead to two-and-one-half minutes by the second mark, the Outer Automatic Buoy. Captain Ben Pine drove the *Columbia* as hard as he dared, and during the windward race from the second mark to the Sambro Light Ship he succeeded in closing the distance between him and the *Bluenose*. As both vessels passed the third mark, they were neck and neck, with the *Bluenose* to windward and on a course for the shoal off Chebucto Head. It was a dangerous course to follow, but the *Columbia* lay directly alongside and Captain Pine was not about to give up the advantage by falling off to leeward. They passed Bell Rock Buoy to landward and tension grew as the *Bluenose* edged closer to the white water of the shoals. Captain Walters had little choice but to force the *Columbia* over to give the *Bluenose* more sea room. The *Columbia* would not give an inch as the two great schooners closed in together. The *Bluenose*'s bowsprit brushed up against the *Columbia*'s forward shrouds and caught up on a halyard, and for about a minute the *Bluenose* was actually towing the *Columbia*, until the vessels parted company and the *Bluenose* inched ahead. She gained the lead of about one minute by the fourth mark and won the race by the small margin of one minute, twenty seconds. Surprisingly, no protests were lodged by either vessel, but the sailing committee immediately wrote out a set of Special Rules (the 1923 Rules) to prevent such an incident from happening again.

The second race occurred on November 1. In another close contest, the *Bluenose* held the lead and won the race by two minutes, forty-five seconds, but it was not a clear win. The *Bluenose* had ignored the new special rule pertaining to the passing of buoys and had passed Lighthouse Buoy on the wrong side, to landward. Walters argued that the buoy wasn't a distance market, only a channel buoy, and his deviation didn't affect the distance run in the race. The Sailing Committee decided that the *Columbia*'s protest was legitimate, and gave the race to the *Columbia*, making the series tied one-all.

The final and deciding race was called for two days hence, to give the *Bluenose* time to repair a sprung maintopmast, but Walters, refusing to accept the decision of the previous race, left Halifax in protest and headed for Lunenburg. No coaxing would bring him back. Ben Pine, left with the prospect of sailing the course alone to take possession of the Trophy, declined and sailed off to Gloucester, leaving the 1923 series incompleted.

The prize money of $5,000 was split between the two schooners, but the disagreement over the ruling caused a break in the International Fisherman's competition that lasted seven years.

In the next few years the sea took her toll of sailing vessels working on the Atlantic fishing grounds. The *Columbia* and the sister ship of the *Bluenose*, the *Haligonian*, both ran aground within a week of each other in 1926 and both were hauled off safely. But a year later, in August, the *Columbia*, caught off Sable Island in bad weather, sank with all her crew. The *Henry Ford* was lost the next year off Martin Point, Newfoundland. The boats mentioned were only the most prominent because of their involvement in the International Fisherman's Race, but many others followed similar ends. Almost every day the newspapers would relate stories of vessels in distress or missing.

In the storms of April 1926 and August 1927, the Lunenburg fleet was severely battered. One day in April 1926, eight boats returned from the Banks early because of damage from the sea. Among them was the *Bluenose*. She was in relatively good shape, with two anchors lost, 300 fathom of cable missing, all her fishing gear gone, and a badly damaged foresail. The other vessels suffered various injuries and loss of equipment far worse than the *Bluenose*. However, the season had just started, and at the end of April an even fiercer storm hit. This time the *Bluenose* was caught off Northwest Point of Sable Island's southwest exposure during a blinding snowstorm. She had already parted with one anchor, when a great sea swept over forward breaking the second cable, smashing fourteen stanchions and carrying away part of the rail and bulwarks. The only way out was windward working northwest around the point or straight out to sea. For seven hours under jumbo, double-reefed foresail and a riding sail, she kept biting her way windward into the teeth of the gale in what may be considered the greatest race of her life. The wind finally hauled around a bit to the northwesterly, enough for the *Bluenose* to clear South West Point and carry her crew of twenty to safety.

In the fall of 1926 two separate races took place. In Gloucester, the *Columbia* and the *Henry Ford* had one last contest between them before both were lost at sea. In two successive events, the *Columbia* outsailed the *Ford*. It was unfortunate that the *Columbia* never had another chance to compete with the *Bluenose*. By watching her sailing capabilities, many people agreed that she was the vessel that would give the *Bluenose* the most challenge. In Halifax a race was arranged between the *Haligonian* and the *Bluenose*. The *Haligonian* was built in Shelburne in 1925 along the same designs of William Roué as the *Bluenose* and was thought to be a good match. The *Bluenose* took the races, winning by such a long margin that people wondered what was wrong with the *Haligonian*.

In 1930 another race was held in Gloucester with the *Bluenose* competing against a new schooner, the *Gertrude L. Thebaud*, captained by Walters' old rival Ben Pine. The race was run for the Sir Thomas Lipton Cup. The *Bluenose* lost badly in, perhaps, the worst race of her career. Speculation was made that the *Bluenose* had taken unseen damage after being aground four days off Placentia Bay, Newfoundland, earlier in the year.

In the second race the *Bluenose* rallied her old spirit and led the boat across the finish, but in the third and final race, the *Bluenose* was soundly beaten. Walters reported that they had hit Round Rock Shoal three times but 'wouldn't stop and use it as an alibi for defeat'. Nor would he 'cast any reflections to the three Gloucestermen on board as crew at the time, one who was handling the wheel'. New England was jubilant and immediately plans were being made for a return competition to decide the winner of the International Fisherman's Trophy. Due to the lateness of the season and the fact that the race was funded by public subscription the Race Committee decided to leave the race until next year.

After a lapse of seven years, the International Fisherman's Race was revived in 1931. The *Bluenose* was accepted, unchallenged, as the Canadian defender. In Gloucester, after an elimination race with the *Elsie*, the *Gertrude L. Thebaud* was chosen as the American challenger. Captain Walters was confident of another win, as he quoted a ten-year-old belief: 'The wood is not grown yet, that will build a boat which will beat the *Bluenose*.'

The first race took place in Halifax on October 17, 1931, and although the *Bluenose* won the race by a very wide margin, the race exceeded the official time limit of six hours and was called 'No Race' by the committee. Two days later in the second race, the *Bluenose* appeared to be racing against the clock and not against the *Thebaud* as she cross the finish line a mere six minutes, eleven seconds ahead of the deadline, with the *Thebaud* following far behind. The next race was much closer, and the *Bluenose* beat her rival across the finish by twelve minutes, thus retaining her title as 'Queen of the Atlantic Fishing Fleet'.

In 1932 the fish markets were depressed and many vessels were left to lie alongside their wharfs rather than put out to sea and return with catches that would bring in little or no money. This was the time when the *Bluenose* started her tour as a showboat. If no money could be made fishing, perhaps she could earn something off her name. She had already become a legend across the country, after her likeness was placed upon the Canadian 50¢ stamp in 1928. She was first to represent the Maritime provinces in the Chicago Exposition of 1933. Smartly painted and outfitted, with her fishermen crew dressed in naval uniforms, she started on a voyage into the Great Lakes. Her welcome to ports like Montreal, Toronto, and Chicago was enthusiastic, for her reputation had preceded her. People looked forward to visiting this popular vessel, and they did it by the thousands. The owners of the vessel helped to pay for the trip by organizing charters and cruises. She wintered in Toronto and spent part of the next season barnstorming various ports on the Lakes.

At the time of the *Bluenose*'s stay in Chicago, there was a race from that city to Mackinac. The *Bluenose* was too large to participate for the Mackinac Cup, but arrangements were made for her to race alongside the event with any other vessels that cared to join. An alternative prize of a 300-pound American cheese was put up for the first vessel to cross the finish line, regardless of size. Twenty-seven boats competed in the 331-mile race to Mackinac, and the *Bluenose* led the fleet across the finish line, winning the token prize.

In 1935, the *Bluenose* crossed the Atlantic Ocean for the first time to attend the Silver Jubilee of King George V and Queen Mary. During the Spithead review of the fleet, Captain Walters was invited to visit the King, whereupon the Monarch presented the Captain with a set of sails from the Royal yacht *Britannia*. The *Bluenose* was also invited to compete in one of the traditional races around the Isle of Wight. Although the *Bluenose* was not designed for yacht racing, she did put up a good show coming in third after Davis's *Westward* and Runciman's *Altair*.

The *Bluenose* left England in September to sail back to Canada, but two hundred miles from Falmouth she encountered a fierce storm, which laid her over and caused considerable damage. The crew and passengers had to work non-stop to move the iron ballast forward in order to relieve the pounding on the stern. Both lifeboats were smashed, the foreboom, mainboom jaws and part of the bulwarks were carried away, and the galley housing was uprooted. The vessel was forced into Plymouth for a thirty-day layover to effect repairs. She then returned, unhampered, to rejoin the fishing fleet in Lunenburg.

In 1938 the last International Fisherman's Cup race was held off Gloucester and Boston. Many realized this would be the last time they would see a race between such vessels. Fishing under sail had all but ended, replaced by motorized vessels. The newspapers stated, 'Power has crowded sail from the fishing fleets. We have seen about the last of the topsails above the headlands. It is all oil today in Nova Scotian fishing ports that used to know the forests of tall spars and towering canvas of the Banks schooner.' Even the *Bluenose* was forced to compete with this new age by having twin diesels installed in 1936 at a cost of $12,000. And most vessels that had competed in the Fisherman's Race were lost, the *Elsie* having sprung a leak and sunk off St Pierre in 1935, leaving her crew to row forty-eight miles to shore. No longer were the big Banks schooners being constructed.

The *Bluenose* motored into Gloucester on October 2, 1938, seventeen years old and showing signs of strain. She was old and her qualities uncertain after so many years at sea. She was most certainly hogged, the bow and stern sagging slightly from the middle. Ten years was usually the normal working life of a salt-banker, after which the boat was abandoned or sold for coastal trade. She spent one week having her engines removed and her gear outfitted and repaired for the race. With her rival of eight years, the *Gertrude L. Thebaud*, she sailed to Boston where the first race was to be held.

The first race was held on October 9 on an eighteen-mile course which was to be circled twice. The *Thebaud* established a good lead on the first round and held onto it, crossing the finish line two minutes, fifty-six seconds ahead of the *Bluenose*. The Canadian vessel had fractured her foretopmast during the race and was forced to douse her jibtop and foretopsails. This was the first of many mishaps that the *Bluenose* encountered during the series. Captain Walters protested that the 'merry-go-round' course was not fit for fishermen. The committee 'tried to mollify the peppery Angus Walters . . . that they were trying to protect the vessels from the dangers of twelve miles off shore.' Walters reminded them that 'the *Bluenose* and the *Thebaud* were accustomed not to waters twelve miles from land, but hundreds, and that the racing committee's concern was not appreciated.' The next race did not occur until the 13th, because the weather had been considered too light. The *Bluenose* found her speed in the lighter airs and drifted across the finish line almost twelve minutes ahead of her rival. During the second half of the race, the *Bluenose* blew her staysail in half and had to replace it with a smaller one until the first could be repaired.

Several days later the next race was staged. In the meantime Ben Pine became ill with sinus trouble and was replaced by Captain Cecil Moulton. The *Thebaud* was taken out of the water because it was found that her old paint was peeling off in giant strips and causing drag. The race on the 20th was run over a smooth sea and the *Thebaud* beat the *Bluenose* by a mile, but they had exceeded the official time limit of five hours, so it was declared 'No Race'.

There was concern that the crew of the *Bluenose* had been shifting ballast between races because it was found that over three hundred ingots had been moved onto the *Bluenose* from the dockside. This activity contravened the regulations under the 'Deed of Gift'. The *Bluenose*'s trim was poor and had been commented upon during the races. Her ballast when built was seventy tons, but after seventeen years at sea had been reduced to about fifty tons. It was common knowledge that the crew had been shifting ballast, but the press got wind of the story and caused an uproar. The head of the Race Committee, Captain Lyons, brushed aside the protest saying, 'I told them to get their boats to the waterline required by the "Deed of Gift" and I don't care how they do it.'

The *Bluenose* was measured and found to be too deep on the waterline, so a lighting plant, air tank, and five tons of oil were removed. The *Bluenose*, now lighter, was found to handle far better. In the light winds of the next race on October 23, she had her second victory over the *Thebaud*, crossing the finish line six minutes and thirty-nine seconds ahead of her rival. On the following day, the fourth race was run on a 35½ irregular triangle off Nahant Bay. The *Thebaud* handled well in the boisterous seas, but the *Bluenose* had trouble with her gear. Her backstay parted and caused her to come up into the wind, leaving the *Thebaud* to speed ahead and take the race by five minutes.

Storm warnings postponed the next race for a day and on October 26 the last race was held. Light winds forced postponement early in the day and finally at 12:05 the gun sounded the start of the race. The *Bluenose* sailed well in the light winds and held onto the lead throughout the race. As she neared the finish her topsail halyard block gave way, but she was too near victory to be stopped and crossed the finish line in 4:04:10, followed by the *Thebaud* in 4:07:00, giving the race and the final championship to the *Bluenose*.

All the Captains were upset with the progress of the series. Captain Moulton asserted, 'The *Thebaud* was not beaten by the *Bluenose*, but by Captain Lyons [head of the Race committee]. He sent us out day after day when there wasn't enough wind for a real race and kept us in port when there was a good wind.' Captain Pine stated that he would not challenge again. 'We took two races sailed in a good breeze. The *Bluenose* took three in weather I don't consider fit for a fisherman's race.' And Captain

Walters told reporters that 'the *Bluenose*, as long as I am Master, will never race again in the United States.'

Captain Moulton, dismayed by the outcome of the races, sent a telegram to Captain Walters: 'I hereby challenge you to a race in Massachusetts waters over your own course in any breeze of twenty-five knots or over, you and I put up $500 each and race vessels under "Deed of Gift". Please advise immediately. Put up or shut up. Winnings go to the winning crew.' Walters replied to the telegram stating that he had 'more important personal things to think about'. And indeed he had, for he was returning home to Nova Scotia to be married. But Walters could not resist a further challenge and he replied the next day to the press: 'Five hundred dollars, bah! that's only poker-chip money those Gloucester people are talking about. Let's get this thing settled for once and for all. Let's race for $5,000, from Boston to Bermuda, around the island and back to Halifax, winner take all. Let them think that over instead of spouting chicken feed.' Neither challenge was accepted.

In the middle of all this the International Trophy was stolen. It had been on display in a Boston department-store window, but when time came to retrieve it, the cup was missing. It was thought to be the work of pranksters, and this was confirmed three days later when the coveted Trophy was found on the steps of a foundling home with a poem attached.

> Here's to Angus, good old sport,
> Whose challenge sort of takes us short.
> Send us a gale that blows at Thirty,
> And we'd bet our shirts on little Gerty.

There also appeared to be some question of the prize money, as it was not available at the Cup presentation. In fact, it took some months to recover it with the help of lawyers, so Walters, sarcastically, ordered the *Bluenose* to return home 'before she too disappeared'. The Trophy was presented and Captain Walters returned to Lunenburg. Both he and his crew were received in grand style, celebrations were held, and the *Bluenose* feats were lauded. The Lunenburgers even replied to the Gloucester poem with one of their own:

> And here's to Gerty, who tried in vain,
> The Fisherman's trophy to regain.
> The Bermuda challenge she also shirks,
> So make better use of your Yankee shirts.

The excitement was not to last. The *Bluenose* was not in demand as a fisherman; she was in debt for payment on her engines; war was brewing in Europe; and attention quickly became focused elsewhere. She sat idle at a Lunenburg wharf until put under the auctioneer's hammer in 1939. But Walters attempted to forestall the inevitable by putting up $7,000 to take full possession of the *Bluenose* and by trying to spark public interest in her preservation. Times were against the old vessel. She was of no use or interest, so in 1942 the *Bluenose* was sold for coastal trading in the Caribbean to the West Indian Trading Company. With World War II at its height, large motorized vessels were prime targets for submarines, but small vessels like the *Bluenose* went by virtually unnoticed. Under the command of Captain Beringers, the *Bluenose* spent the next few years shipping needed supplies to the islands of the West Indies.

Navigation in the postwar Caribbean was tricky at best, systems of buoyage and lights were not in extensive use, and the tides varied greatly. During a dark January night in 1945, the *Bluenose* overran her time and distance. At 7:20 p.m. the lookout yelled that there was water breaking ahead. The warning was too late. Minutes later, the *Bluenose* struck a reef off Ile à Vache, Haiti. She was wrecked beyond repair, her keel was broken, and she was split completely across her breakbeam, with water flooding her interior. The crew managed to lower boats and put ashore safely. The next day they found the *Bluenose* still clinging to the reef. Help was found and they returned to the schooner to salvage what they could. The precious diesel engines were hauled out and brought ashore. Later the *Bluenose* slid off the reef and onto the bottom.

It is perhaps fitting that the *Bluenose*'s oldest rival sank not far away in the Caribbean. The *Gertrude L. Thebaud* rammed a breakwater and sank in the port of La Guadera, Venezuela, in 1948.

In 1963 a Nova Scotian brewery launched a replica of the Bluenose *for use in sales promotion; but it grew in public affection far beyond the huckstering of beer, and now is owned by the Nova Scotia government as a tourism draw and symbol of the province's rich sea heritage. It is likely that when this replica ends its career, a new replica* Bluenose *will slip down the ways, to keep alive a special Canadian memory.*

There was another, earlier Canadian-built ship that caught public fancy; not so much in the way of love, but a good deal in the way of excitement, and respect—for the ship she became, and for the unique and colourful character of the men who drove her.

The Ship That Wouldn't Sail
Joseph Schull

No one in Saint John paid any particular attention when James Smith began to clear ground and stake out a 'lanch' in his sprawling shipyard along the Marsh Creek flats. It was April, 1850, and along New Brunswick's Fundy shore the sight of rising ship-frames was a familiar part of the spring awakening.

James Smith was one of the men who had seen that there was money to be made in ships. He had already built a drogher or two, and everyone supposed that this was to be another. If Smith had anything else in mind he had told no one. He was a close-mouthed man, and he was by no means sure that the idea which possessed him was a good one. Why, he had asked himself a year ago, should the short road to England be the only road for a Canadian ship? Why should timber be the only cargo? Why not design a ship that would carry any cargo anywhere, carry a lot of it, and carry it fast?

Through the winter at his work-bench, with a clutter of delicate tools about him, he had begun to carve out from blocks of clean-grained, flawless wood, the seconds of a mould. Each section, measured with hair-line accuracy, differed from the other, and all of them when put together would make his half-round, the miniature model of a ship's hull. He had it together at last, as spring came round and the ground outside was ready to be cleared for the slipway. In his mind's eye he already saw the ship herself. She looked good to him; good, but a little frightening.

In the museum at Saint John you can still see the half-round that James Smith made that winter. It is darkening a little with age now, and unimpressive to a landsman. You would recognize it as a model of the hull of a sailing-ship. You would say it seemed fat in the middle, square at the stern, and a bit on the thin side underneath. You might notice the sharp inward curve of the bow. Unless you were a very knowledgeable sailor, you would have no idea how the various curves would affect her when she sailed. Even the best of sailors, and even James Smith when he began to build from that model, could not be sure.

'At the eastern end of Saint John,' says a writer of the time, 'a small, swampy river empties its scanty water onto the mud flats of Courtenay Bay at low tide. When the tide is high—and high tide in Saint John sometimes rises twenty-eight feet—mud flats and creek are filled with the waters of the Bay of Fundy. It is the most God-forsaken hole possibly discovered.' This was Marsh Creek, and here in April the 'lanch' was completed— the slipway that would hold the ship while it was building and carry it to the water when finished. Timber was hauled into the yards, workmen began to arrive, the forge was lighted in the blacksmith shop, and the whine of saws mingled with the thud of mauls in the carpentry shed.

Idlers from along the shore drifted down to watch as the keel-blocks were laid, and the timbers bolted home. The visitors were elbowed aside by bustling workmen and ignored by James Smith, but they stayed longer than they had intended. Their eyes grew wide at the size of those timbers swinging down to make the keel. They paced off its length. The ship was to be a hundred and eighty-four feet long, the largest vessel ever built in Saint John.

That was the first of James Smith's surprises for the town. More followed as the stem and stern-posts rose, and the ribs were hoisted on pole-and-tackle. Each rib settled into place along the keel, taller than a house and almost as heavy. Each was a massive, gracefully curving section of wood, made up of many sections fitted together and locked into place by wooden pegs. It was the curve of those ribs that had the watchers open-mouthed as they looked up at the finished skeleton. Timber droghers were fat, capacious, slab-sided, built to smash solidly into the waves and wallow through them. This ship, for all her great mid-section, seemed planned to cleave and glide. She carried the belly of an alderman on the legs of a ballet dancer. She was going to be a box with bows, they said—a huge, unhappy cross between a cargo carrier and a yacht. Many of the watchers were seafaring men themselves. They loved good ships and loathed bad ones, and the more they looked at that gaunt skeleton and imagined her clothed the more they began to dislike her. She was already taking on a personality for them, and she seemed not merely ludicrous but an evil thing.

James Smith was conscious of their feelings, and he heard their talk. And it must have seemed to him, one night in early summer, that the worst forebodings were justified. The ship's frame was completed and the timber for her hull was ready. Workmen had laid down their tools in the evening, expecting to commence the long task of bolting on the inner and outer hulls in the morning. But as darkness came a wind rose. Toward midnight a full gale was sweeping in from the Bay of Fundy. In the shipyard a weird groaning began to rise above the screaming of the wind. It could be heard a long way off, and it brought people running down to the shore, breathless from the wind, still rubbing the sleep from their eyes.

They saw a sight they would long remember. The towering skeleton of the ship, revealed as a pale half-moon broke free of scudding clouds, was a thing alive. Its ribs swayed and moaned before the wind, and sud-denly—sharp on the stroke of twelve, according to the superstitious ones—there was a last loud groan of splintering timber, and the whole enormous structure came crashing to the ground. As James Smith looked at his wrecked creation, the other watchers drew away from him. They drifted out of the yard in muttering groups. There was a ship, they said, that didn't want to be born.

Whatever James Smith felt, he started next day to salvage the work of months. The frames went up again, more strongly anchored than before. Through summer, autumn, and on through the winter whenever they could work, shipwrights fitted the planks of the outer and inner hulls, bolted them to the ribs. The decks were laid, the lower masts were stepped. By the time spring came again, the lower stays and shrouds—the first of the rigging—were in place; and 'James Smith's folly' as the town knew the ship now, was ready for launching.

No one in the town or the country around it was going to miss that spectacle. From dawn on Thursday morning, April 17, 1851, the yard began to fill with excited, sceptical watchers. Later on came the town notables and their wives. James Smith, anxious and preoccupied, ushered them to the launching-platform he had built at the ship's bow. The guests were politely enthusiastic, but their eyes were as sceptical as those of the com-moners crowded along the launching-ways below.

The monster which had been a year in growing now stood lifeless on the stocks, her upper deck level with their feet. 'She was a great, thick lump of a black ship,' one man wrote afterward, 'with tremendous beam, square as a brick fore and aft, with a bow like a savage bulldog.' The great spars of the lower masts, supported by a network of stays and shrouds, rose sixty feet above the decks. The hull was painted dead black, except for a wide white band encircling her at the level of her ports. She gave an impression of enormous strength, of sullen ugliness. The only hint of the dreams which James Smith had for her was the figure-head, the carved image of a famous world traveller set in her bow. The figure looked back from the water toward the town, for the ship was to go stern first down the ways and into the waters of Marsh Creek.

The launching hour neared. The great spring tide of Fundy came rolling in over the mud flats, climbed to twenty-six feet, twenty-seven, twenty-eight. The lady on the platform, chosen to perform the ancient rite, looked at James Smith and he gave her a tight-lipped nod. She raised a bottle of champagne in her hand, smashed it across the bow, and cried out in a voice thin with excitement: 'I christen this ship—*Marco Polo*!'

Spaced along the ways below, workmen brought down their axes on the blocks that held the ship in place. The crowd held its breath, waiting for the first shiver of motion and the surging, smoking rush that would take the monster to the water. But nothing happened. The *Marco Polo* sat where she had grown, a lifeless mass of timber. There was deathly silence, a nervous laugh or two, and then an ominous, rippling whisper ran through the crowd. Here was another warning from this sullen, squatting thing. It did not want to go to sea.

James Smith was already down from the launching-platform. With John Frederickson, his foreman, he was running along the ship's sides, shouting at his workmen. They were missing the high tide. They would have to batter the ship down the ways with a ram of logs rigged on a staging.

The ram slugged at the ship as the water below them dropped its first inches with the ebbing tide. Still there was not a sign of motion. John Frederickson, feverishly inspecting the ways, found nothing forgotten, nothing left to hold her, except one small cleat overlooked by a careless workman. It could not possibly have held that mighty mass, but he knocked it out anyway—and leaped back with a gasp, the mallet falling from his hand. The black sides were shuddering above him, the lifeless wood was a thing in motion, roaring down the ways. The cloud of smoke behind her became a cloud of steam as her stern ran off the foot of the ways. The hull lifted with the first thrust of the water cleaving from her sides, and suddenly *Marco Polo* was a living thing with a will of her own. A great, involuntary cheer burst from the crowd, and turned as quickly to a groan. For the ship, possessing herself now, indifferent to all the plans and hopes of men, had shot across the creek and buried herself in the mud of the far bank. She shuddered a little as her stern burrowed deeper with the ebbing tide. Then she leaned to one side, her masts swept down in a slow arc, and she favoured the people of Saint John with a little mocking bow.

For two weeks after that the population of Saint John was divided into sceptics who laughed and friends who sympathized. James Smith was too busy to care about any of them. He had gathered together every man, mule, drag and shovel he could find, and he was out with them on the far bank of Marsh Creek, digging in the noisome mud. The incoming tides billowed about the prisoned ship, diving the men ashore. Fresh crews followed the ebbing waters back. Tons of new mud had to be shovelled at each return, but the trench along the sides deepened with every back-breaking day. At last James Smith called for a tug. The little *Sea Lion* came puffing up the shallow stream, made fast her hawsers as the men in the mud did their last frantic digging before high tide. The flow began, the tug lifted and turned her head upstream. Water rose about the wooden monster, the hawser tightened, and suddenly a great shout rose from the banks of the creek. *Marco Polo* was stirring. Her masts quivered a little, then came slowly upright as she rolled onto her keel. She shook herself casually, lunged forward with a chuckling gurgle, and walked out into the stream.

She was afloat at last, but she was and always would be a ship under a cloud—a 'hogged ship'. Somehow, in that first plunge from the launching-ways into the mud, she must have wrenched and strained herself. The timbers of her hull had been pulled out of their planned alignment—they must have been. She would never sail now according to the will of her designer. Maybe she'd sail better, James Smith protested—there were stories of ships like that. 'Old wives' tales!' snorted the men who had put up money for the ship. The townspeople laughed and agreed with the backers; but James Smith was going to send his vessel to sea.

She was towed to the rigging-wharf and the riggers came aboard: the men with the sure feet, the deft, gnarled hands, the way with rope and tackle. They swayed up her yards, rode her stays, walked like flies among her soaring shrouds. A wilderness of coiled hemp possessed the deck, dissolved above it into magic symmetry—lifts, stays, braces, halyards, sheets—a forest, a maze, a baffling, beautiful spider-web of rope. The great, jute-covered rolls of the canvas thudded over the side, were broken out, bent on. Tackle-blocks smoked, braces tautened, yards ran up and down. Pulleys, bunt-lines, clew-lines, leaches and gaskets—the numberless fittings to keep rope running and canvas flying—were in place at last, and tried. The ship moved away from the wharf and out into the stream, rigged and ready for sea.

It was time for her cargo now and the first cargo, as always, would be timber. The rafts floated up to her great black sides. Her bow and stern ports gaped open. Slimy and huge, the square-cut baulks swayed up from the water on her tackle. The sweating stevedores ran them in through the ports, fought them into place in the monstrous lower hold with handspikes, cant-hooks and peaveys. The deals and planks followed to stuff her upper holds. Another mountain of timber was lashed above the holds as deck cargo. The ship settled easily into the water, fully loaded at last. And at last the watchers from wharf and shore observed a curious thing. Somehow, at work and in her element, the *Marco Polo*'s ugliness disappeared. She still seemed huge and squat beneath her towering bare masts; and yet there was a rough, hard-hewn something about her that was almost beauty.

Sailing-day approached and the crew came swaggering over the side, tough men all and chancy men, the men for a chancy ship. The day she was to go, all Saint John gathered at the water's edge. James Smith stood among them looking at that creature of his in the stream, watching the tumult on her decks dissolve into tense, ordered quiet. 'Break out the hook'—the first bark of a Bluenose mate drifted from the water to the shore. The anchor heaved from the bottom to the stamping, chanting march of men round the capstan. The tug puffed out from under the *Marco Polo* figure-head. The towing-hawser lifted from the water as the slack was taken up, and the ship began to move. She lurched down the harbour behind the tug, cleared Partridge Island. There was a stirring in her lower yards as the three topsails rose and the fore-topmast staysail was set. They seemed forlorn handkerchiefs amid the bare forest of her spars, but her pace quickened. She began to gain on the tug, the towing-hawser slackened then splashed in the water as it was cast off. The ship was free.

There was a light, quartering wind—it was safe to carry all her kites— and perhaps James Smith had ordered his captain to give this doubting town a defiant show. Suddenly the topgallants blossomed white above the topsails, one by one on each of the masts. The great squares of her foresail and mainsail, forty feet tall, seventy feet across, dropped billowing below the topsails. They swelled, hardened round and full to the heave of men sweating on her halyards. Staysails lifted between each mast. Flying jib, outer jib, inner jib broke at her bow, steadying her, lifting her head as she lunged forward. Above the topgallants the three royals whipped out, grew taut, were sheeted home; and still above them, one by one, a man swayed out on the foot-ropes of the skysail yards. Once, twice, once more the watchers saw the white flash and flutter, the tautening-home of soaring canvas, and the three skysails reached to the mast-peaks for the last whisper of the wind.

Men forgot that great, bluff, ugly stern, still high out of the water in spite of the enormous cargo weighing her down. They forgot the signs and portents, and the secret twist in her spine. That towering, billowing pyramid of canvas held their eyes until it glimmered below the skyline, and lingered in their memories while they lived.

The *Marco Polo* made Liverpool in fifteen days. It was a sensational passage for those time, but it did not impress the Liverpool ship-buyers. They did not like her looks, she was built of Canadian soft wood, and gossip had come ahead of her. Everyone along the waterfront knew the story of her launching and of the hog in her spine.

She obtained one cargo for Mobile, Alabama, went out with it in record time, and returned with a great load of cotton. She was a good-natured, well-behaved ship, reported the men who sailed in her—a mighty work-horse. But no more cargoes came along. The broom went up to her mast-head, indicating that she was for sale. She lay in the Mersey idle, waiting for a buyer—a ship with a sour name.

One pair of sharp blue eyes, however, looked at her hungrily from shore. They belonged to Paddy McGee the rag-picker, a shabby little elf of a dock-side Irishman. Paddy had spent his life on the Liverpool wharves. He knew everybody, and everybody knew him; and he had in his time picked up a great deal more than rags. The story of every ship that came and went through the port was an open book to him. Every snatch of seamen's gossip found its way to his ears. It all helped to make a little money go very far in the business of ship-chandling which he sometimes practised, and it made him a rare hand at bargaining. One morning he walked into the office of *Marco Polo*'s Liverpool agent, and announced that he was prepared to make a modest offer for the hogged ship.

The offer was insultingly low, but it was distasteful to bargain with a rag-picker. There were no other offers, and after all the ship was only a New Brunswick timber drogher. Paddy walked out on to the docks again, the new owner of the *Marco Polo*.

He returned the very next morning with an acquaintance somewhat above him in station. James Baines was in his thirties, an eager, peppery little man whose mother kept a cake-and-sweet shop on Upper Duke Street. Baines, however, had turned from shop-keeping to ships at a very early age. He already owned a small fleet of vessels which he operated, rather precariously, as The Black Ball Line. Money was not plentiful with James Baines, but he had taken some long chances successfully and he could obtain credit when he needed it. He was in the market for another ship, and he had been impressed by the secret excitement bubbling in Paddy over his new possession. He snorted with disgust, however, when the rag-picker pointed to the black ship squatting in the stream.

She was the hogged New Brunswicker, he protested—everybody knew New Brunswickers built bad vessels. And even if she were a good ship, she was a timber drogher. The Black Ball Line was looking for a passenger ship.

The little Irishman endured the protests patiently. Hogging was a strange thing, he said—it sometimes brought with it a queer underwater witchery that made a ship sail better. And would Mr Baines just take another look at the lines of her? Baines looked again, and grew silent as he ran his eyes along that capacious belly, that racing bow. He wanted a ship to carry emigrants to Australia. The gold-fields were opening up out there, and all the world seemed mad to get to them. Paddy knew that well enough. Could it be that he had conceived the idea of converting this monstrous timber drogher to a passenger ship?

It was exactly the idea which Paddy had been nursing; and James Baines' eyes were thoughtful as he turned away from the dock. He returned the next morning with the man who would be known all his life as the man of the *Marco Polo*, and would wear her name on his tombstone when he died. His name was James Nichol Forbes. He was a Scot, thirty-one years old, tall and swarthy. He walked with a lithe roll that carried a shade more than necessary of the seaman's swagger. He had sailed timber droghers from the Saint Lawrence in his younger days, and seen the other seas since then. In ports all round the world, good seamen kindled and the stiffs and hoboes cringed at the mention of Bully Forbes. He was known as a coldly reckless driver who pushed both ships and men a little beyond their limits. But he had made some great voyages and some good profits for The Black Ball Line, and Baines was looking for a new command for him.

At first sight of the lumpish monster riding in the stream, Forbes stiffened with dislike, just as Baines had done. Then he too looked again. The ship was standing high and empty; it was possible to get a hint of her underwater lines. Forbes had already heard the talk of clippers, and knew the theory of speed through cut-away lines. This great box, narrowing so swiftly to a wedge, was certainly no true clipper, but there was something about her which made one think of the word. Abruptly, Forbes lunged forward to collar a boat, motioned Baines into it, and they rowed out to the ship.

Five hours later they returned. Forbes had been over the vessel from stem to stern, from keel to truck, and he looked back at her from shore with the eyes of a lover. The marriage of a man and a ship had been arranged. Paddy McGee got his price from James Baines, and *Marco Polo* went into dry-dock. When she emerged, months later, her bottom wore a glittering copper sheath. Her sides shone white, edged tastefully at the ports with black. The workmen of Saint John who had had a part in her building would have gasped at the transformation in her interior. The rough-timbered holds were now maple-panelled cabins and lounges, connected from deck to deck by wide stairways ankle-deep in red carpet. Rich paintings lined the stairways; red upholstery, glass pillars, mahogany, gilt and silver glistened in her dining-saloon. Everywhere, she was rich and reeking with Victorian splendour—the pride of The Black Ball Line—the most elegant passenger ship in the business. By sailing-time she was the talk of all England, and she had booked nine hundred and thirty passengers for her first voyage to Australia.

Other seamen and shipowners, however, were not impressed by the gaudy change. She was still the *Marco Polo*, the hogged New Brunswicker. If James Baines was mad enough to convert this timber drogher to a floating hotel, that was his affair. He would learn, and Bully Forbes would learn, that it took more than gilt and upholstery to get a ship to Australia ahead of the fast American windjammers and the new steam packets.

Baines heard the talk, and it worried him. He had gone deeply into debt to fit out this monstrous drogher with which his captain had fallen in love, and he was beginning to have troubling afterthoughts. At the banquet which was always held on the eve of the sailing of a new ship, he and Forbes were the targets of a good many thrusts from rival captains. Bets, as always, were flying thick and fast. The owner was not too surprised when he heard Forbes bet Captain Thompson of the steam packet, *Australia*, that he would beat him to Melbourne. Sailing-captains often bet against steam, and sometimes with luck they won. He sat bolt upright, however, when Forbes went on to announce with blunt Scotch matter-of-factness that he would be back in the Mersey with his ship just six months from tomorrow morning. The Scot must have gone mad! Good ships had taken a year to make that world-round passage to Australia and back. For the best of ships eight or nine months was a reasonable passage, and anything less a thing to exclaim over. Forbes was making a fool of himself and of his owner.

The captain, however, took every bet that was offered at the banquet, and he was unrepentant at sailing-time next morning. *Marco Polo* was walking down the harbour, under sail for the first time beneath his hands. The tug had cast off and the worried James Baines had gone ashore, still reproaching his captain for that ridiculous boast. Forbes stood smiling by the helmsman, dreamily savouring the first stir of the timbers beneath him. There seemed already some mysterious intimacy between the swarthy master and his vessel. The waving relatives and the sirens and the cheers were left behind now; captain and ship were alone. Alone with nine hundred and thirty passengers and sixty of the best and toughest seamen in the merchant service. But still alone, for she answered only to him, and he alone was answerable.

Nearly thirty thousand sea miles lay ahead of James Smith's timber drogher. There was no Suez Canal yet, and no Panama Canal. The great horseshoe-shaped route would take her down through the North and South Atlantic, on through the width of the Pacific below two continents, and up again through the Atlantic home. And not only the fortunes of the passengers now, but the reputation of The Black Ball Line, of Bully Forbes and of James Baines depended on the heart which James Smith had built into her.

She ghosted easily down Saint George's Channel, left Cape Clear on her starboard hand, and swung to the south. South and a little west, to clear the bulge of Africa on the seven-thousand-mile leg to the Cape of Good Hope. The timbers shaped on the banks of Marsh Creek whispered smoothly past the Azores, past Madeira and the Canaries. The great square stern rose and fell evenly, the bow bit cleanly into the Atlantic rollers. Passengers left the gilded saloons and lounges. They idled about the deck, beginning to be a little bored as the ship nosed down below the thirtieth degree of latitude and reached for the tropics. She was moving now under the gentle push of trade winds from the northeast.

This was easy sailing. The test would come later. Day after day, as Bully Forbes lounged on the poop beside the helmsman, the passengers looked at him and wondered if he ever really did anything. The indolence did not fool MacDonald, his mate, who had sailed with him before. It didn't fool the sailors. The captain's eyes missed no ripple on the sea. The slightest shift of air was answered by a shift of sail. Soft-voiced orders from the poop, followed by the bellowings of the mate, kept seamen aloft through every hour of their watches. When the wind held steady they were still sent up to check the run of the yards and 'slush them down' with grease to make them run better. The helmsman got a word with a stinging lash in it if he slipped a fraction of a point from his course. Bully Forbes, said the men in the forecastle during their off-watches, was waiting for the big winds but he was letting none of the little ones get away.

The ship came round the shoulder of Africa and rolled slackly in the doldrums for three days. Then the southeast trade winds took her on the beam. Yards came round against the stays to send her slanting south. Canvas climbed in tier on tier to catch the last thrust of the gentle, everlasting breeze. She glided down below the tropic of Capricorn, and into the thirties south. The crew still sweated in the rigging, but the passengers began to bundle up and shiver as they ran below the tropics. The captain still smiled and lounged on the poop. It was tense and tiresome, this search for the little airs, this trapping of every breath that came along. But it had to be done. Meanwhile a man could watch, wait, learn the ways of his ship.

The latitude of thirty-one south fell behind, then thirty-three, and thirty-five. The trade winds were lost to the northward. Canvas hung slack in baffling airs, while the days of that six-month wager ticked away. Then, early one morning, came the first whiff of the westerlies, the great winds that sweep round the bottom of the world.

The captain straightened on the poop, and the ship came alive beneath him and above him. MacDonald's voice boomed out and the men raced for the halyards. The great yards came round square. Whipping canvas billowed forward, hardened out round and full. They were round the Cape of Good Hope, 'running their easting down'. Mainsails, topsails, topgallants, royals and skysails climbed and stiffened in the breeze. Then came the sails she had never worn before—studding sails—the 'suicide suit'. They ran out on great booms beyond the ends of the lower yards, sixty feet above the water, fifty feet out from either side of the ship. And the passengers saw the captain in action at last. They came to the deck, drawn by the commotion above them, shivered at the wind and the long swells driving by the side. Then they looked up, and gasped.

High out over the sea, on the far end of the studding-sail boom, Bully Forbes stood with his cap off and his black hair flying in the wind. The canvas strained out iron-hard before him, the timber of the yards creaked and groaned under the enormous strain. One extra puff, one careless twitch of the helm, could explode the sail, split the boom and send Forbes plunging to the sea. MacDonald grimaced as he watched. It was an old trick of Bully Forbes. He was well enough aware of the pop-eyed passengers, and not averse to impressing his crew. But he was not thinking of them now. He was a seaman in his element, in reckless, exuberant communion with the wind he loved and the ship he trusted.

The ship did not fail him. Day after day he climbed out on that leaping spar, willing her along. Day after day she leaped forward to the great gusts of the westerlies. Her canvas strained to the last thread, her masts groaned and fought against the stays. The endless shriek of cordage, the roaring sigh of cleft water and captured wind tore at men's nerve ends, but the captain drove his ship and the ship responded.

Yards snapped high above and canvas burst like cannon shots, but Forbes had men bending on new sail while the old was cleared away. Day after day the figures mounted in the log. Three hundred and ten miles in twenty-four hours, three hundred and twenty, three hundred and thirty. In great, relishing gulps, the Bluenose timber drogher was eating up the last of her fourteen thousand miles to Melbourne. The hard wind lifted to a gale, but not a stitch of canvas was taken in. For ninety-six hours, as the crew grew sullen under the strain and the passengers scared, the ship drove down the last thirteen hundred and fifty miles of her course. Early on the morning of September 18, 1852, just as the gale showed signs of abating, she raised Port Philip's Head. Two hours later she nosed into Melbourne and she had beaten the steam packet *Australia* by a week.

Not many on board noticed that as she came up the harbour she was flying the police flag. Forbes had ordered the passengers to wait below, and mustered the crew on deck. As *Marco Polo* reached her berth a squad of Melbourne police trooped on board, summoned by the flag, and Bully Forbes pointed to his crew. 'Lock them up,' he said, 'for insubordination.'

There had been no insubordination, and there never was on a ship commanded by Forbes. But there was the lure of the gold-fields, and many a sailor had jumped ship to go to them. Forbes had made a record run to Melbourne but the hardest part of the voyage lay ahead, and he was going to keep his men.

For twenty-one days they stormed and threatened in the custody of the Melbourne police. But by sailing-time on the morning of October 11, 1852, they were all on board again, sober and in comparatively good humour. Forbes had let them want for nothing except the chance to desert, and they knew already they were men of a famous ship. But there was still the captain's boast to live up to, and they were fifteen thousand miles from Liverpool.

Marco Polo moved down the harbour, bound round Cape Horn on the homeward passage. On the twelfth of October she passed Banks Strait. The Auckland Islands fell astern on the seventeenth. *Marco Polo* rolled south and eastward into the latitudes that sailors call 'the roaring forties', south still into the white fifties. It was a bitter, heaving desolation of icy water. Only seamen kept to the decks now. The few homeward passengers shivered on the red upholstery below.

Again the westerlies came on astern, and the ship leaped forward. Evil grey seas towered over her sides and smashed inboard to sweep along the decks as high as a man's head. The sails climbed dirty grey and glazed with ice. Men on the yards were hidden from the decks by blizzards and low-scudding clouds. They slipped on the icy foot-ropes, wheeled in tremendous circles as the mast-peaks answered to the plunging of the ship, leaned far out above the roaring sea to claw home loosened canvas with their frozen fingers. Watches went by uncounted in this world of thundering gloom and tossing spars; sleep was a rare hour snatched in a sodden bunk amid the everlasting thud of waves against the sides.

The fierce winds shifted with an evil cunning, but Forbes tacked with every gust, reached for every gale. Exhausted men began to break. He saw the signs and ordered MacDonald to padlock the sheets, the ropes that might loosen straining sails. For ninety-six hours, standing on the poop with a pistol in each hand, he drove his men to their stations and his ship toward the Horn—three hundred and sixteen miles in one day, three hundred and eighteen the next. The next run dropped to three hundred and six, but that was hardly logged before the wildest gale of all caught them from astern. It drove them three hundred and fifty-three miles in a single day, and sent them round the Horn. There she loomed, the nightmare of all sailors—old Cape Stiff, scowling on the port bow. Then she was abeam, and then astern, and they were reaching northward for the Trades and home.

It was December 26, 1852—Boxing-day in Liverpool. James Baines had left his comfortable fireside and come down to the Salthouse Dock, summoned by an employee who had heard a wild rumour. He was not in a good mood. During the past five and a half months he had wearied of the jokes of rival shipowners. They had never let him forget Forbes' ridiculous boast for the dressed-up timber drogher. Some new jokester must have spread the word that she had been sighted off Holyhead, and it would only bring more ridicule on The Black Ball Line.

He stood looking up the Mersey, unhappily conscious of derisive glances from the idlers around him. There would be no ship coming today, and everyone knew it. Baines turned stiffly away for home, but a sudden incredulous stir made him turn back. Round the bend in the river the topmasts of a vessel were coming into view. As Baines recognized them, they seemed to him the most beautiful sight in the world.

He was looking with the eyes of a shipping magnate, not an artist. His ship was only beautiful when she was driving before a Cape Horn wind. At this moment, dingy with crusted salt, beaten by twenty-nine thousand miles of sea and storm, with all sticks bare, she was sauntering up the Mersey behind a belching tug. And strung between her masts, adding to her ugliness, yelling with vulgar triumph, was a great, flaunting sail-cloth banner. 'Marco Polo', it read, 'Fastest Ship in the World'.

But if the Bluenose won love and the Marco Polo respect, another vessel put its name into Canadian history for the sorrow and sense of loss that surrounded its name. On October 25, 1918, the steamer Princess Sophia struck on Vanderbilt Reef in southern Alaskan waters. At first the situation did not seem threatening; and then a horrifying sequence of events took place which saw the ship, and all in her, go to a frigid death. As the authors of the major study of Sophia's sinking point out, the ship took down with it so many of the promising, gifted, and important people from Canada's north that it is likely the country suffered a grievous blow to an extent not recognized even today.

The Sinking of the 'Princess Sophia'
Ken Coates and Bill Morrison

In the early hours of Friday, 25 October, the north wind howled relentlessly down the Chilkoot Pass, along Lynn Canal, and over Vanderbilt Reef and the ship it had captured. The *Princess Sophia*, though firmly stuck for more than a day, moved with the waves that pounded against it. The grinding of her plates on the reef added to the passengers' apprehension. Because of the power failure, the darkness was total, except for the occasional lantern that marked the preparations being made for the rescue attempt. Captain Locke directed the crew to give out life-jackets, assign passengers to lifeboats, and explain the rescue procedure. Nearby the *King and Winge* had stood watch all night, its engines turning steadily. It had no wireless, so it was unable to maintain contact with the stranded vessel. But its captain, J.J. Miller, felt that at least one ship should stay near the *Sophia* in case of a sudden emergency.

A few miles away, the men aboard the *Cedar*, tossing lightly in the lee of Benjamin Island, prepared for their part in the impending drama. Their plan was simple. The next high tide, due at about 5.00 a.m., would cover Vanderbilt Reef with several feet of water. If the wind abated sufficiently, the *Sophia*'s lifeboats could be lowered and the passengers transferred to safety. There were enough vessels in the vicinity to take all the passengers and crew, and Lowle had arranged for their reception at Juneau. Still, there was nothing routine in taking over 350 people off a stranded ship, particularly in total darkness.

The rescue effort began at 4.00 a.m. Aboard the *Cedar*, Captain Leadbetter weighed anchor and steamed slowly up the channel, bucking intermittent squalls of wet snow and a strong northwest wind that was increasing at times to a moderate gale. The trip took about half an hour. At 4.35 the *Cedar* approached the *Princess Sophia* and the *King and Winge*, which still hovered nearby.

When Leadbetter ordered the *Cedar*'s spotlights turned on the *Sophia*,· the sight was disquieting. The ship hung like a faint image in the snow-filled darkness, the spotlights partially breaking through the snow and spray to reveal details of her structure. Despite the tide, now almost at its peak, she was still helplessly stranded. Her bow was completely out of the water; Leadbetter claimed that he could almost see her keel. The ship was facing south by east, which meant that the wind, now increasing to gale force, was striking her between midship and stern. Nearby, on the *King and Winge*, Captain Miller noted that the *Sophia* was lying 'just as she would be in dry-dock, not a particle of list on'.

Leadbetter soon realized that the rescue attempt would have to be postponed. He circled the *Princess Sophia* several times, taking comfort in the fact that there at least seemed to be no sign of damage. But as the north wind continued to rise, dashing breakers against her hull, Leadbetter, Miller, and Locke all agreed that the planned evacuation was too dangerous, and that though the passengers' position was precarious, they were safer aboard the *Sophia* than they would be in the lifeboats. Leadbetter wired Frank Lowle in Juneau to say that nothing could be attempted until at least dawn.

Daylight came slowly on Friday, 25 October, the weak sun of late autumn penetrating with difficulty through the blowing snow and heavy clouds that hung over Lynn Canal; the north wind showed no sign of abating. By 8.00 a.m. the *Sophia*'s crew had fixed the broken steam pipe and restored electrical power. Captain Locke immediately established radio contact with Leadbetter. The first message he received was from Captain Troup in Victoria. Sent at 9.00 the previous morning, it had been stalled along the line before being passed on to E.M. Miller, wireless operator aboard the

Cedar. Troup had asked, 'Do you think she will back off at next high water?'—an ironic question, given the long night the ship had just passed on the reef.

Leadbetter, Miller, and the other captains anxiously awaited news of the *Sophia*'s condition. The news from Locke was bad, but not as serious as had been feared. Water had entered the forward compartment, but the engine room, fire room, and afterhold remained dry. The exact extent of damage remained unknown, although the limited flooding suggested that the hull was not badly torn.

As he circled the reef, Leadbetter noticed that Locke had again ordered the lifeboats swung out on their davits in anticipation of the rescue attempt. Several of the crew were loading small parcels into them; Leadbetter assumed they were provisions placed there in case of a forced evacuation. The lifeboat covers were still on, in deference to the snow that continued to swirl about the ship. The boats dangled invitingly, seeming to offer safety and freedom to the few passengers who braved the wind to stand on deck. But the hope was false. Below them the breakers crashed over the sharp rocks of Vanderbilt Reef, promising almost certain disaster if they were lowered.

As dawn broke, the passengers aboard the *Princess Sophia* tried hard to keep their spirits up and establish some semblance of normality. The hours dragged on, the sense of danger waxing and waning with the wind. The repeated false starts—Locke's confident assertions that the next high tide would provide the opportunity for escape—added to the tension fuelled by mixed fatalism, frustration, anger, and hope. The cold wind and driving snow kept most of them indoors, but from time to time the waiting rescuers saw a couple venture out on deck and, arm in arm, make their way around the ship. For the watchers, the scene was filled with pathos—endearment contrasting with imminent peril.

While they waited, some of the passengers wrote letters to friends and relatives, mostly messages of hope rather than despair. Auris McQueen wrote to his 'Mama':

> It's storming now, about a 50-mile wind and we can only see a couple of hundred yards on account of the snow and spray . . . .[S]he is now . . . on the rock clear back to the middle and we can't get off. She is a double-bottom boat and her inner hull is not penetrated, so here we stick. She pounds some on a rising tide and it is slow writing, but our only inconvenience is, so far, lack of water . . . I reckon we will be quarantined as there are six cases of influenza aboard. The decks are all dry, and

this wreck has all the markings of a movie stage setting. All we lack is the hero and the vampire. I am going to quit and see if I can rustle a bucket and a line to get some sea water to wash in. We are mightily lucky we were not all buried in the sea water.

The flurry of activity in the waters surrounding the *Sophia* no doubt brought some reassurance to her passengers. Early that morning, the *Sitka*, a small halibut fishing boat, arrived at the scene, and like the others began to circle the reef. Other vessels were kept away by the foul weather. The *Estebeth*, *Peterson*, and *Lone Fisherman* had gone to anchor the previous evening, and now found conditions in the channel too rough to leave their shelters.

Ominously, by mid-morning the wind, already strong, was picking up and shifting to the northwest, so that it struck the *Sophia*'s stern more directly. Soon it was blowing a full gale. The *Cedar*, which had arrived as planned before dawn, was having increasing difficulty maintaining her position near the reef. About 9.00 a.m. Captain Leadbetter moved to the lee of the reef and attempted to find anchor about 500 yards downwind of the *Sophia*. He hoped to run a line to the stranded ship and use it to transfer passengers to safety by way of a breeches buoy. But the effort failed. Twice he cast anchor, and twice it would not hold. He remained at the mercy of the wind.

Watching the *Cedar*'s struggle, Captain Locke realized that the rescue attempt would have to be postponed once more. At 10 a.m. he wired Leadbetter, 'No use, too rough, wait until low water.' Leadbetter replied, 'I cannot make anchors hold, could not row boat to you at present, believe your passengers are perfectly safe until wind moderates, will stand by until safe to make transfer.' Although conditions were getting worse rather than better, the two men believed—they had no other choice—that the passengers were better off aboard the *Princess Sophia* than risking a dangerous transfer across the reef. At 11.30 a.m. Leadbetter wired the decision to Juneau: '*Sophia* resting even keel on high part Vanderbilt Reef, blowing strong northwest wind, will transfer passengers as soon as possible to *Cedar*.'

It was around the same time that E.P. Pond, the photographer on board the *King and Winge*, took his dramatic photographs of the *Princess Sophia* sitting on Vanderbilt Reef. Though badly seasick, Pond managed to capture the helplessness of the ship's situation and the danger she was in. The photos show a heavy swell, and the smoke cutting abruptly off at the ship's funnel indicates the force of the wind. The ship is perfectly level and looks at first glance as though she is steaming safely towards Juneau, but the sharp peak of Vanderbilt Reef just forward of the bow reveals her true situation.

Leadbetter's progress report was only one of many messages exchanged between Juneau and the rescue scene that Friday. With the *Cedar* to relay messages, Frank Lowle in Juneau was able to get regular reports on the condition of the *Sophia*, a welcome change from the confusion of the previous day. For Captain Troup, isolated in his Victoria office, the communication problem eased more slowly. On Thursday the 24th he had ordered Lowle to 'send all possible assistant to *Sophia*'. Lowle had done so, but he did not receive the message until 7.50 the next morning. The tangle in communications up the west coast had all but cut Juneau off from the south, and messages continued to flow in both directions at a frustratingly slow pace.

Early on the morning of the 25th, Lowle received a first-hand report on conditions at Vanderbilt Reef. The *Amy*, its crew without water or food for twenty-eight hours, arrived in Juneau harbour at 7.00 a.m. She had left the *Princess Sophia* the previous evening, had anchored for several hours at Tee Harbour, and had then pushed on to Juneau. Edward McDougall, master of the *Amy*, passed his log on to Frank Lowle, provided a short description of events, and departed in search of a long-overdue meal.

In Juneau Lowle did was he could to help the stricken ship. For the most part he accepted the optimistic forecasts he received from Locke, Leadbetter, McDougall, and others that the *Sophia*'s passengers would soon be removed, probably on Friday afternoon. With that in mind he continued his preparations for their arrival, arranging to have the water, heat, and light in Juneau's abandoned Orpheum building connected and laying on a hot meal for them.

Meanwhile, Captain Troup in Victoria was becoming increasingly frustrated. For a man of action, the lack of precise information and the impossibility of influencing events was maddening. He sent several messages, each one more abrupt, demanding that Lowle let him know the condition of the *Sophia*. On Friday morning he telegraphed: 'You have not replied to my wires. Please make every effort to get suitable boats to *Sophia* for transferring passengers moment it is safe.' Cut off from events in Juneau, and receiving no answer to his enquiries, Troup thought that Lowle might be in Skagway, where he regularly travelled on official business, leaving no one in charge of the necessary preparations in Juneau. He thus wired John Pugh, the US Collector of Customs in Juneau, asking for the assistance of United States ships. His message was answered by an assistant, for Pugh was on board the *Princess Sophia*. The first message from Lowle to Troup did not arrive in Victoria until 12.29 p.m. on the 25th, more than twenty-seven hours after it had been sent. It bore the news that evacuation plans were in place, and asked if transportation could be arranged to bring the passengers south from Juneau after the expected rescue. Troup would rather have learned that the danger had passed and all aboard were safe in Juneau; however, it was encouraging to know that something was being done.

Many along the coast shared Troup's desire for more information. On the morning of 25 October the regional papers carried the first news of the accident. 'Passengers Still on Board' read a page-one headline in the Vancouver *Daily Province*, with a sub-head noting 'Wind in Lynn Canal Prevents Transfer from the *Princess Sophia*'. The story conveyed little of the drama and no sense of the impending tragedy, ending with the comment that the *Sophia* was 'resting easily as far as can be gathered, and there is no danger to the passengers unless the weather becomes worse'. In the article, Captain Troup attempted to sooth worried friends and relatives: 'The passengers are our first consideration, and we have done everything in our power to relieve them, even to the extent of disorganizing our gulf service.' Most newspapers in the coastal towns repeated the optimistic pre-dictions of an early rescue.

Aboard the *Sophia* many of the passengers and crew, realizing that word of the accident must have spread along the Pacific coast and farther, tried to reassure their friends and relatives that rescue was imminent. David Robinson, the wireless operator, telegraphed his mother in East Vancouver, 'Still ashore, all well.' He then passed on the same report for Charlie Beadle, a purser, and for second officer Frank Gosse, third officer Arthur Murphy, and one or two others. There was no time on the wireless for the passengers' messages, and with the exception of Customs Collector Pugh, no one other than the crew was able to send word out. It mattered little, for none of these reports reached its destination.

David Robinson had his hands full with messages to and from Captain Locke. Because of power outages and problems with the storage batteries, the *Princess Sophia* did not communicate directly with the outside world. Robinson sent his messages the short distance to Elwood Miller, wireless operator on the *Cedar*, who the relayed them to Juneau or to Victoria, often by way of other ships. For instance, at 1.00 on Friday afternoon Miller wired a message from Captain Locke to Troup in Victoria, telling him that the ship's bottom was 'badly damaged but not [t]aking water. Unable to back off reef; main steam pipe broken.' At the same time he forwarded a message to Lowle in Juneau: the Captain of the *Sophia* 'cannot do anything until the weather moderates. *Cedar* and *King and Winge* standing by. How is weather at Juneau?' The message reached the *Cedar* at 1.00, was relayed to the *Atlas* at 4:45, and finally arrived in Lowle's hands at 7:30 that night.

But in the end none of this helped. The weather did not improve. Some time before noon the barometer began to drop, and the wind, already strong, blew even harder. Some later estimates put it at 100 miles per hour; by the next morning, the barometer at Sitka had dropped to 28.92 inches–proof of a major storm. Captain Leadbetter, worried about the safety of the *Cedar*, saw that he could be of little use to the passengers of the *Sophia*, and asked Locke if he could withdraw to anchor behind Sentinel Island. He promised to return to Vanderbilt Reef later in the day if the weather im-proved and again stand by during the night. Locke agreed and said he would call at 4.30 p.m. The *Cedar* then ran for shelter, reaching anchorage at 1.45 p.m.

For Robinson and Miller, the wireless operators on the *Princess Sophia* and *Cedar* respectively, the break was a chance for some much-needed rest. Robinson had been battling with power problems on the *Sophia* and struggling to maintain contact with the rescue ships. Both men had been at their posts for nearly forty hours. They agreed to break off contact until 4.30. Robinson returned to work on his batteries. Miller lay down with his headphones on, but could not sleep. After half an hour he tried un-successfully to establish contact with the *Sophia*, and then began to pass a backlog of messages via the *Atlas* to Juneau.

Captain J.J. Miller of the *King and Winge* followed the *Cedar* to anchor and safety. He brought his ship alongside her and shouted up to Leadbetter for instructions. Leadbetter told him that Locke had postponed the transfer of passengers until the weather improved. Later in the afternoon, Captain Miller crossed to the *Cedar* in a dory to discuss the rescue plans with Leadbetter. The two agreed that it was safer to leave the passengers on board the *Sophia* than to risk their lives attempting a rescue in such foul weather. In more than a day on the reef the ship had shifted hardly at all, and they believed that even in the worsening storm it was not likely to shift much more. As J.J. Miller later testified,

> she had stayed on all the morning, which was a higher tide than the afternoon, and she had never moved on the reef, according to the message that the captain of the Cedar had received. As she hadn't moved with the higher tide at the time, I didn't figure she would pound off with the smaller tide, unless the sea would get some enormous hold of her.

On the *Cedar* Leadbetter and Miller laid new plans for the evacuation. As the *Cedar*'s anchor had failed to hold after several attempts, it was agreed that the *King and Winge*, carrying a 350-fathom cable, would anchor to the northwest of the *Sophia*. The cable would be slowly let out until the *King and Winge* got as close as was safely possible to the stranded ship. A line would be run between the two vessels while the *Cedar* stood off to windward, making a lee for the lifeboats. The passengers would be lowered into the *Cedar*'s waiting lifeboats–the *Sophia*'s boats would not be needed–and then be transferred, through the relative calm created by the *Cedar*'s windbreak, to the waiting *King and Winge*. The plan seemed workable, but it required a moderation of the weather.

Through the afternoon everyone waited and watched the skies. Lowle in Juneau and, particularly, Troup in Victoria still had problems getting up-to-date information. Lowle continued his preparations for welcoming the passengers. He contacted the CPR agent in Skagway, Lewis Johnston, asking for a breakdown of the first- and second-class passengers, assuring him at the same time that although the seas were too high to remove them, ships were standing by: 'everybody happy'. Not far from Lowle's office, however, there were those who knew better. The oil tanker *Atlas* left Juneau harbour and retreated to Taku Inlet, a safer sanctuary in a really bad storm. This augured ill for those aboard the *Princess Sophia*.

For Captains Miller and Leadbetter, the darkening skies and gusting winds meant that the rescue would have to wait until the next morning. Around dusk Miller prepared to return to the *King and Winge*. Just as he climbed into his dory, he heard the clatter of the *Cedar*'s wireless. Knowing that Robinson on the *Sophia* had agreed to call the *Cedar* twenty minutes earlier, he assumed that all was well and, without waiting to hear the latest news, continued back to his vessel. His assumption was wrong.

It was 4.50 on the afternoon of Friday, 25 October. 'Ship Foundering on Reef. Come at Once.' The message from Robinson spelled out the impending disaster briefly and dramatically. Elwood Miller scrawled the message on his note pad and passed it to Captain Leadbetter, who immediately prepared to steam to the reef. Miller wired the *Atlas* and asked her to join the rescue, then re-established contact with Robinson on the *Sophia*.

On the *King and Winge*, Captain Miller, just back aboard, heard two whistles from the *Cedar*, indicating that the ship had weighed anchor. Unsure of what Leadbetter was up to, Miller went below for a quick meal, confident that the *Cedar*'s captain would let him know if there was an urgent problem.

Aboard the *Cedar*, wireless operator Miller waited anxiously for further word from the *Princess Sophia*. Nothing came for half an hour. Suddenly, at 5.20 p.m., the static broke with a horrifying message: 'For God's sake hurry,' David Robinson pleaded, 'the water is coming in my room.' There was more, but Miller could not follow it. He told Robinson to conserve his meagre battery power, and to come back on air only if absolutely necessary. 'Alright I will,' Robinson replied, adding anxiously, 'you talk to me so I know you are coming.' That desperate plea for reassurance was the last word heard from the *Princess Sophia*.

Meanwhile, Captain Leadbetter took his ship alongside the *King and Winge* and shouted over the storm to Captain Miller: 'I am going out there to try and locate him. If the snow should clear up, you come out and relieve me.' Miller responded, 'I will give you an hour to find him.' With this understanding and, in the face of the worsening storm, considerable trepidation, Leadbetter ordered his ship out of its shelter behind the island and into the full force of the northwesterly gale.

It was a brave but hopeless effort. As soon as the *Cedar* emerged from its shelter it was battered by heavy seas and snow that blew almost horizontally across the water. Leadbetter knew that his ship was within 500 yards of the Sentinel Island lighthouse, but in the whiteout and the screaming wind he could neither see the light nor hear the blast of the foghorn. For thirty minutes he battled with the weather, pushing very slowly northwards towards Vanderbilt Reef. The farther he went, the greater his danger, since he had only a rough idea of his actual position. Finally, and with great reluctance, he had to admit that the effort was in vain. He wired the *Atlas*: 'We can't do a thing now—thick weather, heavy sea running and gale. Can't even see the *Sophia* or get our boats to her. Will have to stand by until weather clears.'

Now Leadbetter's main concern was the safety of his own ship. Captain Dibrell, the Lighthouse Inspector for that part of the coast, was on board, and advised him either to steam north to Port Hilda or to try and return to his safe anchorage. Leadbetter chose the latter option, though neither was a particularly safe bet. Navigating more by intuition than by observation, he headed south again, sounding his whistle repeatedly in an attempt to locate his position. Eventually J.J. Miller on the *King and Winge*, still at anchor behind the island, heard the whistle and responded repeatedly with his own, guiding the *Cedar* back to safety. The storm and darkness were such that Leadbetter took his ship to within 20 feet of Miller's before he saw her. As he told Miller, 'I was in danger of losing my boat and crew out there tonight.' Much as they hated to do so, they were forced to admit defeat and wait for better weather before renewing the rescue attempt. He wrote in his log: 'terrific seas were running together with a blinding snow storm. Made it impossible to see our bow. Green seas were continually breaking over bow of *Cedar*.'

The two ships rested safe at anchor, their captains desperate to learn the fate of the *Princess Sophia*. Frustrated by his inability to act, Leadbetter wired the *Atlas*: 'Attempted to reach *Sophia* five p.m. blinding snow storm, could not make her. Will advise you soon as weather permits. Blowing a gale and snow.' Others in the area, though unaware of the present emergency on the *Sophia*, feared for the safety of those aboard her. J.P. Davis, master of the *Estebeth*, had passed much of the day circling Vanderbilt Reef, but, like the others, he had headed for shelter as conditions deteriorated. After dragging anchor several times behind Mab Island, he decided to retire further to the safety of Bridget Cove for the evening. At 7.00 p.m. he recorded that a heavy blizzard had descended on the region, obscuring all vision and making navigation all but impossible. He noted in his log book, 'God help those aboard the wreck.' But by that time it was too late.

Among the *Sophia*'s passengers the tension had mounted throughout the morning and afternoon. The repeated delays in the rescue effort, the increasing wind and snow, and the disappearance of their rescuers to shelter added to their anxiety. They were not poised by the lifeboats, however, nor did all of them have life-jackets on. It was obvious that rescue would be delayed, and since all aboard believed that the ship was secure on the reef, there was no sense of acute peril.

A few minutes before 4.50 p.m., when Robinson wired his first desperate message to the *Cedar*, the final disaster struck. For nearly forty hours the *Princess Sophia* had sat firmly wedged on Vanderbilt Reef, her stern pointed approximately north into the wind and her bow in the general direction of Juneau. Now the wind and waves began to lift the stern off the reef. Under their force the *Sophia* rose, then swung slowly around in a 180-degree turn, as if on a pivot. The weight of the ship as it turned ground the rocks beneath it 'white . . . as smooth as a silver dollar'. Now her bow faced up the channel, into the storm, and the *Princess Sophia* began inexorably to move off the reef into deep water. As she began to turn, passengers and crew ran to the lifeboats. Several were launched, others partly lowered, and a number of passengers clambered into them.

Slowly the *Sophia* turned and then, twisting and grinding, slid backwards off the reef. The rocks ripped gaping holes in her hull, tearing out virtually the entire bottom. Heavy bunker oil poured into the sea and frigid water rushed in, flooding the engine and boiler rooms. The boilers exploded, devastating the lower decks. A number of passengers who had sheltered from the storm below decks were killed by the explosion and the flying debris. Portholes were shattered, allowing the sea to enter even faster. The explosion pushed upwards as well, blowing off part of the deck. As the ship settled and began to slide beneath the waves, the wounds in her hull releasing thousands of gallons of oil into the sea, the dark, cold waters of Lynn Canal reached up to claim their victims. In a matter of minutes—just long enough for Robinson to send his last, panicked message—the water had reached the pilot house. And then the entire ship was engulfed.

The exact sequence of events aboard the *Princess Sophia* that dark afternoon will never be precisely known. Some of the passengers and crew were dressed for an evacuation, and many were wearing life-jackets. Others, however, were in their cabins, some even in bed. Clearly Captain Locke had not called a general alert, and there was no planned abandonment of ship underway at the time she sank. The uneven preparation shows how quickly the final crisis had developed.

Many of the passengers were caught unawares. Ilene Winchell had remained in her stateroom with Sarah O'Brien, but some of her belongings were scattered about the ship: her pocketbook was found in a man's coat and—here was the stuff to titillate rumour-mongers—her baggage was found in another man's room. The rest of the O'Brien family were separated in the chaos. Louise Davis was trapped between the saloon and the social hall. W. Lidgett, second cook on the WP&YR steamer *Yukon*, grabbed 4-year-old Sidney Smith and in a desperate attempt to save the child from the rising water, hoisted him onto his shoulders. They died together. Some parents tied their children with lengths of rope to the additional 'flotation devices' that had been provided. The children either drowned or suffocated.

Many seemed entirely unprepared. Several children were found carefully tucked in their beds. Five people, perhaps confused by the noise and tumult, were found in the washrooms, fully dressed. In all there were almost a hundred people trapped below decks. The reason is not to ascertain. There was, after all, half an hour between the first SOS, at 4.50 p.m. and Robinson's last despairing plea at 5.20. Most of the watches found on the bodies had stopped around 6.50, or 5.50 Alaska time, indicating that another half hour passed between the last message at 5.20 and the time when the watches were stopped by oil and sea-water. This evidence suggests that it took as much as an hour for the *Princess Sophia* to sink: first the tide and waves

gradually lifting her stern so that she bumped on the rocks, then the terrifying pivot so that her position on the reef was reversed, then the slow
slide backwards. With thirty minutes, and possibly as much as an hour,
to get on deck, it is difficult to understand why anyone was found in
a stateroom. Perhaps the boilers exploded before the ship sank, trapping
people below. It seems that Captain Locke either left the order to abandon
ship until the last moment, or never gave it at all. Over the previous two
days there had been several false alarms; perhaps those below deck believed
the shifting of the ship's position was no cause for alarm. Yet at 4.50 it
must have been evident that they were in grave trouble. It has been suggested
that some people realized they were doomed, and composed themselves
calmly, in their cabins, for the end–but such resignation is rare in human
nature. This part of the episode is the greatest mystery of the disaster.

It is clear, however, that the majority of the passengers had feared the
worst. These may have been the ones who had been seen on deck many
times, ready to take to the lifeboats with or without Captain Locke's order.
Those who did get off the ship were, almost without exception, wearing
life preservers. Several of them had evidently made preparations in expectation of the worst. Lulu Mae Eads, the former 'Queen of the Klondike',
had placed all her jewels–later valued at some $5,000–in a chamois bag
and strung it around her neck. Like her, most people had their valuables
with them, usually in a coat pocket. Several women had dressed in overalls,
abandoning fashion in favour of protection against the frigid ordeal they
faced. John Maskell tucked his will and some last-minute letters into his
pocket; Auris McQueen carefully pocketed a letter to his mother. Yet there
was no organized evacuation. Several of the lifeboats were lowered, but
later examination of the davits by divers suggested that this was done in
the final desperate seconds, as the *Sophia* slid from her resting place into
the sea.

As the ship started to sink many aboard panicked, either jumping directly
into the water or scrambling into one of the few lifeboats freed from the
davits. Most surely paused for at least a second to consider the odds. To
stay on the ship meant certain death, but their chances in the sea were
little better. Visibility in the driving snow was scarcely twenty feet, and
the shrieking wind and the crash of the waves breaking against the doomed
vessel emphasized their peril. All semblance of order lost, passengers and
crew jostled at the rail—mothers separated from children, husbands from
wives. Now, singly at first, and then in larger numbers as the *Sophia* began
to slide down, people leapt off the deck. What they could not see was

the bunker oil pouring from the shattered hull, covering the water with a viscous mass that already stretched many feet from the reef.

Death came quickly for most who jumped. The water was bitterly cold. Jack London, in his most famous story, captured the essence of a plunge into the north Pacific:

> The water was cold–so cold that it was painful. The pang, as I plunged into it, was as quick and sharp as that of fire. It bit to the marrow. It was like the grip of death. I gasped with the anguish and shock of it, filling my lungs before the life-preserver popped me to the surface.

This natural gasping reflex filled the mouths and lungs of the victims with oil congealed by the cold. Blown by the spray and the wind, it stuck to clothes, weighing them down. Those who may have made it into the lifeboats were no better off, for as the captains of the rescue ships had predicted, the boats were immediately swamped on the reef, throwing their human cargo into the water. The two wooden lifeboats capsized and floated upside down; the eight steel ones sank. The extra flotation devices–simply hollow rectangular wooden buoys with ropes attached to them–were useless; the idea that people could cling to them until they were rescued was practical in the Caribbean, perhaps, but absurd in the Lynn Canal. One of these devices was later found smashed on the rocks of Lincoln Island with the bodies of four women tied to it. Mercifully, whether by drowning or choking and suffocating on the oil, within a few minutes nearly all were dead. Some were in the steel coffin that the *Sophia* had become; other floated inert in their life-preservers, an oily mass coating their lungs, mouths, and nostrils. The howl of the storm echoed over Vanderbilt Reef. The *Princess Sophia* was gone, only a few feet of its forward mast visible above the water.

Some had behaved heroically in those last moments. James Kirk of Dawson, travelling in charge of Herb McDonald's horses, had been heading for Vancouver to consult a specialist about his eyes. A native of Wentworth in Cumberland County, Nova Scotia, he was 50 in 1918, but apparently still a strong swimmer. During the *Sophia*'s last moments, he tied himself to a younger man, wrist-to-wrist, evidently in an attempt to save him from drowning. The newspapers later acclaimed him as 'one of the most heroic, if not the most heroic man, of the *Sophia* wreck'.

And at least one man probably survived those first few moments after the ship went down. Frank Gosse, the ship's second officer, clambered into a life boat that somehow did not swamp, but made it to shore. The boat grounded, and the first rescuers on the scene claimed to have seen footprints leaving it. Gosse, they speculated, might have landed safely and, in climbing the rocks to shelter, slipped and cut his head; it was badly gashed, and he was found with his coat covering the wound. Perhaps he had lain down to wait for rescue, and died of exposure. Others claimed that no one could have made it to shore, that the footprints belonged to rescuers, and that his body had floated to shore with the rest. But if Gosse did not make it to safety, he likely came closer to doing to than anyone else.

In fact, there was one survivor. An English setter–who had owned it was later hotly debated, though it likely belonged to Captain Alexander–did get to shore. Half starved and covered with oil, the dog must have swum to Tee Harbour, eight miles from the reef. From there it struggled another four miles to Auk Bay, where residents discovered it, terrified but alive, two days later.

Unaware of the catastrophe, Lowle and Smeaton at Juneau persevered in planning for a rescue that would never happen. Knowing only that the weather had deteriorated, Lowle tried again to contact the *Princess Sophia* and Troup in Victoria. The same evening he received messages from both. Troup's had originated a full day earlier, the one from Locke, sent via the *Cedar*, was six and a half hours old. If Lowle was out of touch with events, Troup was even more so. In the early hours of 26 October, just after midnight, he received a wire from Captain Locke: 'Steamer *Cedar* and three gas boats standing by unable to take off passengers account strong northerly gale and big sea running–ship hard and fast on the reef with bottom badly damaged but not [t]aking water. Unable to back off reef. Main steam pipe broken–disposition of passengers normal.' By the time Troup received it, they were all dead.

There are other ships whose stories could be retold, or deserve to be: the Half Moon *of Henry Hudson; Cartier's* La Grande Hermine; *Vauquelin's* Aréthuse; *Mulcaster's* Royal George; *the RCN's* Haida *and* Labrador; *the indomitable coastal steamers of Newfoundland and Labrador, or the ships of the B.C. Ferry System. All are part of a tapestry of storytelling that deserves to be rewoven far more than has been attempted here.*

c h a p t e r   s i x

Going It Alone

In the long course of Canadian maritime history there have been some who
have chosen to make a solitary acquaintance with the sea, or at least with
a few companions, if any, rather than the press of a large ship's company.
The first man to sail alone around the world, Captain Joshua Slocum of Westport,
Nova Scotia, came to such a solitary business late in life. At the turn of the
century he could not find work as a sailing vessel captain. Given a crumbling
little sloop as a gift, he rebuilt the boat and sailed it singlehandedly around
the world. The boat's name was Spray, and her story and name were to beome
legend. The following account of the passage of the Spray from Gibraltar to
Brazil gives an insight into the self-reliance and skill that made Slocum's name
a byword for such qualities amongst seamen.

Sailing Alone Around the World
Joshua Slocum

MONDAY, August 25 [1895], the *Spray* sailed from Gibraltar, well repaid for whatever deviation she had made from a direct course to reach the place. A tug belonging to her Majesty towed the sloop into the steady breeze clear of the mount, where her sails caught a volant wind, which carried her once more to the Atlantic, where it rose rapidly to a furious gale. My plan was, in going down this coast, to haul offshore, well clear off the land, which hereabouts is the home of pirates; but I had hardly accomplished this when I perceived a felucca making out of the nearest port, and finally following in the wake of the *Spray*. Now, my course to Gibraltar had been taken with a view to proceed up the Mediterranean Sea, through the Suez Canal, down the Red Sea, and east about, instead of a western route, which I finally adopted. By officers of vast experience in navigating these seas, I was influenced to make the change. Longshore pirates on both coasts being numerous, I could not afford to make light of the advice. But here I was, after all, evidently in the midst of pirates and thieves! I changed my course; the felucca did the same, both vessels sailing very fast, but the distance growing less and less between us. The *Spray* was doing nobly; she was even more than at her best; but, in spite of all I could do, she would broach now and then. She was carrying too much sail for safety. I must reef or be dismasted and lose all, pirate or no pirate. I must reef, even if I had to grapple with him for my life.

I was not long in reefing the mainsail and sweating it up—probably not more than fifteen minutes; but the felucca had in the meantime so shortened the distance between us that I now saw the tuft of hair on the heads of the crew—by which, it is said, Mohammed will pull the villains up into heaven—and they were coming on like the wind. From what I could clearly make out now, I felt them to be the sons of generations of pirates, and I saw by their movements that they were now preparing to strike a blow. The exultation on their faces, however, was changed in an instant to a look of fear and rage. Their craft, with too much sail on, broached to on the crest of a great wave. This one great sea changed the aspect of affairs suddenly as the flash of a gun. Three minutes later the same wave overtook the *Spray* and shook her in every timber. At the same moment the sheet-strop parted, and away went the main-boom, broken short at the rigging. Impulsively I sprang to the jib-halyards and down-haul, and instantly downed the jib. The head-sail being off, and the helm put hard down, the sloop came in the wind with a bound. While shivering there, but a moment though it was, I got the mainsail down and secured inboard, broken boom and all. How I got the boom in before the sail was torn I hardly know; but not a stitch of it was broken. The mainsail being secured, I hoisted away the jib, and, without looking round, stepped quickly to the cabin and snatched down my loaded rifle and cartridges at hand; for I made mental calculations that the pirate would by this time have recovered his course and be close aboard, and that when I saw him it would be better for me to be looking at him along the barrel of a gun. The piece was at my shoulder when I peered into the mist, but there was no pirate within a mile. The wave and squall that carried away my boom dismasted the felucca outright. I perceived his thieving crew, some dozen or more of them, struggling to recover their rigging from the sea. Allah blacken their faces!

I sailed comfortably on under the jib and fore-staysail, which I now set. I fished the boom and furled the sail snug for the night; then hauled the sloop's head two points offshore to allow for the set of current and heavy rollers toward the land. This gave me the wind three points on the starboard quarter and a steady pull in the headsails. By the time I had things in this order it was dark, and a flying-fish had already fallen on deck. I took him below for my supper, but found myself too tired to cook, or even to eat a thing already prepared. I do not remember to have been more tired before or after in all my life than I was at the finish of that day. Too fatigued to sleep, I rolled about with the motion of the vessel till near midnight, when I made shift to dress my fish and prepare a dish of tea. I fully realized now, if I had not before, that the voyage ahead would call for exertions ardent and lasting. On August 27 nothing could be seen of the Moor, or his country either, except two peaks, away in the east through the clear atmosphere of morning. Soon after the sun rose even these were obscured by haze, much to my satisfaction.

The wind, for a few days following my escape from the pirates, blew a steady but moderate gale, and the sea, though agitated into long rollers, was not uncomfortably rough or dangerous, and while sitting in my cabin I could hardly realize that any sea was running at all, so easy was the long, swinging motion of the sloop over the waves. All distracting uneasiness and excitement being now over, I was once more alone with myself in the realization that I was on the mighty sea and in the hands of the elements. But I was happy, and was becoming more and more interested in the voyage.

Columbus, in the *Santa Maria*, sailing these seas more than four hundred years before, was not so happy as I, nor so sure of success in what he had undertaken. His first troubles at sea had already begun. His crew had managed, by foul play or otherwise, to break the ship's rudder while running before probably just such a gale as the *Spray* had passed through; and there was dissension on the *Santa Maria*, something that was unknown on the *Spray*.

After three days of squalls and shifting winds I threw myself down to rest and sleep, while, with helm lashed, the sloop sailed steadily on her course.

September 1, in the early morning, land-clouds rising ahead told of the Canary Islands not far away. A change in the weather came next day: storm clouds stretched their arms across the sky; from the east, to all appearances, might come a fierce harmattan, or from the south might come the fierce hurricane. Every point of the compass threatened a wild storm. My attention was turned to reefing sails, and no time was to be lost over it either, for the sea in a moment was confusion itself, and I was glad to head the sloop three points or more away from her true course that she might ride safely over the waves. I was now scudding her for the channel between Africa and the island of Fuerteventura, the easternmost of the Canary Islands, for which I was on the lookout. At 2 p.m., the weather becoming suddenly fine, the island stood in view, already abeam to starboard, and not more than seven miles off. Fuerteventura is twenty-seven hundred feet high, and in fine weather is visible many leagues away.

The wind freshened in the night, and the *Spray* had a fine run through the channel. By daylight, September 3, she was twenty-five miles clear of all the islands, when a calm ensued, which was the precursor of another gale of wind that soon came on, bringing with it dust from the African shore. It howled dismally while it lasted, and though it was not the season of the harmattan, the sea in the course of an hour was discoloured with a reddish-brown dust. The air remained thick with flying dust all the afternoon, but the wind, veering northwest at night, swept it back to land, and afforded the *Spray* once more a clear sky. Her mast now bent under a strong, steady pressure, and her bellying sail swept the sea as she rolled scuppers under, courtseying to the waves. These rolling waves thrilled me as they tossed my ship, passing quickly under her keel. This was grand sailing. September 4, the wind, still fresh, blew from the north-northeast, and the sea surged along with the sloop. About noon a steamship, a bullock-drogher, from the river Plate hove in sight, steering northeast, and making bad weather of it. I signalled her, but got no answer. She was plunging into the head sea and rolling in a most astonishing manner, and from the way she yawed one might have said that a wild steer was at the helm.

On the morning of September 6 I found three flying-fish on deck, and a fourth one down the fore-scuttle as close as possible to the frying-pan. It was the best haul yet, and afforded me a sumptuous breakfast and dinner.

The *Spray* had now settled down to the trade-winds and to the business of her voyage. Later in the day another drogher hove in sight, rolling as badly as her predecessor. I threw out no flag to this one, but got the worst of it for passing under her lee. She was, indeed, a stale one! And the poor cattle, how they bellowed! The time was when ships passing one another at sea backed their topsails and had a 'gam', and on parting fired guns; but those good old days have gone. People have hardly time nowadays to speak even on the broad ocean, where news is news, and as for a salute of guns, they cannot afford the powder. There are no poetry-enshrined freighters on the sea now; it is a prosy life when we have no time to bid one another good morning.

My ship, running now in the full swing of the trades, left me days to myself for rest and recuperation. I employed the time in reading and writing, or in whatever I found to do about the rigging and the sails to keep them all in order. The cooking was always done quickly, and was a small matter, as the bill of fare consisted mostly of flying-fish, hot biscuits and butter, potatoes, coffee and cream—dishes readily prepared.

On September 10 the *Spray* passed the island of St Antonio, the north-westernmost of the Cape Verdes, close aboard. The landfall was wonderfully true, considering that no observations for longitude had been made. The wind, northeast, as the sloop drew by the island, was very squally, but I reefed her sails snug, and steered broad from the highland of blustering St Antonio. Then leaving the Cape Verde Islands out of sight astern, I found myself once more sailing a lonely sea and in a solitude supreme all around. When I slept I dreamed that I was alone. This feeling never left me; but, sleeping or waking, I seemed always to know the position of the sloop, and I saw my vessel moving across the chart, which became a picture before me.

One night while I sat in the cabin under this spell, the profound stillness all about was broken by human voices alongside! I sprang instantly to the deck, startled beyond my power to tell. Passing close under lee, like an apparition, was a white bark under full sail. The sailors on board of her were hauling on ropes to brace the yards, which just cleared the sloop's mast as she swept by. No one hailed from the white-winged flier, but I heard some one on board say that he saw lights on the sloop, and that he made her out to be a fisherman. I sat long on the starlit deck that night, thinking of ships, and watching the constellations on their voyage.

On the following day, September 13, a large four-masted ship passed some distance to windward, heading north.

The sloop was now rapidly drawing toward the region of doldrums, and the force of the trade-winds was lessening. I could see by the ripples that a countercurrent had set in. This I estimated to be about sixteen miles a day. In the heart of the counter-stream the rate was more than that setting eastward.

September 14 a lofty three-masted ship, heading north, was seen from the masthead. Neither this ship nor the one seen yesterday was within signal distance, yet it was good even to see them. On the following day heavy rain-clouds rose in the south, obscuring the sun; this was ominous of doldrums. On the 16th the *Spray* entered this gloomy region, to battle with squalls and to be harassed by fitful calms; for this is the state of the elements between the northeast and the southeast trades, where each wind, struggling in turn for mastery, expends its force whirling about in all directions. Making this still more trying to one's nerve and patience, the sea was tossed into confused cross lumps and fretted by eddying currents. As if something more were needed to complete a sailor's discomfort in this state, the rain poured down in torrents day and night. The *Spray* struggled and tossed for ten days, making only three hundred miles on her course in all that time. I didn't say anything!

On September 23 the fine schooner *Nantucket* of Boston, from Bear River, for the river Plate, lumber-laden, and just through the doldrums, came up with the *Spray*, and her captain passing a few words, she sailed on. Being much fouled on the bottom by shellfish, she drew along with her fishes which had been following the *Spray*, which was less provided with that sort of food. Fishes will always follow a foul ship. A barnacle-grown log adrift has the same attraction for deep-sea fishes. One of this little school of deserters was a dolphin that had followed the *Spray* about a thousand miles, and had been content to eat scraps of food thrown overboard from my table; for, having been wounded, it could not dart through the sea to prey on other fishes. I had become accustomed to seeing the dolphin which I knew by its scars, and missed it whenever it took occasional excursions away from the sloop. One day, after it had been off some hours, it returned in company with three yellowtails, a sort of cousin to the dolphin.

This little school kept together, except when in danger and when foraging about the sea. Their lives were often threatened by hungry sharks that came round the vessel, and more than once they had narrow escapes. Their mode of escape interested me greatly and I passed hours watching them. They would dart away, each in a different direction, so that the wolf of the sea, the shark, pursuing one, would be led away from the others; then after a while they would all return and rendezvous under one side or the other of the sloop. Twice their pursuers were diverted by a tin pan, which I towed astern of the sloop, and which was mistaken for a bright fish; and while turning, in the peculiar way that sharks have when about to devour their prey, I shot them through the head.

Their precarious life seemed to concern the yellowtails very little, if at all. All living beings without doubt are afraid of death. Nevertheless, some of the species I saw huddle together as though they knew they were created for the larger fishes, and wished to give the least possible trouble to their captors. I have seen, on the other hand, whales swimming in a circle around a school of herrings, and with mighty exertion 'bunching' them together in a whirlpool set in motion by their flukes, and when the small fry were all whirled nicely together, one or the other of the leviathans, lunging through the centre with open jaws, take in a boat-load or so at a single mouthful. Off the Cape of Good Hope I saw schools of sardines or other small fish being treated in this way by great numbers of cavally-fish. There was not the slightest chance of escape for the sardines, while the cavally circled round and round, feeding from the edge of the mass. It was interesting to note how rapidly the small fry disappeared; and though it was repeated before my eyes over and over, I could hardly perceive the capture of a single sardine, so dexterously was it done.

Along the equatorial limit of the southeast tradewinds the air was heavily charged with electricity, and there was much thunder and lightning. It was hereabout that I remembered that, a few years before, the American ship *Alert* was destroyed by lightning. Her people, by wonderful good fortune, were rescued on the same day and brought to Pernambuco, where I then met them.

On September 25, in the latitude of 5° N., longitude 26° 30' W., I spoke the ship *North Star* of London. The great ship was out forty-eight days from Norfolk, Virginia, and was bound for Rio, where we met again about two months later. The *Spray* was now thirty days from Gibraltar.

The *Spray*'s next companion of the voyage was a swordfish that swam alongside, showing its tall fin out of the water, till I made a stir for my harpoon, when it hauled its black flag down and disappeared. September 30, at half-past eleven in the morning, the *Spray* crossed the equator in longitude 29° 30′ w. At noon she was two miles south of the line. The southeast tradewinds, met, rather light, in about 4° N., gave her sails now a stiff full breeze, sending her handsomely over the sea toward the coast of Brazil, where on October 5, just north of Olina Point, without further incident, she made the land, casting anchor in Pernambuco harbour about noon: forty days from Gibraltar, and all well on board. Did I tire of the voyage in all that time? Not a bit of it! I was never in better trim in all my life, and was eager for the more perilous experience of rounding the Horn.

Another Canadian sailing vessel captain, John V. Voss, equally down on his luck a few years later, bought a West Coast native log canoe and set it up as a three-masted little schooner, with a small cabin. Named the Tilikum, *it sailed under Voss's hand westward from Victoria, British Columbia, to England, and survives today in the Maritime Museum of British Columbia in Victoria near another epic little circumnavigator, the sloop* Trekka. *But* Tilikum's *voyages were not without incident that tested the mettle of both Voss and his log canoe, as Voss's account relates.*

To the Australian Continent
John V. Voss

On October 20th Mr Luxton came to me and said, 'Look here, John, I have got a good seaman to take my place for the run with you to Sydney, and if you are willing to take him along I propose to take passage on a steamship, and on your arrival there I will join you again and complete the voyage, as I am satisfied now that the *Tilikum* is quite able to make it.'

I accepted his proposal, and the next morning my new mate came on board. By the looks of him he appeared to be what he later on proved himself, a first-class seaman. His name was Louis Begent, aged thirty-one, a native of Louchester, Tasmania. I told Begent to go to work and get the boat ready for sea, saying that we were going to sail during the afternoon. However, having made quite a few friends in Fiji, we did not get away till the following afternoon at three o'clock. Captain Clark was good enough to give us a tow out as far as the lighthouse. An hour later he turned back with his launch, and we, with a moderate south-easterly breeze, shaped our course for Sydney, a distance of about eighteen hundred miles. Just about sunset, about seven miles outside the bay, we got into a channel between two islands, and as this looked very dangerous for navigation, I ran close to a beach in smooth water and anchored.

The following morning, at daybreak, when we were in the act of getting under sail again, we found that our anchor was foul of the bottom, and were therefore unable to get it up. My mate offered to dive down to clear it, but as the water was full of sharks I cut the anchor rope instead, and with a fresh easterly breeze we steered again on our westerly course. The wind kept fresh and the weather clear until the morning of the 27th, when the sky became cloudy, and during the day the wind freshened up to a strong breeze. At ten o'clock that night, I took in the foresail and spanker, and under the mainsail and staysail, with a strong easterly wind, and steering south-west the *Tilikum* went along quite comfortably, now and then taking over a little water, but nothing to speak of.

It was my watch on deck from eight till twelve, and about half an hour before midnight the compass light went out. As the night was quite clear, with a good many stars shining brightly in the south-west, I picked out one of the stars nearly ahead of the boat and steered by it till my watch came to an end, when I called my mate, who got up and took my place at the rudder. I told him to keep the boat going by the star ahead till the light was fixed up. I then took the box, which contained the compass and light, down to the cabin. My mate was well able to keep the canoe on her course by the stars, so there was no particular hurry about the compass, and instead of getting the lamp lit at once, I lit a cigar for myself, another for my mate, and passed it out to him. I then set to work on the compass light. While I was thus employed my mate was telling me how he enjoyed the sailing in the *Tilikum* and how he would like to make the trip to London in her.

'If we keep this wind,' he said, 'we will be in Sydney in time for the Melbourne Cup Race. I expect my brother-in-law to be in Melbourne by that time, perhaps you know him? His name is Castella, and he is in command of the American ship *Hawaiian Island.*'

'I am well acquainted with Captain Castella and his wife,' I answered. (The ship in question was at that time the largest and finest steel ship under the American flag.) After that I became very much interested in my mate, and for a minute forgot all about the compass, till he said, 'It is getting cloudy ahead of us, so will you pass the compass out?'

While were were chatting away the *Tilikum* went along at her best, answering her helm beautifully. I had lit the lamp and handed the binnacle out to my mate, who, for a second, let go the tiller in order to place it in front of him on the seat of the cockpit, and just as he put the binnacle back in its place, I saw a large breaking sea coming up near the stern of the boat. Knowing by the appearance of the sea that it was a bad one, I shouted loudly, 'Hold on'; but before I had the words out of my mouth the breaker had struck us.

I had braced myself in the cabin door to keep the water out, but when the sea struck it knocked me down. However, I was up in a second to see if any damage had been done on deck. I could not see my mate, and the boat was just about half-way round coming up to the wind. I peered forward, thinking that my mate was getting the sea anchor out or doing some other kind of work, but he was not to be seen. I shouted, but got no answer. I knew then that he was overboard, and of course that he must be to windward, as the boat had been going very fast, and therefore must have left him some distance astern ere she came to the wind. To try and beat back to where he had gone overboard was an impossible task owing to the strong wind and large seas. Therefore I put the helm hard down, lowered the sails, and put the sea anchor out to prevent the boat drifting too much. Thinking that he might be able to swim to the boat, and that this was the only way his life could be saved, I continued calling him by name, but got no reply. All my shouting and calling, which I kept up for a long time, was in vain. Nothing but the sound of the wind, and now and then a breaking sea, was to be heard. Ten minutes passed; twenty minutes; thirty minutes; an hour, and still no sign of my unfortunate companion. Then I knew that he was dead.

The loss of my mate was partly due to negligence, as I always had a life-line, one end of which was fastened to the boat; the other end to be put round the helmsman's body. I told him, when he first came on board, never to neglect to put that life-line around himself whenever he took the rudder, as I always did, and if he had followed my advice he may have gone overboard from the effects of the sea, but would never have got away from the boat.

The sea that took my mate overboard was by no means very dangerous. Of course there was water enough in it to carry a man away if he was not holding on to anything. However, later on during the cruise the boat shipped larger seas than this one, but I never again had a deplorable accident of this kind.

After I had given up all hope of ever seeing my mate again I went down to the cabin, and there found everything afloat. The bedding was soaked and everything else in the cabin was very wet. I then bailed the *Tilikum* out, after which I went on deck again, and sat down in the cockpit thinking over the loss I had sustained. I was approaching the southern limit of the south-east trade wind, but instead of a trade wind it developed into a howling gale during the morning hours. I was just going to have a look at the compass to see if the wind was still in the same direction when I discovered to my dismay that the compass and binnacle had gone too!

When daylight came, and the sun made its appearance on the eastern horizon, I got on top of the cabin deck and took a good look round for my missing mate. But there was nothing to be seen but the large seas with their breaking summits, and the passing clouds in the sky above, while the *Tilikum* under her sea anchor and a storm sail over the stern, rose bravely to every sea as it came along.

At eight o'clock I hoisted my little Canadian flag half-mast, and then proceeded to search for a small pocket compass, which I knew my former companion had, when we were hunting in the forest of Vancouver Island. Being unable to find it, it struck me that Mr Luxton kept the same one in one of his valises, and doubtless without thinking of it took the compass with him when he left me in Suva. Consequently, I was alone at sea without a compass.

My position was then about six hundred miles southwest from Suva, and about twelve hundred from Sydney, isolated, no compass to steer by, everything soaking wet, and the boat hove to in a gale. For some time I was completely taken aback, and did not know what to do or what would become of me. The first thought that occurred to me was that I might wait there for a passing vessel. Then again, it struck me that I was out of the track of vessels and might lay there for months and not see one.

During the forenoon the wind abated somewhat. At midday the sun was shining brightly. I took my quadrant, and getting on top of the cabin deck, with one arm round the mast to prevent myself from falling overbard, tried to get the noon altitude. While standing there watching the sun slowly rising to the meridian to the north of me, I said to myself, 'Well, there is north.' By facing north the wind was about ten points to my right and the sea running from the same quarter, which of course made the direction of the wind and sea from the E.S.E. The latter observation almost satisfied me that I could make a fairly good course by steering in clear weather by the sun, moon or stars, and in thick weather do the best I could, steering by the ocean swell.

A little after noon the wind had moderated considerably and the seas had lost their breaking tops. I hauled in my sea anchor, and under the forestaysail swung the *Tilikum* on her course to the south-westward, steering by the ocean swell which was running from the E.S.E. By steering the boat so that the E.S.E. swell would strike her two points abaft the port beam, was to give her a S.W. course.

The guides I had to steer by were the sun, moon, stars, and the ocean swell, but I soon discovered that the ocean swell was by far the best to keep the boat making a good course. Then, again, I was obliged to use the heavenly bodies to get the set of the swell. The only trouble I had in finding the course was when after I got up from a sleep and found the weather thick and overcast. Still worse, when there was a cross swell I was helpless, and obliged to heave to until the weather cleared up.

For two days after the accident it kept blowing from the E.S.E., and as I was unable to sleep I kept her going night and day until the third day, when the wind died out and I lay becalmed.

From the time of the accident till the calm was two and a half days, during which time I had no sleep, and very little to eat, and that cold; I may say that I was just about played out. I therefore went to work and made myself some warm food, and after a fairly good meal, laid down to have a sleep. I laid in my little bunk for quite a while, turning from side to side and thinking over the past few days. However, I eventually dozed off only to dream about all kinds of things. I thought I saw my lost companion look in at the cabin door, and it gave me an awful start. On looking up the time I found to my surprise that I had only been asleep about ten minutes. I tried again and again to sleep, but in vain. However, I laid down for a few hours; then I fancied I felt a breeze come in through the cabin door, and sure enough when I got on deck there was a moderate breeze from the south. The great trouble was that whenever I retired to my bunk to sleep I could not do so, and when sailing, especially in light winds, I could not keep awake. Still, I set sail and did the best I could to keep the *Tilikum* going towards Sydney.

The wind and weather kept about the same till the following day. It was in the afternoon, while I was nearly asleep, when a heavy southerly squall struck the *Tilikum* under all sails, and over she went on her beam ends. So did I; it was only through a piece of luck that I did not go overboard, for the boat was on the port tack, with the sheets hauled by the wind. I was sitting on the port side dozing when she went over on her beam ends. Landing against the lee washboards, which kept me from going overboard, I nearly broke my neck. As luck happened the foremast snapped, and the boat righted at once.

From the fall I got a kink in the neck, and laid for a little while in the cockpit before I was able to realize what had happened. When I came to my proper senses, I looked round and saw the foresail, part of the fore-mast, forestaysail and all the head gear hanging overboard. The mainsail and mizzen were still set, and these, with the aid of the fore gear hanging overboard, kept the vessel nicely head to wind. After stripping her of the mainsail, and hauling in the mizzen sheet, the *Tilikum* laid as well as if she was riding to her sea anchor.

For the next few hours, while I was thinking of my miserable plight and what would next happen to the *Tilikum* and myself, I let her drift as she was. By and by I came to the conclusion that while there is life there is hope, and where there is a will there is a way; and being still in the possession of both, I went to work and picked up all the head gear and sails that were hanging overboard, secured it on deck, and as it kept blowing hard for two days I let the boat drift under her sea anchor and storm sail. All that time I was, of course, unable to do anything toward repairing the damage, but by keeping a riding light on deck during the night I got all the sleep I possibly could.

During the second night the wind gradually died out, and at daybreak the weather was calm and clear. After the large seas had gone down I went to work to splice the foremast and put everything back in its place, and in the afternoon I was ready for another breeze. I did not have to wait long for it, a moderate breeze coming up the same night. From then I experienced light winds and weather until October 14th, and when my position was about a hundred and fifty miles north-east from Sydney a strong breeze came in from the rear. I kept running before it as long as I thought it safe to do so, but when the wind increased to a howling gale and the seas commenced to break I hove to in the usual way. I put a light on deck, and then turned in 'all standing' (with all my clothes on). Now and then I would get up and see if the light on deck was burning.

About midnight I got up to see if the light was all right, but to my surprise it was extinguished, and, to make matters worse, a green, red and bright light appeared ahead. Of course, I knew at once that these were a steamer's lights, and that the vessel was coming straight towards me. There was no time to lose. I had to let the lookout on the steamer know that I was ahead of her or in another five minutes she would have run me down. I knew that I had no time to fix my light, so pulled off one of my socks, soaked it with kerosene, and set it ablaze. I felt a good deal better when I saw the green light disappearing from my sight. They had seen my signal, and in less than five minutes a large steamer passed by.

The gale kept up its fury for three days and nights, after which the wind moderated, but as I had seen neither sun, moon nor stars, and had completely lost my position, I kept the boat under her sea anchor till noon, when I got the position, which put me about a hundred miles south-east of Sydney. By that time the wind had died down and the sea became quite calm. Two hours later the sky was as clear as crystal, with the exception of a very heavy cloud rising from the south-west. I watched this as it grew larger and larger. In a little while, when it rose to about forty-five degrees above the horizon, it looked like a huge arch supported on the bosom of the ocean, one abutment in the south-west and the other in the south-east, and it certainly appeared to be a long, sharp point forming underneath the centre of the span, which was gradually approached by a similar point rising out of the ocean, and as soon as the two points met they formed a large waterspout. I at once made a dive down into my cabin to get my rifle on deck, which did not take longer than half a minute, and by the time I was on deck again there were two. Then, one after the other they formed until, in a very short time, there were six, the nearest at the very most, one mile from me; but there they stopped, and owing to the perfect calm I could hear the water rushing up in the cloud, which sounded something like a distant waterfall. Shortly afterwards one of the spouts broke; then another; then another would rise; and so they kept on rising and falling, one after the other, for about three hours. The cloud got larger and larger till six o'clock, when the last spout dropped.

I may mention here that I had sailed across the South Pacific several times, and on different occasions I have seen water-spouts of the same nature. All other water-spouts I have seen moved more or less in a slanting position, while those in question were all perfectly vertical.

During the afternoon, from about three till six o'clock, there must have been at least thirty spouts that I saw from my boat, and the nearest at any time I should judge was about a mile distant. I fired several shots at the spouts, and one of them broke shortly after I fired, but whether it broke from the effects of the vibration of the shot or from natural consequences I cannot say. I have been told by ship-masters who have had experience with water-spouts that they will break every time from the vibration of a gunshot, if it is discharged within two hundred yards. I, however, was well pleased that they kept where they were, as, had they come near my vessel, and had I been unable to break them with my gun, the *Tilikum* and I might still be sailing in the sky.

At six o'clock the bank that had up to then formed a large arch, and by the looks of it had imbibed from the ocean thousands upon thousands of tons of water, broke up and covered the sky in a few minutes with dark and threatening clouds. At the same time the weaather still kept calm but I heard light thunder; then a flash of lightning was followed by a loud peal of thunder, and I then experienced a very severe thunderstorm. There was no wind with it, but occasionally very heavy rain squalls. The lightning was apparently very near my boat, for it would make the dark and cloudy night as bright as day. I knew I was absolutely unable to prevent the lightning from striking my boat, so went below and laid down in my bunk to await further developments.

The thunderbolts seemed to be very close to the *Tilikum*, and I was apprehensive that the next flash of lightning would strike the canoe and put the two of us out of existence. However, nothing happened to me or my boat, and later the thunder diminished, until at midnight it stopped altogether. I got up, opened the cabin door, and took a look round. There was then no cloud to be seen anywhere, and the sky was dotted with stars. There was also a light breeze from the south-east, and as I had all the starts I wanted to guide me on my way, I at once got sails on the *Tilikum* and directed my course for Sydney.

The south-easterly breeze kept light during the night, but freshened in the morning. At noon I had as much wind as she could stand under all sails, and this condition continued until dark, when the breeze gradually moderated, and at nine o'clock I said to myself, 'If my reckoning is right I should see the Sydney light before long.'

From that time I kept looking for the light, and in fifteen minutes sighted it.

Personal encounters with the sea were, and are, not always a matter of dramatic or lethal confrontations high aloft on the yards or under gunfire from an enemy.

Yet they could lead to personal growth and eventual inspiration equally as much as life in the forecastle of a South Seas copra schooner. The distinguished Canadian writer Thomas Raddall's first taste of the sea suggested a more civil, if no less challenging, first encounter when he signed on a steamer after completing his wireless operator training.

A Quiet Way
Thomas H. Raddall

Armed with this certificate and the letter to prove that I had passed the first-class exam, I signed the crew list of *War Karma* as 'Jn. W. Opr.' on May 17, 1919. She was an iron stemer of about two thousand tons, built at Three Rivers in 1918 for the British Ministry of Transport. Canadian yards had been turning out many like her, usually of bigger tonnage, and all named *War*-something. Some were built of iron or steel, some of wood. Most of the wooden ones were built in British Columbia yards and brought around to the Atlantic via the Panama Canal. They were not made to last long, and they didn't. A lot broke down after a few voyages. The iron *War Karma* was sold in France a year or two after my voyage in her, and eventually she went to the Greeks, who have a knack of buying supposedly worn-out ships for little money and keeping them staggering about the seas for years afterward. Incidentally, *Karma* is from the Sanscrit, meaning 'fate-by-deeds' or something like that. If I needed a motto for my life, there it was.

Our captain was Charles Hunter of Tusket, Nova Scotia, a master of Bluenose square-riggers who had gone from sail to steam before the war. He had now shipped his son Walter as an ordinary seaman with a view to a career in the Canadian merchant marine, coming up the hard way as he had himself. Walter had been born at sea in his father's barque, returning from the voyage to India. He was a few years older than I, blond and stocky, cheerful and easygoing, and we became chums. Eventually he became a wireless operator himself and spend the rest of his lifetime in the Canadian sea service.

The senior wireless operator of *War Karma* was a tall gangling fellow of twenty-six, known as Skin because, as his shipmates said, he was as thin as a fathom of pump water. He knew his job well and spent his lifetime at it. Shortly after War Two, still pounding brass aboard a freighter, he died and was buried in the Caribbean Sea.

The Halifax tailors were booked up far ahead because men were pouring out of the armed services eager to get into 'civvies' again. Consequently I had no uniform when *War Karma* sailed from Halifax twelve days after I signed the ship's articles. I was conspicuous in the officers' quarters for that reason and because my age and inexperience were obvious. I came in for a lot of good-natured ribbing. In those days, like a middy in the navy, a merchant service brasspounder was considered, and frequently told, that he was the lowest form of marine life. He sailed the sea in a chair, fiddling with knobs and switches and making noisy electrical sparks. So Sparks was his nautical nickname. In uniform he wore the wavy gold braid on his cuffs, but on Marconi pay he got less money than the navigating officers and engineers. Indeed, as the greenhorn junior operator at forty-five dollars a month I was paid less than a seaman or fireman.

Skin and I shared a little cabin across an alleyway from the radio room. At sea we kept continuous watch, each doing six hours on duty and six off, around the clock. The ship ran into stormy weather soon after Halifax. Deeply laden, and carrying a large deck load of timber, she rolled and pitched unmercifully. For forty-eight hours or more I was miserably seasick and homesick, but I never missed a watch. Whenever Skin came to rouse me I got up at once, clenching my teeth and staggering to the radio room. For the next six hours I sat at the instruments, bracing myself against the violent movements of the ship and dutifully making a log entry every fifteen minutes, recording the names or call letters of ships engaged in wireless traffic.

In our passage across the sea we frequently 'spoke' other ships by radio and exchanged information about the latest navigation warnings. The war had left a lot of floating wreckage in the North Atlantic, including dangerous wooden derelicts. Also, a multitude of mines had gone adrift from their moorings about the North Sea coasts during the war and now were floating far and wide. Each night we tuned in to broadcasts from Poldhu, Cornwall, and 'FL' (the Eiffel Tower in Paris) and copied long lists of such sightings, with latitude and longitude given to the last fraction of a degree. From Cape Race, Newfoundland, we had similar warnings of icebergs in the northerly routes to Britain.

We wrote our log entries on long yellow sheets with a carbon copy. At the end of a voyage the log sheets, together with copies of all messages sent and received, had to be mailed promptly to Canadian Marconi headquarters in Montreal, whose code name was ARCON. The logs were subject to scrutiny at ARCON, and any lax or faulty operation brought a sharp reproof.

In the whole Canadian Marconi service, ship and shore, Atlantic and Pacific, a message from ARCON was a word from God. ARCON could pluck a man from a comfortable shore station like Montreal or Vancouver and send him to some desolate cape or island far up the map towards the Arctic. On the other hand, it could take him off a deadly dull post like the Lurcher lightship in the Bay of Fundy and place him aboard one of the smart new CGMM freighters bound to South Africa, India, Australia and other strange romantic places. It could take him from the barren sands of Sable Island and set him down at North Sydney, say, where the raadio station was right in town and he could live like a blooming gentleman.

I made personal entries in a small pocket diary. This got soaked in a boarding sea, and anyhow it was inadequate. Eventually I copied the contents into a larger journal and went on from there. The diary habit stayed with me the rest of my life. When I became a writer the diaries gave story material here and there, and after I reached the age of fifty they became intensely interesting, bringing back clearly people, places, adventures and misadventures that had faded or slipped away from my memory altogether.

Part of my diary entry for June 3, 1919, says: 'On watch . . . very homesick but no longer seasick.' In fact I now had sea legs which seldom failed me afterwards. Like many other sailors, including Lord Nelson, when I put to sea in rough weather after a long stay in port I got a headache and didn't care to eat on the first day, but never again did I have to run for the lee rail.

Small and overloaded, *War Karma* took the weather badly. One midnight after taking over the watch, I slipped along the deck to fetch the usual 'mug-up' from the galley. I was on my way back to the radio cabin with a sandwich and a mug of hot cocoa when the ship rolled deeply to starboard, and a huge sea came out of the darkness as if it had been waiting for that moment. In a moment I was neck-deep in the North Atlantic and would have been dragged over the rail if I hadn't been able to fling one arm about a stanchion and hang on. After what seemed a very long time the ship recovered and rolled the other way, and I made my way, chilled and soaked, to the cabin. The sandwich was gone and so was the cocoa, but I was still clutching a mug full of sea water.

Later that night another sea poured a lot of water down the open skylight of the engine room, filled the stokehold with steam, and injured one of the firemen. The engineer of the watch, feeling the violent jar to the ship and seeing the in-pour of water, thought we had struck a floating mine. With his wartime instinct he shut off steam to the engines to stop further headway, and the ship fell off broadside to the sea and took several in succession.

The blows and sounds were tremendous. Half the deck cargo and part of the bridge were carried away, portholes and doors were smashed, alleyways were awash to the full height of the door coamings. Roused thus from sleep, Skin stepped over the coaming into our alleyway, intending to take charge in the radio cabin. When his bare feet plunged into something like twelve inches of water he thought the ship had sunk that far, and he burst in on me with his mouth agape and his pale blue eyes popping. This surprised me, and I had a silly feeling of triumph over my superior officer. The truth was that he and others in the ship's company were still on edge with the long tension of the U-boat war, while I was just too green to be scared.

Our first destination was 'Fastnet for orders', Fastnet being a lone rock, bearing a famous lighthouse and signal station, that stands out of the sea off the southwest tip of Ireland. From the remote days of the transatlantic trade this rock, or Brow Head on the coast beyond, was the chosen landfall of vessels bound to English ports or to continental ports along the Channel and North Sea. Our final destination had been given us by wireless, and when we sighted the Fastnet's flutter of signal flags they merely confirmed what we knew. We were to proceed to Manchester by the normal peacetime route.

In a mild June night we passed up Liverpool harbour and entered the first lock of the ship canal to Manchester. The next day we went up the canal, a strange sensation after our stormy ocean passage, steaming slowly inland for thirty-five miles and passing small villages, farms, and pastures with grazing cattle. We moored in Salford, the dock district of bustling Manchester, and lay there two weeks while the cargo was unloaded and the ship repaired. With the aerials lowered and coiled out of the way of the cargo derricks there was nothing for a wireless operator to do. Day after day, and evening after evening, I walked through the dock gate and explored Salford and Manchester.

My chosen chum was Walt Hunter. He didn't drink but he liked a pretty girl, and Manchester was full of them. Before long he was much attached to a demure little waitress in a café, and as her girl friend also worked there it followed that I made the fourth in a quartet. It tickled me to pose as a man like Walt, strolling along arm-in-arm with a pretty girl. She was Irish and her name was Bridget, but she preferred the diminutive Bridie. She had Titian hair, a soft milk-and-roses skin, violet eyes that sparkled with fun, and what was rare in working girls in England then, she had perfect teeth. When the girls had an afternoon off we went with them to various Manchester parks or to the perpetual carnival of the Bellevue Pleasure Gardens, and in the evening we treated them to meals and movies. None of this entertainment was extravagant, but it took most of the fifty dollars Mother had given me for 'emergencies' as well as an advance on my pay.

Now the captain had further orders. As soon as the ship was ready, *War Karma* was to proceed to Cardiff and load a cargo of munitions for the white Russian army at Archangel. We were told that Archangel was jammed with shipping and some ships, including ours, would remain through the winter, acting as floating storehouses which 'the white Ruskies' would unload over the ice. Meanwhile the red Russian armies were closing on Archangel, and if any of them penetrated to the shore of the bay any time between November and May, the ships frozen in the ice would be sitting ducks for their artillery.

Fortunately for us the Allied governments were now making up their minds to abandon the crazy adventure at both ends of the enormous Russian mass. Towards the end of June, Captain Hunter got orders to pay off the crew and proceed with the Canadian officers to London.

In the custom of wireless operators paid by the Marconi Company, Skin and I had signed the ship's articles (thus bringing us under the ship's discipline) at the nominal pay of one shilling a month. We signed off *War Karma* in the Salford shipping office, and under British Board of Trade regulations we now received the little blue-covered book so important to every British mariner, entitled 'Continuous Certificate of Discharge'. In this is written a description of every voyage you make or period of service you put in, the name of the ship and her captain, the date and place of engagement and discharge, your rank or rating, and the captain's opinion of your ability and general conduct. We also received the Identity and Service Certificate with a photograph.

As usual in Manchester rain was falling, but in spite of it the photographs were taken in the little courtyard of the shipping office. Mine was a quick head-and-shoulders. I have these documents before me now. In the picture I show my opinion of the fuss and the Manchester weather, and I look much older than the boy on the back of the Naval Department's second-class ticket. Not merely the frown and set mouth but something else, the mark of a hard voyage and the conquest of homesickness and *mal de mer* all at one time.

On the first of July we Canadians left the ship and caught a midnight train jammed with people, including a lot of glum Tommies returning from leave to rejoin the army on the Rhine. Early in the morning we arrived in London at St Pancras station and found quarters for ourselves. Walt and I shared a room at the Imperial Hotel in Russell Square.

While Captain Hunter and the others reported at the Furness Withy offices for orders, Skin and I reported at Marconi House in the Strand, which was international headquarters for all seagoing Marconi personnel. We found ourselves in a throng of other brass-pounders sitting in a long waiting room on plain wooden chairs. The routine was this: you registered your name and last ship and took a seat if you could find one empty, and you listened to an intermittent stream of dots and dashes from buzzers on the wall, each calling a man by name and summoning him to Office Number This or That. It was an efficient system in those days before the vocal intercom was invented but a bind on the men in the waiting room. They had to be there listening every morning and afternoon as if on watch at sea, until some office type was ready to deal with them. A chap sitting next to me had been there four days without a single buzz from 'those fucking desk-blokes inside'.

Skin and I were more fortunate. A buzzer snapped our names within two hours. In one of the offices a very brisk desk-bloke ordered us to join the transport *Prince George* at Southampton and gave each of us an advance of five pounds on our pay. When I rejoined Walt at the hotel I found that Captain Hunter and the others were posted to *Prince George* also. Before the war she and her twin ship *Prince Arthur* had been smart little freight-and-passenger liners on the run between Boston and Yarmouth, Nova Scotia. In 1916 the British Admiralty leased them for the Channel run between Southampton and Le Havre, carrying mails and soldiers on leave. Now the Admiralty was returning them to the owners in Boston, and in this way our *War Karma* party would work their passage home.

I took the tube from Euston to West Hampstead and called on my aunt Jessie Raddall, much to her surprise. The Raddalls have a chronic aversion to writing letters, so she didn't even know that I was out of school and off to sea. She and another teacher shared a flat near Hampstead Heath, and the two ladies bombarded me with questions. My aunt kept saying, 'How you've changed!' As I told her truly, a lot of things had happened since she saw me last, more than six years ago.

Our party of *War Karmas* arrived in Southampton on an afternoon train and found the twin ships tied up at adjoining quays. Our captain and son Walter were familiar with them from pre-war days. Each had two funnels and a lean look in its naval grey paint, and they had a speed of twenty knots. Because they were designed for the Boston-Yarmouth run and could not carry enough coal for the transatlantic passage, carpenters were boarding up the rails on the lower decks to stow extra coal. Even with this the ships could only reach Horta in the Azores, where they would coal again for the run to Boston. The Hunters shook their heads over the condition of the ships after three years of troop carrying. Most of the crewmen were. RNVR types at a loose end after the war, glad to work a one-way trip to the States and then get a paid passage home. We made bets with the officers of *Prince Arthur* that our twin would beat theirs to Horta and again from Horta to Boston.

Both ships left Southampton together, with a crowd of friends and relations waving on the quays and the crews singing the chorus of a wartime song, 'Goodbye-ee, goodbye-ee, /Wipe the tear, lady dear, from your eye-ee. /Though it's hard to part I know, /We're just tickled to death to go.' The weather was warm, the Channel calm, and the English coast lovely in the evening light. By the next evening we were rolling heavily in a beam sea out of the Bay of Biscay, which gave me a headache and twinges of nausea, like Lord Nelson long before me, but I kept my watch. On orders from London we listened carefully for radio signals from *R-34*, a British copy of the Zeppelin, which had crossed over the Atlantic to the United States and was now on its way back. We heard nothing. On July 13, Poldhu station advised all ships that *R-34* had returned safely.

Besides the shortage of bunker space there was a shortage of tank space for fresh water, so all hands were rationed to a quart a day. This had to provide for meals, washing, shaving and drinking. At midsummer the latitude of the Azores was hot; with a cloudless sky and burning sun we minded the water shortage. Less than six days out of Southampton, however, we sighted the first of the Azores, a wide sprawl of volcanic peaks that stand out of the sea in tall green cones. In a few more hours we anchored off Horta, a pretty little town in pastel colours with the steep green vineyards of Fayal island for a backdrop. We had won the first half of our bet, for *Prince Arthur* was just passing Hera Cruso island, miles astern. It meant that we would have first turn at the coaling equipment and thus a head start for the second bet to Boston.

The coaling method was primitive. The Welsh coal came off to us in lighters from the storage heaps, and a gang of chattering Portuguese workmen rigged wooden stages up the ship's side. Two ragged fellows stood on each stage and swung the coal up in two-handled baskets to the deck, where it was dumped into the bunkers. Horta was a sleepy out-of-this-world place in those days. Men returning from a brief run ashore, or chaffering with bumboats alongside, brought aboard a lot of cane furniture, lace, wine, plaited grass basketwork, and caged canaries. By nine that evening we had finished coaling and topped up our water supply. We left the anchorage at once, and *Prince Arthur* took our place

A precocious romanticist wrote in my diary, 'The lights of Horta twinkling farewell. A perfect night, warm and voluptuous, a big moon peeping over the black bulk of São Miguel, and the faint music of the military band drifting over the water. Walt waxing sentimental again. A senhorita this time.'

Captain Hunter, a sportsman, notified *Prince Arthur* that he would wait off the west end of the Fayal Channel so that the second half of our race to Boston would start fair and square. The captain of *Prince Arthur*, a very different kind of sportsman, played his second bet strictly to win. He drove the stevedores hard in the night and then slipped away by the east entrance of the Fayal Channel which lies between the islands of Fayal and São Miguel. he ordered his wireless operators to keep silent and headed for Boston at full speed. When he failed to appear at the west entrance, and when our wireless calls got no reply, Captain Hunter guessed the game, and we were off. By the next afternoon we had dropped the peak of Corvo astern, our last view of the Azores.

It was a pleasant voyage. There was some excitement, a fire in one of the bunkers, and the stokers and trimmers toiled for hours to get at it. Early one morning I picked up dot-and-dash signals from Sable Island, like a voice from home. After many clear hot days and nights we were now in fog, and the fog became thicker as we drew towards Cape Cod.

Here I must mention RDF (Radio Detection Finding), then fairly new and in the minds of many merchant skippers a very doubtful contraption. During the war, U-boats surfaced at night to charge their batteries and communicate by radio with each other and with Germany. Consequently in 1917 the British Admiralty set up RDF stations. When U-boats began to raid the east coast of Canada in 1918 the Canadian Navy built RDF stations at Chebucto Head (Halifax), Canso, Nova Scotia, and Cape Race, Newfoundland. Any two of these stations could take bearings on a radio transmitter within their range and thus get a 'fix' on it. The system was imperfect. It was bothered with night variations which often made a fix impossible; but in daylight it could locate a transmitter with ease, and usually the fix was sharply accurate.

At the war's end it was obvious that RDF would be of great help to ships in fog or snow and for any reason doubtful of their position, so the RDF stations remained in operation. The difficulty now was to convince the old-fashioned captains that anything contrived by 'those wireless blokes' could be worth a damn in the field of navigation. Skin and I had told Captain Hunter about this new aid to navigation. I happened to have the watch as we approached Cape Cod in a wet blanket of fog, and the captain asked me with a sceptical grin to get him a position by RDF.

If any US naval RDF stations were manned for general use at this time we were not advised of it, but I had picked up good signals from the Canadian stations at Chebucto Head and Canso. In our position far to the south this meant an acute angle for the bearings, not the broad angle that gave best results. The method was for the ship to transmit the figure two (two dots and three dashes) for a full minute. This gave a good signal for RDF purposes. Then the two shore stations compared notes, and the nearer one (in this case Chebucto Head) gave the cross-bearings.

I carried the message up to the bridge and watched eagerly as the captain and chief officer drew the bearings on the chart. A smile spread over the Old Man's face. He thumped a big fist down on the chart table and declared, 'They cross between my funnels!' The RDF fix was near enough to his own reckoning at any rate, and from that moment he was sold on the newfangled and indeed fantastic idea of getting a ship's position actually through the skull of Sparks.

Naturally this position of ours was picked up by *Prince Arthur*, and next morning she broke her long silence and called the Canadian RDF stations for a fix. We copied it and sent it to the bridge. The Old Man worked it out on his chart and said cheerfully, 'Well, the bastards are ahead of us. Not far, mind you. But we can't catch 'em now.' When we slipped out of the fog and into the sunshine of Boston harbour on July 25, we found *Prince Arthur* neatly tied up at an East Boston dock and her officers calling out to us, 'Where've you been?'

Walt and I explored Boston and its environs in the next three or four days. The most interesting place to me was the Harvard campus, whose open spaces had been covered with wooden barracks during the war as the chief training school for US Navy radio operators. We inspected and admired the equipment, which was about to be dismantled along with the barracks. At the end of the month our two crews signed off, and the British personnel went home by passenger liner. Captain Hunter and Walt remained a day or two longer to visit friends and relatives around Boston. Skin and I took train for home.

So ended my brief service with the British Ministry of Transport. My first experience of the sea in *War Karma* had been a rough one, and then came the warm and pleasant voyage in *Prince George*. I had enoyed working at my job. I had enjoyed the illusion of being a man full grown (in spite of Mr Desbarats) and seeing strange towns and people. But what I enjoyed most was that brief glimpse of lush green islands in a sea of marvellous blue and their easy-going olive-skinned people, all placed beyond an enormous reach of ocean as if for the reward of way-worn sailors, like the Isles of the Blest in Masefield's ballad. I knew there were many such places in the world. Bermuda, for instance, or Tahiti, magic name, or Hawaii, or Conrad's enticing East as he sniffed it first from a small boat in *Youth*. I loged to set my feet on such places, to feel myself part of them for a time and then go on to the next. Why else do young men go to sea?

In the scores of young men and women who sail today in Canada's sail training ships, or in the yachtsmen and yachtswomen who point their bowsprits at Georgian Bay or Sambro Head, but dream of Rum Cay or Moorea, it is likely that Raddall's closing sentiment still lives, and burns as brightly as ever.

Dark Shadows:
Modern War at Sea

The great wars of the 20th century found Canada's naval service poorly prepared to meet the threat of the German naval forces which were the enemy in both the First and Second World Wars. In the First World War, the small Royal Canadian Navy played a minor role; but in the Second it was forced to grow into a formidable fighting force, with all the attendant agony and difficulty that rapid growth brings. Canadians served in the vessels of the parent Royal Navy, in flotillas of motor gunboats and torpedo-boats and launches; in corvettes, destroyers, and escort carriers in the anti-submarine and surface war of the Atlantic and elsewhere. The Royal Canadian Navy came of age quickly, and Canada's naval forces remain since that baptism of fire professional and competent. But the baptism was not a gentle one.

The Motor Gunboat War in the English Channel, in heavily-armed, high-powered wooden boats that clashed in raucous shoot-outs with their German counterparts, had a particular flavour.

Early Patrols
Hal Lawrence

'There are E-boats in your sector attacking convoy NB 121. Sail units of the 6th Flotilla chop-chop.'

'Right. I have the convoy on our plot; they're just entering our bailiwick. I'll sail the second division. Hichens has it tonight.'

An autumn night in Felixstowe, Suffolk, England; the water flat and black, the air still and silent except for tinny music of the BBC light program coming from one of the looming hulls of three squat silhouettes at an MGB jetty; a low gibbous moon in the southern sky throws long shadows from cranes at the dockside. Outside the harbour a convoy of merchant ships is ghosting along, one in the endless chain carrying war materials from the north of Scotland to the south of England. On this night in 1941 Holland is occupied by the Germans; indeed, since May, 1940, enemy *Schnellboote* (we called them E-boats) have sunk several destroyers and many merchantmen. Tonight would tempt any E-boat flotilla: the North Sea calm ruffled only by light airs, with good visibility. Against a westering moon our convoys will stand out nicely—a night for E-boats to hunt. Those from the Hook of Holland and the Scheldt estuary sailed after sunset; at eleven p.m. they attack. Our convoy escort swings out to intercept and bleats the warning to the Commander-in-Chief of the English Channel and the North Sea area—C-in-C the Nore—Admiral Commanding, Dover. His operations room telephones the warning to Staff Officer Operations (SOO) at HMS *Beehive*.

The alarm sounds; three boats are on immediate notice; captains rush to the operations room for a quick briefing by SOO; an engine coughs into life; pounding feet, slamming hatch covers, first lieutenant barking.

'Let go head and stern lines; let go after spring; hold forrard spring.'

The first engine roars to a crescendo, shattering the silence of the village. The second and third destroy all talk unless yelled in your ear. Acrid fumes and blue smoke curl upward. The captains run back, charts and notes in hand, and leap on board.

'Slow ahead starboard.'

Three boats surge ahead, sterns angling out.

'Slip. Slow ahead port. Port wheel. Slow ahead starboard.'

The boats move into the harbour.

'Midships. You see the harbour entrance, cox'n?'

'Aye, sir.'

'Steer for that.'

'Steer for the entrance, sir.'

In column they steam to the gate vessels. The net swings open. They pass.

'What's the first course to intercept, pilot?'

'North-48-East, sir,' replies the navigator.

'Revolutions for thirty knots.'

Throttles are lifted, the roar of the engines deepens, spray flies from the bow, the fore-foot lifts, and the boats begin to plane. Over the wireless telegraph (w/t) is babble and chatter of attacking E-boats and defending escort.

'Sounds as though there's a lot of them out tonight, pilot.'

'Yes, there should be plenty for us.'

'How far to go, pilot?'

The navigator replies, 'Forty-two miles, sir, sixty-nine minutes.'

The moon sinks, mist is forming, the boats are in three-quarter line, each off the starboard quarter of her next ahead. Three white wakes plume astern pointing back to home and going on to battle. The senior officer of the half-flotilla is Lieutenant-Commander Robert Peverell Hichens, RNVR, until recently a country solicitor; he has a few months' more experience than the rest. Hitch leads his boats across the North Sea to the fray a few miles ahead. The hands are at action stations, tactics agreed on, battle plans rehearsed time and again over the past months. The stage is set. In command of the two following boats are RNVR Lieutenants L.G.R. Campbell, known as 'Boffin', and G.E. Bailey, known as 'George'. Both have over a year in coastal forces and before the war were a tea planter and an insurance agent. Now Hitch settles down to a blank state of watchfulness, the least tiring way of passing long hours under way. It is midnight; his mind drifts.

' . . . moon still up, sea flat calm. Like this, motor gunboating is sheer joy; station-keeping is easy; boats fly along with a powerful sense of speed . . . very beautiful . . . one of the most lovely sights . . . setting moon showing orange . . . a gun boat unit at speed in moonlight, with white pluming wakes, cascading bow waves, the thin black outline of guns starkly silhouetted, figures of gunners motionless at their position . . . carved out of black rock, and all against the beautiful setting of a sparkling moon-path on the water . . . between moving billows of mist . . . fog bank ahead . . . '

The smell of rubber burning breaks his reverie. The motor mechanic sticks his head up the hatch, 'Will you stop, sir, please; a pendulastic is going.' (This fantastic name is for a piece of equipment between the engine and the gearbox—unreliable and temperamental.) Engines cut; a deafening silence descends on the moonlit sea. The dilemma now is that there is a certain chance of action ahead, yet if he goes on it will have to be at reduced speed, and he is needed next night for an important job. It is a difficult decision, the kind captains are paid to make.

'There are lots of E-boats ahead. Do you think those damn pendulastics will hang on for eight hours if we don't exceed eighteen knots?'

'I'll keep an eye on them, sir, let you know if trouble gets worse. Probably all right. Let's give it a go.'

The peace of the night is rent again as the boats slide off. Hitch's engine-room troubles are not over; George Bailey signals he has an excessive quantity of water in the carburetor and filters of his starboard engine. He can't clear it and will have to return to harbour. He peels off at reduced speed and fades into the mist. Boffin and Hitch continue on North-48-East.

'How far to go now, pilot?'

'Thirty-six miles, sir.'

Mist is forming low on the water, a common occurrence in quiet weather. The moon sinks, and from the sound of the radio chatter there are lots of E-boats ahead, probably two groups out tonight, six to a group—plenty of targets. We're the only British unit clear of convoy routes, so anything we see will be enemy and we can fire on sight, and this course should intercept them as they head home. Visibility is getting worse, making it hard to see them over a hundred yards, but it's a good night to hear them.

'How much longer to go, pilot?'

'Fifteen and a half minutes, sir.'

All on the bridge peer anxiously.

'Two minutes, sir.'

'Let me know at thirty seconds.'

The guns swing to a forward bearing; the ammunition-supply hands follow.

'Thirty seconds, sir.'

A lamp flashes to Boffin astern; the two boats slow.

'Cut engines.'

Silence. The bows sink, the rush of water fades. What a relief after hours of noise! The exquisite absence of noise. Homey sounds, the clink of a cocoa mug, a muffled laugh. It's now two a.m. From the silence of the convoy and escort w/t it would seem the attack is over. The E-boats are returning but won't be here until about four. The MGB crews settle down to a listening vigil. Hitch goes below for a doze. At a quarter to five he is called.

'Distant sound of engines, sir, bearing about west.'

At last, the murmur of engines, growing louder, louder. Music to their ears. Have they not flogged these waters for nearly a year without being able to meet E-boats head on, fairly and squarely, see their bows and not only their arse, and that through the smoke made to cover their retreat. Yes, the boats making that noise are approaching, heading home to Holland. Can we intercept and cut them off? If only we had more than eighteen knots. The rumble is increasing.

'The bearing is west-southwest now, sir.'

'E-boats all right, moving east; they've moved from west to west-southwest. I'll plot them for a while and get a course and speed. With luck we'll head them off. *Damn* this eighteen knots and damn all pendulastics to hell!'

The North Sea is wide; the moon has set and the night has grown dark and misty. The rumble grows to a full-throated growl. All hands peer into the dark as the growling, thudding mutter grows and grows; but even as close as 200 yards they could pass unseen. Should we edge forward a bit? No, better to stay silent.

'Bearing is south 50 west now, sir, time 0553.'

'Then we've heard them now for eight minutes, say twenty-seven knots, four miles; in another six minutes we'll be on the beam of their line of advance.'

Captains can't keep from theorizing, yet so much was a matter of estimate, of chance. One last look at the rough plot.

'Start up. Steer south 25 east, cox'n.'

But now you can't hear them; where *are* they now? The boats go on a few minutes. He *has* to get another sound bearing; but if he stops to get one they might pass ahead and draw away. He flashes Boffin; the throttles are slammed down; Boffin, caught short by the suddenness of the order, surges up on the beam. Silence, only silence; then the louder rumble of enemy engines to the south'ard. If the bearing is the same as before, then the intercept course is okay. No, it has drawn a little eastward, we are falling astern, slightly; we must alter.

'Start up, steer south 50 east, cox'n.'

Seconds go by, then a minute.

'Flashing light to port, at red three oh, sir.'

Yes, there it is, a little blue light winking, then the blur of a low hull, a faintly darker shape in the mist. The challenge flashes out; the reply is garbled; then all doubt is removed. There they *are*—five low, white hulls nuzzled together, stopped. A rendezvous? Why? Never mind—there they *are*! Four are off to port, the fifth dead ahead.

'Sparks, send a w/t report giving our position and that we're engaging the enemy.'

'Open fire. Hard a-port.'

Guns crash out toward an E-boat, now drawing aft to starboard. Boffin's guns are firing, too. The range is fifty yards and hits are steady, a constant red flicker as our shells explode. The E-boat to port is at the same range and now both MGBS are pumping a steady hail of shot into her as well. Neither E-boat replies; they are dead before they know we're there. Hitch and Boffin pass the port E-boat at twenty yards, pouring fire into her.

By now the other three E-boats are wide awake and firing vigorously, some rounds zipping overhead, some tracing small spouts of water across the bow, some hitting. The vivid streams of tracer arch between the British and German boats, and the fourth E-boat is getting good. Hitch's forward gun is smashed and its stand shot from beneath the gunner's feet. The scene is confused—'the fog of battle'. Hitch weaves this way and that; Boffin stays faithfully on his stern. The sounds and sights of the mêlée suffuse us—a constant roar of our own and the enemy engines; the spitting of the small, chatter of larger, and thudding the the largest guns; creaming, crisscrossing white wakes; flames from barrels, arcs of amber and green tracer; the red wink of hits. The enemy skims along at thirty knots, we at our more sedate eighteen. The after gun jams, but the fourth E-boat is on fire aft. And then they're scattering! Which to follow? There's one to starboard, same course as ourselves, about sixty yards.

'Open fire, clear that damn after gun, the forrard one is finished. *Must* I fight an E-boat with only a Lewis gun? Firing .303 bullets? Damn *rifle* bullets?'

This E-boat is strangely silent. The Lewis gun opens up; her tracer points out the target to Boffin, who opens up with larger guns. The silent E-boat is stung into activity and chatters back with commendable dexterity and accuracy. Then she peels off, heads for Holland, making smoke, still firing her after gun, which falls silent as she works up to thirty-five knots. She is gone. Nothing is now in sight—time to stop again and listen.

'Stop engines.'

Silence is complete and nothing is near; 5:45 a.m., still dark.

'Sparks, crank up your w/t again and tell the Admiral our position and that we've been in contact with five, three damaged.'

Sparks jumps to it. As with all other wireless telegraphists, it is his greatest pleasure to send an enemy report like this. While he is sending it all tels in the area must listen; the repeated prefix—ER ER ER: Enemy Report—silences all others and while transmitting it *he* is the star of the airwaves; his chums in other ships will recognize his 'hand' on the key.

On the bridge the vigil goes on.

'I think I hear something, sir, over there,' pointing.

'Quiet everyone. Do you hear anything, Boffin?'

'Yes, in the southwest, I think.'

'Let's go and see. Start up. Steer southwest.'

It is not nautical twilight but it now somehow seems less dark, the mist thinning. They steam in for ten, fifteen minutes. Then, following the proper naval procedure, a lookout reports:

'Vessel bearing green four five, sir,' followed by the unorthodox but heart-felt, 'It's one of them bloody bastards!'

She is lying black and still about 200 yards away; what can this mean? Is she abandoned? Is it a trap? Will she open fire any minute? Slow speed. She is obviously badly beaten up but is she crippled? Boffin appears out of the dark from astern, introduced by a burst of Lewis gunfire. Boffin roars, 'Cease fire!' and the cease-fire bell is heard shrilling out. Some bloody-fool gunner too worked up!

'I'm going to send a boarding party over. Stand off a bit so we don't get in each other's crossfire if we have to open up. When we get close put your searchlight on her. If she opens up, plaster her.'

So, in a glimmering dawn, they approach.

'Snottie, you speak the lingo. Ask if they surrender.'

'Gelben Sie auf? Gelben Sie auf?'

No answer.

'Gelben Sie auf? Do you surrender?'

Silence.

Boffin's light blazes on the E-boat. Nobody appears on deck, and the swastika flag droops from the yard arm. The boarding officer jumps over, and a burst of a 20mm gun breaks the silence. Christ, they *are* there. No. That's our own after gun that was jammed; it's now cleared. The silly bugger must have pulled the trigger. The gunfire ceases, and the boarding officer ruefully looks at the line of holes just ahead of him that his own gunner has put there. Then the looting starts—everything that's not fastened down. Yes, the E-boat *is* empty; the crew must have been taken off by another E-boat. Nearly all hands swarm on board. Their boarding stations ('looting stations') have been detailed from the day they joined the boat. The motor mechanic heads to shut off the sea valves, which will certainly have been opened by the Germans before they abandoned ship. The German-speaking midshipman looks for demolition charges—and finds one, a fuse leading down the ladder. Follow it.

'Where does it go?'

'Wait a minute . . . here . . . there's a wooden handle at the bottom, sir.'

'Is the fuse lit?'

'If it is, sir, then it's a long fuse. How long have they been gone? Fifteen minutes? Twenty?'

'About.'

'Wait, here's the plunger, the detonator, it says, "Remove handle to fire".'

'Yes, of *course!*'

'Then leave the handle in.'

'*Naturally*. Do you think I'm a . . . I'm chucking the *whole lot* overboard.'

The engine room is flooded with water and diesel oil and it is impossible for the motor mechanic to get at the sea cocks; other compartments are filling, and she rolls sluggishly. 'Bring them back alive,' Admiralty had said, but perhaps not this one. She is too deep and heavy to take in tow. It would only ruin our engines, and without a power pump we cannot empty her. Still, we'll try and save her. I'll ask that a power pump be sent by motor launch; an ML can get here in time. Meanwhile, let's see what we can get. Charts, books, logs, revolvers, ammunition, pictures (one of Hitler). Sparks takes all the w/t equipment he can move; the gunners take all the small guns they can lift; others grab a compass, a searchlight, a long sausage, black bread, sauerkraut, binoculars. The stern is lower. Jot down all the external features of the E-boat we can see; we must give Their Lordships as much as possible. But it doesn't look as though they're going to get *this* boat. No, she's lower in the water, her smoke-making gear is fizzling and emitting tentative whisps. She is going under.

'Abandon the E-boat. Get back to your own boats.'

Her bows lift high, higher, as she slips back, bows pointing to the sky as if in supplication. She is gone. All hands watch, silent. It's a sad thing to see a ship die—her crew have lavished her with as much care as we give this old girl.

'Oh Lord, our boats are so small and Your sea is so large.'

The ML bringing the power pump is turned back. It would have been nice to bring in a prize of war but we didn't do too badly. A victory, certainly. And in this case there are no deaths to mar our victory, only four wounded, none seriously.

The two MGBS head for home and make a triumphal entry into harbour. The sun is high and it's nearly time for up-spirits. The swastika flag is flying inferior to the white ensign. As we reach the convoy route we pass the destroyers who had engaged our friends the night before and had listened with rapt interest to our signals. The crews of the destroyers and trawlers cheer as we steam through the gate and up to the base. The word is out; the dockside is crowded with enthusiastic mateys, sailors, Wrens from the maintenance shops, the transport pool, and the offices; white handkerchiefs flutter. The Captain of the base, who is always there to see us off, stands out in front to see us safely in. He looks pleased.

'I've got to go and make a preliminary report, pilot; you start writing the final. I'll check it when I get back. Number One, get tingles *only* on the lower holes; no time for bloody refit, we've got to get out again. And get that sodding gun replaced; and see if you can finish ammunitioning early so the hands can get their heads down for a few hours. The other boats will help with ammunition and stores. We have to sail again at sunset.'

Far different, with its own nerve-grinding routine of cold, endurance, seasickness, and death lurking in the form of either the killer ocean itself or the hidden U-boat, was the war experienced by the men of the RCN's corvettes on open ocean escort.

Slip and Proceed
James B. Lamb

'Four-thirty, sir!'

We are snatched from the warm world of sleep by the rough hand on our shoulder and start up, blinded by the light, to find the quartermaster, cowled and hooded like a medieval monk in his fleece-lined watch-coat, bending over us. For some reason which we never understand, Operations ashore always sail escorts at some ghastly hour, never quite night or quite day; it is part of the traditional horror of sailing day. Always it is the same; the stuffy cabin, the dazzling light on the white paintwork, the oppressive, all-pervading sense of foreboding, the certain knowledge of misery to come.

Pull on the old sea-going uniform; hump yourself into the heavy winter sheepskin, stiff with salt, and the zip-fastened flying-boots, while overhead the thumps and muffled bumpings tell that the deck party is going about its work of 'singling up'. The heavy ropes, stiff with frost and black with use, are being lifted off the wharfside bollards in readiness for departure, leaving us secured by only a single set of warps to the shore: head and stern lines, breasts and springs. The after winch gives a few appropriately hollow groans before reluctantly settling down to its task of reeling in the frozen weight of the stern lines; you can hear the voice of the leading hand as he directs their stowage under the pom-pom bandstand. Bells clang deep in the bowels of the ship; they are testing the engine-room telegraphs and bridge communications as His Majesty's Canadian Ship *Trail* prepares for sea.

Out on deck it is black as Toby's arse, as a cowled figure remarks as we make our way forward; that is Bill Harvey, the sublieutenant in charge of the quarterdeck party. There is a light dusting of snow on the steel deck, making it dangerously slippery, and as we climb the steel ladders up to the bridge we become aware of the biting wind whistling in from the east. God, it'll be nasty outside with this gale still blowing! The sudden serenity of the asdic cabin is welcome; Clarke, the HSD and the senior asdic rating aboard, is checking out his set, and the chart table behind its black-out curtains is a warm pool of light. It's all there, just as it was laid out yesterday: the chart, with its pencilled course from St John's to the rendezvous point where we're to meet our convoy well out in the Atlantic, south of Cape Race; the notebook, with its estimated courses and speeds and times of arrival, in accordance with the secret signal received from Operations the day before, its traditional preamble going back to the days of Pepys's navy: 'Being in all respects ready for sea, slip and proceed at 0500 . . . .'.

'Hands to stations for leaving harbour!' That's the bosun's mate making the pipe through the crowded messdecks, and already the fo'c'sle is alive with hooded figures. There's the captain coming up onto the bridge, and we make way for him as he peers over the dodger into the icy blackness. The tug has hauled off the two sleeping corvettes that have been berthed outside us; at the corvette berths, ships are crowded three and four deep alongside and at the trot-buoys in the centre of the harbour. Figures take their accustomed places; the yeoman of signals takes charge of his signalmen, and from the bridge-wing voice-pipe a steady voice announces from the wheelhouse: 'Coxswain at the wheel, sir!'

The engines are rung to standby; at a word from the captain, all the lines aft are cast loose and hauled in, the headline is taken in, and men stand by with fenders along the break of the fo'c'sle as the captain orders slow ahead. We are steaming against the spring line, which alone attaches us to the shore; the torque of the propeller turning over slowly walks the stern out from the wharf. When it is well clear, the captain stops engines, then orders slow astern, with the helm amidships. Responsive as a motorboat, the ship begins to gather sternway; the wharf slips by with gathering speed as the siren blasts three times to warn any traffic that we are proceeding in reverse. The helm is put over and the stern moves obediently to starboard until we lie in midstream, our bows pointing toward the wharf, where the tug is already returning the two outer corvettes to the berth we have just vacated. The engines are stopped, and we lie silently, still turning, our sidelights gleaming red and green in the oily water beneath. Then 'Half ahead', and the ship swings rapidly as the rudder bites under the impetus of our new momentum, and we steady with our head pointing directly at the distant harbour entrance. Now the wind is strong and cold, blowing directly into our faces. Below us the fo'c'sle party is already stowing lines and fenders, securing for sea; in daylight, they would have been fallen into line, facing to port, like the seamen on the quarterdeck, ready to honour the Admiral's flag when the bosun's pipe shrilled the 'Still'.

Ahead of us, a confusion of dim lights shows where our sisters of the escort group are leaving their berths; we stop and wait while they sort themselves out. That will be HMS *Montgomery*, the old four-funnelled former American destroyer, built late in the First World War and handed over to the Royal Navy in the destroyers-for-bases deal. Her captain, a professional RN lieutenant-commander, is our senior officer, and he leads the parade as he takes us out to sea: five Canadian corvettes and a Juicer four-stacker, a typical mid-ocean escort group in this winter of 1941–42.

All about us is the sleeping city of St John's; the barren hills of the South Side rise unseen to starboard; the snow-dusted streets gleaming fitfully in the lights of a passing car are all we can make out of the city itself, climbing its hills all along our port side. There is enough light to pick out the rocks of the narrow entrance: the dim, flashing light of Chain Rock to port and the concrete bulges of the entrance battery burrowed into the rock to starboard. As we reach the entrance, a red signal-light blinks blearily from the ship ahead: 'Order One, speed 12 knots.' We find our place in the line-ahead formation, crank up the engine revolutions for 12 knots, and we are off and running.

In Newfyjohn, as the sailors call St John's, you are either in the harbour or out of it; there is no long estuary leading to the sea. The transition is brief and dramatic; one moment you are trundling along in the comparative serenity of harbour, and the next you are in open ocean, amid all the fury of the North Atlantic winter. As we leave the narrow entrance, we stick our bows into a great black sea, and we climb upwards, only to come crashing dizzily down in a welter of breaking water. We ship the end of a sea over the bows just as the fo'c'sle party is putting the finishing touches on the securing of the upper-deck gear, and they scuttle for safety in their sodden sheepskins, in a flurry of boots and bad language. The sea is getting up under the impetus of that shrieking wind; for the next few hours we shall be punching into the teeth of the freshening gale, and already a lot of us are having sudden doubts about our stomachs. There are retching sounds from behind us on the bridge, where one of the new signalmen is bringing up his innards as he greets his first Atlantic gale; in anticipation, the yeoman has thoughtfully provided a bucket lashed to a stanchion, and I can feel my own stomach heave in sympathy.

I mentally review what I had for dinner last night. We'd had a couple of rums in the Crowsnest, that marvellously contrived club for seagoing officers on the draughty upper floor of a Water St warehouse, before going on to the Newfoundland Hotel for the traditional last-night bang-up dinner. We'd dined in sombre state in the great, glacial dining-room, topping off a fine dinner with Drambuie, sipping that amber ambrosia in order, we assured ourselves, to settle the stomach. Two of our five at dinner had Scots blood in them, and they assured us that Scots never drank for pleasure; it would be contrary to their dour Presbyterian upbringing. But it was only prudent, mind, to take a wee drop to whet the appetite or settle the stomach, to aid digestion or steady the hand, so to speak. We had, accordingly, taken prudent precautions, but as the ship crashed and plunged into the rising head sea and the signalman behind retched and gasped, I wondered if we had been prudent enough.

Once clear of the harbour, the watch closed up to begin the seagoing routine which would last until we berthed on the other side of the Atlantic; one-third of the ship's company manning the engines, boilers, wheel, asdic, wireless, and lookout positions, the other two-thirds below trying to catch what sleep they could before their own four-hour stint began. It is my watch until eight, but the captain lingers anxiously, worried about the rising wind and sea.

A green one crashes aboard; peering over the dodger we can see its dark shape engulf our foredeck, and we crouch for shelter as the ship plunges thunderously into it. A wall of water, tons of it, sweeps across our fo'c'sle to hurl itself against our bridge structure with a resounding thump. Water sweeps overhead; even in the shelter of the dodger we are drenched, and from below comes a series of bangs and crashes, from mess-decks and galley and upper deck, where a hundred items, big and small, have bumped and smashed and clanged and rattled under the impact of the heavy sea. A great murmur of protest, of oaths and groans and bitching, rises from the ventilators and voice-pipes, and from the wheel-house we hear the bosun's mate, loud and clear: 'This effing bucket! Roll on, our refit!'

The captain grins, catches my eye: 'Hearts of oak!' he grunts.

But it is clear that we cannot go bashing into it at this speed. Up ahead *Montgomery* must be semi-submerged, those old four-pipers being notor-iously the world's worst sea-boats. Sure enough, back comes the signal: reduce speed to 10 knots. It is going to be a long run, just to meet our convoy, and it has all the earmarks of another sticky crossing.

For us, our watch eventually comes to an end, as they always do; we hand over to Bill Harvey, his face still puffy from sleep, and give him our course and speed and show him our position on the chart. A last look round before going below. A grey, lumpy sea, flecked with white, fills our universe, under grey, scudding clouds. There is no land to be seen, anywhere, only our little handful of ships in all this mad world of wind and sea and driven water. We are steaming in line abreast now, at intervals of a mile. There is *Arvida* to starboard, and to port are *Chilliwack* and *Dauphin* and *Kamsack*, with *Montgomery* just visible, now and again, far on the horizon beyond. But although the sea is worse than ever, the wind seems to be dropping, not quite so fierce as it seemed at the beginning of our watch. But then, the wind never *does* seem so bad at the end of your watch as it does at the beginning.

Breakfast in the wardroom below is a cheerless affair; the deadlights dogged down over the ports and the carpet stowed away, as it will be until we make port again, reduce the cheerful clubroom of our dockside days to a sort of clinical tank. The big armchairs are lashed to stanchions to keep them from crashing about, and we eat our greasy egg and tomato, our burnt toast and marmalade sitting bolt upright on the hard leather settee which runs along one side of the table. Number One is just finishing his breakfast as we arrive for ours, and is off to go rounds of the messdecks with the coxswain.

Better him than me! The messdecks of a corvette in bad weather are indescribable; it would be difficult to imagine such concentrated misery anywhere else. Into two triangular compartments, about 33 feet by 22 feet at their greatest dimensions, are crammed some sixty-odd men; each has for his living space—eating, sleeping, relaxing—a seat on the cushioned bench which runs around the outside perimeter of each messdeck. There is a locker beneath the seat for his clothing, and a metal ditty-box— something like an old-fashioned hatbox—holds his personal things in a rack above. The space where he slings his hammock—carefully selected by the older hands and jealously guarded—is 18 inches beneath the deck-head, or another hammock, which are slung in tiers between stanchions and beneath pipes, wherever there is room. Most of the deck space is taken up with scrubbed deal tables, one to each mess, where you eat or write or play interminable games of cards.

Crowded in harbour and stuffy, the messdecks at sea are like some vision of Hades. There is absolutely no fresh air; all the ports, open in harbour, are dogged down and blanked over at sea, and in heavy weather even the cowl ventilators from the upper deck have to be sealed off. Dim emergency lights, red or blue, provide the only illumination in the dark hours, and around the clock there is always at least one watch trying to catch a few hours of oblivion, while about them the life of the mess goes on: men coming and going from outside, or snatching a meal before going on watch. With the hammocks slung, there is hardly room anywhere to stand upright, and there is moisture everywhere—water swirling in over the coamings when the outside doors open, sweating from the chilled steel of the ship's side, oozing from the countless pipe joints and deck-welds and rivets and deck openings, and all the other manifold places where water forces an entrance from the gale outside. Plunging into a head sea, the noise and motion in the fo'c'sle must be experienced to be believed; a constant roar of turbulence, wind, and water, punctuated by a crashing thud as the bow bites into another great sea, while the whole little world is uplifted—up, up, up—only to come crashing down as the ship plunges her bows over and downward, to land with an impact which hurls anyone and anything not firmly secured down to the forward bulkhead. With a rolling, corkscrew motion, the nightmare world of the fo'c'sle starts to climb again, up, up, up. . . . In their navel pipes, the twin anchor cables rattle and clank at each movement, a dominant note in the endless, maddening din.

In such a place, under such conditions, corvette crews endure for days, weeks, years, a degree of discomfort and hardship which they could not have sustained for an hour in civilian life; wet, cold, bruised, sleeping in their clothes, with never a moment's privacy or quiet. When they are keeping watch, getting up at all hours to brave the elements, night blurs into day in a misery too great for words. In everyone's mind is the surcease to come when we make port, when the motion and misery stop, and everyone can sleep, sleep, without interruption. No one thinks beyond that; to endure this crossing is our chief aim, and the ship is impelled onward by the mind and heart of every soul aboard.

But there are degrees of misery, as with anything else; when eventually the long bash to windward is done and we reach the point of rendezvous, we turn to comb the track along which the convoy will come. We are taking the seas on the quarter now, and while the ship rolls heavily, right over on her ear, there is no more pitching, and the surcease is like a kind of heaven. The wind is easing and everyone is more cheerful. Life settles into its accustomed seagoing routine; the seasick are either better now or beyond hope. In every escort, there are always one or two individuals, the chronically seasick, whose endurance becomes a matter of proud boasting by their shipmates, and who live at sea in a sort of half-world, between life and death, sustained only by a handful of crackers or soup for all the days and weeks of a voyage. Seasickness—real seasickness—is endured by these few with a resolute bravery that sometimes awes their heedless and healthy shipmates.

We have arrived at our rendezvous on time, but the convoy is a little late, delayed by weather. We are now at Westomp—Western Ocean Meeting Point—where the convoys change escorts, much as trains change crews ashore at divisional points. Our eastbound convoy here will shed the Local Escort Group which has brought it from New York, Boston, and Halifax to this point, to be replaced by us, the Mid-Ocean Escort, who will stay with it until relieved by the United Kingdom escort somewhere south of Iceland and west of Ireland.

And suddenly, there they are. First the cluttered mast of a destroyer pierces the horizon right ahead, then her whole bridge heaves into view; her signal lamp flashes a greeting, to which *Montgomery* responds. Now, right across the horizon, masts and funnels appear, rapidly climbing over the heaving seascape to reveal themselves as merchant ships; out on each flank is the tiny silhouette of an escort.

A convoy at sea is an awe-inspiring sight, even to us, who spend most of our days at sea hanging about the flanks of them, and as we draw rapidly up to this one, even off-duty crewmen climb out on our deck to have a close-hand look at HX 142, as it has been officially designated—

forty-two ships, bound from Halifax to the United Kingdom with food, weapons, machinery, oil, petroleum, and all the manifold munitions of war.

A convoy is a live thing, a collective entity greater than the sum of its parts. There is an unmistakable sense of purpose about this enormous collection of ships as it forges relentlessly to the eastward, its vast bulk covering the sea from horizon to horizon. Its ships are in nine ordered ranks, its flanks five ships deep, and as we draw closer to its starboard wing we can make out the individual ships, the characters of the convoy, so to speak, whose eccentricities of appearance and behaviour are to become a part of our lives in the long days and nights ahead.

It is always a thrill to see a convoy at sea in the brief role of spectator before one's horizon becomes limited by responsibility for some single sector, and as we pass down the side of the great armada we are again moved by its sense of might and purpose, and by an appreciation of the enormous human energy and miracles of organization which have assembled this force of great ships, flying the flags of virtually every maritime nation, bound from ports all over the world to an embattled island, now besieged and surrounded. Here is one of the concentrations of power that are shaping our destiny; here in these ships are the essentials which can sustain a whole nation: food for millions of people, and fuel and arms for their defence. Millions upon millions of dollars are represented by these ships and their cargoes, the accumulated man-hours of countless men and women toiling in farms and factories in a score of countries, in hundreds of towns and cities.

This convoy, manned and escorted by more than a thousand seamen, assembled and equipped and directed by staffs who even now are plotting its position in operations rooms on both sides of the Atlantic, represents a significant portion of the wealth of the free world, the end result of dedicated man-hours and a triumph of human organizing genius. More to the point, it represents a very important factor in the war between freedom and tyranny, and as we watch it surge past us we are reminded yet again of our own responsibility for its safe arrival.

The sense of power invests this collection of rusting ships with an almost elemental quality; one can sense that it will steam on, regardless of loss, regardless of weather or attack, like some great leviathan scorning the assaults of lesser creatures of the deep.

At the head of the centre column is the commodore's ship, a fine 'Blue Funnel' cargo liner, one of Alfred Holt's great ships, her halyards a mass of bunting as she signals a pending course change to her charges. Behind her, sheltered by the columns on either side, are the three precious tankers carrying the fuel oil and petroleum that is perhaps the most valuable of all the varied cargoes being carried here to a besieged Britain. They are so deeply laden that they seem at times to be largely submerged, like some half-tide rocks, but as they forge into the great rollers they occasionally rise ponderously, like monstrous sea-beasts from the depths, streaming tons of water from their rusting decks.

Some of the leading ships in the columns have Spitfire and Hurricane fighters mounted on long catapult structures on their bows; these are to give us some measure of air protection as we cross 'The Pit', that enormous sector of mid-Atlantic which lies beyond the zones of air-cover extending east of Newfoundland, south from Iceland, and west from the British Isles, Strictly a one-way trip for their pilots, of course; once their job is done, the enemy aircraft shot down or driven off, they must either crash-land in the sea close to an escort and hope to be rescued from their sinking plane, or simply abandon their aircraft at a safe altitude and bail out by parachute, hoping to be plucked from the sea by an escort. Normally, escort commanders try to conserve them until sea conditions give the pilot a fighting chance of ditching or bailing out safely.

The escort carriers, converted merchantmen able to fly on and off a handful of aircraft and thus provide air cover to the convoy all the way across, are still a year in the future in this winter of '41–'42.

The ships themselves represent the whole spectrum of maritime trade. Although we do not have the older, smaller ships that sail in the slow 'sc' convoys, there are ships here of every class and vintage, from trim Blue Star and Ellerman liners, still with their peacetime promenade deck amidships, to the ugly ore-carriers and the new utilitarian 'Empire' and 'Fort' wartime-built ships. Mostly they are painted grey and streaked by rust and salt, but here and there are trim Scandinavians, bright in peacetime livery, with huge flags painted on their sides. Some of these neutrals still sail independently, trusting to their lights and flags to earn them safety from U-boat attack, but so many have been lost that now they tend to sail in convoy through the dangerous North Atlantic along with Allied ships.

Here and there, one can see an exotic newcomer to the grey Atlantic: a Ben liner from the Far East, a Fyffe banana boat, a Royal Mail ship from the blue Pacific, the little English Channel packet steamer sailing as rescue ship to the convoy.

We notice something missing: there's no battleship escort to give big-gun protection against a surface raider. We've grown accustomed to having one of the old 'R'-class battleships, usually HMS *Revenge*, along for the ride across, but this time we've got an armed merchant cruiser, a former liner armed with six-inch guns, to add a bit of punch to the escort. Somebody makes out her name; it's *Worcestershire*, the fine old Bibby liner, and the name brings a grin all around on the bridge. For *Worcestershire* is famous for an incident involving her doctor's hideous revenge on a group of Canadian army officers who had taken passage aboard.

The doctor, who, as is traditional in HM ships, was secretary of the wardroom mess, had cautioned the Canadian army types against what he considered excessive drinking, and muttered darkly about damage to the kidneys and other possible effects. The Canadians, enjoying a respite from their usual responsibilities, were in no mood to heed these mutterings from the doctor, and when they discovered that he was a teetotaller and at the same time in charge of wardroom wines and spirits, their merriment knew no bounds. Goaded by their incessant teasing, the doctor determined to wreak a horrible revenge. With the considerable resources of the ship's big peacetime passenger dispensary on hand, he began to introduce into the Canadians' drink and food a chemical compound which turned their urine a bright orange.

This had no noticeable effect on the Canadians, other than a marked aversion to oranges and citrus fruits, so the doctor played his second card. He switched to a compound which changed his victims' water to a vivid green, and after a few days, to a rather attractive electric blue. He was now producing real results; green slowed the Canadian drinking to a trickle, and blue brought it to an absolute standstill; the Canadians sat about the wardroom morose and silent, each man alone with his thoughts, and waving away any proffered drinks which the doctor, now assiduous, pressed upon them. Pale and wan and worried, they were a pitiful sight.

But by now the doctor's blood was up; not content with the sad state to which he had reduced his hapless victims, he determined on one final brutal stroke to complete his revenge. Overnight he changed their urine to a deep black.

It was the last straw. With half-remembered tales of black-water fever crowding into their fevered minds, and pale from lack of sleep, the Canadian officers one by one called in at the ship's hospital in the morning 'to have a word with the doctor'.

The doctor claimed that he then made it clear to his victims that it had all been a harmless prank, but the Canadians had versions of how they had extorted details of the plot from him under duress, and with promises to have him disgraced by his fellow practitioners for violation of his Hippocratic oath. However that may be, the doctor's ingenious plot has established him as a character, and has made his ship a famous and welcome addition to any North American escort force. We are pleased to have *Worcestershire* sailing with us.

Our escort group breaks up on a signal from *Montgomery*, and each of us heads for an allotted place in the screen. We work our way gingerly across the front of the oncoming herd to take our station out on the starboard flank. *Montgomery* has positioned herself, *Arvida*, and *Chilliwack* across the front of the convoy, with *Dauphin* opposite us on the port side and *Kamsack* as Tail-End Charlie covering the rear. We are stationed so as to be able, in theory at least, to cover our sector with our asdic beams overlapping, zigzagging but maintaining station on the eight-knot convoy.

We are rapidly closing *Fort William*, a steam Bangor designed as a fast fleet minesweeper but converted into an ocean escort; she is making heavy weather of the big sea still running, shipping a good deal of water over her short fo'c'sle and low quarterdeck. Her skipper is an old friend of our own captain, and as we take over from her and begin our outward leg, our captain signals: 'THERE IS A VERY YOUNG, VERY PREGNANT GIRL ON THE JETTY ASKING AFTER YOU.'

Back comes the prompt response: 'SHE'LL JUST HAVE TO WAIT HER TURN LIKE ALL THE OTHERS.'

It raises a smile as the Local Escort hauls away for the fleshpots of St John's, and we settle into the familiar routine of convoy escort. Quickly our little world takes on its distinctive shape: the diminutive silhouette of *Chilliwack* far ahead, and the five ships of the wing column stretching down our port side. We come to know each detail of those five ships: their silhouettes, their peculiar groupings of funnels, masts, and derrick booms, their varying colours, and even their distinctive rust streaks and patches. There is one in particular, the third in line, which is of special significance; a modern motorship, she is fitted with goalpost masts to handle her cargo, and it is the distinctive silhouette of these great rectangular projections and the thick, squat funnel which makes our job of night station-keeping easier. *Montgomery* has the only radar yet fitted in the group; the rest of us keep station visually, zigging outward until the convoy becomes invisible behind us, then altering course in until, at the limits of our inward leg, the convoy becomes visible to us again. On a black, rainy night or in a shrieking blizzard, a glimpse of those ungodly goalpost masts helps to put things in proper perspective, and a quick bearing tells us whether we're in proper station.

Another help to station-keeping, but a nuisance in every other way, is the inevitable Smoky Joe, the last ship in our line. An old coal-burner, and only just able to keep up with her newer, faster sisters, she frequently commits the cardinal convoy sins of straggling and making smoke, often at the same time. She is a case-hardened tramp of First World War vintage, her overworked stokers attempting to keep her antiquated engines running at close to her maximum speed on inferior coal, and she quickly establishes herself as our particular problem child. Once she falls behind, it is all she can do to catch up, emitting clouds of black smoke which can be spotted by a questing U-boat far over the horizon, thus risking the survival of every ship in the convoy. Yet if she falls back beyond the escort coverage, she is herself a sitting duck to be snapped up by the first U-boat which sights her.

Time after time, in those first days, we close her with our loud hailer going and signal flags flying from our yard-arm—cautioning, cajoling, pleading, threatening. To all our exhortations, we receive the same response: a wave of acknowledgement from her skipper at the open door of her wheelhouse. We want him to do the best he can, but of course we know what he is trying to cope with, and for all our lecturing we feel a deep sympathy for his predicament. But he is Trouble, the weak link which could mean disaster for us all, and we curse the officer ashore who included him in our lot instead of grouping him with the slower ships where he belongs.

Slowly, painfully, HX 142 inches eastward; the noon positions crawl across the chart of the western ocean in half a hundred chart rooms. Each day at noon Howard Wallace, our diminutive red-bearded navigator, emerges, sextant in hand, in the hope that the constant cloud cover will thin enough for him to get a noon altitude and thus establish our latitude, to complement the occasional star shot he may sneak in a clear patch in the night watches. On a rolling, pitching corvette bridge, with a horizon lumpy with heavy seas, it takes both luck and skill to produce satisfactory results, and for days on end bad weather reduces us to estimating our position simply on course steered and distance run. Each midday the convoy commodore, operating from the stablest platform and with the best facilities, indicates by a flaghoist his observed or estimated position, which automatically becomes the official one of the convoy, but every self-respecting escort and merchantman commander likes to arrive at his own independent calculation, which allows them to sneer at the figures arrived at by the commodore.

In good weather the commodore may exercise his ships in convoy evolutions, carrying out turns by signal, or exercising gun crews in firing close-range weapons.

A convoy is like a small city at sea, full of minor or major crises: a man is injured or falls sick, and the destroyer's doctor may have to be transferred to a merchantman—not fun in bad weather; one ship has engine trouble, another has a bad leak, or problems with cargo shifting. There is a constant flow of information back and forth between commander and convoy, convoy and escort. Daily our senior officer checks out the fuel remaining to each escort; under the best of conditions some of them, particularly destroyers, can only just make the other side on a mid-ocean crossing with a slim margin of fuel remaining, so that bad weather or prolonged high-speed steaming means refuelling at sea, always a bit dicey in bad weather. But the overriding concerns, overshadowing all else, are weather and U-boats, and threatening situations in connection with either call for consultation between commodore and escort.

Each evening our wireless office gives us the latest Admiralty appreciation of the U-boat situation. Daily, with Teutonic punctuality, each U-boat at sea tries to signal Doenitz's headquarters its position and situation, so that the master in his Berlin bunker may guide them to a chosen target. These U-boat transmissions are monitored by shore stations in Britain, their messages decoded by the secret 'Ultra' deciphering machine, and the position of each U-boat is plotted and broadcast to Allied escorts. Each evening, as we crawl steadily eastward, we plot the positions of known U-boats on our chart, and it becomes ever more apparent that we are in for a brush with them; half a dozen are scattered right across our path, and although we are routed ever more to the north, up toward the Arctic Circle itself, no amount of course alteration seems able to take us clear. Bad weather, which makes it impossible for U-boats to operate on the surface, may yet see us through. And bad weather there is in plenty.

Gale after gale shrieks down upon us, howling out of the north as we approach Cape Farewell, southernmost tip of Greenland. Fierce winds tear at our rigging, snatch the tops off waves and send them flying above our mastheads, stinging our faces and blinding our eyes. Mountainous seas crash inboard, making our upper decks impassable, sweeping over our forward gun and crashing against our superstructure with an impact that jars us to the keel. Life below is a hell of wet clothes and fitful sleep, of sandwich meals and constant, violent, bruising motion. Even the plumbing is impossible; to use the toilet is to risk a cold douche as the head seas overpower valves and piping.

On a wild night watch, I see the lighter rim of the sky blotted out and realize, in a moment of mind-numbing panic, that the wall of blackness that towers ahead of us is an enormous, an unbelievable sea, the '67th wave' dreaded by every sailor. I duck beneath the dodger as the bows rise, and commend my soul to God. There is a thunderous roar, and the whole world is blotted out in water, filled with a myriad crashes and crackings. Miraculously, the wave passes, and I emerge, soaked and scared yet unscathed. But in the sudden silence I can sense something wrong; the ship is falling off into the trough and I can get no answer from the wheelhouse voice-pipe. Mad with fright—if the ship falls broadside to the waves in this mountainous sea we shall surely be rolled right over—I dash down the ladder and burst into the wheelhouse, and into a scene of utter chaos. The rogue sea had burst in the shutters and windows of the wheel-house, flooding and gutting it and knocking helmsman and telegraph rating against the after bulkhead. They are still there, paralysed with fright and shock, but at the wheel is the captain, brought from his tiny sea-cabin off the wheelhouse, now spinning the wheel hard over to get the ship back head to sea. I ring the engines to emergency full ahead, and we wait, frozen in an agonized tableau, our eyes riveted on the pool of light that is the steering compass. The ship rolls heavily, deeply, right over on her side; if she gets another sea in this position we are all gone for sure. But the engine beat quickens; we can hear the stokehold bell below as the engine room opens all the taps, and at last we can see the compass card begin to move. The crisis is past; it is just a matter of shoring up our shattered wheelhouse covers and we are back in business.

The wild weather may be keeping the U-boats down, but it is also taking its toll of the convoy; under its thunderous blows, HX 142 begins to dis-integrate. The gaps between ships increase as ships seek greater sea-room. There is a tremendous collision near the centre as a great bulk carrier becomes unmanageable and sheers out of line, her bows colliding with those of a new Empire vessel in the adjoining column; in the black night we hear the rending screech of fractured metal above the howling of the gale.

Fortunately, it is a glancing blow, but even so it has torn a gaping hole in the starboard bow of the Empire ship, and although the hole is well above the water-line, in this wild weather it is a dangerous wound. Both ships fall astern to examine and repair damage as best they can, and *Kamsack* is told off to stand by them until they can rejoin the convoy. But there is no respite; all the next day the gaps between ships steadily widen, although the commodore has reduced speed to a signalled four knots, which is more like two over the ground. At this speed some ships are virtually unable to maintain a proper course; they fall out of line and peel off to either side, seeking sea-room. They give us in the escorts some grey hairs, for there is nothing which can bring one's heart into one's mouth faster than the sight of a great black shape looming out of the night when one fancied oneself safely distant a mile or so from the nearest merchant-man. Next morning Smoky Joe is far behind, now just a smudge of smoke astern on the horizon, and *Kamsack* is directed by *Montgomery* to take him under her wing as well. By the morning of this third day of the gale, HX 142 is scattered over miles of ocean, its shattered ranks broken into two shapeless huddles of storm-lashed ships, its escorts now running dangerously low on fuel with a thousand miles of stormy Atlantic still ahead and the U-boat gauntlet still to run.

Fortunately, at this desperate juncture the wind begins to ease; by afternoon it is no more than a fresh breeze and by nightfall the enormous sea has begun to subside. Dawn next day reveals a North Atlantic restored to something like normalcy. Immediately *Montgomery* drops back to fuel from the aftermost tanker in the centre column, signalling as she goes the rotation in which we, the other escorts, are to leave the screen to top up our depleted tanks. By mid-afternoon our turn has come; we steam down through the re-forming ranks of the convoy and approach the tanker from astern. Our fo'c'sle party grapples and picks up the long grass-line streamed behind the huge tanker, together with the empty water-breaker used as a buoy on the end of it, and haul it on the empty fuel hose, filled with air so it will float, which the tanker pays out like a great serpent astern. We close up until we are broad on the tanker's quarter, the buoyant hose streaming astern of the tanker and then up into our fo'c'sle in a deep U-shape. The hose end is quickly fastened to the pipe-nozzle which had just been fitted for the purpose at our refit last fall, and at a flag signal from us the oiler begins pumping. We steam along at convoy speed, protected from attack by ships all about us, keeping station easily by maintaining the U in the bight of the hose, which in effect cushions any small failure in station-keeping caused by wind or sea.

This is a method of fuelling at sea developed by mid-ocean escorts in the teeth of regular-navy opposition, for in peacetime oiling had been regarded as an evolution, something to be carried out on calm seas as a display of smart seamanship. Destroyers were required to close the tanker alongside and to steam, beam to beam, a few feet apart, while a short length of hose was passed directly across. Station-keeping had to be perfect;

the slightest yawing resulted in a broken hose or a collision, sometimes both together, so that the evolution became impossible with any sort of sea running. Even the astern method had its dangers; more than one escort had been covered with thick black oil from bows to bridge, from masthead to waterline, as a result of a hose breaking during fuelling and the broken end, flying madly about under great pressure, squirting tons of heavy bunker oil over everything. Such a nightmare was always possible in bad weather, but the large amount of slack in the fuel hose represented by the deep U-shaped bight provided a safe degree of leeway for any well-handled ship. In less than an hour we have topped-up, had pumping stopped, let the hose blow clear, capped it, and cast it off, and we are on our way back to our screening position on the starboard flank of the convoy.

All day HX 142 has been re-forming, the commodore maintaining slow speed while stragglers hurry back into position, and the ranks slowly close up and regain cohesion. Last to return is Smoky Joe, clouds of smoke belching from his tall, thin funnel. As night closes in, convoy speed is increased.

Next day brings a new enemy. We are approaching the area, just beyond reach of air cover from Iceland or Ireland, where the U-boats maintain their patrolling line. It is a thin affair nowadays, as more and more U-boats are hurried down to the happy hunting grounds off the American coast where American shipping, unprotected by convoy as a result of an almost unbelievable miscalculation by Admiral King and his staff, can be butchered like so many sheep. But the evening U-boat report shows plenty of activity still in our area, and the Admiralty, in a special signal to us, warn that at least three U-boats are in the immediate vicinity of our convoy.

We take every precaution; lookouts are especially vigilant, guns and depth-charges are checked out, and we close in to abjure Smoky Joe to throw on his best lumps of coal in order to keep in station and make the minimum amount of smoke. We receive the mandatory wave of the hand—reassuring? resigned? resentful? Who could say?—and return to our position on the screen, maintain our zigzag in meticulous station. The night passes without incident.

Next day it becomes clear that we have been spotted. Unusual U-boat activity from our immediate area indicates we are being tailed by at least one U-boat, and the pack is gathering. Late that afternoon, as visibility fades, *Montgomery* leaves her station and sweeps astern at high speed; half an hour later the commodore alters convoy course drastically to the north-ward. *Montgomery* hopes to force any shadower to submerge and thereby not be in a position to detect our new change of course. *Montgomery* returns early in the evening without having spotted anything, but it is hoped that we have shaken off, at least temporarily, any U-boat attack. It is standard practice for U-boats to maintain contact at visibility limit astern, on the surface or at periscope depth according to circumstances, steering convoy course and speed by day and surfacing at nightfall to overtake at high speed and gain an attacking position on the bow of the convoy. Attack is usually from this position on the surface, the boat trimmed down so that virtually only her conning tower is exposed. A spread of torpedoes is fired, with the attacker then either running right through the convoy, or turning to escape at high speed on the surface while the convoy steams on.

It is black night; there will be a moon later on, if the cloud cover permits, but meantime the darkness favours us in our attempt to avoid detection. We steam on, everyone on tenterhooks; on the bridge and in the messdecks the tension is almost palpable. Yet at sea we are all fatalists; when I turn in after an austere supper—all our fresh supplies are long gone and we virtually live on Spam—I quickly fall into deep and dreamless sleep.

Good God, what was that? I sit upright in the pitch-black cabin. There it is again, the rumbling bang against the ship's side of an underwater explosion, and as I switch on the lamp there is another one. Not depth-charges, these; they can only be torpedoes, and as I fling my legs over the side of the bunk and pull on my seaboots, the alarm bells suddenly go off overhead, sounding action stations, and the whole sleeping ship explodes into pandemonium. Racing for the bridge, I cannon into dark figures, bulky with lifejackets; the night is filled with drumming feet, muttered curses, the metallic sounds of clips being loosened, hatches flung open, guns and depth-charges cleared away, and over all the insistent, mind-maddening clangour of the alarm bells.

Up on the bridge the atmosphere is tense with suppressed excitement; the captain is at the voice-pipes, bringing the ship around to point directly away from the convoy, his voice clipped, controlled, urgent. And the convoy, ah God, the convoy—

We must have been at the inner limit of our zigzag when the torpedoes struck; the dark shapes of the outer column tower darkly above us, seeming frighteningly close. But just beyond them is a terrifying sight: the leading ship of the second column is afire, and flames can be seen all along her upper deck. Even as we watch there is a blinding flash, and suddenly she bursts into a towering pillar of flame. Across the water comes the sound of the explosion, and a new, horrifying sound: the roar of the inferno that has engulfed her. She must have been carrying high-octane petroleum as deck cargo; only this could have turned her into such a tremendous torch. It is as bright as day; the flames light up the sea all around us, throwing the ships of the intervening column into bold relief, illuminating the pale, tense faces on the bridge behind me. All eyes are on the doomed ship; nobody speaks, we are struck dumb by the fearful majesty of the terrible scene before us, by the unbelievable roar of the holocaust. Slowly, serenely, she passes down the column, isolated now from her grubby sisters in the splendid beauty of her destruction. It is a voice up the pipe from the wireless office which breaks the spell: 'From *Montgomery*, sir: Raspberry!'

It is an order to all escorts to turn outward and illuminate their sectors with star shell—one of the new group tactical evolutions embodied in the escort 'Bible', the big blue-bound volume known as Western Approaches Convoy Instructions, or simply 'Wackey'. From our inward position, the captain swings our bows around until we are steaming directly away from the convoy, and at a word from him Falconer, our gunnery officer, calls down the foregun voice-pipe: 'With star-shell and reduced charge, load! Load! Load!' There are orderly scufflings from the gun's crew, and we can hear the breech being swung open and closed, and then Falconer passes down the arc to be covered. 'Illuminate from red 45 to green 45.' The gun is trained and reported ready, and as all glasses on bridge are readied and we cover our eyes with our hands, there comes the order 'Shoot!' A blinding flash, a hot whiff of cordite, and in the sudden blackness that follows, everyone peers intently out into the dark void on the port bow. After what seems like ages, the shell burst, high and far, and instantly turns night into day. As the magnesium flare, dangling from its parachute slowly descends, it lights up the empty sea beneath it. Even as we watch, the gun fires again, and after another ageless interval, a second flare appears, further ahead, and now higher than the original, which has been drifting evenly down. And then another, and another; in the space of a minute we have hung a curtain of star shell over a wide arce of the sea, and as the flares drift lower they light up the surface in unbelievable detail, throwing into relief every tiny wavetop. All around the convoy the other escorts are lighting up their sectors; already we can benefit from the out-ermost star shell fired by *Chilliwack* ahead and *Kamsack* far astern. If, as *Montgomery* believes, the U-boat attacking us is making her escape on the surface, we should be able to catch a glimpse of her, with any luck. Luck, because the area to be covered is huge, and the arcs can never be simultaneous; the first star shell are dipping into the sea, to be snuffed out before the arc can be half completed, and the gaps between areas covered by individual escorts are many and large. And yet—there is a lot of light up there, a lot of sea laid bare for the scrutiny of hundreds of searching eyes. *Montgomery* has radar, a sort of Stone Age contraption; one of her officers told me that they don't put any faith in any object it reports unless they can actually see it, and that its main use was giving a distance off the convoy for station-keeping, but for all of that they'll be chasing every back-echo and will-o'-the-wisp wavetop it reports right now.

And then—there it is! Far out to the right of the last star shell I catch a glimpse through the binoculars of something in the wavetops, and as my heart almost stops with excitement I see, for the first time, the unmistakeable outline of a U-boat conning tower. My shout is simultaneous with that of the Captain: 'There she is; green 45!' and then everything happens at once. The captain cannons into me, leaping for the voice-pipe. 'Starboard twenty!' Falconer calls for another star shell on the same bearing as the last, and Harvey rushes for the asdic set to give his operators the bearing of the surfaced enemy; the moment he dives he becomes their responsibility. As the ship steadies on her new course, heading directly for the submarine, the captain issues a string of orders. A sighting signal is cracked off to *Montgomery*, the gun's crew bangs off its last star shell and then loads with high-explosive shell and a full charge, and down in the waist and quarterdeck the depth-charge crews rush to put shallow settings on their first pattern of charges, for we hope to be up with the U-boat before he can dive deep. The captain calls for emergency full ahead, and even on the bridge we can hear the double ring of the engine telegraphs in the wheelhouse, and up the stokehold ventilators behind us we can hear the answering bells ringing and the stokers shouting as they open all the taps.

I keep the glasses glued on the U-boat, now brightly illuminated as the star-shell flares fall closer; under our feet the ship vibrates madly as the engines reach for their full power. We are closing rapidly, but suddenly there is a welter of white water all about the tiny black conning tower towards which we are charging.

She's diving! I turn to the captain, but he has already seen for himself.

'She's blowing ballast tanks,' he mutters, and calmly takes a bearing of her over the standard compass.

In a matter of seconds, she is gone, her position marked by a swirl of foam, and moments later our last star shell dips into the sea and blackness locks us in on every side. The captain moves into the asdic house to direct the search, and as we approach the diving position we reduce speed to ten knots, our asdic beam searching beneath the surface for the vanished enemy.

'From *Montgomery*, sir; *Kamsack* to close and assist *Trail* in hunting U-boat,' reports the signal yeoman from the wireless cabin voice-pipe. This is welcome news; with two escorts, one to hold contact while the other attacks, we should be able to kill this U-boat. On the silent bridge, on the darkened decks, men stand in attitudes of tension, all minds on the softly lit compass in the asdic cabin, where a ray of light and the persistent ping! of the set indicate that our supersonic beam is probing the blind depths for the hidden killer of our ships.

'Echo bearing red 10, range eleven hundred yards!' Out on the windswept bridge, I hear the report we have been aching to hear on the chart-room voice-pipe. The report is from the operator on the set; from Clarke, his leading hand the ranking asdic rating on the ship, comes the qualifying report: 'Echo low,' and then, after the cut-offs have been established, the confident, unequivocal report: 'Target is submarine, sir, on an opening course.'

From the captain, then, the low words that put it all together: 'Start the attack!'

The attacking signal is made to *Kamsack* and *Montgomery*, we accelerate to a fifteen-knot attacking speed, settings for depth-charges are confirmed and their crews put on standby for firing. As officer of the watch I keep a lookout on the bridge, but my mind is with the little group huddled about the soft-lit instruments inside the cabin behind me, where the operator is holding contact. Clarke, our senior specialist, is keeping the captain posted, and the deep black marks of the chemical traces mark the roll of paper on the set each time an echo is received back from the U-boat, and thus indicate its range on the marked scale.

Bang!

Jesus, what was that! I whirl around toward the convoy, and then, seconds later, comes the sound of yet another explosion. Lord, more torpedoes; we've walked into a second submarine. I pass the word to the captain inside, who simply nods, too intent on our own developing attack to waste words. Moments later, *Kamsack* is diverted from us by *Montgomery*, and detailed to sweep astern for the second U-boat. The commodore reports the pennant numbers of the latest ship attacked, and corrects an earlier report; despite those first three explosions, only two ships have been torpedoed in the earlier attack—the extra bang was just one of those things.

At six hundred yards, the captain makes a bold throw-off, based on reports from the set and our plot, where the courses of target and ship have been carefully plotted. We alter thirty degrees to starboard in order to cross ahead of our unseen antagonist, so that our charges may sink through the water in his path and, hopefully, explode as he heads right into them.

Now the reports come thick and fast, the whole intensity of our effort stepping up as the range closes quickly. This is the climactic moment of the whole attack, when this ship justifies the purpose for which she was built and for which all her crew have trained and endured. The next few seconds can make it all worth while, can redeem the endless man-hours and effort which ship and crew represent. Except for the chanted litany of the asdic team, intoning its bearings and ranges, there is utter silence throughout the ship, every man keyed up to the breaking point. In the asdic cabin, the black line of the echo traces will be moving along the paper tape, being aligned with the perspex firing bar; when they coincide with the etched line on the bar the firing will begin.

There it is: 'Fire one!' And seconds later, 'Fire two!' and then 'Fire three!' From the blackness behind us, we hear the splash of the charges from the traps into our wake, the 'whoosh! whoosh!' of the throwers on each side as we drop our charges in an elongated diamond pattern of ten, with six charges in pairs on the centre line and four from the throwers, two on each side.

'Simultaneous echoes!' comes the report from the asdic operator; the target is so close that no ranging is possible, and moments later, as the target passes astern and our transmissions are blanked out by our own wake, 'Lost contact, sir.'

'Boom! Bang! Whoorumph!' The tremendous detonation of our charges is like a giant hammer striking our hull; the whole ship lifts and is borne aloft as a great fountain of water, sensed rather than seen, rises from astern. The ship is given a ferocious shaking, and on deck we clutch for support; in the engine room, we must have broken every pipe we have. The captain reduces speed, and we circle around to give our asdic set a clear field in which to regain contact. But in the asdic cabin there are bitter oaths; the main gyro which directs our compasses has been unseated by the explo-sions, and everyone works desperately to get it back in service, for without it our asdic compass is useless. The captain paces in a fury of exasperation.

How was it? we ask ourselves. In the waist, the depth-charge crews are jabbering with excitement as they reload their mortars, and all of us wait for confirmation of our success. Surely no U-boat could have survived the accurate explosion of three tons of amatol? From the plot comes the confirmation that the attack seemed a good one, but still, as we circle around, comes neither contact with the U-boat nor signs of its destruction. Unless—surely that smell was not there before—surely that is the smell of oil! I call the captain out and he sniffs excitedly, but then the smell is gone, as quickly as it came.

'Not enough for a kill; more likely she's sprung a rivet or two in her fuel tanks,' the captain cautions, and moves back to the set. At long last, our gyro is operational again, and the asdic team buckles to its job. Still no contact; we begin a square search, directed by the plot, and the minutes grow, and with them our chances of regaining contact dwindle. Time is now crucial to us, for if we are not firmly in contact we cannot delay much longer. Our convoy is under attack, our escort hard-pressed, the sea perhaps covered with survivors awaiting rescue or death, men whose life in the sea is measured in minutes.

The issue we are already beginning to agonize over is resolved in a moment by a peremptory signal from *Montgomery*. We are to rejoin at best speed, and sweep astern as we do so while *Kamsack* screens the rescue ship, lying stopped and vulnerable as she hauls shaken and sodden men from the sea.

In dejected silence we huddle at our action stations. In an inspired moment, somebody lays on a cup of 'kye' all around, and as we sip the hot chocolate, so thick that it is barely liquid, we fortify ourselves for the long hours of vigilance which still lie ahead of us before this night is over. Our burning motorship has disappeared, her flames presumably snuffed out by the invading sea, and everything else has been swept away from our world, the dark shapes of the convoy having long vanished over the horizon ahead. We increase to fifteen knots; it will be all we can do to regain station by early morning.

In the event, we come up with part of the convoy earlier than expected. At first light, the air becomes rank with a familiar stink, and as the light grows we find ourselves steaming through a vast pool of oil, a slick of glossy slime that seems to cover the whole ocean. It is fuel from the bunkers of our torpedoed merchantman, and scattered about in it is the indescribable debris left by sunken ships. We pass gratings, and boxes, and nameless hunks of timber, hatchboards, bloated canvas covers, bits of white-painted wood. Boats, too; one of them with bows stove in and half full of water, two others in good shape, but empty of occupants.

In silence we stare from our decks at the debris streaming past; clusters of faces at the break of our fo'c'sle show that even the watch below has come out to look, in shivering silence, at these pitiful fragments from the shattered households of friends and comrades. There are worse horrors to come; my stomach rises as I see, white in the black water, the bloated sacs and torn flesh of what I am forced to recognize as the lungs and viscera and abdomen of a human being, and a little further on, a sudden pointing of arms from our onlookers indicates a man, only his head and shoulders visible in the filthy sea. He is dead, of course; his eyes are open, like his twisted mouth, but he sags lifelessly against his oil-stained lifejacket, his face as grey as the soiled canvas supporting it, his hair and cheeks plastered with the fuel oil which has suffocated him. We steam past in awed silence; for our first-trippers, it is a startling glimpse of the Death which up to now has been one of war's abstractions, distant and impersonal, something to be read about or glimpsed in a distant explosion.

Oppressed by our failure, in the bleak grey dawn we steam through a filthy sea laden with reproach, our decks slippery with disorder of a night action, squalid with dirty cocoa cups, blistered paint, broken glass, and fallen corking. Sullen, sleepless, and silent we rejoin HX 142.

The RCN's sleek, fast Tribal-class destroyers were perhaps the most romantic of all the warships manned by Canadians in the Second World War. The ships served in that war, in Korea with UN forces, and on into the 1960s before being scrapped. They were a kind of bridge between the gruelling, slog-it-out war of the corvette and the gunslinger life of the MGB. But their action—and their end—could have its own excitement, and its own tragedy.

The Tribals—the Loss of 'Athabaskan'
Joseph Schull

A little to the west of the area in which the MTBs operated, three Canadian destroyers were engaged on more extended operations. *Iroquois*, first of the Canadian Tribals and the longest in service, had been sent to Halifax in February for a refit. *Haida*, *Athabaskan*, and *Huron* remained. They had been attached to Plymouth Command in January as part of the 10th Destroyer Flotilla. By April they had become veteran members of a force whose activities were becoming ever more urgently and directly linked with the preparations for Neptune.

Two methodical, long-range programs involving almost nightly missions for the destroyers had been carried on under Plymouth Command for many months. The first, known as Operation Tunnel, was a continuous series of patrols directed against German Biscay and Channel convoys. Groups of destroyers, frequently supported by cruisers, placed themselves athwart the well-known routes in the Bay or the western Channel, seeking to destroy both the merchantmen and the strong escort forces which sailed in company.

Operation Hostile, the second of the two programs, was a minelaying operation in which the destroyers, again frequently with cruisers, served as a covering force. While fast British minelayers went in to mine enemy waters, the covering forces lay to seaward of them, prepared to deal with German ships which might come out to interfere. The mining of enemy convoy routes, and more particularly of the approaches to their harbours along the French coast, was an important feature of the Neptune preparations. As D-day approached, Operation Hostile was stepped up according to a set schedule both in range and intensity. By the time the ships of Neptune sailed, every enemy harbour along the coast was to be ringed with mines of the newest and deadliest type.

By the latter part of April *Haida* had carried out nineteen of the Operation Tunnel or Operation Hostile missions; *Huron* had carried out eleven; and *Athabaskan*, nine. Between missions they had fitted in as they could as series of special exercises in night fighting, navigation, and the radar detection and radar-controlled gunnery which were later to prove of deadly effect. Up to the night of April 25, however, none of their sorties had brought them into contact with an enemy force.

On that night another mission under Operation Tunnel was in train, and was to be carried out by the British cruiser, *Black Prince*, the British destroyer, *Ashanti*, and *Haida*, *Huron*, and *Athabaskan*. The force was to sail from Plymouth at nine o'clock on the evening of April 25, and at one-thirty on the morning of the 26th was to arrive in a position seventeen miles east-north-east of Ile de Bas, about ten miles off the French coast. From that point it was to patrol in an east-northeasterly direction for two hours. Three German Elbing class destroyers were known to be berthed in St Malo and were expected to move out early on the morning of the

26th. If they did so, they were to be intercepted. If nothing was seen of them, the British force was to leave its patrol area in time to arrive within twenty miles of the Lizard before dawn.

Black Prince and her destroyers arrived on station punctually and began their patrol. *Haida* and *Athabaskan* were formed up a mile and a half on the cruiser's starboard bow; *Ashanti* and *Huron* had a corresponding station to port of her. Almost at once the force was detected by German radar stations on the French coast, and flashes of gunfire, apparently from shore batteries, appeared in the distance. No salvoes fell near, however, and for a time the patrol continued uneventfully.

Sharp on two o'clock *Black Prince* got a radar echo at 21,000 yards, dead ahead. A moment or so later *Haida* and *Ashanti* confirmed the contact. At that time the force was steaming in a northeasterly direction. The enemy ships were approaching almost head-on, but the radar picture had hardly been analysed when it changed dramatically. The Germans had reversed their course, increased speed from twenty to twenty-four knots and were steaming back for the French coast. The cruiser and her destroyers gave chase at thirty knots, certain now that they were on the track of the three Elbings from St Malo.

At nineteen minutes after two, with the range reduced to 13,000 yards, *Black Prince* fired starshell over the enemy, while the destroyers raced ahead to engage him. According to the usual plan, *Black Prince* with her superior range would manoeuvre herself into position to provide illumination by starshell while the destroyers carried out the actual attack.

The first starshells from the cruiser burst to the right of the target. *Haida* signalled, 'More Left', and the next burst revealed three destroyers dead ahead at a range now reduced to about five miles. *Haida* and *Athabaskan* opened fire at 2.23; *Ashanti* and *Huron*, at 2.26. The Germans began immediately to make smoke; and soon only wreathing, greyish-white clouds could be distinguished ahead, fitfully illuminated by starshell. Salvoes from the four pursuing destroyers plunged into the murk; and out of it came the return fire of the Germans. The Elbings' gunnery was not particularly good, and they seemed to be concentrating mainly on escape as they zig-zagged through the macabre mists of their screen.

Ashanti scored the first hit at thirty-one minutes after two. Five minutes later another bright red flash spumed up through the smoke, indicating a second hit, although it was impossible to tell which destroyer had scored. The chase continued for another fifteen minutes, with the pursuers closing the range to 7,300 yards but still unable to see their enemy. Difficulties increased a few minutes later when one of *Black Prince*'s gun turrets jammed and the destroyers were forced to take turns in putting up starshell.

By 3.20 the flying Elbings, occasionally running out of their smoke screen and then ducking back, were hugging the French coastline, heading for St Malo. They were within twelve miles of shore; and the outlying rocks not only provided inlets where they might hide but were already confusing radar operators with false echoes. *Haida* had noticed that her three radar targets seemed to have decreased to two, indicating that one of the Elbings had fanned out from the others. At about the same time *Black Prince* saw pass down her port side a torpedo which did not appear to have been fired by either of the two ships ahead.

Suddenly at 3.25 *Haida* sighted the Elbing which had broken away. It was two and a half miles distant on her starboard bow and was making off to the south and west after firing the torpedo at *Black Prince*. With *Athabaskan* following her, *Haida* turned at right angles, crossed a British minefield which had been laid in the area, and sent a first salvo crashing into the afterpart of th German ship. Her second and third salvoes struck amidships, starting other fires; after them more shells came raining down from *Athabaskan*.

In a matter of minutes the Elbing was ablaze from stem to stern, but still firing. He continued his fire when *Ashanti* and *Huron*, having lost their two ships among the rocks of the coast, returned to join in the kill. Each destroyer fired torpedoes, none of which found its mark. Then, circling the blazing enemy at ranges as low as four hundred yards, the ships poured their gunfire into him. Just at the conclusion of the mêlée *Ashanti* and *Huron* collided with each other, doing considerable damage. Gradually the fire from the German vessel slacked. The flames mounted higher about it, then began to be eaten away at their base as the ship settled. At twenty-one minutes after four *Haida* reported to *Black Prince*, 'Enemy has sunk.'

Three days later, on April 28, *Haida* and *Athabaskan* sailed from Plymouth on an Operation Hostile mission. They were to screen a flotilla of British minelayers whose mission was to sow mines about ten miles east of Ile de Bas, near the mouth of the Morlaix River. By two o'clock on the morning of the 29th they had begun their patrol, and by three o'clock the minelayers had finished their work and were on the way home.

Previous to the departure of the minelayers, however, *Haida* and *Athabaskan* had received a signal from Plymouth, ordering them to steer southwest at full speed. It was a night on which radar conditions were exceptionally good, and radar stations on the English coast had picked up echoes which indicated an enemy force passing in a westerly direction across the entrance to the Morlaix River. At 3.13 Plymouth signalled the destroyers again that the enemy force was nearing them and was expected to pass through a position ten miles north of Ile de Bas. Fifteen minutes later this estimate was altered. The German ships were hugging the coast, and it now seemed that they would pass just one mile north of Ile de Bas.

Haida and *Athabaskan*, steaming southwest for the coast, estimated that they could intercept the enemy after he had passed Ile de Bas and while he was still east of Ile de Vierge. At one minute to four in the morning the first echo came. *Athabaskan* reported a radar contact to port, at a range of fourteen miles. Immediately afterward *Haida* obtained a confirming echo. The first indications were of two ships, but by eleven minutes after four the echoes had increased to three, making it appear that a third small vessel had joined the first two.

The range was closing rapidly and by 4.12 it was down to 7,300 yards. *Haida* gave the order, 'Ignite', and *Athabaskan* fired starshell. Two destroyers, both Elbings, were revealed in the orange-pink glow of the burst. Smoke immediately began to form about them as they laid a screen and turned away. *Haida* and *Athabaskan* opened fire, and, as they did so, turned their bows directly toward the enemy so as to present the narrowest possible silhouette for the torpedoes which German destroyers usually fired as they swung round to retreat.

Athabaskan had barely steadied on her new course when a huge sheet of flame shot up from her afterpart into the early morning darkness. She had been hit by a torpedo fired either from one of the two destroyers or from the third smaller vessel, possibly an E-boat, which was never sighted. As the torpedo struck, *Athabaskan* lost way, turned slowly to port and stopped. Probably her propellers or propeller shafts had been smashed and her rudder broken.

Large fires broke out above and below decks, both in the afterpart and amidships. All after guns were knocked out of action immediately, and in a moment or so fire from the forward guns also ceased. As the stern began to settle, the order 'Stand by to abandon' was given. Boats were made ready but not lowered; and as there seemed to be some hope of saving the ship, hands began to prepare cables for towing. The flames began to blaze up more fiercely and were now becoming uncontrollable. A fire party managed to get the ship's seventy-ton pump to the after part where the blaze was worst, and began the work of connecting it. Just as the last connections were falling into place, however, the destroyer's magazine blew up, sending into the sky a column of flame and smoke which was seen by ships thirty miles away.

With the second explosion the destroyer gave a tremendous heave to starboard, swung slowly back onto an even keel, and then listen to port. The men who were still on board and alive and conscious managed to shove a few Carley floats overside and follow them into the water. They had a minute or so to push themselves away from the writhing steel sides above them. Then the blazing wreckage of what had been one of the happiest ships in the Canadian navy upended slowly in the water and slid under amid clouds of steam and the doleful roar of escaping air. On the oily, heaving blackness of the sea there remained only a few bobbing lights attached to the life jackets of *Athabaskan's* survivors, who were floating— many of them barely conscious—within five miles of the German-held coast.

For *Haida*, the grim priorities of sea warfare had to be maintained. When the torpedo struck *Athabaskan*, she had swung sharply to port and run across in front of her sister ship to lay a protective smoke screen. Then she had altered away again at full speed and resumed her pursuit of the Elbings, on one of which she had already scored a hit. Destruction of the enemy still had to take precedence over rescue work, and she was now hard on the heels of the Germans.

As usual her gunnery was magnificent, controlled throughout the action mainly by radar, since the Elbings could rarely be made out through their smoke. Just at the moment when *Athabaskan* blew up five miles astern, a salvo from *Haida* landed squarely on the Elbing she had already damaged. It banished all prospect of escape for the German, and he ran in at full speed to ground himself among the off-shore rocks of the coast. He still continued to fire, and *Haida*, coming in as close to the rocks as she dared, poured salvo after salvo into him until he was hopelessly ablaze. Then, with dawn breaking and the other Elbing beyond her reach, she turned back to do what she could for the men of *Athabaskan*.

As she reached their position *Haida* was five miles off the French coast, within range of shore batteries and liable to air attack at any moment. The destroyer stopped and dropped all her boats and floats. Scramble-nets were lowered over the side and word was passed from the bridge that the ship would remain for fifteen minutes. Her own men went down the scramble-nets to drag up dazed and exhausted survivors. Her motor cutter also went over the side, manned by a party of three volunteers in charge of Leading Seaman W.A. MacLure.

Haida remained stopped for fifteen minutes and during this time thirty-eight men were rescued. After that, as day broadened, she was under the absolute necessity of departing. Aircraft might be arriving in force from the German-held coast at any minute; and the first responsibility of *Haida*'s commanding officer was to assure the safety of his own ship and her company. Word was passed along that the ship would go ahead in five minutes. The warning was repeated at one-minute intervals to the rescue parties labouring along the side and on the quarter deck. Sixty seconds after the last warning, the order 'slow ahead' was given.

The water began to boil back along the destroyer's sides as she moved past clusters of men who raised an occasional faint cheer. Hands clutching at her scramble-nets lost their grip. Two of her own crew who had gone down the nets were washed off by the backrush and remained in the water with the survivors they had not been able to reach. Then, as *Haida* disappeared in the distance, three German mine-sweepers put out from the coast to make prisoners of the men who were left.

MacLure and his men in *Haida*'s motor cutter had been cruising about picking up any survivors not on Carley floats; and they had now eight in their craft, including their two shipmates who had been washed from the scramble-nets. They were not disposed to accept capture if it could be avoided, and when the mine-sweepers appeared, they set off in the direction of England. One of the German ships chased them briefly, and then for some unaccountable reason turned away. Unpursued, but with a very baulky engine, the men in the motor cutter began a cross-channel voyage alone.

They had fuel for thirty hours and some emergency rations, but for a while it seemed that their chances were not good. Three times the motor failed entirely; even after a leaky feedline had been patched, the best they could get out of their craft was a tedious three knots. In mid-afternoon a flight of bombers passed over them, but failed to observe their Verey lights and hand signalling. A little after four, three planes which they took to be Spitfires came toward them flying very low. Amid a flurry of waving hands the aircraft roared in at a height of about twelve feet, then zoomed upward to give the men in the boat a view of the black crosses of the *Luftwaffe* on the under side of the wings. In the early evening two more planes appeared; and were greeted more circumspectly. This time, however, there was no mistake. The planes were Spitfires; and, as they nosed down for a look, semaphore flags from the cutter spelled out, 'Athabaskan, Canada, Navy'. The Spitfires acknowledged the signal, and remained wheeling overhead until they were relieved by two more Spitfires and a Lancaster. Later in the evening a rescue launch of the Royal Air Force came charging out from the British coast; and by midnight the three men of the cutter's crew, together with the eight passengers, were being protestingly hospitalized 'for observation' in Penzance. Their arrival brought the total number of *Athabaskan* survivors to forty-four. The commanding officer and 128 of the ship's company were missing and eighty-three were prisoners of war.

After the Korean War, Canadian naval vessels were not involved in serious hostilities until the Gulf War, which pitted a coalition of forces against those of Saddam Hussein's Iraq. The Canadian ships deployed with the coalition forces established a reputation for efficiency and daring, and a respected Canadian officer, Commodore Duncan Miller, was placed in command of the huge Coalition Logistic Fleet, carrying off the task with skill and efficiency. Both that man, and those Canadian ships, drew on and confirmed the reputation and foundations established in the bloody North Atlantic days of the Second World War, when the Royal Canadian Navy learned, inch by painful inch, how to do its trade. The postwar RCN, and the Maritime Command which succeeded it, have never let waver the bright flame of professionalism lit with such difficulty and sacrifice on the dark, war-shadowed seas of the North Atlantic.

The Modern Sea:
Harsh Workplace,
Beckoning Playground

To a Maritime trawler fisherman, or a British Columbia salmon fisherman, the sea remains a harsh and unforgiving workplace, with the concerns of storm, tide and collision added to now by the worries of dwindling fish stocks, pollution, overseas competition, and skyrocketing expenses. The sea has become the highway of the fast turn-around container vessel or the enormous VLCC (Very Large Cargo Carrier) behemoths, run by computers and crewed lightly by men and women who rarely tread a deck. Canadians are involved in this, and lead in certain areas, such as undersea technology. But there are still individual Canadians whose livelihood, however precarious, is earned in an intimate, personal relationship with the sea.

Skiffs, Gillnets, and Poverty-Sticks
Howard White

They've got the dirty thirty blues, Tom and Jack, drifting around the inlet mouth by Salmon Rock in leaky skiffs, trying to scratch a living, and a damn meagre living at the best of times. They only pay seven cents a pound for dressed coho and if the boys hustle five bucks a day they're doing pretty fair.

Tom and Jack are hometown boys from the nearby village but many of the others have come from Vancouver or elsewhere. They live, these transients, in tents and makeshift shacks on the beach, just within the protective hook of the bay where the village lies. They are proud men, choosing to maintain some vestige of dignity in preference to panhandling, stealing, or taking relief. It's a marginal existence. Maybe if they're lucky they can save enough in five or six years to put a down payment on a gas-boat. Then they can head upcoast, get in on the big runs and make some halfway decent money. Meanwhile she's a hand-to-mouth proposition.

It's Sunday but a workday nonetheless. Can't afford any time off at this racket. Their equipment is rockbottom minimal—crude bamboo poles and gut lines—all they can afford. Some of them also carry herring-rakes in hope of striking a school of 'stinkies' for bait. The rakes are used to scoop the thickly-clustered fish into the stern of the boat like so many wriggling leaves.

But the salmon are the money fish. They hook them laboriously, one at a time, whenever the stubborn buggers condescend to bite. There are maybe twenty boats in all, working fairly close together. Tom and Jack are no more than fifteen feet apart. The salmon ain't biting worth a damn.

Lost, lean years when the village is young and the world a simpler place of one-to-one relationships and fixed beliefs. The school science books still hold the atom to be indivisible, and television's an expensive gimmick you've heard the odd rumour about but sure don't ever expect to see. The moon's just a thing in the sky that pulls the tides around—too damn far away to even worry about. Inconceivable war that will end the Depression forever in North America and unleash horror and deprivation of a much more drastic sort elsewhere, waits scant years off. They are holding a bloody dress rehearsal in Spain and someone you know knows someone in the Mackenzie-Papineau Battalion but it is all very remote and doesn't have much bearing on the price of fish.

The price of fish is traditionally as little as the canneries can get away with paying you—two cents a pound for spring salmon, three-quarters of a cent for humpback, ten cents apiece for dogs. A fledgling union—the PFCU—is attempting to organize and negotiate a better shake for the fishermen but it's a tough struggle. Partly it's the inflexible attitude of the operators but another major source of difficulty is the large Japanese fleet whose complacency toward low prices tends to maintain the niggardly status quo.

The skiff fishermen are the worst off of all, making little more than bare grub money on the best of days. There are maybe five hundred rowboats actively working the lower Gulf. Salmon Rock at the mouth of Howe Sound is only one of the spots they frequent. They gather at numerous points—Lasqueti Island, Poor Man's Rock—praying for strikes with considerably more fervour than any Sunday wonder from Shaughnessey Heights with his expensive tackle. They work in as close proximity as possible to the fish buyers, who advance them food and tobacco. Day after day, as long as the weather's even half feasible, they row seaward to woo the elusive quarry—to bob for salty hours and dream of palmier possibilities.

Most of them graduate to gas-boats in time. They are unprepossessing craft with plodding Easthope or Vivian engines, but they beat rowing all to hell. By God, they're mobile at last!

As they head upcoast that first, independent time, they pass their former comrades in their cockleshells, still hauling them in the hard way. They wave in an offhand, superior manner, bound for Smith's Inlet, Rivers Inlet, the Nass, the Skeena—brawling northern waters and big summer runs. The canneries are booming—there are eighteen in Rivers Inlet alone—and they'll process all the fish you can feed them but the money is still a long way from good. If a man can clear six hundred dollars after food and expenses it's a good season. Still, it is a definite step up the ladder, for all that.

The game of gillnetting, while safer than some, is not without its hazards. The obvious one of course is simply falling overboard and drowning. In rough water or when a guy has taken on too much booze this possibility is always present. Crazily enough, in common with other sailors, many fishermen have never learned to swim, but even a good swimmer would have little chance in a coal black blowing sea with no lifejacket and his unconcerned boat thudding farther away from him every second. Another way a man can get it is by asphyxiation from carbon monoxide fumes. Boats are sometimes found circling aimlessly with their occupants unconscious or dead.

In one such incident, slightly more gruesome than most, the man had collapsed against the very engine whose gases had undone him and the flywheel, by the time he was found, had worn half his head away.

Then there is always the chance of being wrecked, for the coastal waters can be a maze of circuitous treachery, especially in fog, mined with dead-heads, hidden reefs and whirlpooling rapids. Many stretches of the jagged shoreline are desolate as the dawn of time, devoid of humanity for miles in any direction. A man cast up in such an area, perhaps shivering in some blind cul-de-sac of a cove walled round with unclimbable cliffs, might wait for days before being found—sometimes forever. Savage storms can boil up without warning in the open waters and high winds charge down the inlets from snowy channelling valleys. There are certainly dangers, but the men face them with philosophy.

Gillnetting by hand is rough, exhausting work. The nets vary in depth and mesh size according to the variety of salmon being fished, but they all share one factor in common—they're heavy as hell to wrestle back aboard with any kind of catch in them. Really gets you in the arms and back. Sometimes you get so gaddamn tired, you feel like chucking the whole business and going back to the skiffs but some old tenacity keeps you going, the same tenacity that has sustained fishermen in all the waters of the world for centuries. Their ghosts pull with you.

When the season is finished, the men head home with wallets, if not bulging, at least comfortably lined. In the off months many of them will put up the poverty-sticks, as trolling poles are wryly called, and, weather permitting, cruise the sheltered sounds in search of spring salmon. Trolling is simply a more elaborate form of skiff fishing. The poverty-sticks are in essence giant fishing rods, jutting out from either side of the boat like wooden antennae. From these hang the trolling lines with hooked steel flashers attached at regular intervals. When the fish are really biting, as many as twelve lines may be used but they are seldom biting with any such gusto, particularly in the sparse winter months. It's slim pickings for the most part, which accounts for the nickname.

Now the war, long threatening, explodes across Europe. It's still a distant thing, however terrible—a misfortune involving a lot of very faraway people who should know better—but the repercussions are not long in being felt, no matter what your leanings or allegiances.

The fishing industry is of course affected along with everything else. Many drop the trade and head overseas, if not to save some great aunt, then for plain, damn adventure. As for the rest, people still have to eat. Fishing, along with logging, pulp milling, mining, farming and other key trades, is soon classified as essential work. Its practitioners are largely made draft exempt and frozen to their jobs. Fish prices at last make a significant jump and the lid comes off generally as far as quota regulations are concerned. It's a mad scramble for wealth. Men who were walking around with holes in their shoes a few months before are suddenly flush.

A whole new branch of fishing evolves during the war and a lot of money is made at it. This is the catching of dogfish—a primitive and highly prolific relative of the sturgeon, hitherto of no commercial value due to the long standing belief among fishermen that its flesh is inedible— fit only for fertilizer—despite considerable proof to the contrary. Now however, diet research burgeons and vitamins become increasingly important. The liver of the dogfish is rich in Vitamin D and it is hunted for this sole organ. The rest is thrown away. They're paying a pretty buck for a chunk of the guts, and the gulls can have what's left.

Apart from the introduction there is no radical change in the general pattern of things for the first two years of the war. The fish still make their coastal migrations on mysterious cue, the men still sail to waylay them—except that there's a lot more money around now and the skiff fleet dwindles noticeably as more and more of its members graduate to gas-boats.

Then comes Pearl Harbor. The hostilities spread like a brushfire around the globe. All at once, they're uncomfortably close to your own backyard. Suddenly those energetic little guys you've been fishing alongside for years are no longer simply your rivals but sinister enemy aliens. And then they're gone, the lot of them, in one fell, Defence Department swoop. The internment of the Japanese will become a subject of much hindsight controversy in the relaxed atmosphere of later years, and will generally be conceded to be somewhat of an over-reaction, although it seemed a reasonable idea at the time.

The hapless Japanese, most of them no more loyal or disloyal than any other citizen, are forced to sell their boats and then shipped to Interior camps to wait out the war under surveillance. Their disappearance leaves many empty gillnetters and a huge gap in the fishing fleet, soon filled by an influx of eager newcomers to the game, many undoubtedly bent on staying out of uniform.

It is a free-booting period of outright plunder. Overfishing reaches scandalous proportions with no thought for tomorrow. Hell, the way they're burning up the world, there may be no tomorrow! This shortsighted don't-give-a-damn attitude results in the near-depletion of some stocks and dangerous thinning of others. It will lead to skimpy runs, impoverished years, but no one considers this. Live for now!

In any coastal town in those war years it is impossible to be unaware of the fishermen. The very tempo and flavour of village life is geared to their comings and going. Years are judged good or bad according to the salmon runs; the economy waxes and wanes to the vagrant rhythms of the fish. In a good year, there are smiles on the most taciturn faces, new clothes for the wife and kids, money for beer and updated equipment like radiophones and power drums. In a bad year, wry faces predominate, belts are tightened, credit extensions awkwardly requested from local merchants. Often the younger men go logging as necessity demands, helping to foul some of the very spawning streams that beckon the salmon shoreward in the first place. The oldtimers put up the poverty-sticks and troll for whatever meagre bounty they can get. They don't believe in mixing trades.

To Rivers Inlet and the other northern meccas all such boats as are able set out in the late spring to hopefully reap their share of the yearly harvest. Often the younger wives go along with their men to work the canneries that still flourish in the upcoast inlets. Most of the sons go too, as soon as they are old enough to be useful.

The fishermen are Scots and Finns for the most part, proud, weather-pummelled men, left wing to the extreme in their political leanings, fond enough of their drink but able to carry it well and given to consuming it in the privacy of their homes. They dress, except for weddings, funerals and other formal occasions, in a similar rough-and-ready fashion—heavy brown woollen pants, police suspenders, thick work shirts with longjohns showing underneath even in summer, mackinaws of various patterns and colours but frequently simple grey, elasticsided fishermen's slippers. For headgear they favour toques or cotton caps. The younger men often add a few colourful variations of their own but the oldtimers are as conservative in their dress as they are radical in their politics. They tend to be close-spoken, a trait learned over many years of lonely, rocking sea hours.

But if most of the fishermen prefer to keep their own counsel, there are always a few who do not. These are the out-and-out reprobates, bachelors for the most part, who scrape only a fringe living from fishing when they bother to go out at all. They spend most of their waking hours sitting, in one state of inebriation or another, around the decks and holds of their invariably ill-kept boats. These unsanitary characters have names like Dirty Alec or Old Swen and thirsts of an extremely catholic nature, but they are never unwilling to pass on their own version of fishing lore—lurid accounts of knife-fights in netlofts, groggy trysts with Indian girls from the production lines, record runs when the fish swam thick as fleas on a dog's back, ghostships, gambling and buddies who came to bad ends.

As the war comes to an end, the fishing business slowly rolls into another phase. The short-lived dog-fishing industry dies with the development of synthetic vitamins, cutting off a valuable source of revenue for many and relegating that much-maligned creature to the status of a nuisance fish again.

Equipment is becoming increasingly more sophisticated. Nylon nets are now coming into general use but they are much more expensive than the old type. Radar and sonar devices are being installed by many boats and some sort of radiophone is becoming almost mandatory. There are holdouts of course among some of the more recalcitrant oldtimers and one such, a grizzled Scot by the name of Kenny Campbell, suffers a rather unnerving experience as a result.

Campbell, an elderly man and semi-retired, has been fishing the coastal waters the better part of his life. On this particular occasion he is on his way home from Rivers Inlet after the summer run. His boat, the *Betty*, is a battered thirty-footer and its 10-14 Easthope, which has been running on sheer nerve for a long time, is on its last legs. When the old engine splutters and dies a few hours out of harbour it's no surprise to its owner, who's dealt with the same situation many times, but this time it appears that no amount of monkeywrenching, coaxing or cursing is going to revive the old girl. Scantily-provisioned and radioless, Campbell watches the coast-line gradually fade from sight as he is swept oceanward by a southeaster, the *Betty* tossed upward and heaved back into giant swells, water rushing in and out of the cabin.

After six days the storm finally abates enough that Campbell can tackle the old Easthope again. After several hours he gets her going again and for two days heads east, but no sooner does the coastline come into sight once more the engine gives up the ghost again. No gas.

But the waves push him relentlessly toward the jagged coast and Campbell is helpless as they crash the *Betty* against a giant reef just off shore. Several hours later he finds himself on the beach, exhausted and half-starved, disoriented, talking to himself. Somehow a benevolent fate leads him to a hunters' cabin in the nearby woods, where, at the end of his rope, he lies down to die. For another week he keeps himself alive there, until he is miraculously spotted by a small plane and the Coast Guard comes to the rescue, forty miles south of Cape Flattery in Washington State. After a period of recuperation in hospital, he return to Vancouver, leaving his unsalvageable boat behind him. He leaves his fishing days behind him too, for after this harrowing ordeal Kenny Campbell has had more than enough of the sea. Later, he will discuss his inadvertent odyssey with a certain dry humour. 'Missed my pipe a hell of a lot more than the grub.'

Few oldtimers make their exits from the business in such dramatic fashion. Most depart the game without fanfare as a concession to advancing years and ebbing energies. There is no shortage of younger men waiting to fill their boots and the number of boats working the B.C. waters remains constant.

Indeed, without the rigorous controls exercised by the Department of Fisheries, many men would enter the trade. But important lessons are learned during the unregulated war years, the chief of these being that fish are by no means an inexhaustible resource. Through development of hatchery programs, the stocks are gradually brought back to an approximation of their former strength and quota regulations are strictly enforced. A system of licensing is instituted whereby individual boats are only allowed to work the salmon runs for a ten-year period. They are then purchased by the government through a buy-back fund, phased out of the industry altogether and re-sold for other purposes. This effectively limits the number of boats working the coast in any given year.

The cost of maintaining a complex of upcoast canneries close to the fishing grounds begins to loom prohibitive. It becomes infinitely more practical to load the fish aboard huge packers and haul them, stored in brine, to modern processing plants in Vancouver and Prince Rupert. Here they are close to shipping facilities and retail outlets. One by one, like snuffed out candles, these rackety old salmon factories with their piling perched shades, their moribund belts, rancid stinks and Iron Chinks, begin to die. One by one, they are abandoned like worn-out toys along the sopping shores of Rivers Inlet and the Nass.

Today things are pretty much mechanized and orderly in the B.C. fishing business. Expensive too. Hell, in the old days you could outfit as fine a boat as you could want for $5,000. Now it costs anywhere from $40,000 on up. Those damn licences keep going up every year too. There's lots of guys around whose licences are worth more than their gillnetters.

The main trouble now is with the offshore fishing. Japanese and sometimes Russian ships with ultra-modern equipment, cutting into the runs beyond the twelve-mile limit. There'll be a good many International Courts of Inquiry before they sort this one out. Meantime, there'll be Cod Wars off Iceland and maybe Salmon Wars here—who can tell?

The game goes on, and for the most part it's all pretty routine. Gillnetting's not half the bullwork it used to be since power drums although these can be dangerous. A guy got caught in his net, wound round the drum and killed a while back. Still, as a general rule, they're pretty safe. Sure beats hand-hauling. Yeah, they're getting her down to a science.

It remains to be seen whether the future of Canadians will be as unknowingly bound up with the sea as it once was; the growth of the Pacific Rim as a major economic arena of the world's economy, and the maintenance of the historic North Atlantic link to Europe, suggest that if anything the sea will grow in importance as a productive workplace for Canadians, even as they commit themselves to the struggle to ensure the world's oceans are not plundered and polluted beyond hope of recovery. It may be that by encouraging a reconsideration of the sea and the other waters of Canada as a vast schoolroom for the pleasurable learning of skills once taught out of harsh necessity, that an awareness can grow for the value of those waters. If a difficult economy does not prevent more Canadians from taking to the waters in this way, in everything from personal pleasure boating to the more serious commitments of youth sail training and marine environmental study, Canadians may in the future be able to reclaim in greater measure the right of place at sea earned at such cost in the past.

The past was not all pain and self-denial, however. There is something wonderfully gentle in this 1900 yachting discovery of Georgian Bay.

On the Big Sea Water
Stewart Edward White

Most of the Lake Michigan and Lake Huron yachtsmen either sail majestically up the middle in schooners, or dodge past sand-bars between ugly piers in smaller sloops.

Neither course is pleasant. In the schooner you have a sailing-master, a sideboard, and many friends. You hoist flags in a punctilious manner when the crew eats pie, or the skipper takes a drink; you bestow much thought on the advisability of shooting small breech-loading cannon; the failure of one of the A.B.'s to coil a line Flemish causes uneasiness, and the boarding of shore visitors on the captain's side of the yacht is a matter of agonized mortification. This is interesting, just as is the purchase of neckties of approved stripe, or the donning of the proper shoes with the proper trousers. But it is not cruising.

Nor is the small boat in much better ease. Therein you dodge large short seas which break over with considerable weight; you are constantly reefing for black squalls; above all, you are on a continual rack of anxiety as to whether you will miss the shoal or whether you can make the next harbour before dark—usually a sandy little river, lumber-flanked, dirty.

We avoided both horns of the dilemma, and this is how we did it.

Just forty-five miles from the Island of Mackinac you may enter Potaganissing Bay. This, in turn, opens into the North Channel. The North Channel contains many islands and a harbour every few miles. It conceals various bass of sporting proclivity, and it leads to the Georgian Bay.

All these waters are deep. The chart of the British Government estimates that the islands which spangle them number 'from thirty to one hundred thousand', which is near enough to the truth not to be troublesome. There are very few shoals, and these few are visible in the clear water many miles. Most of the shores can be dived from, or, what is more to the point, can be tied to with a six-foot draught. The scenery is beautiful. The Chippewa and Ottawa inhabitants are interesting. Up the north rivers are a number of Hudson Bay posts, some of which are still trading. There are no summer resorts. You can sail on open water, with more space abeam, forward, and astern than in Long Island Sound, or you can wind in and out of the island channels, just as you happen to please. Sometimes it seems you are in a great lake eight or ten miles across, the shores of which open before you and close silently behind you as you advance. Again, you need a fair wind and a steady eye, as in the forty-foot passage of the Little Detroit. Or still again, you may be out of sight of land entirely. In that country to the west hangs a horizon of smoke, faintly aromatic, pleasing, and to the north a brown horizon of mountains, rock-browed, bold. The afternoon sun becomes a great red ball, whose track on the waters is of blood, and whose last glance causes the north hills to blush a glowing purple. Above all, it is the northland, and the air is like wine.

Yet, strangely enough, yachtsmen continue to carry out their punctilious etiquette, or to seek their sawmill harbours, while the bays are solitary, save for the Indian fishing boats and the few, the very few, of the elect.

We are of the elect. We claim it with the arrogance of bigotry, if you will, but we claim it emphatically.

The summer of which this narrative speaks we foregathered from several points of the compass. The mate, possessed of a fly-book which he worshipped idolatrously, and a fund of theoretics which everybody else distrusted, arrived on the *Manitou* from Chicago. The dog watch was a lank individual of skilful pencil, small reverence, and ready excuse, summering on the island. The scullion was a fair-skilled, jolly, good-natured young artist from Baltimore. The skipper now speaks.

Our boat was a cutter sloop, twenty-eight by eight, drawing just six feet, and carrying much outside ballast. She was put together for business. Her decks were flush, with the exception of a low deck-house and a small self-bailing cockpit. Her horn was housable. She could be battened down and driven through anything. Her spars were lofty, and her spread of canvas great. She could, moreover, beat under the staysail, which is an unusual and desirable accomplishment.

For six days we ballasted, rove halliards and sheets, slaved in interior depths, and astounded the resorters by our disreputable appearance. At the end of that time we found our work good. The cutter was stocked and equipped.

The skipper distinguished himself just before the start by getting knocked overboard by the boom. He made desperate efforts to save himself, but disappeared amid frantic cheers from the entire crew, who, along with winds, waves and marine gods, were most liberally "cussed" when he climbed over the rail. The wind was light and dead ahead as we tacked, and after getting along a few miles it died entirely, so the best we could do was to haul aft the main-sheet snugly and slap about. The crew made bets as to whether or not the yacht would beat the dinghy going sideways. On examination of our exchequer we found several pennies, one of which the mate threw overboard with the appropriate whistling and scratching of the mast. The gods were at once appeased, and a moment later we heeled over with gunwales awash. The mate turned a pale green. The dog-watch became a dull yellow brown, and lay down.

And now the skipper had his jest.

Directly across the noble reach of Detour Passage (through which each year passes a greater tonnage than through any like waterway in the world), north of Drummond, the waters open out. Near at hand, far away, to the right, to the left, rise hundreds and hundreds of little islands. They are all wooded to the water's edge; they all drop off into deep soundings.

Between them are glimpses of distant blue seas and other islands. As the yacht slowly and steadily cut her way forward, more and more of these dots of rock and earth opened up, revealing enchanting possibilities of exploration. With a northerly gale abeam we bowled along through the islands only too swiftly. We had reefed away down, stowed the staysail, even dropped the peak, not because she would not carry the canvas, but in order to reduce speed. You see, we had never been there before, and though we had charts no one could tell whether they were reliable.

So we sped along, disputing about islands, keeping a sharp lookout for yellow water, and hoping fervently that Providence had its eye on us. Somebody had heard somebody say that a man he knew had heard that Harbour Island was a good place.

Suddenly in a long island some miles ahead, a bight opened up, under the lee of which we perceived a narrow opening. Through the opening there appeared another bight. The chart fiends agreed that this must be Harbour Island, and that in the narrow opening—about a hundred and fifty feet wide—was much water. We derided, but crept in under the jib, sounding energetically, when on a sudden came a sarcastic voice from the shore: 'There is twenty-two feet of water all through there'—and we abstained from further sounding. After a little we rounded a point, the anchor bit, and we drew a long breath and looked around us.

The passage opened into a great lake or bay situated in the very centre of the island. The high woods surrounded it on all sides—even the entrance seemed closed by the point of the outer bay—and in one elbow nestled a house, a workshop, and a dock. We had just dodged in from a three-reef gale, yet here the water was hardly riffled, and we could hear various frogs, tree-toads, and birds assuring each other sleepily that it was almost evening. We stayed days, and even the business man grumbled only softly. Such is Harbour Island.

Now, on Harbour Island there is a king, and his name is Church. He is grizzled and grey. He lives in a house on the knoll. His wife is Ojibway, and his children half-breeds, therefore the Indians do him homage in some sort. King Church knows the language of the native, and can sing therein; he possesses a fund of information concerning Indian customs and manners, which he imparts quaintly between puffs of his pipe; he has much lore of ancient times, and can tell you of the old raid the peaceful Ottawas (accent the second syllable, if you please) made on the Iroquois, and how even to this day they occasionally get into a panic for fear of retaliation, and flee incontinently to the headwaters of the creeks. And then he will pour out into a tin cup near a half a pint of raw Canadian Club. After this he wipes his mouth on his checkered shirt, and discourses of Epictetus and the pronunciation of *Thule*. The capt'n surprises you somewhat.

We floated gently out of the narrow passage, and, turning sharp to port, cruised down a little channel between Harbour and Maple Islands. Navigation at this point became interesting. The mate sat in the cock-pit with the charts spread out before him, keeping an eye on ranges, and the skipper held the stick. We wound in and out between beautifully wooded islands, over waters so clear that shoals fairly stared at us, and we couldn't have run against them if we had tried. In a little while the islands widened out, and soon after leaving Indian Village astern, we gybed and headed up the more open waters of Potaganissing. Some little time later we rounded Chippewa Point and emerged into the north channel of the Georgian Bay, finally dropping anchor behind the peninsula of Thessalon.

On the east side of the peninsula we discovered a cove, surrounded by huge old Laurentian rocks, rounded by the action of water and cracked in symmetrical parallelograms by the frost. In a hollow between several of these some Indians had pitched their wigwams and built kettle tripods. The rover and dog-watch had been so long deprived of feminine society that they hailed with eager delight the advent of two girls on the beach. With a view to moonlight boating, they became clamorous to borrow the dinghy. *Vetoed*: the skipper and mate wanted to turn in.

Next day we made a direct run across open waters under a southeasterly breeze. The air was cool, the sun warm. All the ship's sewing and patching was done, the rover in especial toiling long and loud over his private wardrobe. The mate kept an eye on the chart, and all took tricks at the helm.

About four bells we dropped anchor in Sitgreave's Bay, a large bight of water, hugging a smaller bight under the arm of one of its points. The latter made an ideal harbour, sheltered in every direction. The mate exhumed from his war-bag that precious fly-book and had a try for trout.

The mate was always convincing himself that he had left that confounded fly-book on the beach somewhere. He usually attained that conviction, about midnight, at which time he would rout us all out and detail his suspicions.

'Well,' said we with forced calmness. 'we're anchored. It can't be any farther away by morning.'

'Ah, but I could not sleep until I know where it is!'

He would then haul from his war-bag the following articles, which he distributed over us in our bunks: Two undershirts, two pairs drawers, six pairs socks, one pair shoes, a sweater, a flannel shirt, two pairs ducks, a suit of oil-skins, fishlines, soap, towels, brushes, medicine case, pistol, cartridges, and, last of all, the fly-book. Then putting them all back again, he would sink to sleep like a tired child.

Near the head of a cove we passed through a zone of echoes, remarkable even for this country of many voices. At one place a pistol-shot gave back seven distinct reports. All day long we loafed through the open water, passing successively the False Detour Passage, Cockburn's Island, Mississauga, and the first point of Grand Manitoulin—a huge island, which was to lie to our starboard for many days.

The only breeze we struck next day struck us about breakfast time. It had been perfectly calm, and the skipper was trying to get breakfast. On the oil-stove he had a kettle of 'stirabout'; on the alcohol lamp a pot of coffee. The puff in question wandered idly over the hills of Mildrum Bay, sought what it could devour, and leaned against our mainsail to rest. The coffee emptied into the starboard bunk-locker; the stirabout was saved at the last moment. The alcohol distributed itself impartially and began to blaze. At this the skipper seized a coat (the rover's) and entered earnestly into the business of extinguishing small flames. To accomplish it he leaped madly back and forth soliciting assistance. The crew, puzzled and anxious, could not for some time make out the seeming madman. Their final comprehension arrived about the time the last flame was smothered, and the skipper then had difficulty in averting a deluge of water.

Somebody believed the squall hit pretty hard, but none cared.

One day we beat down Gore Bay, around another point, into a beautiful land-locked harbour. On one side the bluffs rose to a height of over two hundred feet, palisaded like the Hudson. In the curve of the other lay the town, a dusty-streeted little affair, whose establishments were adapted to the needs of farmers.

The dog-watch, the rover, and the skipper climbed the high bluffs, where-from they obtained a beautiful view of the bay and the surrounding country. The latter is well cleared into organized farms, in sharp contrast to the trackless wilderness everywhere else in this northland.

Clapperton Island is what the part above water is called. Thereabouts are large rounded boulders, bigger than houses, wherefrom you could slide on a shovel direct into nine fathoms. Near at hand are the Sow and Pigs, brown-skinned, foam-flecked, threatening. Underneath are bold reefs to be dodged by means of puzzling ranges.

We did these things, and, besides, we managed to admire the great ragged hills to northward, the green islands ahead, the queer, straight-up-and-down formation of Clapperton itself. We took a moment to cuss the dog-watch for letting the jib-sheet run at the most critical moment of all, and to wonder frantically about the location of Reynolds' Rock, water a fathom and a half, big sea. That sea was nasty, three-cornered, wet. It slapped us, and twisted us, and yawed us until the helmsman's life was a burden to him because of the great fear of jibing.

However, once that rock was dodged and that point rounded, we found ourselves boiling along down the lee of Clapperton in a flat sea, but with a puffy wind that often buried our deadeyes. The rover distinguished himself by sitting calmly on the stern in the height of the nervousness sketching the effect of some old lumber schooners against the sky. The wind now swooped over the hemlocks of Clapperton, and fell upon us suddenly. This disgusted the dog-watch, for the sporadic and decided heeling of the craft disturbed his habitual reclining posture.

As we proceeded, we became aware that the objects toward which we were tending, notably a range of perpendicular cliffs and a deep V-shaped bight, were larger than we had at first supposed them to be. The cliffs rose; the bight opened. We consulted the chart. The land proved to be some six hundred feet in height, and the bay eighteen miles deep and five miles broad. Later we learned from the Indians at its foot that we were the first yacht to enter it for twenty years, which goes far to show the unexplored character of these waters. The Indian village just mentioned consisted of perhaps a score of little log-houses scattered over a mile or so of country. They were arranged quite without order. Instead of flanking the road, the road went to them. They seemed to be fairly clean for Indian huts, owing probably to the fact that these were not 'backwoods Indians', but enjoyed the advantages of Christianity. These advantages consist mainly of *ex post facto* marriages, a church with a small tin steeple, and the usual brilliant Roman Catholic prints. That is to the external man. But they mean moreover industry, childlike faith, and a blind trust in the priest. The monthly visits of the latter measure time for the villagers.

In the early morning the wind backed to the north. The skipper paid out cable and let go the second anchor. Later a big sea was rolling down that thirty-mile sweep. We tugged and plunged. 'Kismet,' said we, and hung on. The rain drove down and we had to eat a cold breakfast within the cabin. 'Hell!' said we, and curled up variously, trying to read. The mate took bismuth for a weak stomach. The yacht tried to pull her nose under water by the bitts. The wind shrieked in seven keys.

For untold ages thus it endured. Then with many strange oaths the mate and dog-watch donned slickers and departed in the dinghy. 'We will stretch our legs on the beach, and return anon,' said they.

We issued premonitory advice as to returning into cabins with damp clothes.

Two hours later the skipper uncoiled and looked out the hatchway.

The scuds were scurrying by in ragged grey wisps so low down that they swept the face of the great cliffs opposite. A mist obscured all distant objects. Rain drove in fitful gusts. Great white-crested waves rolled majestically down, lifted the yacht, and finally dashed against the coast with a mighty boom.

The skipper crawled forward. Both anchors held. The yacht rode the great surges easily. He returned to the cabin. The rover and the skipper conversed concerning the mate and the dog-watch. After looking out, the rover gave it as his opinion that both were drowned. The opinion was received with indifference. Both then ate of cold lunch.

Finally, about sunset, those base deserters reappeared, one at a time, wetly and with danger.

They reported much. They had penetrated to the sanctums of sugar-makers, the fashioners of snow-shoes and blanket-weavers and builders of baskets. In one hut the dog-watch had been requested to dance with an Indian maiden of sweet sixteen, but, overcome with sudden and strange timidity, had declined, whereupon the squaws did guy him in strange polysyllables. The mate was hailed as a *Musk-a-wah-wah-ninney*, or doctor, by virtue of his medical studies. The dog-watch agreed to endorse the title, provided the accent was placed on the last syllable. Said *Musk-a-wah-wah-ninney* dosed sick Indians with great satisfaction to himself and them.

During the day on which we left this quaint harbour we shifted canvas just eleven times. We had all kinds of weather, from a vicious black squall to a dead calm. We wore everything, from our skin-tight 'swimming suits' to full lines of slickers.

But when it was all over, how pleasant it was to slip quietly along under the influence of a soft fair wind that scarcely rippled the water! The bird songs of late afternoon sounded clearly as we glided past an occasional little island or skirted the miniature coast of a larger bit of land. Directly astern the sun was setting in the usual blood-red haze. The water was taking to itself the peculiar deep amethyst tinge of the northland, the colour seeming to belong in the very substance of the liquid rather than to be merely reflected from the surface. The yacht cleaved her way onward without a sound. Point after point opened up silently. The dusk of evening fell, and we did not care, for we knew that in the narrow channel of Little Current were situated lighthouses, well ranged, and that with this fair, sweet wind we could nose our way to a little cove we wot of at the head of Goat Island, where the channel turns, and thence by one more easy stage to Killarney.

We went through Little Current like a shot out of a gun, but without mishap. Below the passage the water opens out into many broad reaches, island-starred. With the exception of the North Passage, which we did not attempt this trip, it is the most beautiful portion of the channel. From one point you could look up an opening, mathematically straight, twelve miles long, and but a quarter of a mile wide, composed of many islands ranged side by side. To the south, on Manitoulin, open bays as deep as that in which we had weathered the norther. And toward the pole-star were great ranges of precipitous mountains.

All day long we made time through the islands under a fresh fair wind. Almost before we knew it we were picking our way among shoals off Killarney.

We rather expected letters at Killarney, so we sought out the post-office. It was located in an Indian woman's kitchen cupboard. She presented us with the assortment, with the request that we return what we could not use. From her grandmother's maiden aunt we ordered moccasins, most excellent heavy-weather foot-wear for gripping on slippery decks. On the docks was much Indian bark and quill work, indicative of tourists. Inquiry disclosed that the Collingwood boats touched here twice a week, and our letters made it necessary for our scribe to return to civilization by their friendly aid.

To be an amateur on the waters, as most Canadians perforce must be nowadays, requires some defences beyond the stirling attributes of wintry self-discipline. A sense of humour helps, as perhaps is well illustrated in the following episode in a voyage carried out a few years ago in a small Newfoundland schooner by noted author (and ex-soldier) Farley Mowat, and equally noted publisher (and ex-MGB officer) Jack McClelland. At the very least, one must admire their courage.

The Foggy, Foggy Dew
Farley Mowat

We spent five days waiting for good weather before reaching the conclusion that to wait was vain. Good weather and Trepassey did not go together.

So early on the sixth day we cast off our lines, started the bullgine, and steamed off into the fog. We now had a definite destination in mind, if not in view. We had given up our original intention of sailing to the tropics because it was clear from a scrutiny of our log that, even if we maintained our current rate of progress, it would take us sixteen months to reach the Caribbean; twenty-nine months to reach the Azores; and seven and a half years to reach the South Pacific. We did not have that much time. Consequently we chose as our alternative the island of St Pierre.

While hardly tropical in character, and able to boast of no brown-skinned *wahines*, this little island did offer certain compensations. It was a foreign land, flying the French flag. It was, and remains, famous for having the cheapest and most abundant supply of alcohol to be found anywhere on or near the North American continent. But perhaps St Pierre's greatest attraction for us was that it lay no more than one hundred and twenty miles to the westward of Trepassey and only a few miles off the south coast of Newfoundland. We felt we had at least a chance of reaching St Pierre before winter closed in upon us.

Visibility in Trepassey harbour itself was surprisingly good as we set out. We *almost* saw the fish plant, and we certainly knew where it was because the wind was blowing from it to us. Once, as we thundered through the harbour channel, we caught an indistinct glimpse of land off the port bow. It may have been Powles Head, the entry landmark. If so, it was the last landmark we were to see for a long time to come.

Trepassey Bay was black with fog. We had gone no more than a mile when, faint-heart that I am, I decided it would be hopeless to proceed.

'Jack,' I said as firmly as I could, 'we'll have to put back to harbour. There isn't a chance we're going to find St Pierre in fog like this. Considering the state of that bleeding compass, we're more likely to end up in Ireland instead.'

Jack fixed me with a cold stare and there was no mistaking the threat of mutiny in his voice:

'The hell you say! Mowat, if you turn back now I swear I'll do an Enos. I'll leave you to rot in Trepassey harbour to the end of your born days! Besides, you silly bastard, how do you think you're going to *find* Trepassey again? I'm going below to work out a course to clear Cape Pine. You keep this boat heading as she is or else . . . !'

He vanished and I was alone with my thoughts. I had to admit he had a point. Although we had found Trepassey harbour once in heavy fog we weren't likely to be as lucky a second time, and the rocks and reefs on both sides of the entrance were particularly fearsome and unforgiving. Also I was pretty sure Jack would make good his threat, supposing we did regain the harbour, and the prospect of being marooned alone with *Happy Adventure* in Trepassey was too horrible to contemplate. The lesser of two evils would be to continue out to sea. I held the little vessel 'steady as she goes', but with my free hand I pulled out my own personal bottle of rum from its hiding place in the lazaret, and poured a good dollop overboard for the Old Man. *Happy Adventure* puttered blindly on into the dark and brooding murk and I was soon fog-chilled, unutterably lonely, and scared to death. Since rum is a known and accepted antidote for all three conditions I took a long, curative drink for each separate ailment. By the time Jack reappeared on deck I was much easier in my mind.

By 1000 hours we had run the required distance to clear Cape Pine (distance run was measured on an ancient brass patent log towed astern of the vessel), and were ready to alter course to the northwest, to begin the twenty-mile crossing of the mouth of St Mary's Bay. But now a problem arose—we did not have the faintest idea what our compass error was on such a course. All we could do was alter ninety degrees to the north and hope we were actually sailing northwest despite what the compass had to say about it.

The knowledge that we were by then in close proximity to St Shotts did nothing to bring me peace of mind. Having once been to St Shotts by land, as a visitor, I had no desire to return to it unexpectedly by sea, as a piece of business. The bare possibility gave me such a bad attack of shivering that I had to send Jack down below to check the pumps while I took another cure.

It was a curious thing, but whenever I felt a pressing need to reach for the bottle Jack seemed perfectly willing, and even anxious, to nip below and give me privacy. Sometimes he even anticipated my need. At the time I thought this was only happy coincidence. But at the conclusion of the passage when I was cleaning up in the engine room, I found, under a pile of rags, a bottle that was the twin of the one I kept hidden in the lazaret. Like mine, it was completely empty.

The crossing of St Mary's Bay began uneventfully. There was not a breath of wind. There was very little sensation of movement because there were no reference points for the eye to find. We seemed poised and immobile in the centre of a bowl of calm and leaden water a hundred feet or so in circumference.

This was a region where we knew we could expect to encounter other vessels, particularly draggers and fishing schooners, with the consequent danger of collisions. Being without radar we had to rely on other boats to spot us and keep out of our way. Nor could we have heard their fog-horns above the roar of the bullgine. We ourselves did not need a fog-horn—the engine made more noise than any horn could have done.

Just after noon the fog to starboard suddenly grew black as the shadowy shape of a vessel came into view about fifty yards away. She was a big power schooner on a converging course with us and her rail was lined with gesticulating figures.

We were so glad to see other human beings in this void that we ran close alongside and stopped our engine. The big schooner did likewise and the two vessels drifted side by side.

'Where you bound, Skipper?' someone called across to us.

'St Pierre,' I cried back. 'Heading to clear Cape St Mary's with a five-mile offing.'

There was a long thoughtful silence from our neighbour. And then:

'Well, byes, I don't see how you're going to do it steering the course you is. Unless, that is, you plans to take her up the Branch River, carry her over the Platform Hills, and put her on a railroad train. If I was you, I'd haul off to port about nine points. Good luck to ye!'

The diesels of the big vessel started with a roar and she pulled clear of us and disappeared.

We altered *ten* points to the southward just to be sure. The lubber line on the compass now indicated we were steaming south into the open ocean on a course for Bermuda. As the hours went by we found this increasingly unsettling to the mind. Was the schooner skipper correct, or was he wrong? The compass insisted he was very wrong indeed. We stewed over the matter until mid-afternoon, by which time we had lost all confidence in compass, schooner skipper, and ourselves.

At this juncture the bullgine took our minds off our navigational problems. It gave a tremendous belch. A huge cloud of blue smoke burst out of the companionway. I plunged below and grabbed for the fire extinguisher, expecting to find the entire engine room aflame. However all that had happened was that the exhaust stack had blown off at its junction with the engine, allowing exhaust gases and bits of white-hot carbon to fill the little cabin. The engine continued to run, if anything, a little better, since there was no back pressure from the stack.

There was also no longer anything between the hot exhaust and the bilges of the boat in which floated a thin but ever present scum of gasoline.

I held my breath, screwed my eyes tight shut, groped for the ignition wire, and pulled it off. Then I fled back on deck.

The bullgine wheezed to a stop and Jack and I sat in the ensuing, overwhelming silence and discussed our situation. It was not a cheerful prospect that we faced.

There was no way we could repair the exhaust stack without access to a welding torch. There was no wind and we could not sail, and so without the engine we would be doomed to sit where we were until something happened. That might be a long time but when something *did* happen we could be pretty sure it would be the wrong thing. There was apparently nothing for it but to restart the engine and hope she would not backfire and blow us all to Kingdom Come.

Leaving me to cogitate upon the problem Jack took advantage of the silence to slip below and turn on our small battery radio in an attempt to get a weather forecast. We could not use this radio while the engine was running because it was impossible to hear the tinny, indistinct sound that came out of it. Now, by pressing his ear against the speaker, Jack could hear the strains of cowboy music from Marystown Radio across Placentia Bay. Because it served a fishing community Marystown Radio gave the weather at frequent intervals.

Happy Adventure lay as silent as a painted ship upon a painted ocean—one painted in unrelieved tones of grey. After five or ten minutes Jack reappeared on deck.

'Farley,' he said quietly, too quietly, 'you aren't going to want to believe this, but they're putting out a general storm warning. There's a tropical storm coming in from the southwest and it's due here in ten hours, more or less. They're predicting winds of sixty knots!'

We got out the charts, spread them on the deck, and pored over them. First Jack would pour, then I would pour. This made us feel better, but it did not do us a great deal of practical good because we did not know exactly where we were. In truth, we didn't have a clue as to where we were. However assuming we had cleared Cape St Mary's and were crossing the mouth of Placentia Bay—a fifty-mile-wide traverse—we found by the chart that we could not be less than eighty miles from St Pierre. Under full engine power *Happy Adventure* could manage five knots. In ten hour's time this would have put us thirty miles short of the haven of St Pierre and we knew that if the tropical storm arrived on schedule, thirty miles might just as well be three hundred.

The nearest port in which we could hope to find shelter appeared to be Placentia Harbour, twenty-five or thirty miles to the northward of Cape St Mary's, on the east coast of the great bay.

I was rather afraid to suggest we try for Placentia Harbour, expecting another mutinous response from Jack. But he appeared to have had his fill of excitement, and he agreed that, yes, perhaps we should put in there for the night.

He went below and cautiously started the bullgine. We reset the patent log to zero and put the vessel on what we trusted (trust was all we had) was the correct course for Placentia Harbour.

It grew bitter cold and the fog began to close in tighter and tighter until it was so black that, had my watch not denied it, we could have believed night had fallen. Jack and I huddled together in the steering well, as far away from the engine room as we could get. We had also taken the pre-caution of hauling the dory up close under the stern so we could leap directly aboard it in an emergency; and we had stowed the dory with our last communal bottle of rum and a bag of sea biscuits. There was no room for anything else and, indeed, there was no room for us if it should come to that. We hoped it wouldn't come to that.

Five hours later the patent log showed we had run the proper distance to Placentia. I sent Jack to stop the bullgine so we could listen for the fog-horn at the harbour mouth.

Then a strange thing happened. The engine stopped but the roar con-tinued. At first I thought this must be a physiological reaction of my ears and mind to the endless thunder of the bullgine which we had endured for so many hours, but suddenly the truth came clear to me.

'Start her, Jack! Start her! Oh start her, Jack!' I howled.

Startled, Jack did as he was told and the bullgine caught on the first spin of the flywheel. I shoved the tiller over, hard. *Happy Adventure* picked up way and turned westward, away from the roaring surf that lay unseen but not unheard a few yards off her starboard bow.

We ran for half an hour before I could relax my grip on the tiller, unclamp my jaws, swallow once or twice, and find my voice again.

We had no way of knowing how close we had come to Placentia Harbour itself, but we did know we had come much too close to the east coast of the great bay. We knew we did not want to encounter it again under any conceivable circumstances. So we held on to the westward, knowing we had at least forty or fifty miles of open water ahead of us in that direction. We did not allow ourselves to think beyond those forty or fifty miles.

As we drove away from the land a kind of peace came over us. The bullgine rumbled and the exhaust smoke rolled out of the cabin into our faces. The fog grew thicker and somewhere the sun sank below the horizon, and it was night. We did not bother lighting our oil-burning navigation lights, because they could not have been seen from more than four or five feet away. We sat in our oilskins and blundered on into an infinity of blackness; into a void that had no end. We told each other that this was how the mariners of ancient times, the Norse in their longships, the Basques in their cranky vessels, Columbus in his caravel, must have felt as they ran their westing down toward a dark unknown. Day after day, night after night, they must have learned how to live with the terrors of a long uncertainty. On that black night perhaps we shared a little of what they must have felt.

At midnight Jack got another forecast. The spiralling storm centre had slowed down and was not expected to reach our area until just before dawn. In preparation for its arrival we double-reefed the main and foresail and felt our way over every inch of the fog-shrouded vessel putting all things in order for a blow.

A light breeze had risen from southerly, so we hoisted sail and shut down the bullgine, which had again begun to misbehave. The new checks had not bedded properly in their seats and she had started to overheat again; thus increasing the likelihood of backfires and of even more spec-tacular pyrotechnics.

We slipped along under sail in almost perfect silence in a world reduced to a diameter of not more than fifteen feet. I worked at the pump and Jack, at the helm, leaned over the compass whose card was lit by the dim glow of an expiring flashlight which we had taped to the binnacle, in lieu of a proper lamp.

The thought occurred to me that if we *had* to find ourselves in a situation of some jeopardy, we were better off aboard *Happy Adventure* than aboard a well-found, comfortable, and properly equipped yacht.

'You have to be kidding!' Jack said when I propounded this idea.

'Not all. Look at it this way. If we were aboard a hundred-thousand-dollar yacht we'd have to worry like hell about the prospect of losing her. We don't have that worry aboard *Happy Adventure*. We only have to worry about losing ourselves and she doesn't give us any *time* to worry about that.' I paused to let this sink in. Then: 'Would you mind unstrapping that flashlight from the binnacle and bringing it below? The main pump has jammed again.'

By the time we had repaired the pump and regained control over the leaks the little vessel had developed a new motion. She was beginning to roll. A heavy swell was heaving in from seaward. It gradually built up until we were rolling and pitching hard enough to spill the small wind out of our sails. Booms, gaffs, and blocks charged about, banging and thumping unseen above our heads.

The wind now failed and we lay becalmed on the black, heaving sea in an ominous silence broken only by the complaining noises of our running gear. There was nothing for it but to lower away and risk starting the bullgine once more.

She started with extreme reluctance, but she started, and for once her horrible outcry was welcome music in our ears. We drove on into the hours of the graveyard watch, hauling the patent log every now and again, to make sure we were not closing too fast with the alien coast which lay somewhere off our bows. At 0300 hours the log showed thirty-five miles and, very mindful of our recent experience off Placentia, we decided to stop the bullgine and listen.

At first we heard nothing—then very distant and indistinct we caught the faint moan of a diaphone. We were no longer alone in an empty world.

Each diaphone (fog-horn) has its own signature or code by which it can be identified. One may be timed to blow three five-second blasts at three-second intervals at the beginning of every minute; its nearest neighbour may be timed to blow for ten seconds, every thirty seconds. Jack slipped below to get the official Light and Fog-horn List while I began timing the distant moans. This was difficult because fog has the ability to muffle, distort, and freakishly obliterate sounds. Furthermore the second hand on my watch had a disconcerting way of moving in swift rushes followed by intervals of extreme sluggishness. Jack's watch was not available because some hours earlier the bullgine had struck it a smart blow with the starting handle.

Our first identification of the horn suggested it was on Cape Ann at the entrance to Gloucester, Massachusetts. We did not believe this, so we tried again. The next identification was of Red Rock at the mouth of the Saguenay in the St Lawrence River; we did not believe that one either. Finally by the slow process of elimination we concluded that the horn *might* be on Little Burin Island on the west side of Placentia Bay.

Having perhaps located Little Burin Island, our next problem was to get into Burin harbour. The Newfoundland Pilot Book informed us that the harbour was complicated, with off-lying dangers, and that it should *not* be entered unless one took aboard a pilot. Furthermore it should *not* be entered, even in daylight, unless one possessed local knowledge. The book said nothing about what should *not* be done at night, in a black fog, by perfect strangers. We drew our own conclusions.

We decided we had better stay where we were until dawn. If the storm struck before then we would have no alternative but to head out to sea and try to ride it out. If the storm held off until dawn, and if the fog lightened, there would be a chance of closing with the shore without inviting certain disaster. There was the further possibility that we might encounter a shore-based fishing boat from which we could get a little 'local knowledge'.

According to my watch dawn arrived at 0600 hours, but there was little visual evidence of its coming. True, the fog lightened enough so that we could actually see each other if we stood no farther than six feet apart. A kind of sepulchral semi-luminosity made it possible to read the compass card without the flashlight, which was just as well because the flashlight batteries had burned out and we had no replacements. At first we suspected that my watch was wrong (and we hoped it was), but when an early rising puffin suddenly whirred through the murk and just managed to avoid colliding with our mainmast, we knew that dawn had really come.

For half an hour more we waited, hoping to hear the slow, measured throb of fishing-boat engines. During the hours of drifting the current had carried us closer to shore and the horn was now quite distinct, and it was unmistakably Little Burin. Yet the fishermen of Burin did not seem to be abroad and at their work. We cursed them for being sluggards until Jack remembered that—storm warnings aside—this was Sunday morning. We thereupon gave up hoping for salvation from the fishermen. Being good Christian men they were all ashore seeing to their own salvation.

At seven o'clock we did hear a new noise. It was the first keening note of wind in our rigging. It was the first breath of the oncoming storm.

The skipper of the *Jeannie Barnes* had given us a small-scale and much-worn chart of Placentia Bay. Although it was almost indecipherable at least it told us there were no reefs or rocks off shore from Little Burin Island itself. In our dilemma we now decided to run straight toward the horn and, when we had it close aboard, swing north and try to feel our way behind the island. We would anchor there in whatever shelter we could find until the gale was over or until the fog blew away allowing us to seek a better haven.

The approach run was a ghastly ordeal. In order to keep track of the horn we had to stop the engine every five or ten minutes so that we could take a bearing; each time we stopped her she became more difficult to start. At eight-thirty, when we had worked our way within a quarter of a mile of the horn, the engine absolutely refused to start again. I sweated over it, exchanging igniters and frigging with wires, while the sound of the surf breaking on the two-hundred-foot-high seaward cliffs of Little Burin Island grew steadily louder as the tide carried us toward shore.

It took almost an hour to revive the bullgine and we knew we would not be able to risk stopping her again until we had reached an anchorage. Jack went forward to the bowsprit while I steered. I could only just see him as he waved his arm to signal the direction of the horn, which he could hear even above the thunder of the engine. Suddenly he flung up both arms at once. Confused, I put the helm hard over. *Happy Adventure* spun on her heel and we headed back out to sea.

Jack stumbled aft, a shaken man. He told me that as he stared into the murk the grey wall had suddenly turned pitch black, not only dead ahead, but off to port and starboard too. It took him only a fraction of an instant to realize that he was staring at the shrouded face of cliffs which loomed no more than a few yards from him. Since destruction seemed certain no matter which way we turned he tried to signal to me to stop the engine and so at least ease the final blow when *Happy Adventure* struck. Luck was with us. We had entered a shallow bay to the south of the fog-horn and it was just wide enough to let us turn about and make our escape.

Our immediate reaction was to give up any further attempts to reach shelter and to decide to take our chances with the storm at sea. However a little reflection changed our minds. *Happy Adventure* was leaking so badly that the unreliable pump was barely able to hold its own. The engine was clearly on its last legs. The wind was rising out of the sou'east. We knew we would stand no chance of beating off shore into the teeth of mounting wind and seas. One way or another we seemed destined to go ashore; only the choice of how we did it still remained to us.

We chose to make another pass at Little Burin Island.

Jack went forward again. He told me afterwards that he had an almost irresistible impulse to pick up our boat-hook and to stand poised on the bow with the pole thrust out ahead of him to fend us off the cliffs. It was not such a crazy idea as it sounds. A few days later the light-keeper told me *his* impressions of our tilt with Little Burin Island.

'I heard you fellas out there fer hours and hours. Couldn't make out what you was about. Heard your engine fer a time, then she'd shut off and I'd think you was gone away or gone ashore. Then, bang, you'd be coming at me again. Well, Sir, the last time you come in I thought you'd come right up the cliffs, gone by my door, and fair into my back yard.'

On our final approach our course was indeed dead at the horn. I could even hear it from where I sat at the helm; a bull's bellow above the blatting of the engine. Jack's right arm shot out and I hauled the tiller hard to port. This time I too saw the black loom as we ran parallel to the cliff and not more than a ship's length from it. The horn suddenly boomed, and it was straight overhead. I hauled harder on the stick and the black loom vanished and we were again lost in the world of fog.

That was the way we navigated. I eased the stick over very slowly. As soon as the fog began to darken Jack would wave me off. As the fog lightened and we lost touch with the island, we would turn cautiously inward again until we raised its loom before hauling off once more. Despite the chill of the morning I was sweating like a pig. I was so engrossed that it was some time before I realized that the boom of the horn was now behind me. We had rounded the corner of the island and were running down its northern shore.

I had the chart spread out on my knee and I peered at it trying to make out the water depths behind the island. Eventually I read part of a line of soundings. They showed twelve fathoms right to the foot of the cliffs—and we had just fifteen fathoms of anchor chain.

Up forward Jack was already flaking the chain on deck, ready for my order to let go the hook. I yelled to him and he came aft. I showed him the soundings. We both knew there was no way we were going to ride out a storm with only three fathoms of scope on our chain. Then Jack grinned. A terrible grin.

'The hell!' he said. 'Head for north. We'll run right up Burin Inlet. We'll hold tight up against the western shore and steer by the loom of the land.'

And that is what we did. Fired with an exhilaration that might have been recklessness, or may have just been the fine feeling of already having done the impossible, we ran up Burin Inlet for almost two miles. We never saw a thing. We ran solely by the loom of the black fog on our port bow. When we had run far enough to feel we were as safe as we could ever hope to be we stopped the engine.

Happy Adventure drifted through the grey soup on calm, still waters. Somewhere a dog barked. Somewhere a church bell was ringing. Jack swung the lead over the bows and got four fathoms with a mud bottom. The anchor went over and the chain ran out with a clear, strong song.

After a while we descended into our little cabin and went to sleep.

No collection of Canadian sea stories could exclude at least a passing reference to Canada's own buried treasure mystery: the Oak Island enigma of the so-called 'Money Pit'. Oak Island is—or was, until the bulldozers got at it— a pretty island set in amongst others in Mahone Bay, Nova Scotia, a picturesque place of beautiful, evergreen islands and snug coves. But over the years, the possibility that a huge hoard of treasure might be buried on the island has lured numbers of treasure seekers, some to their doom.

The Money Pit
Derek Wilson

The search for the treasure of Oak Island has lasted almost two hundred years, swallowed up well over a million pounds and cost six lives. Like most other treasure stories of the American seaboard it has persistently been connected with pirates. Oak Island is one of a cluster of islets in Mahone Bay, Nova Scotia, some eighty kilometres south of Halifax. In 1795 three lads from the nearby township of Chester were exploring the deserted eastern end of the island when they came across a tree with a lower limb which had been used to support a block and tackle. The equipment was still in place and beneath it there was a slight depression in the ground. Brought up on popular legends, the boys immediately thought of 'pirate gold'. They came back time after time to dig in their secret pit, only to discover that it was much deeper than they could have expected. It was a well-constructed shaft some four metres across with a succession of wooden platforms. At ten metres they had to give up and seek help. In 1804 the first professional excavation attempt was made. Its backers, like all those who were to involve themselves later with the Oak Island mystery, worked on the simple principle that since someone had gone to considerable trouble to create an elaborate pit they must have concealed something of great value in it. Just how elaborate the shaft system was they soon discovered to their cost. They penetrated to thirty metres, removing successive platforms. Then the hole began to fill rapidly with water. Some of the tightly fitting obstruction had acted as airlocks. Unknown to the excavators, two tunnels connected the money pit with a nearby beach. When the air pressure was released sea water flooded into the diggings.

Over the years various expeditions went to Oak Island, digging a succession of fresh shafts all around the original money pit and turning the whole site into a muddy morass. It was not until 1845 that the secret of the flooding was discovered. A succession of drains and filters had been constructed beneath the high water level of a cove—work demanding considerable skill and hard labour. Efforts to dam the tide failed and fresh excavations caused a collapse in the Money Pit which, the excavators believed, carried treasure chests to the bottom of the flooded workings.

More and more syndicates came and went, equipped with drills, cranes, mechanical excavators and explosives. In 1894 a drill went through a barrier of cement at about fifty metres and came up with fragments of wood, metal and parchment attached ot it. But the seekers could not reach whatever lay at the bottom of the shaft. By then the whole area had become so pockmarked with deep holes that further excavation was rendered very hazardous. This did not deter hopeful seekers after the 'obviously' important Oak Island Treasure. The twentieth century brought wealthy treasure-hunters equipped with electric pumps and expensive mining gear, as well as cranks armed with 'gold detectors', divining rods and radar devices. In 1965 four excavators were buried when their shaft caved in. In 1971 a Canadian company working the site lowered a television camera to the bottom of the shaft. Dimly it revealed what appeared to be the outline of chests— wooden treasure chests? Intact after 200 years most of which they had spent under water?

The work goes on. The eastern end of Oak Island is by now totally devastated. The only people to profit from the excavations are the businessmen who run the Buccaneer and Captain Kidd motels and the Oak Island Museum; the fishermen who take visitors on sightseeing trips; and the locals who in sundry ways supplement their incomes from tourism.

Yet the tantalizing facts remain that the shaft and tunnel complex was constructed by someone, and constructed for a purpose. The favourite candidate is, inevitably, William Kidd. Some support seems to be given to this identification by the marked similarity of Oak Island to the 'Skeleton Island' of the Kidd maps discovered earlier this century. But there is no evidence to show that Captain Kidd travelled as far north as Nova Scotia, nor that he possessed the skill and leisure necessary for so elaborate a construction as the Money Pit. Another theory requires us to believe that the American seaboard pirates joined forces to create a communal bank and that the Money Pit was their vault. It seems an unlikely solution; collaboration and making provision for the future were not common characteristics of pirates. If not buccaneers, then perhaps the crew of a Spanish bullion ship: this idea, convassed as recently as 1978 in a well-argued book [*The Money Pit*] by D'Arcy O'Connor, envisages a damaged mid-seventeenth-century galleon limping homewards. Her captain realizes she will never reach Spain with the heavy cargo so he has it landed and concealed on Oak Island, elaborately safeguarded from pirates by the system of shafts and tunnels. The ship sets sail again and is overwhelmed by Atlantic storms. No one survives to reveal the secret or reclaim the treasure. This scenario fits most of the known facts but is quite incapable of proof. And would a random Spanish ship have had aboard the necessary equipment and men with the requisite engineering skills? Wilder theories which connect Oak Island with Incas, Vikings or the lost manuscripts of Francis Bacon can safely be jettisoned.

Rupert Furneaux [*The Money Pit Mystery*, 1972] has presented what appears to be the most plausible solution offered so far. He dates the construction to about 1780, when the War of American Independence was in full swing. The British garrison at New York was under pressure and might have to withdraw hurriedly to Halifax. In order to safeguard his war chests, the British commander-in-chief had a secret repository prepared by the Royal Engineers. If this is the explanation, did the British ever have to use the pit? If they did, did they came back for their treasure? Whatever solution one accepts to the Money Pit mystery, it only seems to lead to new questions.

One would like to hope that something dramatic may be found in Oak Island's pits. But like every other treasure of Canadian waters, it has proven to be not easy to obtain, and demands a sacrifice of risk, effort and courage before it grudgingly yields up its bounty. In that sense, Oak Island's wealth is a very characteristic Canadian treasure indeed.

Summary

Over the seas of the world, as elsewhere, a technological age of post-industrial computerization is dawning, moving toward networks of world-wide information access. Increasingly the computer monitor screen becomes the window to knowledge, and as concepts such as Virtual Reality (VR) are explored, to experience itself. At sea, the technologies of transportation are moving toward enormous, multi-hulled vessels of hundred-knot speed computer-navigated to precise locations on the face of the globe, and carrying their crews farther and farther away from the most elemental struggle of passagemaking and landfall. If economic woes or environmental degradation do not slow this process, the sea is becoming an alien environment across which such stabilized, air-conditioned and GPS-fixed vessels move with little confrontation or accommodation to the sea. To the degree that this process may lower, or even end, the loss of human life in Canada's seas is commendable.

But Canadians were shaped in the past by a direct struggle against hostile elements, both in the land, and the seas. There may be a danger in giving up too soon an appreciation of that fact, and relying too much upon the electronic circuit board to ensure existence. The struggle to come to terms with what our northern oceans demanded of Canadians was part of the shaping of Canadian human qualities, giving a good deal of what is valuable in Canadian views of what societies should be like. The sea gave, for all its harsh price, a theatre as well where romance and adventure could dwell. In the stories of this volume the reader has glanced at a far greater treasure trove of tales that await discovery. One may hope that Canadians will never turn away from such stories and the mirror to their own character that can be found there. Not everyone can set a topsail aloft in a square-rigger, or grip the wheel of a destroyer knifing through northern seas; but to seek to relive that experience, even if only in print, may keep alive a spark of human adventure that may serve us well when the manufactured experiences of the computers fail us. One should never forget what once took place on the glittering waters that surround Canada, and that it will always be there to be discovered again, if so wished.